About t...

USA Today bestselling auth... graduate and former intell... lives with her husband, so... New York. She writes sexy, humorous books that have been published in more than twenty countries. Her novels have won the *RT* Book Reviews Reviewers' Choice Award, the Golden Leaf, the Book Buyer's Best, and the New England Readers' Choice. You can sign up for her newsletter at annadepalo.com

Karin Baine lives in Northern Ireland with her husband, two sons, and her out-of-control notebook collection. Her Mother and Grandmother's vast collection of books inspired her love of reading and her dream of becoming a Mills & Boon author. Now she can tell people she has a proper job! You can follow Karin on X, @karinbaine1 or visit her website for the latest news – karinbaine.com

Taryn Leigh Taylor likes dinosaurs, bridges and space, both personal and of the final-frontier variety. She shamelessly indulges in cliches, most notably her Starbucks addiction, her shoe hoard and her penchant for falling in lust with fictional men with great abs. She also really loves books, which is what sent her down the crazy path of writing one in the first place. For more on Taryn, check out tarynleightaylor.com, her Facebook @tarynltaylor1 and X @tarynltaylor

Sports Romance

December 2024
On The Stage

January 2025
On The Ice

February 2025
In The End Zone

March 2025
In The Saddle

April 2025
On The Pitch

May 2025
On The Track

Sports Romance:
On The Ice

ANNA DePALO

KARIN BAINE

TARYN LEIGH TAYLOR

MILLS & BOON

All rights reserved including the right of reproduction in whole or in part in any form. This edition is published by arrangement with Harlequin Enterprises ULC.

This is a work of fiction. Names, characters, places, locations and incidents are purely fictional and bear no relationship to any real life individuals, living or dead, or to any actual places, business establishments, locations, events or incidents. Any resemblance is entirely coincidental.

This book is sold subject to the condition that it shall not, by way of trade or otherwise, be lent, resold, hired out or otherwise circulated without the prior consent of the publisher in any form of binding or cover other than that in which it is published and without a similar condition including this condition being imposed on the subsequent purchaser.

® and ™ are trademarks owned and used by the trademark owner and/or its licensee. Trademarks marked with ® are registered with the United Kingdom Patent Office and/or the Office for Harmonisation in the Internal Market and in other countries.

First Published in Great Britain 2024
by Mills & Boon, an imprint of HarperCollins*Publishers* Ltd
1 London Bridge Street, London, SE1 9GF

www.harpercollins.co.uk

HarperCollins*Publishers*
Macken House, 39/40 Mayor Street Upper,
Dublin 1, D01 C9W8, Ireland

Sports Romance: On The Ice © 2025 Harlequin Enterprises ULC.

Power Play © 2019 Anna DePalo
Reforming the Playboy © 2017 Karin Baine
Playing to Win © 2016 Taryn Leigh Taylor

ISBN: 978-0-263-39776-5

MIX
Paper | Supporting responsible forestry
FSC™ C007454

This book contains FSC™ certified paper and other controlled sources to ensure responsible forest management.

For more information visit: www.harpercollins.co.uk/green

Printed and Bound in the UK using 100% Renewable Electricity
at CPI Group (UK) Ltd, Croydon, CR0 4YY

POWER PLAY

ANNA DePALO

For my editor, Charles Griemsman.
Your editorial guidance has been invaluable!

One

Sera disliked smooth operators, bad in-laws and unwelcome surprises.

Unfortunately, Jordan was all three, and his sudden appearance in her offices on a sunny spring day in Massachusetts meant she'd better start preparing herself for the unthinkable.

"You!"

The exclamation was out of Sera's mouth before she could stop it. It had been just another day at Astra Therapeutics until Mr. Hotshot-NHL, Underwear-Ad-Hottie Jordan Serenghetti had crashed the party like an errant puck arcing through the air.

Jordan smiled lazily. "Yes, me."

Arms folded, he lounged against the treatment table, as if striking sexy poses was second nature to him—even when propped up by crutches, as he was now. Clad in a casual long-sleeved olive T-shirt and jeans, he emanated charisma. The shirt outlined the hard muscles of his arms, and the jeans hugged lean hips. Not that she was noticing. Not in *that* way.

Sera was wary of men who were too good to be true—as if everything came easy to them. Nowadays, Jordan Serenghetti would be at the top of her list. He was smoother than a skate blade hydroplaning over ice. With dark, ruffled hair clipped short, moss-green eyes, and a sculpted face with a chiseled jaw, he could score anywhere.

Sera had seen him in underwear ads, showing off his package on supersized billboards and fueling thousands of dreams. But she'd learned the hard way to deal in reality, not fantasy.

"What are you doing here?" she blurted, even though she had a sinking feeling she knew. She'd been told her next appointment was waiting for her in room 6, but she'd had no idea it was Jordan.

She'd heard he'd suffered a sports-related injury, but figured he was in good hands with the New England Razors hockey-team staff. She *so* was not going to worry about him, even if her *second-worst mistake* was now related to her by the marriage of her cousin to Jordan's brother. In the annals of her bad history with men, Jordan ranked number two, even if it had become clear to her that he didn't remember their chance encounter in the past.

She eyed his wrapped left knee. She wasn't used to seeing Jordan Serenghetti vulnerable…

"Now, that's a refreshing change from the usual greeting. Too often I get enthusiastic fans yelling my name." He shrugged. "You're an antidote to the monotony, Angel."

Sera sighed. Fans? Women screaming his name was more like it. *Terribly misguided, deluded women.* "Don't call me Angel."

"Hey, I'm not the one who named you for a heavenly being."

She'd never had occasion to rue her name so much. *Se-*

rafina served as a topic of easy cocktail-party conversation, but the nickname Angel irked her, especially when uttered by Jordan. So what if she was named for the seraphim?

"Your type of angel is supposed to be heavenly and fiery," Jordan went on, unperturbed. "Someone had a kismet moment when they named you. Beautiful and hot-tempered."

Serafina rolled her eyes, refusing to be swayed by the way *beautiful* rolled off Jordan's tongue. "Am I supposed to be impressed by your grasp of biblical trivia...or backhanded compliments?" Then she scowled at the thought that her response had just proven his point. She dropped her clipboard on the counter. "So you're here for a physical-therapy session..."

"Yup."

She quelled her irritation. "And I'm supposed to think it's mere chance that you were assigned to me?"

Jordan held up his hands, a smile teasing his lips. "No, I'm not going to lie about that part."

"Oh, good."

"I want the best—"

Sera was sure Jordan was used to the best in women. No doubt eager females were waiting for him when he exited the New England Razors' locker room.

"—and you've already got a great reputation. The clinic manager couldn't stop singing your praises."

With a pro athlete of Jordan's caliber, Sera was sure Bernice had given him his choice of staff. And the clinic's manager probably thought she was doing Sera a favor...

Sera thought back to her conversation earlier in the week with Bernice. *We're trying to land a contract with the New England Razors. Their management is looking to outsource some therapy work and supplement the team's staff. They're auditioning three outfits, including us. If we land this deal, it could open the door to work with other sports teams in the area.*

Ugh. At the time, she'd dismissed her chances of encountering Jordan, even though he played for the Razors. The gods couldn't be so cruel. Apparently, however, gods laughed at angels. Jordan had been sent—or volunteered—to test the quality of the clinic's services. With her. She should have known the minute she stepped into this room, but she'd been in deep denial.

"You asked for me?" Sera said slowly.

Jordan nodded and then cracked a grin. "The fact that, when I booked my appointment for today, your receptionist couldn't stop extolling your cooking skills just sealed the deal for me."

"She mentioned my cooking?"

"And baking," he added. "Apparently, the homemade dishes that you sometimes bring in for the staff earn you brownie points. So you were clearly the right choice."

"Let me remind you of something…we don't like each other."

"Correction," Jordan said, lips quirking. "You don't like me. I have no problem with attractive and passionate women. You, on the other hand, have issues—"

"Right." She narrowed her eyes.

"You should feel safe around me," Jordan said easily. "We're practically related."

Right. Jordan's older brother Cole had recently married Sera's cousin Marisa Danieli. Jordan loved to joke about the couple's long and winding path to the altar. At one point, Marisa's former fiancé had been dating Cole's ex-girlfriend, and Jordan had kidded that his brother and Marisa were engaged by proxy. It did *not*, however, mean that *she* and Jordan were related in any meaningful sense of the word.

Up to now, Sera had done her best to ignore the fact that she and Jordan were technically cousins-in-law. Marisa and Cole had had a surprise wedding, so she'd been spared having to be the maid of honor to Jordan's best man.

"I'll drive you into the ground, Serenghetti," she harrumphed, changing tactics. "You'll sweat like you've never worked before."

It was only a half-idle threat. She expected a lot from her patients. She was good, she was understanding, but she was tough.

Jordan's smile stayed in place. "I wouldn't expect any less."

"Are you always so sunny?" she grumbled. "Do the clouds ever come out in Serenghetti Land?"

He laughed. "I like to rile you, Perini. I may not have clouds, but I can rock your world with thunder and lightning."

There it was again. The sexually tinged double meaning. And then a traitorous voice whispered, *You already have. Once.* The fact that he didn't remember just made it all the more galling. "You don't want to get involved with me." *Again.* "I'm not a woman you can conveniently walk away from." *This time.* "I'm your sister-in-law's cousin."

He arched a brow. "Is that all that's stopping you?"

She threw up her hands—because no way was she going to remind Jordan about the past. *Their past.* And with her bad luck, in the future she and Jordan would be named as godparents to the next Danieli-Serenghetti offspring. As it was, they'd dodged that bullet the first time around since Jordan's brother Rick and his wife Chiara had done the honors. It seemed Cole was going down the line by order of birth in naming godparents from among his siblings.

Jordan shrugged and then glanced around. "At least we'll have the memory of a few good physical-therapy sessions."

"All you'll be remembering fondly is the pain," she practically snarled.

"I'm a good listener if you ever want to…you know, talk instead of spar."

She swept him a suspicious look—unsure if he was joking or not. *Better not to take chances.* "As if I'd open up to a player like you," she scoffed. "Forget it."

"Not even when you're off duty?" he teased. "It could be therapeutic."

"When I need to unwind, I'll book a vacation to the Caribbean."

"Let me know when you're going. I'll reserve a seat."

Argh. "It's a vacation—as in, I don't want to be irritated!"

He quirked an eyebrow. "Irritated isn't your natural state?"

"No!"

"So where do we go from here?" he said. "You're irritated..."

As he said the words, Jordan watched Serafina with bemusement and not a little lust. With blond hair swinging past her shoulders and amber eyes, she was a knockout. He'd been around plenty of beautiful women, but Sera's personality shone like an inner light. Of course, she directed snark at him, but he enjoyed tangling with her.

She was a puzzle he was interested in solving. Because if he'd ever met a woman with a boulder-sized chip on her shoulder, it was Sera Perini.

"Listen, I'll make you a deal," he joked. "I'll try to behave if you stick around and help me out."

"You will behave," she said firmly. "And your coupon is valid for today's session only. After that, the sale is over."

His eyes crinkled. "Hard bargainer."

"You have no idea."

"But I guess I'm going to find out."

"True, but first you need to sit on the treatment table so we can take a look at that knee." She paused. "Let me help you."

"No need."

Even though they were now related by marriage and had

seen each other at the occasional family gathering, they'd never come close to touching. Not a pat, not a brush of the arm, and certainly not a peck on the cheek. *Nada*. It was as if by tacit agreement boundaries had been drawn, because they were more like warring in-laws than the friendly kind. And maybe because they understood that, it was dangerous to cross some unspoken line.

Now, bracing his arms, he hopped up onto the table using his good leg.

"Nice stunt," she commented drily.

He tossed her a jaunty grin. "More where that came from."

With a last warning look, she turned her attention to the paperwork he'd brought with him to the appointment and had dropped on the counter before she'd walked in.

He took the opportunity to study her again. Today, she wore nondescript, body-concealing light blue scrubs. When she'd sometimes waitressed at the Puck & Shoot, the popular local sports bar, she'd usually kept her hair pulled back in a ponytail or with a headband and had had a black apron tied around her waist. But thanks to the fact that they were now related by marriage, he'd seen her in other getups: body-skimming dresses, tight-fitting exercise attire… She had an hourglass figure that was fuller on top, so everything flattered her. More than once he'd caught himself fantasizing about what it would be like to run his hands over her curves and skim his palms over her endless legs.

Yet he didn't know what to make of her. He was attracted as hell, but she was an in-law…and she didn't like him. Still, the urge to tease her was as natural and unavoidable as breathing, and as irresistible as the impulse to win a hockey championship. And on top of it, he needed her physical-therapy skills. Already the companies behind his endorsement deals were getting nervous because he'd been off the ice. For the umpteenth time, he pushed aside the thought that his career could be over. He'd work like hell in therapy to make sure that possibility would never become a reality. Sure he'd made some savvy business investments with his earnings, but his plans depended on continuing to play.

With a grimace, Jordan turned and stretched out his legs in front of him on the treatment table.

Sera looked up, seemingly satisfied with what she'd gleaned from his intake papers. "So how did the ACL tear occur?"

"A game three weeks ago against the New York Islanders. I heard a pop." He shrugged. "I knew what it was. Cole's been through this before."

His older brother had suffered a couple of knee injuries that had ended his professional hockey career. These days, Cole was the head of Serenghetti Construction, having taken over after their father's stroke had forced Serg Serenghetti to adopt a less active lifestyle.

"You're lucky it happened at the end of the hockey season, and the Razors didn't advance in the playoffs this year."

"I've never thought of getting knocked out in the playoffs as a lucky break," he quipped. "Especially when I wasn't there to help."

"It's a tear, not a break," she parried. "So who performed the ACL surgery on your knee?"

"Dr. Nabov at Welsdale Medical Center, and it was last week. In-patient for a day. They insisted I stay overnight. I guess they didn't want to take any chances with my recovery. Hockey fans, you know."

"Mmm-hmm." Sera flipped through his paperwork again. "Did you sign autographs while you were there?"

He cracked a smile and folded his arms over his chest. "A few."

"I assume the nursing staff went wild."

He knew sarcasm when he heard it and couldn't resist teasing back. "Nah, they've seen it all."

"You've been icing the knee?"

"Yeah. The staff at the hospital told me what to do post-surgery."

"Until you could get yourself into more expert hands?"

He flashed a grin. "You. Right."

She might totally be his type if she wasn't so thorny… and since she was related to him by marriage, a casual fling was out of the question. Still, there were layers there, and he enjoyed trying to peel them back.

Sera set aside his paperwork and approached him, her expression all business. "Okay, I'm going to unwrap your knee."

For all her prickliness up to now, her touch was light as she removed his bandages. When the bandage was off, they both studied his knee.

"Good news."

"Great."

"No signs of infection and very little bleeding." She pressed on his knee as he remained in a sitting position on the table but leaned back propped up by his arms.

"Am I hurting you?" she asked, not looking up.

"Nothing I can't handle."

"Manly."

"We hockey players are built tough."

"We'll see." She continued to press and manipulate his knee.

"I'm your first. Otherwise you'd know."

"I've never been curious about how tough hockey players are."

"You're mentally disciplined."

"We physical therapists are built tough."

Jordan smiled. "Built pretty, too."

"Behave."

"Right."

Then she reached over to the counter for an instrument. "I'm going to take some baseline measurements so we know where you are."

"Great." He waited as she straightened his knee a little, measured, and then bent his leg and measured again.

After putting the measuring instrument aside, she said, "Okay, not a bad starting point considering your knee has been wrapped since surgery. Our goal today is to improve your quad function and the mobility of the patella, among other things."

"What's a *patella*?"

She tucked a strand of hair behind her ear. "Your kneecap."

"Of course."

"Let me know if I'm causing you too much pain."

Her tone was surprisingly solicitous, so he joked, "Isn't that what you promised? Pain?"

"Only the intended and expected variety."

He was a high-level athlete—he was used to pain and then some. "How many ACL tears have you treated?"

"A few. I'll let you know at the end if you were my best patient."

He stifled a laugh because she'd deftly appealed to his competitive instincts. He wondered if she used the same technique to cajole all her patients. Probably some played sports—since a torn ACL wasn't too unusual an athletic injury—even if she'd never treated a professional hockey player like himself before. "Will you dock me points for irreverence?"

"Do you really want to find out?" Methodically, she taped two wires to his thigh. "I'm going to set you up with some muscle stim right now. This will get you started."

In his opinion, they'd gotten started with the electricity when she'd walked in the room. But he sensed that he'd teased her enough, and she wasn't going to take any more nonsense, so he kept mum for the next few minutes and just followed her directions.

After the muscle stim, she taught him how to do patellar glides. He followed her instructions about how to move his knee to gain more flexibility. They followed that up with quad sets and heel slides, which she told him to do at home, too.

Overall, he found none of it too arduous. But at the end of half an hour, she announced that his ability to bend his knee had gone from around ten degrees to eighty.

He grinned. "I'm your best?"

"Don't flatter yourself, Superman. Your knee was wrapped in bandages that interfered with motion until now, so you were bound to make some significant improvement."

"I'll take that as a yes."

"You're impossible."

"No, I'm very possible if you'll consider your options. Now, insufferable, that's another thing…"

Sera seemed to grit her teeth. "You'll need weekly appointments."

"How long will my therapy last?"

"Depends on how it goes." Her expression was challenging—as if she'd been referring to his behavior, good or bad, as well as his recuperation. "Usually three to four months."

"Nothing long-term, then?"

She nodded. "What you're used to."

A fling. The words drifted unspoken between them. She'd met his double entendre and raised him. *Ouch.*

Two

"I can't do it. There's no way I can be Jordan Serenghetti's physical therapist." Sera drew her line in the sand. Or rather, on the hockey ice—or *whatever*.

"You have to," Bernice, the clinic's manager said, her short curly brown hair shining under the overhead fluorescent light.

"He needs a babysitter—" *of the centerfold variety* "—not a trainer. Or a physical therapist."

"We're counting on you to help us land this client."

And Jordan Serenghetti was counting on landing her. His appointment had ended over an hour ago, and still she was suffering the lingering effects. Annoyance. Exasperation. Indignation. She'd spent the time since naming her emotions.

True, Jordan emanated charm from every pore. She wasn't immune. She was still a woman who liked men, and she wasn't dead. And okay, maybe she was the one with long-suppressed needs. But that didn't mean Jordan was getting anywhere with her. *Again.* She still remembered the feel of his lips on her. And he didn't have any recollection—*none whatsoever.* She'd just been another easily forgotten face in a cast of thousands. That much had become clear once she'd reencountered him years later while waitressing at the Puck & Shoot, and there'd been not even a flicker of recognition in his eyes.

She knew the score these days, and this time she was determined that the game would end Sera 1, Playboy 0.

Endure months of close contact with Jordan? It would test her nerves and more. So after her session with him had ended, Sera had sought out Bernice in her office to plead her case. Standing just inside the doorway, she focused on the bobblehead dolls lining her boss's bookshelves. All the major sports were represented there—including hockey. Scanning them, Sera didn't see Jordan. It gave her hope that she had a small chance of convincing Bernice. How big a fan could her boss be?

"How about you reassign me and I bring you another baked lasagna to thank you?" Sera cajoled.

"Ordinarily I'd consider a small bribe," Bernice parried, her desk chair turned toward the office's entrance, "especially if it's one of your homemade dishes. But this time, no. The staff has been enjoying the big pan of baked ziti you brought in for lunch today, though."

Sera lowered her shoulders.

"If we do a good job," Bernice continued, "we should get regular business from the New England Razors. It'll be a huge boost for Astra Therapeutics and for your career."

Sera held back a grimace. As far as her boss was concerned, there'd be no getting out of this gig.

Bernice tilted her head. "You've dealt with difficult clients before. We all have."

Sera opened and closed her mouth. This was different. *But she could hardly explain why.* "Isn't this like nepotism? I get the plum client because he's related to me by marriage?"

Bernice chuckled. "The fact that you're practically family should make this assignment a piece of cake." Her manager looked thoughtful. "Or if he's a bad in-law, well then, we've all had those, too."

Sera pressed her lips together. *Damn it.* She'd worked so hard to get her physical-therapy degree. She'd moonlighted as a waitress and endured three grueling years back at school for a graduate degree. And now Jordan Serenghetti stood in the path of her advancement.

Bernice gave her an inquisitive look. "On the other hand, is your problem that Jordan has too much magnetism? Some people get starstruck by celebrities and have a hard time focusing on the job."

Sera spluttered. "Please. The fake charm is a big turn-off."

Her manager raised her eyebrows.

Sera's face heated, and she quickly added, "I'm not taking it personally. There isn't a woman alive Jordan doesn't try to charm."

"You know, if I were a little younger, and my husband would let me, I'd consider dating Jordan Serenghetti."

"Bernice, please! You've got gold with Keith. Why trade it in for pyrite?" Sera knew her manager had just celebrated her sixtieth birthday and thirtieth wedding anniversary.

"What makes you think Jordan isn't genuine?" Bernice countered.

Sera threw up her hands. She wasn't about to dig into her past with her boss—and explain how she'd honed her instincts about men the hard way. She was wise enough these days not to be taken in by ripped biceps—hadn't she seen them up close an hour ago?—and hard abs. Probably those lips were still magic, too. "The problem is he knows he has the goods."

Bernice laughed. "There's nothing wrong with a man who's confident."

"Try arrogant." Sera knew she had to talk to Marisa. Perhaps her cousin could convince Jordan that this work arrangement wasn't a good idea. If she couldn't get out of this assignment herself, maybe Jordan would back out.

Knowing she wasn't going to get anywhere with Bernice, Sera decided to back off and change the subject. But when her workday ended at four, she made the short drive from Astra Therapeutics' offices outside Springfield to Marisa and Cole's new home in Welsdale.

Sera pulled up to a classic center-hall colonial and thanked her lucky stars for May in western Massachusetts. The breezy, sunny day could almost erase her mood. She had texted Marisa in advance, so when she got out of her beat-up sedan, her cousin was already opening the front door.

Marisa wore a baby sling and raised a finger to her lips but exchanged a quick peck on the cheek with Sera. "Dahlia just fell asleep. I'm going to lay her down in her crib and be right with you."

"You and Cole have gone all Hollywood with the baby naming," Sera remarked wryly, because even months later, the baby's name brought a smile to her lips.

"If Daisy is acceptable, why not Dahlia?" Marisa said over her shoulder as Sera closed the door and followed her into the house.

"And here I thought Rick and Chiara would go all name crazy, but no, nope, they had to settle on something traditional like Vincent." Frankly, it wouldn't have surprised her in the least if the middle Serenghetti brother and his new wife, actress Chiara Feran, who resided in Los Angeles most of the time—home to the weird Hollywood baby-naming craze—had come up with something like Moonlight or Starburst.

Sera bore only a passing resemblance to her cousin. They shared the amber eyes that were a family trait, but she'd grown a shade taller than Marisa by the time she was fourteen—and her dark blond hair set her apart from her cousin, who had long curly brown locks. When Sera had been younger, she and Marisa had been deep in each other's pockets, and sometimes she'd wished the similarities had been strong enough that they could easily pass as sisters.

"I'll be right back," Marisa said as she started up the stairs from the entry hall. "I'll meet you in the kitchen."

As Sera made her way to the back of the house, she noted once again that it bore the stamp of domesticity. The new home was still sparsely furnished, but the signs of baby were all around. She figured that Jordan must break out in hives here.

When her cousin came back downstairs moments later, Sera put down her glass of flavored water and braced her hands on the granite kitchen countertop. She wasted no words. "Marisa, Jordan is about to become a client of mine."

Her cousin's expression remained mild as she turned on a baby monitor. "They're sending him to you to help recover from his torn ACL."

Sera didn't mask her surprise. "You know? And you didn't warn me?"

"I found out just this morning. Cole happened to mention Jordan was heading to Astra Therapeutics. But I wasn't sure he would definitely be assigned to you." Her cousin wrinkled her brow. "Though, come to think of it, he did make an offhand comment to Cole about possibly asking for you..." She shrugged. "We thought he was teasing because, ah, you two have always seemed to rub each other the wrong way at family gatherings."

"Well, it's no joke, but someone has made a mistake." Wanting to spare her cousin any awkwardness with her in-laws, and because, frankly, her first encounter with Jordan had been embarrassing, she'd never mentioned to Marisa that she and Jordan had briefly crossed paths in the past. It was bad enough that others could sense tension between her and the youngest Serenghetti brother.

"If anyone can whip Jordan into shape, it's you," Marisa teased.

Sera scowled as she pushed away from the kitchen counter. "This isn't funny."

"Of course not, but maybe you've met your match."

Sera shuddered. "Don't say it."

The last thing she needed was for anyone to think Jordan was a work challenge that she couldn't conquer. First off, she didn't want to conquer anything—especially him. Second, no way was he her *match* in any other sense of the word—not that Marisa could mean *that*. The fact that Jordan had found her infinitely forgettable at twenty-one was evidence enough that they weren't fated *in any way*.

Her cousin glanced down at some paint chips fanned out on the kitchen counter. "Who knew there were so many shades of beige for a guest bedroom?" she asked absently. "I just want a soothing tone, and Cole is kidding me about using Diaper Brown."

"Is that the name of a paint color?"

Marisa pinked. "Paint colors are a running joke in this house ever since Cole and I redid the kitchen cabinets in my old apartment."

Her cousin and her husband had only months ago moved into the new colonial in Welsdale that Cole had built for their growing family. They'd moved in right before Dahlia was born, and Sera knew that the process of decorating weighed on Marisa, especially as a new mom. "Most of us can use a professional. Get a decorator."

Marisa looked at her thoughtfully. "Isn't that why Jordan is coming to you? Because you're a professional?" She tugged on the hem of her top and rubbed at a stain. "Why are you so reluctant to help him?"

Sera opened her mouth and then clamped it shut. Because...because... No way was she getting into any embarrassing past *incidents*. "He's obnoxious."

"I know you two have a testy relationship, but he'll have to do what you tell him."

"He's a smooth operator." *Happy-go-lucky*. With a bad memory to boot. And he didn't know the meaning of struggle.

Marisa glanced at her keenly. "You're protesting too much."

"Paraphrasing Shakespeare? Spoken like a true English teacher."

"Former English teacher. And I'm on maternity leave from the assistant principal position at the Pershing School." Marisa yawned. "Something to eat?"

"No, thanks. And you're doing great in your leave as a new mom."

Her cousin gave a rueful laugh. "I know, but family history and all. At least Cole is on board."

Sera gave her cousin a reassuring pat. Marisa had been raised by a single mom, Sera's Aunt Donna. Marisa's father had died before she'd been born—having already made clear that a baby didn't factor into his plans for pursuing a minor-league baseball career and maybe getting to the majors.

Men. These days, Sera didn't need more confirmation that they could be fickle and untrustworthy. Her awful experience with Neil had taught her enough. Jordan had just been the start of her bad track record—one she seemed to share with the women in her family. *Must be in the genes.* "You and Cole have to convince Jordan this is a bad idea."

"Sera—"

"Please."

* * *

Jordan shifted in his seat next to his brother and glanced around the crowded bar. Business was humming as usual on a Thursday evening at the Puck & Shoot. None of his teammates from the Razors were around, partly because many had scattered for home or vacation in the postseason.

Sera also no longer moonlighted here as a waitress—and *that* was a good thing, he told himself. He could still recall his reaction when he'd first discovered, shortly before Cole's marriage, that the hot blond waitress at his favorite dive was Marisa's cousin. The fates had a twisted sense of humor.

Still, tonight, even without his teammates and Sera at the Puck & Shoot, it almost felt like old times. He nearly felt like his old self—*normal*. Not injured and off the ice, with brothers who'd suddenly morphed into fathers—though he was happy for them. It felt good not to be holed up at home, which would have just given him more time to mull his uncertain future and push away his regular companion these days—unease.

If he could only take out his frustration and pent-up energy the way he normally did, things would be better. "Man, I miss our evenings at Jimmy's Boxing Gym."

Cole, sitting on the bar stool next to him, smiled. "I've got better things to do with my after-work hours these days."

"Ever since you got hitched, you've become boring, old man," Jordan grumbled good-naturedly. "And fatherhood has just added to your—" he strangled out the word "—domesticity."

"Dahlia is brilliant," Cole countered. "Did I tell you she rolled over the other day?"

"No, but she clearly takes after Marisa. Beauty and brains."

Cole just smiled rather than giving as good as he got—

and that was the problem. Jordan wished for the old days. It was as if his brother didn't even miss hockey. What was the world coming to?

"The only reason I'm here at the Puck & Shoot is because of Marisa," Cole said. "She's the one who encouraged me to come keep your sorry butt company."

"You owe me one. More than one. You might not be wallowing in wedded bliss if it weren't for me."

"Yeah, how can I forget." Cole's voice dripped sarcasm. "Lucky for you, it all ended well. Otherwise, you could have been sporting a broken nose."

Jordan grinned because this was a spark of the old Cole he was used to. "Luck had nothing to do with it. You and Marisa were destined to be together. And for the record, a broken nose would have just added to my sex appeal."

Jordan had seen how unhappy his older brother had been when his reconciliation with Marisa had headed south, so he'd fibbed and told Cole that Marisa was looking for him—sending his unsuspecting brother to her apartment. Jordan had hoped that once the two were alone, they'd have a chance to talk and patch things up. They'd realize they were made for each other. In fact, Cole and Marisa hadn't made up then, but shortly afterward. And in the aftermath, they'd invited everyone to an engagement party that had turned out to be a surprise wedding.

Sera had been at the event, of course, looking sexy and tempting. He'd only discovered at a fund-raiser a short time before that she was Marisa's relative; there he'd recognized the attractive waitress from the Puck & Shoot whom he'd never had a chance to speak with and who always seemed to avoid him. The physical resemblance when she was side by side with her cousin had been unmistakable.

He'd gone slack-jawed, however, at Sera's transformation from waitress to temptress in a blue satin halter-top cocktail dress. Makeup had enhanced her unique and arresting features—full lips, bold eyes and fine cheekbones that any model would have wept for. And the halter top on her dress had emphasized her shoulders and toned arms before skimming down over testosterone-fueling curves to endless legs encased in strappy, high-heeled sandals. Seeing an opportunity to make his move, he'd approached the two women, but Sera had swatted him away like a pesky fly that night…

Cole slapped him on the back. "You look pensive. Buck up. It's not all doom and gloom."

Jordan didn't think his thoughts were showing, but maybe he was wrong. "Since you got married and gave up the mantle to become nauseatingly cheery, someone has to take over the role. And now both you and Rick are fathers."

Cole's face broke into a grin. "Yup."

"Someone has to uphold the family reputation."

"What reputation are you referring to? Being depressed and down?"

"No. Sexy and single." If he wasn't a professional hockey player and all-around chick magnet, who was he? He gave an inward shudder. Best not contemplate the abyss.

"All right, but from the looks of you, I've got to ask. What's throwing shade on sexy and single?"

Jordan waved his beer. "The obvious."

His latest injury had kept him off the ice for the end of the season, and his corporate partners—with contracts for endorsement deals—were starting to get restless. Not to mention his injury didn't put him in a great position to negotiate his next contract with the Razors. Everyone knew that one Serenghetti had already had a career-ending ACL injury.

"I'm proof there is life after the game," Cole said quietly.

"Yeah, I know, but if I can get over this injury, I should have a few more good seasons left." He was on the wrong side of thirty, but he was still at the top of his game. Or rather, he had been. In the last couple of years, he'd shifted position from right wing to center and had had some of his best seasons ever. The one that had recently ended might have been just as good, except it had ended abruptly for him with a knee injury. Still, at thirty-one, he figured he could squeeze out another half decade at the top—if he had better luck than in the past weeks.

"Speaking of injury," Cole said, nodding to the crutches that Jordan had propped against the bar, "what's your game plan for this one?"

Jordan took a swig of his beer. Fortunately, since it was his left knee that had needed surgery, he'd been able to start driving again this week. "I'm doing physical therapy."

Cole took a swallow of his own beer without glancing at him. "Yup, I've heard. Sera. So you weren't joking when you mentioned it might be her you'd see at Astra…"

"News travels fast," Jordan murmured. "I was just in to see her yesterday."

"And I'm supposed to be here to convince you not to see her."

Jordan tossed his brother a quick look. "Wow, so this is what it feels like."

"What?"

"The first time a woman has tried *not* to meet me."

"Sera is special."

"Tell me about it."

"You don't want to tangle with her. She's Marisa's cousin and not someone you can easily walk away from."

"Hey—" Jordan held up his hands "—all I'm asking is that she cure my knee, not date me." So what if Sera had already made a variation of Cole's argument?

His brother's tone was light, but there was also an undercurrent of warning. He wasn't sure whether the note of caution was because Cole was thinking about Jordan's best interests, or because he was naturally protective of his wife's relative. Cole had always been the responsible one, *relatively speaking*, and Jordan had chalked it up to oldest-child syndrome.

"Face it, Jordan. You can't turn off the charm. You love to get a rise out of Sera."

"I thought I was helping her career by asking for her."

"Apparently she doesn't want the boost."

Jordan twisted his lips in wry amusement. If he didn't have a healthy ego, he'd be feeling a twinge of wounded pride right now. "Look, when the Razors' management discovered I'd need physical therapy, they wanted me to try out a new outfit for them. I remembered Sera worked at Astra Therapeutics, so I mentioned the only name I knew when it was time to set up an appointment."

"Except Sera doesn't want to work with you."

Jordan put a hand to his chest. "Be still my heart," he said mockingly. "A woman who doesn't want me."

"You'll get over it. Trust me, you don't want to get involved with Marisa's cousin. I've seen her in the boxing ring. She throws a mean left jab."

"Which one?" Jordan joked. "Marisa or Sera?"

"Sera, but take my word for it, it's in the genes."

"And you know this how?"

Cole gave a long-suffering sigh. "Marisa and I met Sera at her gym once before having lunch nearby. She was finishing up her workout." His brother's lips quirked. "The rest I know because I'm married to one of the parties involved. Marisa is no pushover herself."

So Sera boxed. Like him. Interesting. She liked to take out her frustrations on a punching bag?

Still, Jordan quieted. He hadn't expected Sera to go to the trouble of recruiting Marisa and Cole to make her case. He'd thought he was doing her a good turn by asking for her by name. He was surprised by her level of opposition, and not for the first time he wondered what was behind it.

Maybe he should let her off the hook about this physical-therapy gig if she was that panicked about it. But possibly not before finding out why she was so dead-set against him…

Three

"Guess what?"

Sera regarded her older brother, Dante, with a wary eye. There'd been many *guess what*s in their lives. *Guess what? I brought your hamster in for show-and-tell... Guess what? I'm dating your volleyball teammate... Guess what? You're getting your own car—my old wreck.* She loved her brother, but sometimes it was hard to like him.

This time, they were at Dory's Café in downtown Welsdale, and she had some major armor against an unwelcome surprise. Namely, she was sitting down, already fortified by morning coffee ahead of brunch. And Dante was lucky—there was a table between them, so she couldn't kick him in the shins as she might have done when she was six—not that she was above trying if things got out of hand.

"Okay," she mustered, "I give up. What is it? Winning lottery numbers? One-way ticket to Mars? What?" She stuck out her chin and waited.

"Nothing so dramatic, sport." Dante chuckled. "New job."

Sera breathed a sigh of relief. "Congrats. That makes two of us in less than three years. Mom will be doing the happy dance." Frankly, her mother could use good news. Rosana Perini was still putting the pieces of her life back together—rearranging the puzzle that had broken and scattered when she'd become a young widow. The whole family had needed to regroup when Joseph Perini had died six years ago when Sera was twenty-three. It was one of the things that had made Sera decide to start a new chapter in her life by going back to school for her physical-therapy degree.

"You're looking at the new VP of Marketing for the New England Razors."

Sera's stomach plummeted as she was jerked back to the present. No, no and *no*. Dante's working for the New England Razors meant only one thing: another connection to Jordan Serenghetti. Still, she managed to cough up the critical word. "Congratulations."

"Thanks, Sera. It's my dream job."

Her brother had always been a sports nut. His teenage bedroom had been decorated with soccer, football and hockey memorabilia. No wonder someone had thought he was perfect for the Razors marketing position.

A dream come true for Dante. A nightmare for her. She didn't need her life further entangled with Jordan Serenghetti's. Her brother would be offering up free game tickets and suggesting a family evening out. Or talking nonstop about Jordan Serenghetti's prowess—on and off the ice.

Dante, though, appeared oblivious to her discomfort. "I wonder if Marisa can grease the wheels for me with Jordan Serenghetti. You know, maybe invite us both to a family barbecue at her house again soon." Her brother shrugged.

"Making sure that Jordan and the Razors are happy with each other is part of my new job description."

"She doesn't need to," Sera managed to get out, volunteering the information because Dante would find out eventually anyway. "I'm seeing Jordan myself."

Dante's eyebrows shot up. "Oh, yeah?"

"Jordan is my new client at Astra Therapeutics. The Razors are farming out some of their physical rehab, and Jordan is their guinea pig."

A grin split her brother's face. "You mean your guinea pig."

Sera tossed her hair. "Hey, I'm a professional."

"Then why do you eye him at family gatherings as if he's the first case of the plague in five hundred years?"

"Professional distance."

Dante snorted. "I'll buy that as fast as a counterfeit trading card on an online auction site."

"Whatever. I'm giving him the boot to another therapist in the office."

"Why?"

"You just said it yourself. We don't get along."

"What about family loyalty?"

"To Jordan Serenghetti? He's only a cousin-in-law." As if she could forget.

"Jordan could end up owing you a debt of gratitude for getting him back on his feet."

Just then, the waitress arrived with their food—a lumberjack breakfast of eggs, sausage and toast for Dante, and an egg-white omelet for her. Sera liked to practice what she preached to her clients—healthy eating and clean living. She also made sure to thank the waitress because she knew what it meant to be on your feet for hours.

Her brother took his first bite and then tilted his head and studied her. "You don't like him because women fawn over him."

"I hadn't noticed, and anyway it's none of my business." She gave all her concentration to seasoning her food with the pepper mill.

"You shouldn't let one bad experience with what's-his-name Neil sour you."

True…if she could trust her instincts. But she still wasn't sure her radar was working right. And Dante had no clue that she and Jordan had shared more than casual conversation in the past. Not that she wanted her brother to ever find out. It was bad enough he knew the basics of her drama with Neil.

Dante waved his fork as he swallowed his food. "You should at least tell Jordan that your attitude isn't personal."

"Never…and you're not going to, either." Because it was personal—and wasn't just about her unsavory experience with Neil.

"Okay, play it your way, but I think you're making a mistake."

She shrugged. "Mine to make."

"Ser," Dante said, suddenly looking earnest, "I could use your help."

"Wow, this is a change."

"I'm serious. I need Jordan back on the ice, and the sooner the better. It would make a great start to my new job if I could claim some credit. Or at least if I could say my sister—the physical therapist with the golden touch—helped get him back in shape."

Sera made a face. "Ugh, Dante. That's asking a lot."

Dante cleared his throat. "I got the position with the Razors…but there's already a higher-up who is gunning for me." He shrugged. "We have some bad history together at a prior employer, and I'm sure he'd be happy if I screwed up."

Sera sighed. "What kind of bad history?"

Her brother looked sheepish. "We were in competition

at a sports agency…and there might have been a woman involved, too."

Great. She took a bite of her omelet. She could just imagine her brother involved in a love triangle. *Almost.* She didn't want any more details.

"Fans come to see Jordan in action," Dante cajoled.

"Whatever." From what she could tell, Jordan was still in fantastic shape despite his injury, and she didn't care how much money he had on the table. The guy had major bank already—what was a few million, more or less, to him?

"Sera, I'm asking."

Sera shifted in her seat. Because, for once, the tables were turned. Her brother needed her help—unlike when he'd stepped in to bail her out when they were younger. Sure, he'd been a thorn in her side with his antics—keeping her on edge—but he'd also cast a protective mantle. Unlike her, Dante remembered the child their parents had lost at birth, and it was almost like he'd absorbed their unspoken worries about losing another loved one. So, he'd issued warnings about situations to avoid at school, stood up for her when she'd been picked on as a kid and, yes, kept some of her secrets from their parents.

On the other hand, Jordan threatened the safe and tidy world that she'd worked hard to build for herself. She knew just how potent his kisses could be, and she was nobody's fool. Not anymore. If she stepped up for Dante, she'd be walking a fine line…

Sera folded her arms as she stepped into the examining room. "So you're stuck with me."

Jordan was leaning against the treatment table, crutches propped up next to him. He was billboard-ready good-looking even under the fluorescent lights of the room. She, on the other hand, was in her usual shapeless scrubs. Clearly, if he didn't enjoy toying with her, she'd be beneath his notice—which ran to models, actresses and reality stars these days, if his press was to be believed.

Jordan's expression turned to one of surprise, and then he gave his trademark insouciant grin. "I'm stuck with you? And here I thought the best part of the day was getting to sample your cannoli bruschetta mash-up recipe along with the rest of the staff. It was delicious, by the way."

"Well, you were wrong," she deadpanned. Why did she feel a thrill at his compliment?

"What prompted the change of heart? Don't keep me waiting. This is the most suspense I've had in ages."

"I'm sure it's a rare occurrence for a woman to keep you cooling your heels."

Jordan's smile widened. "What do you think?"

She ignored the question and gritted her teeth instead. *Best to get this over with.* "My brother, Dante, just got a job with the Razors. Marketing VP, to be exact."

Jordan raised his eyebrows and then his lips quirked. "You Perinis can't seem to stay away from professional hockey players."

She gave him a frosty smile. "Let me remind you that I was initially recruited for this job. I didn't volunteer."

"The end result is the same."

"Now I'm helping out Dante by getting you back on your feet."

"Of course."

Well, that was easy.

"Do I get anything in return for helping you out?"

Sera narrowed her eyes. She'd spoken too soon. This was more like the Jordan Serenghetti she expected. "Don't be evil. The chance to spread some beneficence should be good enough for you."

Jordan laughed, looking not the least bit insulted. "Now I understand why you showed up for my appointment today as scheduled—instead of, you know, feigning typhoid or something."

"Count your blessings."

"So you're going to agree to be my physical therapist, and here I was about to let you off the hook."

"You're not going to make this easy for me, are you?"

"Is that a rhetorical question?"

"The silver lining is that I get to make you sweat."

"Some people pay to see that, you know."

Of course she knew Jordan got paid millions for his skills on the ice. Still… "Don't you ever stop?"

"Not when it's this much fun."

"Well then, I guess it's time for me to stop making it so enjoyable for you."

"You know, I really was going to let you off the hook today." Jordan shrugged. "Cole came to see me because you were adamant about not being my therapist. Obviously, you've had a change of heart."

Now she looked like an opportunist. She didn't know that Marisa had followed through and told Cole to have a talk with Jordan. "Why didn't you cancel your appointment? Or ask for someone else before your scheduled time?"

"I didn't want you to look bad at the office. I figured it would be better if the word came from you."

Sera lowered her shoulders. She felt bad—guilty… Damn him. She was only trying to help her brother!

Jordan just stood there, being himself—all sexy. Badass abs and chiseled pecs under a formfitting T-shirt, square jaw, magnetic green eyes and all.

Sera gritted her teeth again. She could do this. She… owed him. "Thanks."

He cupped his hand to his ear. "What was that?"

And just like that, they were back to squabbling. She knew she was rising to the bait, but she couldn't help herself. "Thank you…for giving me the opportunity to see you grunt and sweat."

Jordan laughed but then started leveraging himself onto the treatment table. "Ready when you are."

She moved aside his crutches and then helped him stretch his legs before him. When he was settled, she examined his knee. After a few moments of poking and prodding, she had to admit he was coming along nicely. "The swelling is about as good as we can expect at this stage."

"So I heal well?"

She looked up. "You're a professional athlete at the top of your game. It's not surprising." When he looked pleased, she added, "Today we're going to focus on increasing mobility and improving your quad function even more."

"Sounds…fun," he remarked drily. "You know, it's amazing we didn't know each other in high school. You lost some opportunities to kick my butt."

"*Amazing* isn't the word I'd use." *More like a relief.* Her teenage self could have gotten into big trouble with Jordan. As it was…but she was older and wiser now.

"Marisa mentioned you grew up in East Gannon. Right next door."

"And yet a world away." East Gannon was Welsdale's poor cousin. People had small clapboard homes, not mansions with expensive landscaping.

Jordan looked thoughtful. "Welsdale High played East Gannon plenty of times."

"I didn't pay much attention to hockey in high school. I left that stuff to Dante."

Jordan's expression registered surprise. "And you call yourself a New Englander?"

She stuck out her chin. "I played volleyball."

Jordan's eyes gleamed. "An athlete. I knew there must be something we had in common."

Sera stopped herself from rolling her eyes.

"And you also box to stay in shape, from what I understand," he murmured. "So two things we have in common."

"I doubt there are three," she countered, and he just laughed.

She could get used to the way his eyes crinkled and amusement took over his entire face.

"You went to Welsdale High?" she added quickly. "I figured you'd gone to a fancy place like Pershing School along with Cole."

Cole Serenghetti had been a star hockey player at the Pershing School. It was where he'd met Marisa, who'd attended on scholarship. They'd had a teenage romance until Marisa had played a part in Cole's suspension. Then they'd led separate lives for fifteen years until fate and a Pershing School fund-raiser had brought them together again.

"Serenghetti Construction wasn't doing well during a recession, so I decided to take the financial burden off my parents by switching to Welsdale High for my junior year."

"Oh." She tried to reconcile the information with what she knew of Jordan Serenghetti. *Self-sacrificing* wasn't a word that she'd have associated with him. And she didn't want a reason to like him.

Jordan gave her a cocky grin. "I had an excellent run at Welsdale High School. You missed it all."

"No regrets." Then, giving in to curiosity, she asked, "Do you ever wish you'd gone to Pershing School?"

"Nope. Welsdale High had just as good a hockey team, and we were the champs twice while I was there."

This time, Sera did roll her eyes. "No doubt you think it was due to the fact you were on the team."

Jordan smiled. "Actually, I was a lowly freshman for the first win."

She shrugged. "Maybe you thought Pershing School was second-best to Welsdale. After all, the suspension that Marisa earned Cole meant that Pershing hadn't won a championship in a while."

Jordan held up his hands in mock surrender. "Hey, I don't blame Marisa. She had her arm twisted by the fates." He gave her a cheeky look. "And no, I didn't transfer because I thought Welsdale High had a better hockey team. I figured whichever side I played on would have the superior team."

"So I was right, after all. You claim all the credit."

Jordan relaxed his teasing expression. "As I said, since the two teams were about equal, I decided to do my parents a favor by saving on tuition. But I let them believe that the hockey team was the reason for my switching schools."

Sera got serious, too. "Well, it was a nice thing to do. Apparently, you do have a pleasant side…occasionally."

He angled his head. "Want to help me brush up on my manners?"

"I'm not a teacher, and something tells me you'd be a poor student. But actually, right now I have something to show you."

He perked up.

"Heel slides," she said succinctly, all business. "The first exercise for your knee."

"Oh."

She guided him in a demonstration of sliding the heel of his foot along the treatment table, extending his knee for twenty seconds. After that, as he reclined on the table, he did repetitions by himself while grasping a belt that was anchored with the heel of his foot.

"Great," she said encouragingly. "This should improve your quad function."

He grunted as he continued, until she felt he'd done enough.

She took the belt from him and put it aside on the counter. "Now I'm going to teach you something you can do at home by yourself."

He arched a brow, and she gave him a stern look even as she felt heat rise to her face.

"Great," he managed. "I suppose I should be glad that there are no paparazzi around, angling for a picture of me on crutches."

"Exactly." Putting her index finger at the location of one his incisions, she moved her finger back and forth, her touch smooth but firm. "This scar massage is to reduce inflammation. You should continue to do this daily." She started a circular motion. "You can also vary the direction."

Sera kept her gaze focused on his knee, and Jordan was quiet for a change—watching her.

"So I have a question," he finally said, his tone conversational. "Have any of your clients flirted with you? Before me?"

"We haven't flirted. Well, you have, but it takes two to tango." With an impersonal touch, she placed his hand where hers had been on his knee. "Now you try."

He inclined his head in acknowledgment, imitating her motion. "Okay, what about before me?"

She covered his hand to guide him a bit, ignoring the sudden awareness that came from touching him again. "Some have tried, none have succeeded."

"Wow, a challenge."

"You would see it that way. But nope, a futile endeavor is more like it."

He looked up. "Throwing down the gauntlet."

She met his gaze. "You're too incapacitated to bend low enough to pick it up."

"But not for long," he replied with a wicked glint.

"Now we're going to try the stationary bike," she announced, ignoring him.

Jordan raised his eyebrows. "I'm going to be biking already?"

"Your good leg will be doing all the work." She was relieved they were moving to the wide-open gym. Verbally tangling with Jordan Serenghetti while they were alone was like walking a tightrope—it took all her focus, and she needed a break.

He followed her over to the gym on his crutches, and she helped as he gingerly got on the bike.

Because he exuded so much charisma, Sera could almost forget Jordan was injured. She refocused her attention and instructed him in what to do.

He slowly pedaled backward and forward with his right leg, his left knee bending and straightening in response.

"How's the pain?" she asked.

He bared his teeth. "I've had worse in training sessions with the Razors."

"Good. You want to push but not too hard."

"Right."

She watched him for a few more minutes until she was satisfied with his effort. "Good job."

"Effusive praise from you," he teased.

"We're not done yet," she parried.

After several more minutes, they returned to the treatment room, where she instructed him on how to do straight-leg raises while resting on his back. She followed this up with having him do raises from the hip while he was lying on his side. Then she helped him sit up to do short arc quads, raising his leg from the knee.

As he was finishing up his last exercise, she glanced at the clock and realized with some surprise that their time was up.

She tucked a stray strand of hair behind her ear and exhaled. "Okay, that's it for today."

He raised his brows. "I'm done?"

She nodded. "You're making excellent progress. You've gained some more motion in your knee since the surgery, and that's what we're going to continue to work on."

He smiled. Not mocking, not teasing, just genuine, and Sera blinked.

"Glad things are working out," he said.

That made two of them. For her peace of mind, Jordan couldn't get well fast enough.

Four

"The companies behind the endorsement deals need reassurance. When do you think you'll be playing again?" Marvin Flor's worried voice boomed from Jordan's cell phone.

Jordan shifted on his sofa. Marv had been his agent since his professional hockey career had started nearly ten years ago. He was good, tough and a whiz at promotion. Hence Jordan's promotional contracts for everything from men's underwear to athletic gear and sports drinks. Marv was in his sixties and a dead ringer for actor Javier Bardem—and well into his third decade as a top-notch sports agent.

"Why don't you partner with your sister, Mia, for a line of men's apparel? Isn't she an up-and-coming designer?"

Jordan stifled a laugh, pushing aside the thought that Marv's half-joking suggestion—at least, he thought it was only semiserious—might be a sign of desperation. His house phone rang, and he ignored it. "First off, I don't think Mia's ready to branch into men's sportswear just yet.

And second, we'd throttle each other if we worked together. Sibling rivalry and all that."

Jordan gazed at the lazy, late-afternoon sunlight filtering through the floor-to-ceiling windows of his Welsdale penthouse. Usually in the off-season, he was a whirlwind of energy. Vacationing in Turks and Caicos, making personal appearances...working out to keep fit. Now the weights in his private gym lay unused, and he hadn't met Cole at Jimmy's Boxing Gym in weeks. At least he'd been able to shed his crutches the other day, since he was close to four weeks postsurgery.

Marv sighed. "So, okay, what's the latest on when you'll be back on the ice?"

"Doubtful for the beginning of the season. We're looking at three months of therapy at least." Jordan winced. His endorsement contracts had clauses in them, and if he wasn't on the ice, he'd stand to lose a cool few million. And then there was the upcoming negotiation of his contract to continue to play for the Razors...

"What's the prognosis?"

"There's no reason not to expect full recovery." *At this point.*

Jordan could almost hear Marv's sigh of relief.

"Good. Because everyone is aware of the family history."

Meaning Cole. Meaning ACL tears ran in the family. And had been career-ending for at least one Serenghetti already. Not good. "I'm in great hands, Marv. The best." He couldn't complain about his doctors. His physical therapist, on the other hand...

Sera had surprised him at their last session. He was happy to help smooth Dante's way with the Razors. And Sera was going to be his reluctant physical therapist for the duration...even if she sometimes acted as if she wanted to take a few shots at him in the boxing ring. The thought made Jordan smile. In fact, the biggest problem with his prolonged recovery was that his plan for what to do with the endorsement-deal money might be in jeopardy. He'd had a few restless nights about his career hitting the rocks, but he was a fighter.

"Well, if we can't get you on the ice, we need to keep you in the public eye with a positive spin," Marv continued. "That should help keep the companies that you've partnered with happy."

Jordan heard his landline ring again and told Marv to hold on even as he picked up the receiver with his free hand. After building reception announced that his mother was on her way up, Jordan switched back to his agent. His day was about to get more interesting, and Jordan knew he had to wrap things up with some quick reassurances. "Don't worry, Marv. With this banged-up knee, I'm not likely to be partying hard in Vegas."

"Yeah, yeah. But good press with your name attached to it would be better. It's not enough to stay out of trouble."

Jordan knew Marv would love his plan for what to do with the paychecks from his endorsement deals, but he wanted to keep his idea to himself for the moment. He hadn't mentioned his intentions to anyone, and anyway, good publicity and Marv's worries weren't the reason he wanted to go ahead with his plan. No, his reasons were deeper and personal, which was why he'd kept a lid on his goal till now.

"I suppose a semiserious relationship isn't in the cards."

Jordan coughed. "No."

He intended to enjoy his pinnacle of fame and fortune. He'd spent enough years being the sickly kid who'd been stuck at home—or in the hospital. That was, until he'd grown into a solid teenager who could slap the puck into the goal better than anyone.

On top of that, his current lifestyle wasn't conducive to

home and hearth. He was on the road half the time when he was playing, and the NHL season was long in comparison to other sports. He wasn't ready to settle down. He was still Jordan Serenghetti—NHL hotshot and billboard model—despite his temporary detour. He'd spent years on the ice. He wasn't sure who he was beyond the identity that he'd taken a long time to carve out for himself.

Marv grumbled. "Well, at the moment you are staying in one place for a while. There's hope. A relationship with a hometown sweetheart would give us some positive ink in the press. Work with me here."

The only woman Jordan was seeing lately was Sera… and she was hardly the type who'd be mistaken for his girlfriend, given that her typical expression around him was a scowl. She'd probably slam the door in a paparazzo's face—and then issue a vehement denial and threaten litigation about linking her good name to Jordan Serenghetti. The last thought made him smile again.

He figured they could have some fun together—what was the harm in a little flirtation? And he was curious about the basis of Sera's prickliness. At least it should make her happy that he'd been doing the exercises that she'd assigned for him. He was also looking forward to seeing her next week—sparring with her and peeling back some more of the layers that made up the complex and intriguing Serafina Perini.

Jordan heard the private elevator that led straight into the penthouse moments before the door opened and his mother appeared, casserole dish in hand.

"Gotta go, Marv," he said before ending the call on his agent's admonition to keep in touch.

Jordan straightened, lowering his bad leg from where it was resting on the sofa's seat cushions. "Mom, this is a surprise."

Everyone but his mother knew better than to show up unexpectedly.

Camilla Serenghetti smiled as she stopped before him. "I brought you something to eat."

Because his mother still bore traces of an Italian accent—as well as having a habit of mixing words from two languages in a single sentence—the *eat* came off sounding as if there was a short *a* vowel at the end of it.

"Mom, it's my knee that needs help, not my stomach." Still, whatever she'd brought smelled delicious.

"You need to keep up your strength." She moved toward the kitchen where a Viking range was visible from the living area. "Lasagna."

"With béchamel sauce?"

"Just like you like it."

"The staff on the show must adore you if you're always sharing special dishes." *Like someone else he knew.* Except his mother had her own local show, *Flavors of Italy with Camilla Serenghetti*—her name had been added to the title in recent years.

His mother turned back from the kitchen and frowned. "It's not because of the staff that I worry. It's the new television station owners. I'm not sure they like my cooking."

"You're kidding."

"There's talk, *chiacchierata*, about big changes. Maybe no cooking shows."

"They're considering canceling you?"

Camilla's hands flew to her cheeks. "*Per piacere*, Jordan. *Please*, watch what you say."

Jordan knew this show was his mother's baby. And his father had made a guest appearance—finally coming out of the funk into which he'd sunk after his stroke.

"Mom, they're not going to cancel you. They'd be crazy to."

"Not even if they want to bring the television station in a new *direzione*?"

"You mean *take* the station in a new direction." He was so used to correcting his mother's English, it was second nature. She'd been doing a mash-up on her adopted language as long as he could remember.

"*Take, bring*, whatever. *Open* the light means *turn on*. You understand me, *sì*?"

Jordan smiled. "More importantly, your viewers understand and love you. You speak the international language of food."

A look of relief passed over his mother's face. "Years of trying recipes on my family paid off. And you ate my *pastina con brodo*. Always. Good kids make great cooking skills."

He loved his mother's pasta in broth. He'd grown up on it. Even today, the aroma of it brought him back to childhood. He'd been served the dish every time he'd been ill or injured—anything from the common cold to the more serious episodes that had landed him in Welsdale Children's Hospital.

He also knew how much the show meant to his mother as far as giving her a late-life second act. Jordan schooled his expression. "How's Dad? Besides drowning in *pastina con brodo*, I mean."

His mother served the same dish to every ill family member. And because his father had never fully recovered from his stroke, his mother could continue with her culinary cure-all indefinitely. In fact, Jordan was surprised she hadn't brought more of her signature dish with her today on her visit to his apartment.

"Giordano, don't be fresh. Your father is okay with his health. The show, not so good."

Jordan relaxed a little at news of his father. Serg Serenghetti's health had been a cause for concern for his family ever since his stroke a few years ago. For his mother's benefit, however, Jordan teased, "Next you'll be telling me that you're vlogging to build up your audience."

"No, *mia assistente* on the show already does it for me."

"And a star is born." He was surprised his mother even knew what vlogging was, but he supposed he shouldn't be astonished that a cooking show would have already been posting videos online.

"Hmm. Tell that to your father."

Jordan crinkled his eyes. "What does that mean? You just said Dad was fine."

"Yes, with his health."

"Wait, don't tell me… He's having a hard time with the fact that you're the breadwinner now?"

"You know we don't need the money."

"So what is it?" Jordan kept the smile on his face.

For once his mother looked hesitant. "I think—"

"Your star is outshining his?"

Camilla nodded. "He suggested a regular segment about wine on my show. Starring him."

Jordan bit back a laugh. "Delusions of grandeur."

"He built Serenghetti Construction," his mother pointed out.

"Right." Frankly, the wine-segment scheme seemed right in line with his father's outsize personality. "Rope him in, Mom, before he can get away and strike a deal with bigger fish. Cole can get you a lawyer. Tie him up with an exclusive arrangement." He was joking—sort of.

Camilla looked heavenward as if asking for divine intervention. "We already have a long deal. We're married."

Jordan shifted on the sofa, masking a grin.

When his mother's gaze came back to him, she swept him with a sudden, appraising look. "You seem better. More robust. Sera is doing therapy for you."

It was a statement, not a question. His mother was more in the know than he'd realized.

"Yes, what a coincidence," he said cautiously as he straightened, slowly and deliberately.

"Such a lovely woman."

Here we go. But he refused to rise to the bait. "Yup, Cole inherited a great set of in-laws."

"She could have provided rehabilitation for your father."

"Too late. Besides, Dad's stroke happened before Marisa reconnected with Cole." Grimacing, he started to rise, and as he expected, his mother transitioned from hovering in front of him to moving forward, filled with concern.

"Careful, don't hurt yourself. You still need to finish healing."

He waited while she placed a helping hand under his elbow before he stood fully. "Thanks, Mom."

Rick might be the Hollywood stuntman and his new sister-in-law Chiara an actress, but it didn't mean he couldn't call upon his own acting powers when necessary—like diverting his mother from a topic full of pitfalls.

Stepping back, his mother said, "Come and eat."

Mission accomplished.

Why was she here tonight? Her days moonlighting at the Puck & Shoot were supposed to have ended long ago when she'd become a physical therapist. But she was still being roped into helping out from time to time when the bar was short-staffed. She just couldn't say no to the extra cash.

Balancing a tray of beers, she kept sight of Jordan out of the corner of her eye.

Angus, the bar's owner, had called in desperation because they were down two waitresses, and it was going to be a busy Saturday night. The Puck & Shoot was the type of place where the saltshaker was either nearly empty or ready to shower your fries in an unexpected deluge. Still, the regulars loved it.

The part-time gig had helped pay for her education, but at some point, the tables had flipped so that the job was what was holding her back from starting her new life—one which she'd thought involved *not* seeing certain regulars. But she felt she owed Angus.

Jordan sat at the bar, as usual, and held court with a couple of Razors teammates who happened to be around even though hockey season had ended. Sera recognized Marc Bellitti and Vince Tedeschi.

Since Jordan had a habit of not taking a table, she'd almost never had to serve him. It had been years since their brief encounter during spring break in college, and when she'd first started working at the Puck & Shoot, it had become clear that Jordan hadn't recognized or remembered her. She'd been angry and annoyed and then somewhat relieved—especially after Neil had confirmed her opinion about certain types of men. They were players who moved from one woman on to the next, juggling them like so many balls in the air.

Now that Jordan knew who she was, though—Marisa's cousin and his new therapist—even the little bit of distance afforded by his customary seat at the bar seemed woefully small. As she served the beers to a table of patrons, she was aware of Jordan filling the room with his presence. He had that high-wattage magnetism that celebrities possessed. With his dark green gaze, square jaw and six-foot-plus muscled frame, he could make a woman feel as if she were the only one in the room. *Damn it.*

And Sera knew she wasn't imagining things. More than once, she caught his gaze following her back and forth across the crowded bar. It made her aware of her snug-fitting T-shirt and short skirt only partially hidden by an apron. Even though she wasn't dressed up or showing much skin, she wasn't in the shapeless light blue scrubs she wore at Astra Therapeutics, either. And her hair caught back in a ponytail for convenience just meant that she couldn't hide her expression from Jordan.

Already she was regretting her decision to stay on as Jordan's therapist—news that she'd broken to Marisa in a brief text. Only sheer strength of nerves had gotten her through a total of four therapy sessions with Jordan so far—and counting. In the past two weeks, he'd shed his crutches—though he still wasn't close to being completely recovered, of course. In therapy, he'd done the exercises that she'd shown him, including doing hamstring stretches, using a stationary bike and walking on a treadmill. They'd worked on gaining balance, extension and strength in his knee—with a minimum of quips thrown in.

She admired his powers of recuperation. She ought to be pleased. And yet…her only defense was that she was in charge during their sessions. He was all taut, lean muscle—in his prime and in great shape.

After making sure that everyone at her table was satisfied with their order, she wound her way back across the bar with her now-empty tray. She again tried to shake off the prickly sensation of being watched in a sensual fashion. Jordan had done it in the past, before he'd known who she was, but now it was more pronounced—blatant, even. It should have been the opposite since they were in-laws. He *knew* she couldn't be just a casual hookup, because they'd see each other again. Didn't the guy ever obey a DANGER sign?

She frowned. She ought to remind him about what had happened during spring break eight years ago. She'd been tempted to on several occasions, but her pride had stopped her. The last thing she wanted to do was tell Jordan that she'd been one in a long line of forgettable women.

From the periphery of her vision, she noticed a young

brunette sidle up to Jordan and strike up a conversation. After a moment, Jordan smiled and slid into flirtatious mode. *Naturally.*

Sera belatedly recognized the other woman as Danica Carr, an occasional patron. Not too long ago, she'd been approached by Danica with questions about getting into a physical-therapy program. Angus had told Danica that Sera had worked her way through school by waitressing.

Sera determinedly ignored Jordan and his new friend and kept busy as the bar got more crowded. The distraction of work was a relief, but almost an hour later, she had the beginnings of a low-grade headache. It was a lot of effort pretending Jordan didn't exist. And he was *still* talking to Danica.

As she paused at the corner of the bar at the end of her shift, Sera felt her temper spike, or at least lick the edges of her conscious. She untied her apron and stuffed it behind the counter. Once upon a time, she'd been Danica. Young, trusting and on the cusp of making a significant career choice.

These days, she didn't even go on dating apps. All that swiping left at the end of a long day was exhausting. If she couldn't trust her instincts about a guy even after months of dating, how could she put her faith in a mere photo on her phone?

Jordan was probably a dating-app star. The thought popped into her head, and she could feel her mouth stretch into a sour line. Whether Danica knew it or not, Jordan was a lion playing with a kitty, and Sera suddenly knew it was up to her to be the lion tamer. She couldn't stand by and do nothing while another naive young woman got taken in by Jordan Serenghetti.

Sera watched as Danica walked away and rejoined her party at their table. Straightening away from the bar, Sera moved toward Jordan, and at the last moment, he turned his head and noticed her—almost as if he'd known all along exactly where she was.

He was dressed in jeans and a crewneck T-shirt that showed off his biceps—how did he manage to be a walking billboard even injured? His gaze flicked over her, quick but boldly assessing, missing nothing from her breasts to her hips. Still, she refused to be unnerved or to succumb, where most mortal women would be tongue-tied and giggly.

When she stopped in front of him, Jordan remained silent, watchful, his expression for once indecipherable. Fortunately, Marc Bellitti and Vince Tedeschi were caught up in their own conversations at the bar and seemed too distracted to notice.

"Danica is a naive kid," she said without preamble. "Move on. She's not in your league."

Jordan smiled. "You know my league?"

Serafina pressed her lips together. Jordan Serenghetti really was beyond redemption—not that she was in the savior business. "I don't do bad boys. My mother taught me right."

Jordan's expression bloomed into a grin that shot straight through her. "Straitlaced. You need to loosen up."

Ha! Easy for him to say. He was the guy who was nothing but loose…and went over like smooth cocoa butter with most women.

Though not with me, she reminded herself. *Not anymore.* "And for the record, you're my patient. It's all business between us."

He glanced around him. "We're in a bar, not at Astra."

"But I'm still working."

He rubbed his chin and then teased, "You're not a woman who's bowled over by my charm?"

"Of course not. Far too levelheaded." *These days.* It was hard to explain how she'd fallen prey to Neil not so long ago, but maybe she'd been overdue for a lightning strike… Then again, the more she thought about it, the more she wondered whether she'd fallen for Neil precisely because he'd been smooth and worldly and sophisticated. Maybe she'd been determined to prove that she could play in the big leagues and wasn't helpless little Sera who needed protecting.

"And yet, I sense fire and passion in you," Jordan murmured.

"That's because I put you in the hot seat, Serenghetti. I see right through your game."

He made a show of glancing around him. "You've stolen the Razors' playbook?"

Sera placed her hands on her hips. It wouldn't be good if Angus noticed her in an argument with a customer—particularly a famous hometown favorite—but fortunately the bar was packed. "You know what I mean. I know your type, and I can read your plays off the ice."

"Jealous of Danica?"

"Please."

He swept her a look that she felt everywhere. "You shouldn't be, you know. At the moment, prickly waitresses seem to be my type." He regarded her thoughtfully. "Particularly those that might have had a prior bad experience."

Sera sucked in a breath and clamped her lips together. He didn't know the half of it. "I'm not naive, if that's what you're suggesting."

"I didn't claim you were. But you are…wary."

Yup. Once bitten, twice shy.

Jordan searched her expression and then relaxed his. "Danica isn't my type, but I make it a policy to be nice to fans."

As if on cue, Danica suddenly reappeared. "Jordan, I'm leaving—" she looked eager as a puppy "—and I was wondering, do you need a lift home?"

Jordan gave a killer smile that made Sera want to reach for a pair of sunglasses. "I'm good."

"Oh." Disappointment was etched on Danica's face. "I thought with you being injured and all..."

"I'm off crutches and can drive." Jordan waved his hand at Sera, and the other woman noticed her for the first time. "It's what Sera and I were discussing."

Sera tossed him a speaking look. *Oh, really?*

Danica pushed her dark straight hair off her shoulder. "Hi, Serafina."

"How are those physical-therapy program applications coming along?" Sera asked, dropping her hands from her hips.

Danica's face fell. "I still need a prerequisite or two. I'm never going to pass Chemistry 102."

"Sure, you will. With lots of studying. Then you can spend your days bending players—" she gestured at Jordan "—into shape."

Jordan looked amused. "I need to be straightened out apparently."

"More like set straight," Sera muttered, her gaze clashing with his.

"Oh." Danica looked between them. "Sorry, I didn't know."

Sera blinked. "Know what?"

A small frown appeared on the other woman's brow. "Um..."

Jordan got off the stool, and in the next moment, Sera felt his arm slide around her shoulders.

Danica took a step back and then another. "Well, I think I'll be going." Turning back in the direction where her friends were still waiting, she added quickly, "Nice talking to you."

Sera twisted toward Jordan. *What had just happened?* "You let her think—"

"Yeah, but you gave me the opening."

Sera pressed her lips together.

"Thanks for allowing me to let her down easy."

"I didn't—"

Jordan slanted his head. "You warned her off me. Goal accomplished."

"Not like that!" She didn't want Danica to think that she and Jordan were... *Oh, no...no, no, no. Never. No.*

Jordan leaned in, his face all innocent. "Like what?"

She spluttered. "You know what."

He lowered his gaze to her mouth. "It's what you said."

She bit back a gasp. "You're blaming me?"

He gave a slow, sexy grin. "Thanking you. Let me know when you're ready to...explore what's between us."

Sera had never been in a more frustrating conversation in her life. "Nothing more ego-stroking than the idea of two women competing for your attention, huh?"

"If you say so."

Suddenly, she'd had enough. Enough of a guy who could juggle women with dexterity—even injured.

"You don't remember," she snapped.

"Remember what?"

"Spring break in Florida eight years ago."

Jordan's lips curved. "Am I supposed to?"

"It depends," Sera said sarcastically. "Do you keep a running tally of the women you dally with, or do they just run together in one seamless and nameless highlight video in your mind?"

Jordan tilted his head, looking more intent. *"Dally with?"*

She gestured with her hands. "Flirt with. Come on to... Kiss."

"I'm supposed to remember every woman I ever flirted with?"

"Granted, it must be a long list. How about kissed?"

"Including the fans who've thrown their arms around me?"

She drew her brows together. "Including the ones you've

chatted up on spring break and engaged in some lip-to-lip action with after a couple of beers."

Jordan regarded her thoughtfully. "Are you saying we've kissed…and I don't remember it?"

Sera smacked her forehead. "Give the man a prize for a light-bulb moment."

Jordan grinned. "It must have been some kiss."

"You don't remember it!"

"But you do."

Sera felt herself heat. "Only because you've become famous."

He frowned. "I would have remembered an unusual name like yours."

"I didn't give you my name, and anyway, you probably would have thought I meant *S-A-R-A-H*." It was a common mistake that she was used to.

"So you like to operate anonymously?" he said, enjoying himself.

"I'd just turned twenty-one." *I was young and stupid.*

Jordan rubbed his chin. "Let's see, eight years ago… college break. Destin, Florida?"

"Right," she responded tightly. "Hundreds of students clogging the beach. Beer flowing. Dancing. You angled in…"

They'd locked gazes while she'd danced, and the sexual attraction had sizzled. In swim trunks and with all his smooth, tanned muscles, he'd been an Adonis. And she'd never felt sexier than when he'd looked her over in her aqua bikini, appreciation stamped on his face, and had started dancing with her.

She'd known he wanted to kiss her and had met him halfway when he'd bent, searching her eyes, waiting for her cue. Once Jordan had started kissing her, however, they'd been egged on by the crowd. In minutes, they'd been plastered together, arms around each other, making out to an audience.

"Why didn't you say anything when we met again at Marisa's fund-raiser a couple of years ago?"

"Please, I know your type."

"Of course."

She tossed her head, ponytail swinging. "It wasn't important, except for the fact that spring break experience backed up my impression of your reputation since then."

"Naturally."

Her brows drew together again. "Are you humoring me?"

"I'm still processing your bombshell. Our lips have touched."

"Another reason I didn't mention it. We're in-laws. It would make things awkward."

"Or interesting. I've thought that family gatherings could use some spicing up." His lips quirked. "So I knew you in your wilder, younger days, Perini?"

Her naive days—when she was like Danica.

"What went wrong?"

She folded her arms.

"So let me get this straight. Your grudge against me is that I don't remember kissing you?"

"When it was over, you turned away and laughed for the benefit of your friends." As if nothing had happened. As if she didn't matter. Her heart had plummeted. She'd crashed to earth—sort of embarrassed and humiliated. "And then you merged into the crowd."

Her ego had taken a hit back then—only to be run over by Neil a few years later. She had to face it—she sucked at dealing with men.

"Hey—"

"My job here is done," she said, cutting him off and checking her watch.

This time, she was the one to walk away—fading quickly into the crowd. But all the while, she was aware of Jordan's gaze on her back...

Five

Sera gritted her teeth as she made her way to her car in the dark parking lot. It was an older-model domestic sedan that she'd bought used after dealing with a slippery salesman. Slick men—the world was full of them!

She should never have done Angus a favor by coming in to waitress. Her blood still thrummed through her veins from clashing with Jordan Serenghetti. Or rather, she'd clashed while he'd looked underwhelmed—blowing her off as if he were amused by the whole scenario. Typical.

She fumed. She had a bad experience that she'd been nursing as a secret for *years*. And when her big moment had finally arrived and she'd let loose, Jordan's response had been mild. *What was the big deal?*

It all reminded her of…oh, yeah, her confrontation with Neil about his cheating. Or rather his using her, unwittingly, as the other woman in an affair. Even confronted with the incontrovertible truth, he'd been full of justifications and excuses. *You're special. I meant to tell you.* And her favorite: *It's not what you think.*

Serafina still burned every time she remembered how she'd been taken in by Neil's lies. She'd told Marisa and Dante the cursory details. In fact, she probably shouldn't have divulged anything at all and simply said the relationship had ended. In the aftermath of that debacle, she hadn't wanted anyone to think she still needed protecting and couldn't be trusted to exercise good judgment.

She'd told herself that any woman could have been duped by Neil. He oozed charisma and charm. Just like Jordan Serenghetti.

Oh, Neil had lacked fame, but notoriety would have interfered with his twisted schemes anyway. The press would have made it much harder for him to hide the fact that he had a wife and kid tucked away in Boston. *The rat.*

Do you really know a person if you see only one side of him? Sera had had plenty of time to contemplate that question since breaking up with Neil.

She got behind the wheel and pulled out of the lot for the drive home. She lived in a two-bedroom condo on the opposite side of town that she'd inherited from Marisa. When her cousin had gotten married and moved out, Sera had jumped at the chance to buy the apartment for a very reasonable price. Fortunately, because traffic was light and she knew the route well, she could drive practically on autopilot.

As she started on the main road, Sera replayed the evening. The only reason she'd agreed to help Angus was that she had a whole four consecutive days off from her physical-therapy position. What was one Saturday night helping out a friend and former boss? Plus, she was paying off student loans, so she could use the extra wages and tips from a night moonlighting as a waitress, an aproned superhero saving innocent young women who were easy prey for—

Sera snorted. She should have known it wouldn't be a simple favor. *Of course Jordan would be there.* Saying things she hadn't expected him to say. Looking almost... normal...relatable. She couldn't afford mixed feelings where he was concerned. *Danica isn't my type.* It made her wonder who was—and that was the problem.

Sera flexed her fingers on the steering wheel. The last thing she needed was to be mooning over Jordan Serenghetti. She didn't need to be wondering—mulling—what was on his mind.

Suddenly, she spotted a flurry of movement from the corner of her eye. In an instant, a bear appeared directly in front of her car. Sera sucked in a breath and then jerked hard on the steering wheel to avoid hitting it.

Then everything happened in a blur. Sera bounced around in her seat as the car went off the road in the darkness. She heard and felt tree branches hit the windshield and the car doors. Fear took over, and she hit the brakes hard.

An eternity later—or maybe it was just a couple of seconds—the car jerked to a stop, and the engine cut out.

Sera sat frozen with shock. *What...?* It had all happened *so fast...*

She threw the emergency break and then blinked at the debris marring her front window. Taking a shaky breath, she leaned her head against the steering wheel. Tremors coursed up her arms from her grip on the wheel.

Great, just great.

At least she hadn't hit the bear.

Could this night get any worse? She wanted to cry but instead gave herself a scolding. After several moments, still shaken, she raised her head and stared into the darkness. It wasn't safe to be a lone woman stranded by the side of the road at night. On top of it, she didn't know where that bear was, but with any luck, she'd managed to frighten him off with their near miss.

Of course, she could use her cell phone to call for help. Dante or another relative would come if she called. Still, she hated being poor, helpless Sera again in the eyes of her family—which was how they would see it.

Suddenly, headlights appeared in her rearview mirror. Sera shook off the touch of fear. It was just someone driving by. Someone who would most likely simply keep on going—because she didn't even have her hazard lights on. Statistically speaking, it was unlikely to be an ax murderer.

But the car slowed down as it passed. Then, a few yards down the road, the driver pulled over.

When the person behind the wheel got out, she immediately recognized Jordan Serenghetti even with only the dim illumination of his flashlight.

Sera suppressed a groan. Not an ax murderer, but someone even more improbable. Jordan. Though she supposed she shouldn't be surprised, since he'd been at the Puck & Shoot, too, and the bar was minutes away.

Unsteadily, she got out of the car, determined to put on a brave front. His appearance just added to her turbulent emotions.

Jordan's face was pulled into an uncharacteristic frown as he approached, looking from her to her car and back again. *He even looked attractive with a scowl.*

"Are you all right?" he asked, for once not displaying his trademark devil-may-care expression.

"Isn't that my line?" How many times had she asked him the same thing during a physical-therapy session? She raised her chin, but with horror, she realized there had been a slight tremor in her voice. *Not all right. Damn it.* She cleared her throat.

He came close, and she'd never seen him appear more serious.

"What are you doing?"

"Checking you for obvious signs of injury. Relax. I'll

take it as a good sign that you were able to get out of the car under your own power."

His gaze searched hers in the dim light. "Despite what you think of me, I like to give a hand when I see someone in trouble."

She blinked. "Oh."

"Anything hurt?"

"No." And then she blurted, "What are you doing here?"

Jordan managed to look aggrieved—another new expression for him. "I decided to leave right after you did."

"The fun was gone?" Impossibly, she was challenging him, even though she'd just been in an accident—maybe *because* she'd just been in an accident. She didn't like feeling vulnerable.

"You could say that, but I guess it was good timing—" he gave her a significant look "—because I happened by right after your accident."

"I would have been perfectly fine without your help." No way was Jordan Serenghetti her knight in shining armor.

"Well, judging by your mouth, you're not hurt. And I figure you're going to deny being shaken up. So what happened?"

It irked that he could tell she was rattled. "I swerved to avoid a bear in the road." She grimaced and scanned the woods around them. "In fact, I hope it's not hanging around."

"It's unlikely to view you as a threat." His lips quirked. "I, on the other hand…"

She flushed. Considering she'd just tried to stage a takedown of his womanizing ways back at the bar, she could hardly argue. Next, she expected a critique of her driving skills, but surprisingly it didn't come.

Instead, Jordan examined her car, training his flashlight on the front.

She bit back a gasp as the badly dented front fender was

illuminated. And the headlight had been taken out. Her car was a piece of junk, but now she'd have to add automotive repair costs to her budget.

Jordan tucked the flashlight under his arm and pulled out his cell phone.

"What do you think you're doing?"

"Being practical," he responded mildly, walking a few steps away. "I'm getting highway patrol out here."

"You're calling the police?" she said.

His gaze met hers. "So you don't have to. Your insurance may require a police report."

Sera wrapped her arms around herself. The night was warm, but she suddenly felt chilled. She could fume at his take-charge attitude—or grudgingly accept his help, despite what had just happened between them at the Puck & Shoot.

Within minutes, as Jordan continued his inspection of her car, the police showed up. Sera could only conclude there must have been a highway-patrol car in the vicinity.

When the patrolman got out of his car and approached, he paused a moment, and then obviously recognizing Jordan, his expression relaxed. "Hey, you're Jordan Serenghetti."

"Yup."

"Got into a little fender bender tonight?"

"Not me, her."

Sera watched as the police officer's gaze came to rest on her. She gave a jaunty little wave that belied her emotions. So this was what it felt like to play second fiddle to Jordan's star power.

"What happened?" the officer asked, his gaze now on her.

"I swerved to avoid a bear that appeared on the road." She gestured at her car. "And, well, you can figure out the rest."

The officer rubbed the back of his neck. "Uh-huh."

"She may need paperwork for insurance purposes," Jordan put in.

"Right."

The police officer put up flares while Jordan summoned a tow truck.

When the officer got back to her, she had her driver's license and insurance information ready as another patrol car pulled up.

Again the officer—another middle-aged blond guy—did a double take when he saw Jordan.

The first officer patted his colleague on the shoulder as he went by to his car to fill out the necessary paperwork, and Jordan chatted casually with the new arrival, who obviously couldn't believe his luck at running into a sports celebrity during his shift.

Sera was miserable. The night had gone from bad to worse. She should be slipping between bedcovers right now in soft, worn pajamas. Instead, she was in the middle of a Jordan Serenghetti fan moment.

When the tow truck arrived, the driver slowed his steps as he approached Jordan, and Sera resisted the urge to roll her eyes.

"You're—"

"Jordan Serenghetti," Sera supplied. "Yes, we know."

Jordan's lips twitched. "Don't mind her, she's testy." He shrugged. "You know, accident and all."

The tow truck driver's gaze skimmed over both of them. "Well, at least no one was hurt."

Yet. Yes, she was irritable. Sera waved her hand at Jordan. "He is."

The driver and the police officer still standing nearby both raised their brows.

"Knee surgery," Sera supplied laconically. "I'm sure you two gentlemen have heard about it in the sports news."

Before either man could say anything, Jordan added, "Yeah, and my physical therapist is a badass. I go to bed aching."

The men chuckled, and Sera narrowed her eyes. What had she been thinking about no one being hurt *yet*?

Unfortunately for her, it took another half hour for her car to be towed and the police to be done.

As both officers headed to their cars after the tow truck departed, Jordan turned to her. "I'll drive you."

"Please. The last thing the two of us need is to be in the same moving vehicle together." The police had clearly thought she had a ride with Jordan, though—one they no doubt would have loved to take themselves as his fans. Sera gritted her teeth. "I can use the ride-hailing app on my phone to get a car to pick me up. My apartment is on the other side of town."

"Yeah, you moved into Marisa's old place," Jordan said, ignoring the first part of her reply.

"So you know just how far it is." Sera supposed she shouldn't be surprised that he knew where she lived.

He tossed her a sidelong look. "Great, my place is closer. Let's go."

Wait—what? Had he not heard what she'd said? She was not going to Jordan's place.

As if reading her thoughts, he added, "You're shaken up, and I'm not leaving you alone to be picked up in the dark by a driver you don't even know."

"As opposed to you? Because you're the safer bet? And anyway, chivalry is dead."

"So angelic and yet so cynical," Jordan murmured.

"With good reason!"

"I'll get you a car from my place once I'm convinced you're all right."

It was hard to be mad at someone when you owed them a favor.

And the last person she wanted to be indebted to for help was Jordan Serenghetti.

Somehow, she was going to live down tonight's debacle. Somehow, she was going to get through weeks of physical therapy with Jordan. Her mind ping-ponged, hit by a gamut of emotions as she stepped into Jordan's apartment.

His place had the ambience of an athlete…a jock…a celebrity…a sports star living there. But shockingly, Sera couldn't sniff *playboy* in the air as she paused next to the elevator that had just deposited them in his penthouse. Everything was modern, pristine and orderly. White walls, chocolate upholstery and stainless-steel appliances. It was far from the messy fraternity house existence that she'd been expecting.

And then, because Jordan was watching her as they stood just inside his apartment, she said, "So this is how the other half lives."

"It's not that fancy."

Her gaze drifted toward the back of his apartment. "Your Viking range alone must have cost thousands of dollars. And I'm guessing you don't even really cook."

"No, but my mother does. So she has expectations."

The apartment was dim and quiet…and Jordan was standing too close. So much so that she picked up on the scent that she had started to identify as uniquely his.

As a result of their physical-therapy sessions, she was well-acquainted with the reasons why *some* women found him attractive. He was all toned and sculpted muscle—with a lean, hard jaw and wicked glint in his green eyes. Even injured, he exuded a powerful magnetism. This close, she had to lift her head to make eye contact, making her even more aware of just how *male* he was. Now that he was out of his milieu—a sports bar—she could momentarily forget why she didn't like him. *Almost.*

They stared at each other in the dim light.

The corner of his mouth lifted. "Lost for words?"

"I've spent them all."

"Yeah, I know."

All that remained unsaid hung between them.

"Come on in," he said.

"I thought I was getting a car."

"In a sec." He regarded her thoughtfully. "But first you look like you could use a shoulder to lean on."

"Not yours." To her horror, however, her voice wasn't as strong and steady as she would have liked. The hour was late, she was tired and she'd had one roller coaster of a day. Suddenly, it was all catching up to her and was just too much. Right now, she wanted to be in fluffy socks and battered sweats and holding a cup of herbal tea. Not dealing with the complexities of her relationship with Jordan. No, wait—they didn't have a *relationship*.

Jordan searched her face with an annoyingly penetrating gaze. "Are you okay?"

"Fine." Could that high-pitched voice possibly be hers? But fortunately, he hadn't brought up their conversation at the Puck & Shoot.

"Sera."

She felt as if she were drowning.

"Aw, hell," Jordan said.

In the next instant, he'd folded her into his arms, smoothing his hands down her back as he tucked her head under his chin.

She stiffened. "You're the last person—"

"I know."

"I don't even like you. You are irritating and rude and—"

"—ridiculous?"

"This is a delayed reaction," she sniffed, relaxing into his embrace.

"Understandable."

"If you breathe a word about this to anyone, Serenghetti…"

"Not likely. Your reputation is safe with me."

"Great."

She was more shaken up by her accident than she'd thought. More shaken up by *everything*.

He stroked his hand up and down her back, lulling her. She leaned into him. They stayed that way as time ticked by for she couldn't say how long.

It was quiet, and the lights of Welsdale twinkled outside.

Slowly, though, as she regained steadiness, comfort gave way to something else. She became aware of subtle changes. Jordan's breathing deepened, and hers grew shallower and more rapid.

He shifted, dipping his head, and his lips grazed her temple.

She lifted her head and met his gaze. "So these are the famous Jordan Serenghetti moves these days? A hug?"

Their faces were inches apart, and she remained pressed against him—his long, lean form imprinting her, making her *feel*.

"How am I doing?"

She lifted her shoulders. "Do you usually look for a rating?"

"You still have a smart mouth, Perini," he muttered.

"Weaponized? And you're going to disarm me, I bet," she replied tartly.

He bent toward her and muttered, "Worth risking serious injury for."

"I dare you." She tossed out the words carelessly, but she was all taut awareness because she'd never seen Jordan this focused and intent.

"You know that kiss…"

Her brows drew together. "What about it?"

"Since I don't remember it, I'm curious."

She sucked in a breath and then warned, "Since there's no audience to cheer you on this time, why bother?"

He pressed the pad of his thumb against her bottom lip. "Such a loaded question. Let's find out."

And just like that, he kissed her.

She tried for nonchalance. Still, his mouth was lazy and sensual, coaxing hers into a slow dance.

Eventually, the kiss took on a life of its own. In fact, Sera wasn't sure what possessed her. The need to tangle with a player again—and this time be the one who came out ahead? Perhaps a desire to prove that she was older and wiser and not so green—and therefore wouldn't be hurt? She couldn't say—and maybe didn't want to examine the issue too closely.

Jordan cupped the sides of her face, his fingers tunneling into her hair, and held her steady. His mouth was warm, searching…confident.

He swept his tongue around hers, and she met him, every part of her responding. She gripped his shirt, pulling him in, and he made a low sound in his throat.

She'd wondered over the years whether her memory of their kiss had been dulled by time. Had it really been that good? Not that she'd been looking for a repeat lately, she told herself. It had just been idle curiosity sparked by seeing Jordan again. And since he'd been so annoying and able to bring out her snarky best, she'd assumed her recollection was off.

Wrong, so wrong.

Every part of her came to life, sensitized to his touch, his scent, his taste. And there was no lazy humor to Jordan now. Instead, everything about him said he wanted to strip off her waitress clothes so they could both find bliss…

When the kiss broke off, he trailed his lips across her jaw, and she tilted her head so that he could continue the path down the side of her neck. His hand came up to cup her breast, and she strained against him, wanting more, a sound of pleasure escaping her lips.

He brought his mouth to hers again, and his leg wedged between her thighs. She skimmed her hands along his back, feeling the ripped muscles move under her caress.

Jordan's scent enveloped her—the one she'd started to know so well and had fought against. But his casual devil-may-care persona was stripped away, and all he seemed to care about was getting closer to her, exploring the attraction that she'd often dismissed as just smooth moves on his part.

He tugged her T-shirt from the waistband of her skirt as their kiss took on a new urgency. Pushing aside her bra, he found her breast with his hand and palmed it tenderly.

She moved against him, feeling the friction of his jeans straining to hold back his arousal, and he broke off the kiss on a curse.

Lifting her shirt, he looked down as he stroked her breast, his chest rising and falling with awareness.

She glanced down, too, and watched him caress her, her excitement growing.

"So beautiful," he muttered. "Perfect."

He rested his forehead against hers—and their breath mingled, short and deep and fast. "Let me touch you."

Her brain foggy with desire, she didn't understand for a moment, until she felt his hand slide under her skirt. Pushing aside her panties, he began gently exploring her.

Sera's head fell back, her eyes closing.

"So good," Jordan murmured in a voice she didn't recognize. "Ah, Angel, let me in."

She let him stroke her, building the heat inside her. She shifted to give him better access, and he built a rhythm that she enjoyed…until he pressed his thumb against her and she splintered, her world fracturing, filling with their labored breaths and the scent of Jordan all around her.

They stood that way for moments, and Sera slowly came down to earth, her breath slowing.

What was she doing?

With a remaining bit of sanity, she pulled back, and he loosened his hold. Then she laid her hand on his chest as if to underscore the distance she needed. She felt the strong, steady beat of his heart, reminding her of the sexual thrum between them.

He didn't move. His jaw firm, he seemed carved out of stone, his face stamped with unfulfilled sexual desire in the dim illumination.

She felt like a heel—an uncomfortable and new feeling where Jordan was considered. Still, they couldn't, they shouldn't. "This is so wrong. We—"

"Angel—"

"We shouldn't have done that."

And then she ran. Grabbing the purse that she'd come in with, she turned and stabbed the button for the elevator.

"Sera—"

She nearly gasped with relief when the door slid right open and Jordan made no move to stop her.

As the elevator door closed, she called hurriedly over her shoulder, "I'll summon a cab downstairs with my phone."

Six

Jordan came awake. The bedsheets were a tangled mess around him because he'd had a restless night.

Sera. The one-word answer for why he'd been edgy.

He'd dreamed about her after she'd left in a hurry. At least in sleep, he'd gotten a chance to indulge many of his fantasies from the past couple months. He'd guided her and learned her pleasure points with his hands and mouth. He'd whispered all the indecent things he wanted to do with her, and she hadn't blinked. But unfortunately, none of it had been real. In real life, Sera had hurried out of his apartment.

He was still wrapping his mind around all the revelations from last night. Their kiss had been fantastic enough to fuel fantasies all night long. He'd had a hunch they'd be combustible together, and he'd been proven right. More than right. Things had escalated, and if Sera hadn't broken things off, he had his doubts they would have bothered making it from the entry to his bed. She'd been soft and curvy and responsive, just like he'd imagined. *Better than he'd imagined.* She had the softest skin he'd ever caressed.

Sera was soft despite her seemingly hard shell. Who knew?

And how the hell could he have forgotten someone as hot and memorable as Serafina Perini? He racked his brain for memories from eight years ago. Could he really have been as much of a jerk as she'd made him out to be?

Sera had been pissed off at being so easily consigned to oblivion. No question about it.

The only answer was that he'd been young and stupid and immature. Flush with the first victories of a burgeoning hockey career that had put his sickly childhood behind him, and intent on enjoying his new status and image as a chick magnet and sports stud.

Yup. That explanation would go over well with Sera.

She'd have to deal with him, though, at their next therapy session—and to make matters more complicated, she was now driving his car. After Sera had departed in a rush last night, he'd called downstairs and told Donnie at the security desk to offer her the second set of keys to his sedan. She'd need a car until her beaten-up wreck got fixed, and Jordan would be fine driving his pickup in the meantime. Fortunately, Donnie had later reported that Sera had reluctantly taken up the offer.

Jordan smiled over the irony as he stared at the ceiling. His car had been the fastest and easiest way for her to escape from him.

After a moment, he tossed the covers off and headed to the shower. He needed to clear his head and brainstorm a way out of this bind. *What the hell was he supposed to say to her at their next physical therapy session?*

And then there was the other problem he'd been meaning to get to ever since his last conversation with his mother. He bit back a grimace and figured he was overdue for trying to sort out a different Serenghetti family tangle. Plus, it would take his mind off Sera.

An hour later, after downing a quick breakfast, he headed to his parents' house on the outskirts of Welsdale.

He found his father in an armchair, remote in hand, in the large living room that ran most of the width of the back of the house.

"Hi, Dad. Where's Mom?"

Serg Serenghetti looked up grumpily. "At work. The cleaning service just left."

"Yeah, I know. Conveniently, they let me in as they headed out." Jordan smiled gamely. "So it's just us guys, then."

His father glanced at him from under bushy brows. Then he clicked the remote to change the channel from golf to a commercial.

"What are you going to watch?"

"One of those home-improvement shows your generation loves." He guffawed. "As if any of these TV performers really knows the biz."

"Right." Jordan settled onto the sofa next to his father's armchair.

Serg waved the remote. "If any of my children was interested, you'd be helping Serenghetti Construction with a television show."

"Try Rick. He's got the Hollywood ties these days." Jordan looked around. "Quiet here."

"If your mother was home, she'd just be fussing." Serg turned off the TV. "Now it's quiet."

Jordan shook his head bemusedly. His parents' marriage had lasted decades, producing four kids and now grandkids, while riding the ups and downs of Serenghetti Construction. His parents had met when his mother had been a front-desk clerk at a hotel in Tuscany, and Serg had been on his way to visit extended family north of Venice. So the whole feed-and-shelter hospitality biz was in his mother's blood, and the latest incarnation of that was her cooking show. Until recently, his father had handled the sheltering part with his construction business, while his mother was all about sustenance.

Except that had all gotten upended lately. "So what's got you down?"

"If you spent your days out of a job, sitting here watching TV, you'd be surly, too."

"Right."

Serg lowered his brows. "Come to think of it, that's not too far off from where you are."

Jordan shifted in his seat, because it hadn't occurred to him before now that he and his father might have something more in common these days than sharing a passing family resemblance. An extended convalescence had prevented them both from returning to their old lives. In his father's case, permanently. And in his… Chills ran up Jordan's arms.

He'd thought that his days being sick and bedridden were well past him. But being sidelined with his injury brought back the old feelings of helplessness.

His father was nearing seventy. Not young, but not really old, either. Jordan wondered where he'd be at that age. Certainly not playing hockey, but what would his second act be? At least, he had some plans for what to do with his earnings as long as his injury didn't get in the way.

"You need a second act," he said into the void.

Serg grumbled and shifted. "Your mother doesn't like to share the limelight."

Jordan smiled slightly. "Yeah, I heard. You'd like a segment on Mom's show."

"The audience loved me when I did a special guest spot suggesting wine pairings."

"You should revel in Mom's success," Jordan went on.

"But I get it. She's at the top of her game, and you're at a crossroads."

"Since when are you the family psychologist?"

Jordan chuckled. "Yeah, I know. It's a dirty job, but someone in this family has to do it, and I did well running interference for Cole and Marisa."

Serg lowered his chin and peered over at him. "Jordan, your sport is hockey, not football."

"Okay, fair enough. So…back to you and Mom."

"We're out of your league. Don't try to run interference."

"Right." The message was clear, but he had one of his own. "But maybe instead of wanting a piece of Mom's success, you should develop your own game."

Every once in a while, Sera thought it was a good idea to have Sunday dinner at her mother's house. Today was not one of those days.

The simple three-bedroom shingle house with a postage-stamp lawn stood on a tidy side street in East Gannon. Its no-frills white appliances were a world away from the high-end stainless steel in Jordan's sleek, modern penthouse. Here, it was all open bookshelves displaying books, mementos and family photos—not unobtrusive panels concealing high-end electronics, as well as its owner's secrets.

And the contrasts didn't end there. Jordan's place was forward-looking, with very little evidence of the past, as far as she could tell. Her mother's place held a hint of nostalgia—now that the kids had grown and flown the coop—and sadness since Sera's father's death from a heart attack a few years ago. His passing had been the wake-up call that Sera had needed to get on with her life and go back to school for a physical-therapy degree.

At the dinner table, Sera twirled some spaghetti onto her fork. Her mother was an excellent cook, and tonight's chicken parmigiana and spaghetti with tomato sauce was no exception. Ever since her mother had been widowed, Sera and Dante had made it a point to visit regularly. They knew their mother appreciated the companionship.

"I heard you had a car accident." Her mother's brow was furrowed with worry.

Sera cleared her fork and started twirling it again because she'd accidentally put on too much spaghetti. Good thing she hadn't had a mouthful already. On the other hand, maybe she should have welcomed an excuse not to talk... "How did you find out?"

"Dante's friend Jeff happened to be at the auto shop earlier today. He overheard the employee there on the phone with you, taking down your personal information to fix your car." Her mother tossed her an arch look across the dining-room table. "There aren't many women running around with the name Serafina Perini."

For the umpteenth time, Sera rued having a unique name. And she sometimes forgot what a small town Welsdale could be. Still, she was lucky that the most popular local auto body shop had Sunday hours because she'd been able to call and get a status report about when she might get her car back. Unfortunately, the news hadn't been encouraging, and it looked like she was stuck driving Jordan's wheels for a while. Too bad every time she climbed into the car, she was unable to shake his scent.

She'd been surprised when the guy at the security desk in Jordan's building had offered her car keys on Jordan's instructions, but after hesitating a moment, she'd chosen the path of least resistance—one that would solve her immediate problems, whatever the longer-term consequences. She now owed Jordan a favor when she should have been mad at him—and then there was the little complication about what else had happened that evening at his place...

"I assume you got a rental car until yours is fixed," her mother observed, "and that's how you got here today."

"Yes, I have temporary wheels." Jordan Serenghetti's.

"Are you okay?" her mother asked.

She schooled her expression with the help of her reflection in the china closet's glass door. "Fine, Mom."

"Why didn't you tell me about your accident?"

"I just did." Her mother would be even more shocked if she knew how Sera had wound up in Jordan Serenghetti's arms in the aftermath of her fender bender.

"You know what I mean. The mothers are always the last to know." Rosana sighed. "I bet your cousin Marisa would have told your aunt right away."

Her mother knew how to play the guilt card… And if there was one thing that Sera had grown up hearing about ad nauseam, it was the close relationship that Aunt Donna had with her cousin Marisa. Never mind that Aunt Donna had raised her only child as a single mother, making her and Marisa a family of two, relying on each other. Rosana Perini looked up to her older sister, even as she took her sibling's life as a cautionary tale. Ever since Donna had been left pregnant and alone by a professional minor-league baseball player who'd died unexpectedly soon after, Rosana had worried about her. But she'd been thrilled when her older sister had finally found love again with Ted Casale.

"Do you want me to ask Dante to go down to the auto body shop?"

"No. I'm capable of handling my own car repairs."

"Do you need some money?"

Sera deployed a tight smile. "No, I can handle it, Mom."

The last thing Sera wanted was for her family to think they needed to come to her aid. She'd spent most of her twentysomething years trying to shed the image of poor Sera who needed rescuing and protecting.

"Thank goodness you got home okay." Her mother frowned again. "You should have called me."

If only her mother knew that she hadn't gone directly home but had been sidetracked at Jordan's place. A detour that had risked turning into an all-night change of direction, if she hadn't put the brakes on their intimate encounter. Then, to cover her bases, she volunteered, "I was lucky that Jordan Serenghetti happened to be driving by. I got a lift."

Not straight home. But her mother didn't need to know that. Sera had been offering up information on a strictly as-necessary basis to her family for years. But it wouldn't do if word somehow got back to her mother that Jordan had been at the scene of the accident and Sera hadn't mentioned it. Dodging suspicion—that was what she'd been doing ever since she'd been a rebellious teenager cutting the occasional high-school class to hang out with friends.

Rosana Perini shot her a disapproving look. "Another reason I worry about you living alone. Who'd know for hours if you didn't make it home?"

Exactly. Who'd know she'd almost spent last night at Jordan's place? She couldn't believe how quickly things had gotten hot and heavy. She'd been thinking all day about it, in fact. *Reliving the highlights.* He'd brought her to satisfaction right there in his foyer. Sera felt her face flame and hoped her mother didn't notice.

Jordan's power to charm and seduce was beyond her understanding. The realization had unnerved her and sent her hightailing it out of his apartment.

She'd already resolved to treat last night as an aberration never to be repeated. She'd had her guard down and had been running on emotion from an evening capped off by having her car banged up. *Yup, that was her story, and she was sticking to it.* She just needed to convince Jordan to treat last night as if it had never happened and swear him to silence about the whole comforting-embrace-leading-to-fringe-benefits thing.

"It was another story when you and Marisa were roommates," Rosana Perini continued, jerking Sera back to the present, "but now you've got no one nearby."

Except for Jordan. Sera kept her tone light. "I bought Marisa's condo when she got married. I've still got the protective family aura that she left behind."

Her mother heaved a sigh. "You were always sassy, unlike your brother."

"I know. Dante is an angel. I guess you just got the names wrong, Mom."

"Speaking of Dante, he has a new job."

"Yes, I know, he told me." How could she forget? Her brother's new employment was what had gotten her into her current fix. Her gig as Jordan's physical therapist meant she'd have to spend time again and again with the in-law she'd been intimate with.

The doorbell sounded, and her mother got up. "I wonder who that is."

Moments later, Sera heard voices, and then her brother followed her mother into the room.

"Dante, this is a wonderful surprise," her mother said. "We were just talking about you."

Dante filched a piece of bread from the table and bit into it.

Rosana's face was wreathed in smiles as she headed for the kitchen. "I'll set another plate and heat up some more food. I always make extra."

Dante winked at Sera and swallowed. "And today, your just-in-case habit paid off. Thanks, Mom."

As their mother disappeared, Sera regarded her brother. "You made her happy."

"Anything for Mom." Dante took a seat opposite her,

polishing off the last of his bread in the process. "I didn't know you were here. Your car wasn't out front."

"It's there," Sera mumbled. "I parked around the corner."

Dante snagged a piece of cheese from an appetizer plate. "Why would you do that?"

Sera sighed. This was why she was careful around her family. It was always lots of questions—with a subtext of questioning her judgment. And then, because she figured Dante would find out anyway, Sera said, "I got into a little fender bender last night, so I'm driving Jordan Serenghetti's car."

Dante stopped and swallowed. "Whoa, hold up. I'm still processing the cause and effect. How do you go from a little fender bender to driving the Razors' top gun's fancy wheels?" Her brother grinned. "That's some fast work, sis. I'm employed by the Razors organization, and I haven't even had a chance to grab a beer with Jordan yet."

"Hilarious, Dante." She cast a quick look at the kitchen to make sure their mother wasn't coming back. "Jordan drove by right after the accident."

"Just happened to drive by, huh?"

"Yes," she said, holding her brother's gaze but nevertheless lowering her voice. If she couldn't convince Dante there wasn't the scent of a juicy story here, she was doomed with everyone else. "After my car was towed, Jordan lent me his. It was generous of him."

Dante nodded. "Generous."

Sera tilted her head. "What's the matter with you? Have you turned into a parrot?"

Her brother coughed. "Just trying to understand the facts."

Sera smiled brightly. "Well, there you have it. End of story."

"I thought the goal here was to get Jordan Serenghetti

feeling indebted to the Perinis, not the other way around," her brother teased.

Tell me about it.

"By the way, how's it going with my favorite hockey player?"

"Who?" she joked.

Dante bit off a laugh. "Jordan Serenghetti, of course."

Sera debated how to answer. Obviously, *I nearly slept with him* was not the right choice. "He's visiting the clinic weekly and…coming along nicely."

"And you're still his physical therapist?" her brother asked gingerly.

Therapist, in-law, hookup—did the label really matter? "Yup."

Dante relaxed and sat back in his chair. "I knew I could count on you, Sera."

"I didn't say he'd be able to start the season. We're still weeks away from any medical clearance." She took a bite of her chicken parmigiana.

Dante nodded. "But you're helping me get off on the right foot at the office. I've dropped the information into key conversations that my sister is Jordan Serenghetti's physical therapist."

"Yup, you owe me one." Wouldn't Rosana Perini be surprised to know that Sera was helping Dante instead of the other way around? "Don't worry, I'll keep your dirty little secret from Mom. The halo will stay intact."

"You're priceless, sis."

"It's a big favor." Probably the biggest that Dante had ever asked of her, come to think of it. All her instincts had told her to dump Jordan as a client as soon as possible— he was too much for her to handle on every level, and she'd been miserable at keeping it professional—but she was sticking it out for her brother's sake.

"Oh, come on, Jordan Serenghetti isn't that bad. I'll bet

there are plenty of hockey fans in the ranks of physical therapists who'd love to have him as a client."

"I'm not one of them." She just planned to survive the coming couple of months or so at her job—somehow—and be done. Before anyone discovered *her* dirty little secret—which she'd make Jordan swear to take to the grave.

Seven

She could do this. Sera sucked in a breath as she prepared to face Jordan Serenghetti again for the first time since *that night*. It was already Wednesday afternoon and time for their next therapy session. Somehow, she had to do an impossible balancing act between remaining professional and having a frank conversation that addressed moving forward from Saturday's events.

If their families caught even a whiff of this... *situation*, that there was more to it than Jordan just lending her his car, it would be like a powder keg exploding. She'd never hear the end of it, never live it down. Everyone would look at her and Jordan and *know*.

She had to make the potential repercussions clear to Jordan—if he didn't understand them already. *And* she also had to put the genie back in the bottle regarding what happened eight years ago—all in the hour or so they had for their therapy session.

She rolled her eyes. *She could do this.* How hard could

it be? She was dealing with a love 'em and leave 'em type who tossed baggage overboard and bailed... He should have no trouble agreeing to keep things under wraps, right?

But yesterday's delivery from the florist, arranged by Jordan, had made her think she had her work cut out for her.

And unfortunately, she was still driving his car—inhaling his scent and touching his belongings. She told herself that was the reason she couldn't get him out of her mind. And she had to concede it had been a nice thing to do to lend her his ride—a *very expensive* luxury sedan tricked out with leather upholstery and all the latest gadgets that made her beat-up secondhand car look like a horse and buggy. Her own vehicle continued to be in the shop for repairs, and she'd had to make time-consuming calls to her insurance company.

As she stepped into the exam room at Astra Therapeutics, her gaze came to rest on Jordan leaning against the treatment table. Having no need for crutches anymore, he looked even more formidable.

He was dressed in a T-shirt and jeans. Really, what the man could do to a pair of jeans—let alone underwear—was sinful. And he was looking at her as if she were a pint of his favorite ice cream and he was a spoon.

Being this close to him for the first time after Saturday night caused memories to flood back. Her pulse picked up, and she fought the sudden visceral urge to fit back into his arms and pick up where they'd left off. *Have mercy.* This was going to be even harder than she'd thought.

"Hello, sunshine."

"We're here for your rehab." She set down her clipboard. Staying businesslike helped her not lose her mind. She planned to address their never-to-be-repeated Saturday night. *Just not quite yet.* She needed to work up to it and then make it short and sweet.

He looked deep into her eyes. "I missed you after you left."

So much for steering him in a different direction. "Well, I'm here now."

"How's my car working out for you?"

"Fine." And that was the problem. She'd felt enveloped by him for the past four days.

He took her hand, surprising her, and ran his thumb over the back of her palm.

She swallowed. "What happens in the penthouse stays in the penthouse."

He stopped and gazed at her.

She could see herself daydreaming about his changeable green eyes. The whimsical thought passed through her head before she opened her mouth and got back to her script. "You and I are taking what happened on Saturday night to our graves."

Jordan's lips twitched. "The car accident?"

"You know what I mean." She extracted her hand from his because unnecessary touching was a no-no. "The ban includes flowers like those that arrived yesterday." The bouquet had been delivered after she'd gotten home. A lovely bouquet of lilies and… "Achillea Angel's Breath."

Jordan smiled. "I asked the florist for a flower with *angel* in the name."

"Of course."

"You mean a long line of boyfriends has been sending them to you?"

"No, you're the first." *Rats.* Most guys went for the familiar and easy—roses, carnations. She didn't want to give him bonus points for being imaginative. "The flowers were…lovely, but I'm glad you didn't send them to me at work."

Jordan winked. "I'm not going to blow your cover."

"Right." And getting back to the point: "Just erase Saturday night from your mind. Treat it as if it never happened."

Jordan looked amused. "You're asking to rewind the clock. I don't think I can un-remember how soft your skin is, the way you feel in my arms, how you respond to my touch."

She ignored the flutter of awareness at his words. "Really? You can forget eight years ago, but you can't delete last Saturday?"

"Ouch."

She folded her arms. "Save it for when you're doing leg presses."

Jordan sobered. "I'm sorry I came off as a jerk when we first met years ago."

Sera blinked because an apology wasn't what she was expecting. Still, she couldn't let him think it mattered all that much to her, so she waved a hand dismissively. "Please. The only reason I brought it up was because I was annoyed by your smooth-player ways."

Jordan twisted his lips wryly. "The truth is that I've gotten used to laughing off fans' attention or giving them a brief brush with fame and then moving on."

"And those were the moves you were showing Danica at the Puck & Shoot?"

He tilted his head. "As I said, it's easy to fall back on some safe maneuvers."

"So eight years ago, I might have been just another fan coming on to you?" she persisted.

Jordan looked pained. "Okay, that may have been my ego talking."

She dropped her hands. "Exactly."

Jordan held up his hands. "Hey, I'm trying for some honesty here, even if I can't make amends."

Sera lowered her shoulders and sighed. Because, yeah, she'd thought of him as a jerk, but he'd made her look at things from a different perspective. And really, wasn't it best that she accept his explanation and they drop the whole subject—so they could move on as she wanted to?

"So where do we go from here?" Jordan asked, seemingly reading her thoughts.

She pasted a bright smile on her face. "We get started on your physical therapy for the day."

He regarded her thoughtfully for a moment, and Sera held her ground.

"If that's the way you want to play it," he said finally.

"Play is not what I had in mind." Then, seeking a distraction, she concentrated on her clipboard, focusing on her notes and flipping through his paperwork. As if she needed reminding about his file and all the details weren't carved in her memory. Just like Saturday night…

On the fifth page, though, something that she'd initially skimmed over caught her attention. For the question on prior hospitalizations, Jordan had marked *yes* and jokingly written *Too many to mention*.

Hmm. Sera looked over at him. "This was not the first time you've had surgery."

"I'm a professional athlete. What do you think?"

"I think you're familiar with doctors, even if I'm your first physical therapist."

He flashed a brief smile. "I've been giving my mother trouble from day one. Literally. I had a collapsed lung as a newborn. I had some respiratory issues because I inhaled meconium."

She blinked in surprise because this information didn't fit the image she had of Jordan Serenghetti. Cool…invincible.

"And to top it off—" he started counting on his fingers "—a broken arm at age eight, pneumonia at age ten—or wait, was that eleven? And a ruptured appendix at fourteen. I was also in and out of the ER for more minor stuff like an ear infection and a sprained wrist."

"Wonderful."

"Memorable. Just ask the staff at Children's Hospital."

"I'm sure it was for them and you."

He grinned.

Sera felt herself softening and cleared her throat. "Let's get to work."

Jordan followed her from the treatment room to the gym, where they worked on normalizing his gait and improving strength with step exercises and leg presses, among other repetitions. More than a month past surgery, he was regaining mobility.

"So how am I doing?" he asked as they were wrapping up. "Think I'll be able to rejoin the team in the fall?"

Sera tilted her head and paused because, despite his casual tone, she knew the answer mattered to him—a lot. "Mmm, that's a question for your doctor. You're recovering nicely, but there's always some unpredictability post-op. And you're expecting your knee to perform at a high level in professional hockey."

Jordan shrugged. "The PRP therapy that my doctor is doing is helping, too."

"Good. Injections can help speed up recovery." She regarded him, and then offered, "You'll get there eventually. Does it matter when? The last thing you want to do is exacerbate an injury or sustain another tear by getting back on the ice too soon."

"I have some endorsement deals up for negotiation, and my contract with the Razors is coming up for renewal in the next few months. There's a lot on the table."

Oh. Now he told her. Talk about pressure. Not only did Dante need Jordan on the ice—he was a big draw for the fans, obviously—but now there were other deadlines. For a big star like Jordan, his contract and endorsements would be everything.

She'd heard stories about his lucrative investments in business ventures, but still, she was sure that continuing to play hockey was integral to his plans. She knew about other sports celebrities who had gone on to invest in everything from franchises to restaurants to car dealerships, after playing as long as possible.

"Thanks for sharing," she quipped.

Within the four walls of Astra Therapeutics, she'd almost forgotten what a different life he led from the one she did. It was about big money and celebrity and high stakes. Jordan's physical prowess and athleticism had landed him at the pinnacle of professional sports.

"Have dinner with me," he offered, "and I'll tell you all about it. There's a new place in town I've been meaning to try." He shrugged. "But, you know, the knee injury put me off my game."

"Another hockey pub? Angus will be jealous," she parried before getting serious, because she needed to drive this point home. "And we're not dating—remember? Saturday night was a never-to-be-repeated blip on the radar."

"It's not a date. It's friends having dinner. And no, I have someplace a little more sophisticated in mind."

Sera fought the little prick of awareness at his words. He was a master of the segue. "That was smoothly done."

Just like the other night. She'd been replaying the feel of his hands moving over her…again and again. *No…just no.* She wouldn't let herself go there. She was putting Saturday night into a tidy little box and sealing it tight. She took a deep breath. "We're not even friends." *Are we?*

"Okay, in-laws dining out," he responded, but the gleam in his eyes said he recognized she hadn't said no yet.

"We've got nothing to talk about."

"Sure we do." He consulted his watch. "We've talked our way through this therapy appointment. Time flies."

She looked heavenward. Were all the Serenghettis this stubborn?

"There's plenty to discuss. The latest news from our joint family for one," he said, counting on the fingers of his hand again. "And your aversion to hockey and wariness around men."

Around him. "I have nothing against hockey."

"What about men?"

She sighed. "I'm not allergic to men. Saturday night should have put that notion to rest."

He lifted the corner of his mouth. "Yeah."

She took another deep breath. "Obviously, physical therapy isn't the only type you need. We need to add mindfulness because you have to learn to live in the present and stop cycling back to the past."

"I am living in the moment. And aren't you the one caught in a loop about being burned in the past?"

Back to that, were they? Still, she knew Jordan was only guessing if he was referring to anything beyond their kiss on a beach. There was no way he could know about Neil.

"I want to prove you wrong about me."

She was suspicious, cautious…curious. "Why?"

Jordan gave a small smile. "You're funny and smart. You're a hard worker who went back to school to earn her degree while putting up with smart alecks like me at the Puck & Shoot. You're caring. You trained for a profession that makes a difference in people's lives."

She started to melt and then straightened her spine. Still, she couldn't help asking, "Smart alecks? How about glib lotharios?"

He leaned forward, his look intensifying. "I know I have a reputation, but the other night between us was special. I've never felt a connection that fast with a woman before."

"Because I'm good with a comeback?"

"Angel with a smart mouth, yeah. You're one of a kind."

How many times had she wanted to be special and valued for herself? And she especially didn't want to be known as Sera who needed to be protected—as her family saw her. Still, she had to keep these sessions focused on business—she had her work reputation to think about, even if Bernice was the kind of boss to appreciate a good-looking guy. "I'm a therapist, and you're my client. We have to keep this professional."

"We are. I've been doing the homework that you've assigned."

Sera nearly threw up her hands. He was persistent and had a counterargument for everything.

"I hear that you box," Jordan teased. "I'd ask you to meet me for a date at Jimmy's Boxing Gym so we can hit the punching bags together. It's one of my regular haunts but—" he nodded at his knee with an apologetic expression "—I doubt I'm up to that kind of exercise yet."

"Let's take a rain check, then," she said, dodging the invitation before glancing at the clock on the wall. "I'm about to be late for my next appointment."

Jordan looked at her as if he saw right through her.

She wished she could take that rain check for their therapy sessions. Because if Jordan kept on with the charm offensive, it was going to be hard to keep up her walls against him…

By the next week's session on Wednesday afternoon, as he waited for Sera's arrival, Jordan had realized he needed a plan B. The problem was he'd so rarely had to resort to a backup strategy where women were concerned, he wasn't even sure what plan B was. Except that he needed one.

Ever since their fateful Saturday night encounter, he couldn't get Sera out of his mind. Her scent lingered, her touch tantalized, her taste made him yearn for more. Sometimes a great memory was a curse. He must have been an ignoramus eight years ago.

The direct approach—an invitation to dinner—hadn't worked with Sera. She wasn't biting, so he needed to sweeten the offer for her. How? Couldn't Cole and Marisa invite some family over for the baby's sleeping-through-the-night celebration or something? He'd debated his options, had searched his brain during interminable repetitions of his physical-therapy routine at home—when all he could think about was her—and had finally come up with a scenario that involved recruiting his mother.

Needing help from his mother to score a date was as low as he'd ever gone. Frankly, it was embarrassing and humbling...and all part of the new territory he was in with Sera.

When Sera entered the treatment room, her expression was all business. Still, she looked fresh and perky and delicious. He now knew she responded to him as no other woman ever had. She was attuned to him on a level he'd never experienced before. So it made it impossible to even pay lip service to her ridiculous plan to forget that Saturday night ever happened.

"Nice move leaving my car keys with the security desk in my building," he observed.

She swept her hair off her shoulder. "Thank you again for the loan of a set of wheels. My car is out of the shop."

"Congratulations. But I thought I'd at least find some memento of your stay." He shrugged. "You know, a forgotten lip balm or a pair of sunglasses. Or at least your lingering scent on the upholstery."

"I wasn't able to do a complete makeover in a few days," she deadpanned right back. "Your imprint was hard to eradicate."

He loved her sass. "But you tried?"

"I'm sure you'd like to be considered unforgettable."

"I'll settle for immortality," he teased.

She scrolled on the tablet she'd brought to their session this time instead of a clipboard with paperwork.

He eyed her. "I've got a request."

She looked up. "I give you points for being direct."

Jordan laughed as he leaned against the treatment table. If Sera wanted to pretend their close encounter hadn't happened or was an anomaly, then he was willing to play any of the limited cards he had left. "I'd like you to appear on my mother's cooking show."

Sera's eyes widened. "What? You can't be serious."

He shrugged. "Consider it a thank-you for the use of my car."

"Sneaky." She took a deep breath. "Anyway, Marisa may have appeared on the program once, but it's not for me. I've caught your mother's show a few times on television, and I consider it a spectator sport."

"My mother's station is under new management. Mom is worried about being canceled and wants to make a good impression. And I'm trying to help her out by coming up with some ideas."

"Why doesn't she just switch to online? She can go viral." Nevertheless Sera contemplated him thoughtfully. "Still, it's nice of you to try to help her."

"I was an Eagle Scout. Good deeds are my forte."

"Are you sure you want to involve your mother? Who knows what I might tell her?"

He smiled lazily. "That's the point. You'll be on the show, so I'll be on my best behavior…because you'll be doing me a kindness."

"You've thought of everything," she remarked drily.

"And it'll be a good show," he pressed. "Just what my mother needs right now."

"How do you know I'd be appropriate? I might burn the calzones."

"C'mon, you bring homemade dishes to the office, and your coworkers praise your cooking." He'd found a bargaining chip in her baked ziti.

"Remind me to tell them not to be so loose-lipped," Sera grumbled, nevertheless looking flattered. "No good deed goes unpunished."

Jordan snapped his fingers as an idea hit. "You might teach me how to cook. There's no format yet, but the audience would eat up a show about a pro hockey player bumbling his way through the kitchen."

"Well, somehow I doubt any acting would be involved on your part. But anyway, your mother can teach you how to cook on the show." Sera frowned. "In fact, why hasn't she?"

"When the equivalent of Julia Child is at home, why would she let anyone else mess around in the kitchen?" He shrugged. "Besides, I was always at hockey practice. I only made my own breakfast when I slept in. Everyone was doing what they did best. Mom in the kitchen, me on ice."

She smiled too sweetly. "You remember that scene in one of the *Star Wars* movies where Han Solo undergoes carbon-freezing…?"

"I know you'd love to put me on ice—" his expression turned seductive "—but you've heated me up instead."

"Jordan—"

"I like my name on your lips almost as much as your hair down." Instead of her usual ponytail, her hair was swinging loose for a change. Somehow, even with the scrubs she was wearing, the style made her look seductive. He fought the urge to touch her.

As if on cue, she held up a staying hand, and he schooled his expression.

"Right. Behave."

"As if you can."

"I'm trying. And your appearance on my mother's cooking show would help hold me to the bargain."

She sighed in exasperation. "Let's get started on your exercises for today."

He flashed a grin. "So that's a yes? You'll do it?"

"It depends."

"On what?"

"Your behavior. Fortunately, we're already in phase two of your rehabilitation."

"Great, so you're rehabilitating my knee and my playboy ways at the same time. Impressive."

She arched her brows. "I didn't say yes, but just call me a multitasker anyway. Today we'll be focusing on improving your strength base and balance."

As it turned out, the exercises she introduced him to in the gym were some he was familiar with from his pre-injury workouts. He had no trouble with leg squats and glut extensions, and then the various resistance exercises that she threw at him. All the while, Sera evaluated and corrected his body alignment and positioning.

Jordan concentrated on keeping his mind on the exercises. Focus was something that he normally excelled at, but with Sera nearby, he found that his concentration was shot. Instead, his mind wandered to the fullness of her lips, the softness of her skin and the pleasure of her occasional touch.

"We're looking for symmetry of right and left in your gait," she told him.

And he was looking for a *yes* to his proposition, so he aimed to please. At the end of their session, he couldn't resist asking, "So how did I do?"

"Great."

He winked. "And my reward is…?"

"I'll speak to the agent who handles my public appearances and get back to you."

He just laughed—because he was willing to chalk up anything other than an outright *no* as a win.

Eight

Sometimes it was good to catch up with teammates. Marc Bellitti and Vince Tedeschi lived just outside Springfield, where the Razors were based, so even in the off-season, they were good for an occasional beer at the Puck & Shoot, or for lunch like they were having today at another of their customary haunts, MacDougal's Steakhouse.

Except today, Jordan had a motive for asking them to meet up. "I need your help."

With a cooking show. He'd debated how to float the idea of making an appearance on her program to his mother. He knew she'd be delighted to have one of her children back on the air. And Jordan's star power in particular couldn't hurt—just as when his new sister-in-law, Chiara Feran, the Hollywood actress, had gone on the show. Debating what tactic he'd take since talking to Sera and finally getting a tentative commitment, he'd hit upon the idea of a cooking competition—among hometown-team hockey players. Sort of like *Iron Chef* with an ice-puck spin, and Sera as the judge. *Brilliant.* His mother had loved it.

All he needed was to recruit a couple of his teammates—and c'mon, they had to have time to burn in the off-season, and a little positive publicity couldn't hurt.

"When don't you need our help?" Marc joked, snagging a remaining fry from their burger lunch. "Need advice on how to talk to women? I'm your man."

If there was anyone who could best him in the smart-aleck department, it was Marc. But Jordan held his fire, because—as much as this pained him—he needed Marc to play along here. And not in the way his teammate probably imagined. Aloud, he said, "It involves Vince, too."

From across the table, the Razors' goalie held up his hands. "I'm good. Whatever scheme you two are coming up with, count me out."

"Vince, if it's about women, believe me, you could use all the help you can get," Marc shot back.

On that score, Jordan had to agree. Vince Tedeschi was a big, hulking, taciturn guy. He was the team's rock, but he let others do the razzle-dazzle.

"It's 'cause you're such a straight arrow that you're perfect for this gig, Vince," Jordan said.

"Which is?" the goalie asked warily.

"I need you and Marc to cook." Jordan paused. "On air. On my mother's show."

Vince groaned.

"Hey, you're used to being on television."

"But not cooking, man."

"It'll impress the ladies. They'll be calling and writing in."

Vince knitted his brow. "What's the demographic of *Flavors of Italy with Camilla Serenghetti*? My grandmother watches."

Next to Vince, Marc swallowed a snort. "And there's your answer right there."

"You won't be the only ones on it."

Now Marc looked intrigued.

"My physical therapist will be judging our cook-off."

Now Marc burst out laughing. "Great, I'll have a chance to kick your butt on air."

"Yeah, think of it as a golden opportunity," Jordan said drily.

Marc liked to indulge in the occasional prank, and Jordan had had his butt slapped by a hockey stick on more than one occasion.

"You've recruited your physical therapist, too?" Vince seemed perplexed.

"Serafina Perini," Jordan said. "She's an in-law."

Marc's brows shot up. "Do tell."

Jordan shrugged. "She's Cole's wife's cousin."

Vince grumbled. "Jeez."

Marc raised his hand. "Hold up, Tedeschi. Is this Serafina under eighty?"

"Yup." Jordan was tight-lipped.

"Single."

"Yeah." Jordan didn't like the direction this conversation was heading.

"Attractive?"

Jordan narrowed his eyes.

Marc rubbed his chin again. "Sounds like a woman to get to know."

And Jordan was feeling the urge to rearrange Marc's pretty face. He hadn't been able to get Sera out of his mind ever since their night together. Being around her was like a euphoric high that he'd only experienced one other place—on the ice. He was restless to see her, touch her, spar with her again.

"Wait, wait." Marc rubbed his chin. "Serafina Perini is

ringing a bell… Was she the gorgeous ash-blonde poured into a satin dress at Cole and Marisa's surprise wedding?"

The way Jordan saw it, Marc's great memory could be a pain in the ass sometimes. He made a mental note not to invite the Razors' defenseman to any other weddings—not that he was planning to host one himself. "Her hair is a honey blond."

"You noticed." Marc flashed a knowing and triumphant grin.

"Just setting the record straight."

"Hey, is this the same Serafina who recently waitressed at the Puck & Shoot?" Vince suddenly piped up. "That woman you were chatting up during our last time there addressed the waitress as Serafina, and that's kind of an unusual name."

Jordan bit back a grimace—now Vince had to get all verbose on him? "I was not chatting up Danica. She walked over to me, and I was being polite."

"*Polite* is not the adjective that comes to mind, Serenghetti," Marc joked.

Jordan sat back and draped his arm along the top of their booth. "Hilarious."

"Serafina didn't seem particularly friendly toward you at the Puck & Shoot," Vince observed.

Jordan regarded both his teammates. Since when had the Razors' goalie become an astute observer of human interactions? "So are you guys going to do the show?"

Marc looked like he was enjoying himself and not ready to give up the fun. "So this Serafina is an in-law, your physical therapist, a waitress at the Puck & Shoot who, come to think of it, I should have recognized from your brother's wedding even if she was dressed up…and the special guest on your mother's show?" he drawled, rubbing his chin. "Seems as entangled as you've ever been with a woman, Serenghetti."

Jordan shrugged and adopted a bored tone. "Sera cooks, and Mom's liked her since her cousin married Cole."

Marc looked at Vince like he wanted to crack up. "Well, if your mother likes her, I guess that seals the deal."

"Not quite," Jordan replied drily. "I've got to get you two jokers to add some suspense to the whole episode."

"Not romance?" The defenseman adopted an exaggerated expression of shock.

"It's a cooking competition, Bellitti."

"And has this honey-blond physical therapist ever wanted to be on air?" Marc joked.

"No. And she's not into hockey guys." It couldn't hurt to drive the point home.

Marc's eyes crinkled. "Meaning you've failed with her? The legendary Jordan Serenghetti charm hasn't worked."

"I haven't tried." He hadn't tried to get to bed with her. Not really. Not yet…

"This I might have to see," Marc said, warming to the subject.

"If you go on the show, I'll prove that I can make Sera melt." A little extra motivation would be good for Marc.

The defenseman laughed again.

"Guys…" Vince said warningly.

"You're on, Serenghetti," Marc said, his eyes gleaming. "I'll let my agent know. Because I think you're not going to win."

"Don't be too sure."

"And when you do lose," Marc persisted, "what do I get?"

"The satisfaction of knowing I failed."

The Razors' defenseman laughed again. "I'm magnanimous. I'll hold to my side of the bargain, even if you haven't accomplished yours by the time the show tapes."

"Merciful is your middle name, Bellitti," Jordan remarked drily.

Vince shifted in his seat and muttered, "I've got a bad gut about this…"

"We know, Vince. You're out of this bet," Jordan said resignedly. "As far as you're concerned, you've seen no evil, heard no evil. Just do me a favor? Show up and do the program. And if you can outcook Bellitti, it'll be a bonus."

Sera couldn't believe she'd agreed to this. But here she was, in Camilla's office, eyeing Jordan and waiting to tape a cooking show. They'd already gone through the necessary paperwork with producers, and they'd met with Jordan's mother. Camilla Serenghetti was her usual bundle of energy.

Tipped off by Jordan, Sera had dressed in what she considered appropriate: a solid blue sweater and slacks—soon to be covered by an apron, anyway. Jordan had mentioned, and she'd known herself, that busy patterns didn't work on camera. She'd donned some delicate jewelry and had done her own hair and makeup—though she figured the show's staff would do some touch-up before she went on air.

They were in a lull while Camilla spoke with her producers on set and they waited for other guests and the audience to arrive and taping to begin. After she'd reluctantly committed to doing the show—thinking of Dante, Camilla and the favor she owed Jordan after her car accident—Jordan had informed her that the taping would be a cooking competition with him and a couple of Razors teammates as contestants *and her as the judge.* It had been too late to back out, but she couldn't help feeling a little bit like the star of *The Bachelorette*, being asked to choose among several single men.

Still, she felt poised, professional…and sexy under Jordan's regard. She had to put that night behind her—even though every time she was near him now, she had to fight the urge to touch him, slip back into his arms, and… *No, no, no.* Still, his magnetism was so strong, she could feel the pull as if it were a tangible force.

Ignoring the frisson of awareness that coursed through her at the thought, she focused on a framed photo of Jordan and his brothers when they were younger that rested on a nearby windowsill. Picking it up, she asked, "Is this you around age ten?"

Jordan tossed her a surprisingly sheepish smile. "No, that was me at twelve. I've hidden that photo every time I've been to Mom's office, but she keeps setting it back out." After a pause, he added, "I was a late bloomer."

Sensing a chance to rib him, Sera felt her lips twitch in a smile. "In other words, for the longest time, you were an underdeveloped, small and scrawny kid?"

"Going for the jugular with three adjectives, Perini? How about we leave it at *small*?"

"Wow, so you came late to your lady-killer ways…"

He bared his teeth. "How are they working?"

She resisted reminding him that he'd agreed to be on his best behavior today—her sanity depended on it. And she was still processing this new bit of information about Jordan. She'd assumed…well, she didn't know what she'd thought, but she'd always figured he'd sprung from the womb as a natural-born charmer. Apparently, she'd been—and, wow, it hurt to admit this—*wrong*.

"Braces on your teeth?" she asked, setting the photo back down.

"Check."

"Glasses?"

"Sometimes, until laser-vision surgery."

"Acne?"

He nodded. "I'll cop to the occasional teenage blemish."

"Nose job?"

"Now we're going too far."

She smirked. Rumor was, back in the day, all the Welsdale girls got boob jobs and cars for their birthdays—because they could.

"I leave the cosmetic surgery to the models and Hollywood starlets," he added, as if reading her mind.

At the reminder of the types of women he'd dated, she folded her arms. Because now they were back on comfortable ground. He'd started late, but he'd made up ground in the playboy arena with a vengeance. "Making up for lost time these days?"

"Let's not get all pop psychology on me."

No way was she backing off. She was enjoying this. Nodding at the picture, she asked, "How many of your dates have seen this?"

"None, fortunately. Not one has been in Mom's office. But *WE* Magazine ran a Before They Were Famous feature not long ago, and they dug up an old Welsdale newspaper article of me posing with my team in a youth-league photo."

"Horrors," she teased.

Jordan shrugged easily. "I got over it. Not even a nick in the public image."

"The carefully constructed persona stayed in place?"

"Fortunately for my sponsorship deals. Image is everything."

Sera widened her eyes. "Wow, so I just put it all together…"

"What?"

"Doctors, nurses, therapists. They're all uppermost in your subconscious."

"Hold on, Dr. Freud."

"You have a fixation with those in the health-care field because of your own sickly childhood."

Jordan arched a brow. "So you're saying that the reason I'm attracted to you is because you're a physical therapist?"

"Bingo," she concluded triumphantly, feeling a tingle of awareness at his admission that he wanted *her*.

"How much psychology have you studied?"

"I took a few courses on the way to my PT degree, but that's irrelevant."

"Right," he responded drily. "Here's another theory for you. I like blondes. See? My theory even has the beauty of simplicity."

Sera dropped her arms. "You're not taking me seriously."

Jordan tilted his head. "Don't you want to argue that my attraction to blondes stems from the newborn period? You know, when I might have been placed next to babies with wisps of light hair in the hospital?"

Sera resisted rolling her eyes.

"Hey, you started this. Anyway, does it matter? You're here, about to go on television—"

"Don't remind me."

"—and whether I like your physical-therapist scrubs or just women with cute blond ponytails is beside the point."

Sera reluctantly admitted he had a point. Still, if she could pigeonhole and rationalize their—uh, *his*—attraction, it would be easier to manage. Aloud, she said, "Why do you like me? You shouldn't, you know. We're bad for each other. I come with strings attached as an in-law, and that's contrary to your MO. And you're the type of on-and-off the field player that I think should come with a warning label."

"Maybe it's the forbidden aspect that drives the attraction."

"Maybe for you." *Damn it, he was right.*

"Okay, for me," he readily agreed and then checked his watch. "Ah, I've got to warn you before you go on—"

"What?" Sera's sublimated nervousness kicked up a notch.

"My father will be in the audience, and he has delusions of getting on television."

"He doesn't know your mother's show may get canceled?"

Jordan shook his head. "After his one guest appearance, he thinks he can make it better by becoming a staple on the program."

"And why not?" Sera asked. "He's about the only Serenghetti who hasn't been on television regularly."

Cole and Jordan had both been on televised NHL games, not to mention postgame interviews. Their brother, Rick, was a stuntman with movie credits who was married to a famous actress. Jordan's younger sister had done fashion shows that had been broadcast. And Camilla had her own television program, of course. Sera could understand why Serg felt left out of the limelight. He wasn't only dealing with his poststroke infirmities but also with not appearing on the marquee alongside the rest of his family. As a physical therapist, she'd seen his frustration in plenty of patients and could sympathize.

"If he wants to be on television, he should consider commercials for a construction industry supplier instead," Jordan muttered.

"Then why hasn't he?"

"Because he fancies himself a sommelier these days."

Sera felt a tinkling laugh bubble up. "A wine expert?"

"Bingo. And guess whose show he thinks would be perfect for a regular guest segment."

"Oh."

"Right."

"Your father just wants to be understood."

Jordan snorted. "He's tough as nails and ornery."

Sera tilted her head. "So you're telling me this because he might spring up from his seat in the audience and shout something?"

"He can't spring up from anywhere these days," Jordan muttered. "And believe me, the only reason he'd shout a comment is to tell me I'm doing something wrong."

"Does he do that at your hockey games, too?" Sera asked, amused.

"If he does, he's too tucked away in the stands for people to really notice. Anyway, my point is he may try to insert himself into the show somehow, and I don't want you to be surprised by anything…unexpected."

"How does your mother feel about this turn of events?"

"Like the breadwinner who has a temperamental kid on her hands."

Sera laughed.

"Suddenly she's the star, and he's cast in her shadow. Though, I don't think he'd even admit to himself that's what he's feeling."

Sera tapped a finger against her lips. "There's got to be a solution to this."

Jordan shrugged. "If there is one, I haven't thought of it."

Just then, one of Camilla's producers stepped into the room to call them on set.

"Ready?" Jordan asked, searching her gaze.

Sera shrugged. "As ready as I'll ever be."

Showtime. In more ways than one…

Nine

She was supposed to have had one rule: never get involved with a player.

Except Jordan actually seemed kind of cute and endearing at the moment wearing an apron, but still looking masculine. He was prepared to make a fool of himself under the bright television-studio lights. All for the sake of his mother. *Aww.*

Sera straightened her spine against the traitorous thought. She needed to get him in top shape and marketable for Dante and his team—and his sponsors. *Nothing more.*

"Hi, Sera!" Marisa waved as she stepped into the studio with her husband and scanned for an empty seat.

Sera's eyes widened. "What are you doing here?"

"Returning the favor," Cole replied, shooting a look at Jordan.

"What favor?" Sera knew she sounded like a parrot, but she couldn't help herself.

She'd avoided mentioning her appearance on the show

today to Marisa, which meant... She focused her gaze on Jordan, who wore a bland mask.

Cole cast his brother a sardonic look. "Jordan came as comic relief when Marisa and I were guests on Mom's cooking show before we were married."

"Oh." Sera remembered teasing her cousin about the significance of that appearance for her relationship with Cole—which was why she hadn't wanted to mention her own cameo today in return to Marisa, who might get the wrong idea.

"We thought about bringing Dahlia," her cousin went on, oblivious to Sera's distress, "but we figured she was too young to—"

"—watch her uncle Jordan get outmaneuvered." Cole chuckled.

"Thanks for the vote of confidence," Jordan replied.

Cole flashed a smile. "Payback, little brother."

"And thanks to the fact that Mom still has a show, you have the chance," Jordan grumbled.

Just then, Serg Serenghetti walked into the studio, all the while chatting with a producer.

"Excuse me," Cole said. "I'm going to help Dad find a seat."

Jordan watched his brother walk away and shrugged. "The Serenghettis have arrived in force."

Sera bit back a groan. *Great.*

As if on cue, more Serenghetti family members entered the studio. Rick and Chiara Serenghetti were followed by Jordan's sister, Mia. Even though Chiara wore glasses and a baseball cap, so as not to be identified as a well-known actress, Sera recognized her immediately.

Sera swung back to Jordan and asked accusingly, "What is this? A Serenghetti family reunion?"

Jordan shrugged. "News to me, too." Then he stepped

forward and addressed his middle brother. "What are you doing here?"

"We're here for moral support," Rick replied sardonically.

"For whom?" Jordan replied.

Sera was wondering the same thing. In this wilder-than-dreams scenario, it was hard to tell who needed help more: her, Jordan or Camilla, whose show might be in the crosshairs of new management.

Mia Serenghetti walked up, holding a cup of coffee and looking on trend in the way only a budding fashion designer could. She caught Sera's gaze. "Nice job bringing my youngest brother to heel."

Sera blew a breath. Despite her best intentions, it was as if she and Jordan wore bright neon signs: *Get These Two Together*. Still, as everyone laughed, Sera pasted a smile on her face. "Thanks, Mia, but I'm not in the market for—"

"—reforming bad boys," Jordan finished for her wryly. "Yes, we know."

Mia's gaze swung from Sera to her youngest brother and back. "Finishing each other's sentences. Interesting."

That comment earned a laugh from Rick and Chiara.

Sera held up her hands. "No, we're not. We're boring. Very, very boring."

"Better hope that's not true for the sake of Mom's show!" Mia replied, taking a sip of her coffee.

Fortunately, Sera was saved from the need for further comment because the studio staff—including the middle-aged producer who'd summoned her from Camilla's office earlier—started hustling everyone into position.

Minutes later, Sera pasted a smile on her face for the cameras and went with the agreed-upon script. "Gentlemen, start your kitchen appliances."

The audience chuckled.

Okay, so she was here as an *alleged* cooking expert to

judge Jordan's kitchen skills against those of two Razors teammates he'd cajoled, charmed or blackmailed into appearing as contestants today.

Jordan was so in trouble. And frankly, so was she. When she'd agreed to this, she'd thought she was volunteering for some sedate affair. She should have known better with the Serenghettis.

"Jordan, let's start with you," Camilla said in a drill-sergeant tone as she stopped at his counter station.

"Playing favorites, Mom?" Jordan asked, and then winked at the camera. "I always knew I was first."

Camilla ignored him. "What will you be making?"

"*Pasta alla chitarra* with fresh mackerel ragù, capers, tomatoes and Taggiasca olives."

Sera couldn't help a look of surprise. She was shocked Jordan even knew what a Taggiasca olive was.

Jordan winked at the audience. "You can call this dish The Jordan Serenghetti Pasta Special."

Sera raised an eyebrow because Jordan seemed not the least bit nervous about his ambitious recipe. *Fine, let him try.* Shouldn't she have known by now that he was always up for a challenge?

Marc Bellitti volunteered that he'd be making a ravioli dish with a secret family recipe for vodka sauce. And Vince Tedeschi said he'd prepare *pollo alla cacciatore* with mussels.

"Thank you, Vinny." Sera tossed the Razors' goalie an encouraging smile because he seemed the most nervous of the contestants.

Jordan's brows drew into a straight line. "That's Vince."

"She can call me whatever she wants," Jordan's teammate responded with an easy grin.

Sera tossed him a beatific smile. "I'm a fan of turf and surf."

"It's *surf and turf*, not *turf and surf*," Jordan said.

Sera ignored him. "Apparently, the only one who is allowed to make up names is Jordan himself."

"Oh, yeah?" Marc asked interestedly. "What does he call you?"

Sera and Jordan stared at each other for a moment, their gazes clashing.

The entire studio audience—including, heaven help her, Marisa, Cole *and* Camilla Serenghetti—seemed to lean in for the answer.

"Angel," she and Jordan said in unison to much laughter.

"Hey, I think this contest is rigged," Vince protested.

"Yes, but not in the way you think," Sera cooed. "I don't like the name."

"Great, we've neutralized the famous Serenghetti charm," Marc put in.

"We'll see," Jordan remarked drily.

Camilla Serenghetti hurried forward. "Let's get down to cooking."

"Before this show degenerates into slapstick comedy," Sera added.

When Vince groaned, Jordan arched a brow. "Don't you mean *hockey stick*?"

"There's no puck," Sera replied crisply.

"We're slapping the joke into the goal for the winning shot."

"Hmm. The only thing you should be slapping is the fish for the entrée you're making."

The show proceeded smoothly after that. And Sera had to give Jordan points for trying. But at the end, after sampling all three dishes, she had to go with Vince's *pollo alla cacciatore* because it was simply superb. For the audience's benefit, she explained, "While I chose Vince's recipe, Marc Bellitti also gets points for a professional-quality family sauce. And Jordan's dish is original. They were all close…"

"I've always said Marc has the secret sauce," Vince joked. "On and off the ice."

"Hey, I thought that was me," Jordan chimed in.

Camilla clapped her hands. "Well, we have a winner—" she fixed her gaze on her son "—and a loser."

"So Jordan is hopeless?" Vince asked jokingly.

Camilla clasped her hands together. "Perhaps Sera would like to give my son a cooking lesson?"

Sera's eyes widened. No way was she signing up for more. "Signora Serenghetti, I—"

Camilla's request was a tall order. And she'd already told Jordan she wasn't into reforming bad boys. But they were on TV with a live audience—and Jordan was contemplating her expectantly. Looking around for a lifeline, her gaze came to rest on Serg Serenghetti in the audience, and an idea struck. "Serg, would you like to come up here and suggest a wine that I could pair with Vince's winning dish?"

She tossed a significant glance at Jordan and Camilla. "After all, if the loser might get a cooking lesson, the winner should receive some recognition, too."

Serg's face brightened.

"Well, *pollo alla cacciatore* is an interesting dish," Serg said, though he was already slowly standing. "It's got many blended flavors that you don't want to overwhelm. You still want to taste the tomatoes and mushrooms."

Cole got up to help him, but the older man batted away his hand.

"Oh, come on, Signor Serenghetti, I'm sure you can suggest something," Sera prompted.

Serg chuckled. "Well, sure, if you insist."

"Oh, I do." Sera was enjoying herself. Beside her, Camilla and Jordan had gone still. *Priceless.* She bit back a laugh as Serg stole everyone's thunder. Jordan was probably wondering whether she'd gone nuts and why she was disregarding his warning from earlier. But she had a plan.

Serg accepted help from a producer who gave him a hand getting on stage and led him to where Sera was standing. "Now, traditional chicken *cacciatore* is made with red wine—"

Sera furrowed her brow at the camera for effect.

"—but Vince went with white instead."

Sera widened her eyes to underscore the point.

"Obviously, he would not have won if the dish wasn't creative and delicious," Serg added.

"Of course."

"Now a Chianti classico is a good red wine to pair with traditional *pollo alla cacciatore*." Serg paused. "But even a white zinfandel would be good paired with Vince's version."

"A Serenghetti who knows his wine," Sera offered approvingly.

"My son—" Serg jerked his thumb at Jordan "—never offered you a glass of wine?"

Sera heated, and Jordan cleared his throat.

"Well, uh—"

"As a matter of fact—"

The older Serenghetti cut them both off. "A travesty."

"We've had catering at family events. I've never had to bartend," Jordan offered by way of explanation to the audience.

"And I like to pour my own wine," Serafina added quickly, trying to cut off the line of conversation, which could end up…who knew where.

Serg just shook his head in disappointment.

Steering the conversation to safer ground, Sera said, "You're a natural at this."

Serg beamed, while Jordan tossed her a questioning look that said *You're creating a monster.*

Ignoring Jordan's expression, Sera went on. "You should have your own gig, Mr. Serenghetti, not minutes snatched from another show. You could tape commercial-length wine segments." She smiled brightly. "I've even got a name. *Wine Breaks with Serg!*"

The audience clapped in approval.

Before Serg could respond, a producer signaled Camilla, who stepped forward.

"Alla prossima volta," Camilla said, giving her signature closing line. "Till next time, *buon appetito*."

Seconds later, the cameras switched off, and Sera's gaze tangled with Jordan's.

He gave a relieved and appreciative grin. "Nice moves. Thanks for giving Dad his cameo and for suggesting something else for him to do. I wouldn't be surprised if he went straight home to build his business plan."

"No trouble," Sera mumbled before looking away in confusion. She had the warm fuzzies from his compliment, and she so didn't want that feeling where Jordan was concerned. Even mindless sexual attraction to a marquee brand, a celebrity face and a bad-boy body was preferable. Because emotion meant wading into dangerous, deeper waters.

"If Dad has his own project, it'll take the heat off Mom." Jordan shrugged. "And who knows? In the future, she might feel comfortable enough to partner with him on air, once he's got his own audience. Good going."

Sera blew some wisps of hair away from her face. Why hadn't she noticed how hot it was under the studio lights when they'd been taping? "I like my entertainment with unexpected plot twists."

Jordan laughed. "What a coincidence. So do I."

His siblings came up on stage then, and Jordan turned away to deal with his family.

Sera found herself at momentary loose ends, until her cousin Marisa stepped close, a teasing expression on her face. "You know you're in trouble, right?"

"I was hoping the trouble was over."

Her cousin shook her head. "Nope. Every woman who has been on this show to cook alongside a Serenghetti has wound up married to him."

Sera felt her stomach somersault, but she strove not to show emotion. "Don't worry. There's no chance of that in this case."

She'd sworn Jordan to secrecy, and in any case, their one recent encounter was eons away from a march down the aisle. Marisa angled her head, scanning her expression. "Are you sure there's nothing more between you and Jordan?"

Sera scoffed. "Of course. Positive."

"Well, I'll just repeat what you said to me," Marisa said, and she mimicked Sera's voice. "'He wants you to appear on his mother's cooking show? That's serious.'"

"That's some memory you have," Sera grumbled.

Her cousin just smiled.

Sera bit back a groan. *Out of the frying pan and into the fire.*

Sera hurried out the front doors of St. Vincent's Hospital to greet the sunny afternoon outside. She'd just visited one of her patients who'd had to have additional surgery.

She was back to business as usual—or so she told herself—after taping Camilla's show two days ago. She hadn't heard from Jordan but she was scheduled to see him again soon for their weekly therapy session. Anticipation shivered over her skin.

She'd known her family would eventually see or hear about her appearance on Camilla's show, so she'd played it off as doing a favor for Jordan and the rest of the Serenghettis. Dante had been thrilled.

Head bowed, she dropped her cell phone into her handbag as she blinked against the bright sunshine, and then collided with a rock-solid chest. "Oomph!"

Strong hands grasped her arms and steadied her. "Easy."

She looked up and locked gazes with the last person she expected to see right now. *Jordan.*

"I didn't think I'd run into you here," he said, dropping his arms and stepping aside.

She followed suit so she wasn't standing in the way of pedestrian traffic. "I just finished visiting an elderly patient of mine who needed surgery." Sera searched her brain for pleasantries even as she drank him in—he looked sinfully good. "What are you doing here?"

"I work with the Once upon a Dream Foundation. I'm visiting the pediatric floor."

She couldn't keep the surprised look from her face.

"Want to join me?" Jordan asked.

Sera looked around and noticed he was alone.

Jordan's eyes crinkled. "I don't normally bring a camera crew with me on these visits." He shrugged. "I prefer not to make it a media event. Sometimes the kids like it when they're on the news, but other times it freaks them out."

"I'd think a kid would freak out just because Jordan Serenghetti showed up in his hospital room."

Jordan grinned and nodded toward the entrance. "Then, come inside with me and calm things down. You're good at puncturing my ego."

Sera flushed. "Yup, you're right."

He was easy on the eyes and, now that she didn't have quite as many of her negative conceptions of him, *dangerous.* Today was another blow to her armor—he did charity work with sick kids?

"So what do you say, Angel? Ready to head back in?"

She couldn't even get annoyed about his use of the pet name at the moment. She was a sucker for people in need—and those who helped them. It was why she'd become a physical therapist. "Another appearance with you in front of a live audience? How could I refuse?"

Jordan gave her a lopsided grin. "Before long, you'll be a pro."

That was what she was afraid of. Nevertheless, she turned to follow him into the main hospital building. He placed a guiding hand at the small of her back, and she felt his touch radiate out from her center, heating her.

Upstairs, the nurses broke into smiles when Jordan appeared. As brief greetings were exchanged, Sera wondered how many other sick kids Jordan had visited in the past.

A portly middle-aged woman in scrubs pulled a hockey stick out of a closet next to the nurse's station.

"Thanks, Elsie," Jordan said, flashing a killer smile as he took the equipment from her.

"Anything for you, honey," Elsie teased. "My husband knows I'm a fan."

Catching Sera's expression, Jordan looked sheepish. "I came by yesterday, but it was the wrong moment for a visit. Elsie was kind enough to hold on to the hockey stick until I came back."

Moments later, another nurse directed them down the hall. When they stopped at an open patient-room door, Sera waited for Jordan to enter first.

He rapped on the door and then stepped inside. Immediately, there was whooping and hollering from a handful of adults in addition to a boy who was sitting up in his hospital bed.

Sera paused on the threshold. Of course she knew Jordan had a fan base, but seeing his effect on people in person was another thing. At the Puck & Shoot, he was surrounded by regulars who weren't surprised when he showed up. And Sera had always dismissed a lot of the rest as just the adulation of adoring, unthinking women. But now, when she saw the frail and bald boy sitting up in his bed—he couldn't be more than ten or twelve—and how his eyes lit up at the sight of Jordan, emotion welled up inside her.

Stepping over the threshold, Sera scanned the crowd. An assortment of adults continued to laugh and smile.

"Hey, Brian. What's going on?" Jordan said casually.

Brian broke into a grin. "Number Twenty-six. I can't believe you're here."

Sera recognized the number as the one that Jordan wore. The local shops in Welsdale sold that jersey more than any other.

"Hey, you invited me," Jordan joked. "Of course I'd show up."

"Yeah, but you're busy."

"Not too busy to visit one of my best fans."

Brian looked uncertain. "I am?"

"You used your wish on me."

A grin appeared again. "Yeah, I did. I just can't believe it worked."

Brian's assorted visitors laughed—including two who, from the resemblance, could be Brian's parents.

Sera felt her smile become tremulous. Damn Jordan Serenghetti. He made her mad, sad and bad by turns—she was always riding a roller coaster in his company.

As the adults talked, Sera learned that Brian's prognosis was good. His leukemia was responding to treatment.

"I brought you something," Jordan said to Brian.

"The hockey stick is for me?"

"Of course. What would a visit be without memorabilia? And I'm going to sign it, too." Jordan fished a marker out of his pocket and placed his signature on the widest part. Then he handed the stick to Brian.

"Wow! Thanks."

"I hope you enjoy it."

Brian looked up from his gift. "Do you think you'll be playing again soon?"

"I hope so." Then Jordan turned to nod in the direction

of the doorway. "Sera's the one who's making sure I'll be back on the ice."

"She's your doctor?"

Sera flushed. Such an innocent question, and such a complicated answer. *Hired professional, in-law and...*

Jordan chuckled. "She's medical. Definitely one of the scrubs."

She cleared her throat as everyone's gaze swung to her. "I'm his physical therapist. We, um, crossed paths downstairs after I saw another patient, and Jordan was kind enough to invite me along on this visit. I hope you don't mind."

Her voice trailed off as she finished her lame and rambling explanation. *Not a girlfriend, not a girlfriend, not a girlfriend.* Thank goodness there were no television cameras in the room.

"Hey, Brian, let's get some pictures of you with Jordan," someone piped up after a moment.

Sera was glad for the change of topic.

Obligingly, Jordan stepped forward and leaned in so that someone could snap a photo. Afterward, Jordan lingered for another quarter of an hour, talking with Brian and the others.

Sera chatted with a woman who introduced herself as Brian's mother and also with a nurse who stopped in. A half hour later, as Brian yawned a couple of times, Jordan took his cue, and Sera followed his lead in saying goodbye.

As she and Jordan made their way toward the elevator bank, she remarked, "You were the highlight of his day."

Jordan sighed, suddenly serious. "It's tough sometimes. Not all of the kids get better, but their courage is inspiring."

"You lift their spirits."

His lips quirked. "It's the least I can do if I'm not going to heal their bodies with physical therapy."

Sera flushed as she stepped into an empty elevator, and he followed. "Do you volunteer here because you were a sick kid yourself?"

"Going all pop psychology on me again, Angel?"

"Just an observation based on the evidence," she remarked as the doors closed.

"Okay, yeah."

"So I was wrong," she joked. "You don't have a fetish for Florence Nightingale types."

Jordan quirked an eyebrow. "I don't? What a relief."

Sera shook her head as the elevator opened again on the ground-floor lobby. "No, my new theory is that you want to be Florence."

Jordan stifled a laugh as they crossed the lobby to the exit. "Great. I guess I have my costume for next Halloween."

When they emerged from the building, she turned to face him. "Would you be serious?"

"Would you?"

"Your visit today was a nice thing to do."

He flashed a boyish grin. "See, I'm not all bad."

"No, no, you're not."

"So I'm making progress?"

"Of sorts."

"Good enough."

"I can't fault a guy who visits sick kids." She cleared her throat. "I had an older sister who died as a baby."

Jordan sobered.

She adjusted her handbag. "She died from a congenital defect." She wasn't sure why she was volunteering the information. "Your family may have hovered because you were always sick. Mine did, too, but for different reasons."

"They were protective because they knew what it meant to lose a child," he guessed.

"Exactly, though it was hard for me to appreciate at the time." She didn't want to understand Jordan Serenghetti, but she did—more and more. It was much easier to label him as just another player.

"My sister Mia could tell you all about overprotective parents." Jordan gave Sera a half smile.

She thought back to her brief conversation with Jordan's sister on set the other day, then sighed as she remembered something else from the taping. "I hope your mother isn't still expecting me to teach you how to cook."

Jordan flashed her a teasing look. "Don't worry—"

"Phew! What a relief." So why did she feel disappointed suddenly?

"I've gotten you off the hook by telling her that I'd ask you to attend a wedding with me."

Sera's mind went blank. "Wait—what?"

"A wedding. I avoid them like the plague—"

"Of course you do."

"—but this one I have to attend. It's a cousin, and Mom is all about family."

Well, that might explain why all the Serenghettis were in town—Mia from New York, where she was based, and Rick and Chiara from Los Angeles. They were here for a wedding—as well as to throw moral support behind Camilla *and* bear witness to Sera's on-screen chemistry with the family's baddest bad boy.

"That is some stealthy maneuvering, Serenghetti," Sera said in her sternest voice.

"It was Mom's idea."

"What!"

"She suggested I bring you to the wedding instead." Jordan shrugged too casually. "Because I was planning to fly solo."

"She makes a good accomplice," Sera muttered.

Jordan gave a short laugh. "She's desperate."

"For ratings, or to get you paired up with a woman who likes to use her brain?"

"Maybe both." Jordan schooled his expression. "You have to come with me to the wedding. I'm too injured to find a date."

"Please. You'd be able to find a date even from a hospital bed."

"You're giving me too much credit."

"Modesty. What a refreshing change for you," she teased. "So I'm a last resort?"

He looked like a kid caught with his hand in the cookie jar. "And a first."

She searched his expression, saw only earnestness and then felt warmth suffuse her.

She didn't want to be number one in Jordan's book—did she?

Ten

The last place Sera wanted to be was at an event with more Serenghettis—and yet here she was.

She'd been to enough get-togethers at Marisa and Cole's house or Serg and Camilla's to know the Serenghettis welcomed everyone and anyone. But once a social event ventured into cousin or—heaven help her—even second-cousin territory, like today's wedding, she knew she was in deep. In fact, she'd just met another of Jordan's second cousins, Gia Serenghetti, so now she knew the family's inside joke about the rhyming Mia and Gia "twins."

Still, Sera had to admit the colonial mansion outside Springfield, Massachusetts, was a picture-perfect setting for a June wedding. She'd decided to wear a sleeveless shimmering emerald sheath dress for the evening affair, and she'd caught back her hair in a jeweled clip for a low ponytail.

Jordan's gaze lit as it settled on her again from across the lawn, where he stood chatting with some fellow guests during the postceremony cocktail reception, while the bride and groom, Constance Marche and Oliver Serenghetti, posed for picturesque photos on the lawn. His perusal was a slow burn, full of promises and possibilities as it skimmed her curves.

As she took a sip of champagne, Sera could almost read the thoughts chasing through his mind. She was a flame dancing in the warm breeze of his appreciation. *Wow.*

Still, she felt like a phony. An impostor. She wasn't really Jordan's girlfriend or even his date. She was here as a fill-in, to avoid a cooking lesson that had been asked for on air. And to help Dante. And…*nothing more.*

She was so far from getting married herself, she might as well have been in a different galaxy. Neil had seen to that. And it wasn't as if she and Jordan would ever walk down the aisle. Her heart squeezed, nevertheless. She'd gotten misty-eyed at the exchange of vows earlier. It had been so beautiful, so perfect. The couple caught in the beams of the evening sun behind them and outlined by a trellis with climbing flowers. She couldn't think of a better arrangement if she'd been planning her own ceremony—not that it was in the cards.

On top of it, Marisa kept shooting her quizzical looks—as if her cousin, too, was puzzled about what to make of today and Sera's agreement to appear on Jordan's arm, especially since Sera had sworn that there was nothing romantic between her and Jordan. An appearance on Jordan's mother's show was one thing; a family wedding was another. *That's serious.* Her cousin's words echoed in her head.

Jordan approached, and Sera noticed again how he filled out his dark tailored suit. Only her well-trained eye could detect any lingering unevenness in his gait, since they were now more than two months postsurgery. In the past couple of weeks, since the cooking show, he'd grown stronger and more able with each physical-therapy session. Even she had been impressed at his progress. She knew from experience that there could be many unexpected stumbling blocks to recovery.

"I should never have agreed to this," Sera murmured as Jordan stopped by her side.

He took a sip from his champagne. "Relax. It's not as if we were caught having sex in the closet under the hall stairs."

"There's a closet under the stairs?" she squeaked. Why was she turned on? She wanted to fan herself and instead took another fortifying sip from her glass.

Jordan gave a strangled laugh. "Every old mansion has one."

"There's already open speculation in your family about what the status is between the two of us. I can read the looks on their faces, and they don't even know—"

"—we got it going already?"

Sera nodded, her face warming. "This is getting complicated."

"No, it's simple. You don't like me, and I've got a hard case of lust for you."

"I've been rethinking that part," she muttered.

"What?"

She cast him a sidelong look. "The part about how I don't...don't like you."

Jordan fiddled with the knot of his tie. "Now you tell me?" he joked. "We're at a wedding surrounded by a couple of hundred people. Some of them even related to me."

"And whose fault is that?" she replied. "Isn't there a closet under the stairs where we can hide?"

Jordan gave her a look of such longing and heat that Sera felt as if her clothes evaporated right off her.

He leaned close and whispered in her ear. "Hiding isn't exactly what I had in mind."

"Oh?" she asked breathlessly.

"What's under that dress?"

"It's got a built-in bra," she answered hesitantly.

"Even better. One zipper? I want to know how easy it is to peel you out of it."

"It's on the back. But don't you want to explore and find the exits on your own?"

Jordan took a deep swallow of his drink. "We could do this."

This was so crazy. They were actually contemplating if they could duck inside the mansion for a quickie.

"Dinner will start soon," she tried.

"We won't be missed."

"Is that why you waited till now? Because disappearing from the ceremony would have been too noticeable?" She really needed a fan.

One side of his mouth rose in a slight smile. "You think you were saved by the wedding bell?"

"Maybe you've been." Jordan was a no-strings kind of guy—it would be lethal if he was caught getting it on with her, of all people, and here, of all places.

"Angel, it's not salvation…yet. It's purgatory right now."

Sera forced a laugh. "Hey, you invited me to this event. I'm sure all your relatives aside from your mother are surprised you're here with a date." *Me*.

"Let them wonder all they want. It's been way too long."

"Since you've been at a wedding?"

"Since the two of us have been all over each other with lust," he responded bluntly.

Sera sucked in a breath.

"Don't tell me you haven't been wondering, too," Jordan continued in a low, deep voice. "Fantasizing about whether the chemistry that night in my apartment was a fluke or we're really that good together."

In fact, she had. She'd been working hard to keep up

her defenses, but it hadn't worked. She was having trouble remembering why she shouldn't like him. "Okay, I have. But it's unprofessional of me—"

Jordan gave a dismissive laugh.

"—and wrong." Dangerous, even. To her peace of mind.

He took the champagne flute from her hand and set it down on a nearby table along with his own glass. Then taking her hand, he said, "Come on."

She looked startled. "What? Where? Why?"

"You forgot *when* and *how*." He tossed her a wicked glance as they headed toward the back of the mansion. "*When* is now, and the answer to *how* is that there's a cloakroom off the main hall on the ground floor that isn't being used because it's summer and no one brought a coat. It's also bigger than the closet under the stairs."

Sera's quick indrawn breath was audible. Still, excitement bubbled up within her. They were playing with fire, but she felt alive, all her senses awakened.

They slipped inside the house without drawing attention, and in line with Jordan's expectations, the short hallway to the cloakroom was deserted. He opened the half door and then led her toward the shadowed recesses.

The minute they reached the back wall, his mouth was on hers.

Finally. She exulted in being in his arms again. She'd fought the good fight against his charm, but everything except this moment receded into the background.

Their mixed sighs filled the empty room as the kiss deepened. She tunneled her fingers into his hair, and he pulled her closer. All her soft curves pressed into his hard, lean physique, molding to him.

His scent was so good, his taste even better. And her senses stirred with his kiss, which was hot, warm and enticing.

When the kiss finally broke off, Jordan skimmed his

mouth across her cheek and nuzzled her temple before his breath settled around the delicate shell of her ear, giving her goosebumps and making her weak with awareness.

"Your dress has been driving me crazy all evening," he muttered.

"It's not meant to make men wild with lust."

He gave a strangled laugh. "That keyhole cutout that shows your cleavage. All I wanted to do was this—" he reached to her nape, and her zipper rasped downward "—and bare your gorgeous breasts."

She leaned against the wall, her breath hissing out of her as the top of her gown sagged. She wanted—

In the next moment, Jordan unerringly gave her what she was seeking—cupping her exposed breast and running his thumb over the pebbled peak.

"You're so responsive, Sera," he whispered, his voice reverent.

She shifted, brushing against his erection, and they both sighed.

Jordan bent and covered her breast with his mouth, and her hands tunneled through his hair as she gave herself up to waves of sensation that carried her closer to a shore of paradise...

Suddenly, there was the sound of a door opening, and Sera froze, yanked from a wonderful reverie.

Jordan straightened, and they hastily moved apart.

Sera's gaze met Jordan's in the shadows, and he pulled her closer, yanking the top of her dress back into place as he did so.

"Shh," he whispered into her ear.

Obediently, she stood still, hoping not to be noticed.

"I'll be back in New York on Monday," a woman's voice said. "We can discuss it then."

Jordan relaxed, his hold on her easing.

Sera thought it sounded like—

"Thanks, Sonia." There was a rustle, as if someone was fiddling with her purse.

In the next moment, the cloakroom was flooded with light as someone flipped a switch.

"Jordan."

Sera suppressed a groan. It was definitely Jordan's sister. "Mia."

While Jordan stayed pressed against her for obvious reasons, Sera looked sideways over her shoulder at his sister, who wore an amused expression.

"I was just helping Sera with her dress." Jordan shrugged. "Stuck zipper."

"Of course," Mia played along. "You don't need to tell me. As a fashion designer, I've seen dozens. Hundreds, even. Those darn zippers. The pesky things give the worst trouble at the most inconvenient moments."

"Right," Jordan agreed.

"Sometimes a zipper will open easily but get stuck closing, or the reverse. Was the zipper going up or down?"

"For God's sake, Mia."

Sera's face flamed. Could things get more mortifying? And of course, it had to be one of Jordan's siblings who walked in on them.

"What are you doing here, Mia?" Jordan asked, going on the offensive.

"I could ask the same thing of you, big brother. But for the record, I was looking for a quiet place to take a call and just wandered in this direction right when the call was ending." Mia arched a brow. "And I'm going to assume you two came this way looking for a sewing kit…to fix Sera's dress."

Sera's hands flew to her cheeks.

Mia laughed. "Don't worry, your secret is safe with me." She gestured near her mouth as if turning a key in her lips and throwing it away.

"Thanks, sis."

Mia winked at them and then flipped the light switch and threw them into darkness again.

A moment later, Sera heard footsteps receding down the hall. She collapsed against Jordan with a small sound of relief, even though she wasn't sure how much longer she could stand their sexual frustration.

As Jordan drove her home after the wedding, Sera was a bundle of tingling awareness. They'd managed to keep their hands off each other and the PDAs to a minimum through the wedding dinner and dancing and socializing, but the tension had built…and built.

Yes, she'd been embarrassed about being caught in a clinch by Mia. And she hoped that Jordan's sister could keep a secret. But she and Jordan were playing with fire, and it just fueled their sizzling attraction.

They got out of his car and made their way to her building, enjoying the fresh air on this warm and balmy night. There was no question she was inviting him upstairs and inside. In the hall outside her front door, she handed him her keys, and the gesture—a mere brush of the fingers—was electric.

When Jordan pushed open the door, Sera entered the silent apartment and turned on a dim lamp. She hadn't changed much of Marisa's decor for the two-bedroom apartment, which had a retro vibe—right down to the Unblemished Yellow wall paint that her cousin had used to give a face-lift to the old kitchen cabinets. She was home, and yet her place had never felt less relaxed. Instead, the air was charged with sexual tension.

She heard every rustle as she set down her evening bag on a console table and Jordan followed her. With a remote, she switched on some flameless candles that sat on a chest in her living room and then turned and nearly collided with Jordan's chest.

He ducked his head and kissed her—all sexy and lingering.

Sera leaned into the kiss. She wanted to taste him, lick him, be enveloped by him.

When they broke apart, he gazed into her eyes. "I want you, Sera. I can't stop thinking about you."

And just like that, the shackles broke, and Sera was in his arms, kissing him back and pressing closer, desperate to pick up where they had left off earlier in the evening.

"Jordan," she breathed.

He smoothed his hands along her curves and skimmed kisses from her mouth to the side of her neck.

She'd resisted him for weeks but had nevertheless felt herself sliding into an attraction that she could not deny. He'd been hard to ignore—at physical therapy, on his mother's cooking show, in the hospital, and now at a wedding—and impossible to resist. He'd seduced her in the process, teasing her out of her shell.

He tugged on the zipper at the back of her dress and it rasped downward, her breasts spilling against him out of the built-in bra.

Bracing his good knee on a nearby ottoman, he bent and drew her closer. Running his hand up her calf in a light caress, he pulled one breast into his mouth.

She held his head close, her eyes falling shut. *Bliss.* The sensations were so acute, so exquisite, and she knew it all had to do with him and their burning, simmering desire for each other.

Jordan transferred his attention to her other breast, and Sera moaned.

He slid his hands up her legs, pushing up the hem of her dress, and then hooked his hands inside the band of her panties and pulled them down.

Sera braced her hands on his shoulders.

He murmured sweet encouragement and words of appreciation. "I've wanted you so long. Waited for you."

Me, too.

It was her last thought before he tugged her down to the ottoman, where she lay back, bracing herself on her elbows as he bent in front of her.

He ran his hands up and down her thighs in a delicious caress. Eventually, he found her with his mouth, and a strangled cry was torn from her lips. She lost all sense of time, just letting herself feel all the wicked things that he was doing to her. And then suddenly, her climax was upon her in a bright burst of energy.

She spasmed, riding an intense crest of pleasure that went on and on until she floated down and went limp against him.

Somehow, after that, they found their way to the bedroom, where they both stripped off the rest of their clothes.

She loved him with her mouth and hands until she could sense Jordan was on the brink of losing control.

"Ah, Sera," he groaned.

"Too much?" she teased as she settled back on her bed.

"Just right." He sheathed himself in protection and braced himself over her.

She quirked a brow at him. "Came prepared, did you?"

He flashed a quick grin. "Wishful thinking, but thank you. It's because of your therapy that we're even able to use this sexual position."

"Sure, blame me," she teased again.

He gave a strangled laugh. "No, I'm going to love you until we're both mindless."

In the next instant, he stroked inside her, and they both sighed.

She took up the tempo that he set. Sera had never felt so close to anyone before.

She'd rationalized away their first encounter on the night of the car accident as the product of adrenaline, annoyance and more.

But this time, there was no denying the truth. She came again, clinging to him as he sent her soaring on a wave of pleasure right before he found his own release.

In the aftermath, she lay in Jordan's arms, content as she'd ever been, until sleep claimed them.

When she came awake, she was surprised to see sunlight streaming through her bedroom windows, but the bed beside her was empty.

Frowning, she looked around the room, but then heard sounds from the kitchen. She cleaned up in the bathroom, donned some sweats and pulled her hair into a messy ponytail before padding out to find Jordan.

He was in the kitchen—at the stove, no less. She let a mix of emotions pass over her—pleasure and, yes, worry. Had she never fully shucked her fears about being disappointed by a man after Neil?

"Hey, sexy." Jordan held a spatula in his hand, and mouthwatering aromas filled the kitchen.

"Back at you."

Sera eyed him; he was tousled and edible-looking. He'd donned last night's suit pants but otherwise he was barechested—all rippling, lean muscle. Sera drank in the view of what was covered up during therapy.

Jordan smiled at her. "Hungry?"

How could he be so cheery so soon after sunrise? Okay, the sex had been spectacular. She felt like a well-sated cat. But still, mornings were mornings. She yawned and moved toward a cabinet to pull down a coffee mug.

"You know, I once asked if the clouds ever come out in Serenghetti Land," she muttered. "I guess the answer is no."

Jordan laughed. "Angel, I'm guessing I'll always need to be the one in charge of breakfast for us."

Retrieving her mug, she answered, "You got that right."

And then she realized...*always?* She hadn't blinked at his allusion to a next time—more than one, in fact—for them. She tested the idea and registered that it made her... happy. Butterflies-in-the-stomach happy, actually. Last night, her relationship with Jordan had taken a big step toward *complicated*, but right now, she wanted to shut out the world for a little bit longer and just experience the moment.

"Grumpy in the morning?"

"Yes." *Well, until seconds ago, anyway.* She poured herself a cup of dark brew that he'd had ready for her.

"I'll file that information away for future reference."

"I bet you've always dated the kind of woman who sleeps in her makeup so she can wake up camera-ready," she grumbled before savoring her first sip of coffee.

Jordan just smiled again. "Don't worry. You're cute in the morning—"

"Only in the morning?"

"—in a tussled-in-the-sheets kind of way."

"Hmm." *Thanks to him.* She looked at the stove. "What are you making?"

"The Serenghetti Brothers Frittata."

"So you do cook."

"Breakfast, sometimes. I think I mentioned it before. Since I often slept in, it was the one meal where Mom wasn't ruling the kitchen."

"Late-night carousing, I bet. I'm guessing you were having a lot of breakfasts later than everyone else. Closer to noon, maybe?"

He tossed her a meaningful look. "I'm not going to incriminate myself."

"Of course."

"When I started living on my own, making breakfast became a survival skill."

"Along with getting the right meal partner?"

"Jealous?"

"Please."

He looked boyishly charmed by her denial. "Something tells me you're going to be my best...meal partner ever."

"Oh?" She kept her tone casual. "Well, you're about to find out."

In fact, his frittata was delicious. And afterward, not least because it was her kitchen, she took charge of cleanup, while he headed to the shower. Wiping down the kitchen counter minutes later, she heard the water running and gave in to the urge she'd been resisting since she woke up.

She stripped off her clothes and headed in the direction of the running water.

Opening the bathroom door, she could see him in the shower stall. He held a disposable razor in one hand and one of her cosmetic mirrors with the other. As he shaved, she slipped up behind him and rested her hands on his hips and her cheek on his back.

When he reached for the shampoo, she stopped him and instead poured a dollop into the palm of her hand and went to work massaging his hair.

He tilted his head back in order to help her reach. And after several moments, he said, "Ah, Sera. Are we going for round two here?"

"Feels good?" she murmured.

"Feels great."

"Mmm." She could feel her body humming and vibrating to life.

"How about you go to work on the ache that's flared up?"

Her brow puckered. "Your knee is bothering you?"

"Right now, I could use your hands on me, Angel."

Concerned, she rinsed the suds from his hair and then bent down to place her hands on his knee.

Laughing, Jordan grasped her arm and pulled her up and around to face him.

Immediately, she realized he was aroused. "I thought you said your knee injury was bothering you."

He gave her a quick peck on the lips. "I didn't mention my knee, but I'm aching in other ways."

She realized she felt the same.

When had she started agreeing with him?

Eleven

Jordan couldn't stop thinking about her. He'd always stuck to casual relationships. What was the saying about best-laid plans?

The sex…it had been fantastic. Mind-blowing, even though that sounded trite. She'd been so responsive, and he'd been able to relieve a sexual frustration that had gone on forever—building up to the breaking point at his cousin's wedding, of all places. Not that he felt relief—now he itched to spend every moment with her.

He'd fantasized about her last night, reliving their evening together, except he'd woken aroused…and to an empty bed. Still, the memories had been vivid. The way she'd looked at the moment of her release—her back arched, her breath coming audibly between parted lips, her eyes half-closed.

Jordan almost groaned aloud, shifted on the bar stool and tightened his grip on his beer. He took a deep breath. If he wasn't careful, he'd embarrass himself or race to find Sera.

Usually weddings like the one the other day were a reminder that he wasn't looking to make a serious commitment himself. He liked his life just fine. At his cousin's ceremony, though, every thought had fallen by the wayside except getting closer to the woman he'd wanted to seduce.

He was pensive this evening even though he'd come to the Puck & Shoot to relax. He couldn't even manage more than distracted conversation with Vince, who occupied the next stool.

On days like today, he had to wonder whether the whole sports celebrity gig was worth it. Because, on top of it, while he'd gotten a reprieve from the press during the off-season and because he was out of commission with a bad knee, lately they'd acted up again.

"Serenghetti." Marc Bellitti slapped him on the back as he walked up. "It's good to see you nearly looking like your old self."

"Yup." Jordan took a swig of his beer.

"Sera must be miracle worker." Marc flashed a grin. "She almost makes me want to have a bum knee."

Jordan's hand tightened on his drink again—because he had a sudden inexplicable urge to get in Marc's face. Once, not so long ago, he'd been like his teammate—unable to remember names, but always able to recall a pretty face and a body to match. But things had changed. *He'd* changed. Maybe it was the injury, maybe it was Sera, maybe it was the two together. After all, he had her to thank for his amazing recovery.

Marc propped his forearm against the bar. "You haven't even glanced at the blonde at table six throwing hot-and-heavy looks your way. So I have to say you're only *nearly* back to normal."

Jordan glanced over his shoulder. "She's not my type."

"Serenghetti, they're all your type. What's wrong with her?"

"Too young."

Marc gave a mock gasp and clutched his chest. "Be still my heart. You cruised past thirty, and suddenly twenty-five is too young?"

"How do you know how old she is?"

Marc gave a sly smile. "On my way over here to keep company with your sorry cooking-competition-losing self, I happened to find out she's already got her degree and is going for another in marine biology."

"As I said, not my type."

"Well, well," Marc drawled, "look which kitty cat has changed his stripes."

Vince laughed.

"Maybe you're still thinking about that physical therapist," Marc commented.

"Appearances can be deceiving," Jordan responded, refusing to be drawn in.

He'd rather eat a hockey puck or two than admit to… *feelings*. He'd never hear the end of it from his teammates.

"Meaning?" Marc prompted.

Jordan raised his eyebrows but made sure to keep his tone nonchalant. "Maybe Sera's just my biggest challenge yet."

Or he was hers. Damn. He and Sera had never discussed the future, and he'd been content to live in the moment. *And what moments they'd been…* Still, the last thing he needed was for his teammates to latch onto the idea that his relationship with Sera was anything more than casual. Although, how he and Sera were going to continue to keep things on the down low after shattering the final barrier in their relationship on the night of his cousin's wedding, he had no idea. Sera hadn't said anything, but they were already skating on thin ice with Mia in the know.

"What about our bet that you could make her melt?" Marc asked. "Are you conceding defeat?" His teammate tut-tutted. "You're on a losing streak, Serenghetti. First, the cooking show, now—"

"I'm not conceding anything." Jordan made a motion indicating he was zipping his lips and throwing away the key. Let Marc speculate all he wanted. He wasn't going to admit anything—or divulge intimate details.

When Marc just laughed, Jordan glanced over his shoulder and then sobered. "Hi, Dante."

He wondered how long Sera's brother had been standing there and what he'd heard and then shrugged off the thought. His words could be read in many ways.

She'd never felt this way about a guy. There, she'd admitted it. He'd been a laundry list of her *never*s, but Jordan had somehow become her *must-have*. She couldn't wait to see him again, jump his bones and float in a happy bubble of coupledom.

Her former self would have found it all ridiculously saccharine instead of cause for a goofy smile. Few would be able to tolerate her right now—even her own past selves.

Take Marisa, for example.

She'd just run into her cousin in the produce aisle of the local supermarket, Bellerose. Pushing her cart and daydreaming, she'd almost jumped when Marisa had called out her name.

Her cousin knit her brow. "Are you okay?"

"Just peachy," Sera managed, even though all she wanted to do was throw her arms wide and twirl. In the middle of the produce aisle. "It's been ages since I've run into you here."

"That's because I'm normally trapped in the baby aisle comparing package labels and feeling guilty about not pureeing everything myself," Marisa quipped and then tucked a stray strand behind her ear. "These days, if I manage to get out of the house without spit-up on my shirt, I'm good."

Sera smiled. "And where is the marvelous Dahlia?"

"At home with Daddy and, with any luck, napping. Cole had the day off."

As they continued to chat, lingering in the aisle, Sera shifted from one foot to another.

She knew her cousin had to be full of speculation about her appearance on Jordan's arm at the wedding. Plus, this was no longer simply one amorous encounter with Jordan that she'd told him to swear to take to the grave. Any last shred of professional distance was gone. She and Jordan had done the deed, and short of amnesia, she was never likely to forget that night—in all its pyrotechnic glory.

As if on cue, Marisa said, "So how is Jordan these days?"

Sera made herself shrug nonchalantly. "He's been recovering nicely."

"Mmm-hmm." Her cousin looked amused. "He seems to be in great shape. Enough to attend a wedding."

With you as his date. The unspoken words hung in the air.

"I went with him because it got me out of giving Jordan the cooking lesson that his mom suggested," Sera blurted and then could have bitten off her tongue. There was no need to clarify why she'd been with Jordan, and being defensive definitely made it seem like a date. Her face heated.

"Mmm-hmm."

"Will you stop saying that?"

Marisa smiled. "Please. The guy's been tracking you with his eyes."

Sera felt a hot wave of embarrassment. "I didn't even want to be his physical therapist. I tried to get myself out of it."

"Yeah, but the attraction was so strong, maybe you were just afraid to go there."

Sera bit her lip. *Afraid.* She hadn't given more than a passing thought to Neil in…it was probably a new record.

Instead, her mind—and heart—had been consumed by Jordan. She supposed it was all a sign of how far she'd come since her bad breakup. Sure, she'd had boyfriends before, but nothing serious until Neil—or so she'd thought. But her relationship with Neil had been skating on the surface in comparison to the depths she'd plunged into with Jordan.

Jordan had wrung every emotion out of her—annoyance, exasperation, nervousness, need, hunger, joy, pleasure. It was like living life in an explosion of color, especially in bed.

Just then, another shopper came by, and Sera and Marisa separated in order to let the older woman through with her cart. Sera took the opportunity to glance at her watch to try to extricate herself from this tricky conversation. If she lingered, she expected more gentle probing and teasing.

But her cousin just winked at her. "Keep me posted."

Sera rolled her eyes. "Right."

Saying goodbye to Marisa with a promise to catch up another time, she headed to the checkout line.

Minutes later, after she'd loaded the groceries into her car and had gotten behind the wheel, her cell phone rang. Noticing it was from Dante, she turned off the ignition and took the call.

After a brief exchange, during which Sera wondered why Dante was calling, her brother asked, "How are things going with you and Jordan?"

"Great." The trending topic of the day: #JordanandSera.

Dante cleared his throat. "Just be careful."

"Don't worry," she replied, hoping to keep this conversation light, "I promise not to let him break a bone on all that physical-therapy equipment." She hadn't confided in her brother about her true relationship status with Jordan these days, so she wondered what her brother was getting at. Unless Mia had been loose-lipped, despite her promise to button it? Sera tightened her hold on her cell. "Is there anything you're not telling me?"

"No. Yes. I heard you went as his date to a family wedding."

"I did. He needed one. He's injured…and not getting around much." It wasn't a total lie, but she added quickly, "I didn't mention it to you or Mom because it was casual." *And I didn't want you to make too much of it.*

There was a pause. "I know I'm going to regret this, but my loyalty to my little sister is bigger—"

"Than what?"

"I ran into Jordan at the Puck & Shoot."

Sera forced nonchalance. "And so? He was flirting with Angus?"

"You know Angus has been married fifty years."

"Thirty-five."

"Who's counting?"

"He is. When he skipped over his wedding anniversary two years ago, his wife never let him forget it."

"No, Angus is out of the picture. But listen, I overheard Jordan joking with some Razors about you being his biggest challenge yet."

Well, she was. Or did Jordan mean she was just another conquest? It was an ambiguous statement, but the fact that he'd been joking with his teammates when he'd said it wasn't a good sign.

"Right before that, I heard Jordan tell Marc Bellitti that appearances can be deceiving."

Hadn't she thought the same thing about Jordan recently? She'd discovered he volunteered with a children's charity. And she'd been basking in the realization that he wasn't quite the player she'd thought he was. "In what context did he say this?"

"To be honest, Marc was ragging Jordan about being hung up on you."

Even Jordan's teammates were onto them? She strove to keep her voice neutral—bored even. "I've been a waitress at the Puck & Shoot. I've heard it all. They were probably just shooting the breeze."

"Jordan and Matt had a bet—"

"Players often do."

"—that he couldn't seduce you. Or, uh, to be more precise, make you 'melt.'"

She froze. It was like Shakespeare's *The Taming of the Shrew*, and she knew what her role was. Her lips tightened. Yes, she was pissed off. But she was going to hold her fire and question Jordan at the appropriate time. Have him explain himself. *If he could.*

She sighed, conceding her brother's good intentions in telling her all this. "Thanks, Dante." She watched a cloud pass in front of the sun, darkening the inside of her car. "I owe you." *Poor Sera, saved by her family again.*

Surprisingly, though, she didn't get an immediate wisecrack from Dante. Instead, her brother matched her tone of resignation. "What are siblings for? Anyway, these days, you've been coming to my aid just as much. More, actually."

Dante's words were almost enough to bring a smile to her face. Because he was right—and there was the small silver lining to her current predicament.

She was a mature and intelligent woman. Or so Sera kept reminding herself.

In the days since speaking with her brother, she'd come up with a plan—once she was done being miffed. She was willing to give Jordan the benefit of the doubt. After all, she'd witnessed plenty of ribbing banter while waitressing at the Puck & Shoot, just as she'd told Dante. The best strategy might be to beat Jordan and his buddies at their own game.

Could it have been only a week since Constance and

Oliver's wedding? So much had happened, including the buildup of sexual frustration. Work and other commitments had kept her and Jordan apart except for physical therapy, and then Dante's news had led her to bide her time until tonight, when Jordan had suggested dinner out at Altavista.

She and Jordan had been served wine but had yet to order their meal. *Time to have a little fun.*

She leaned close, drawing Jordan's attention, so she could keep her voice low. "I've been thinking all week about Saturday night."

Jordan's eyes kindled. "What a coincidence. So have I."

"Hmm." *And not just so he could claim to have won a stupid bet?*

"I don't want to rush you, but, yeah—" the corner of his mouth turned up "—I've wanted a repeat."

She dipped the top of her finger into the top of her wineglass and then, without breaking eye contact, brought that finger to her lips.

Jordan swallowed, his throat working.

She knew him well enough now to recognize the flare of arousal. They occupied a cozy corner table for two, where they could engage in semipublic flirtation without attracting too much attention. She wanted to have some fun while she made him eat his words.

Deliberately, she let her leg brush against his. Her wrap dress clung to her breasts, and she leaned forward, knowing her cleavage would be on full display. "I want to make you melt."

"Sera," he said in a low voice, his gaze kindling, "the appetizer hasn't even arrived, and you're—"

"Ready for dessert?" She trailed the wine-stained finger from her collarbone to the swell of her breasts.

Jordan cleared his throat and lowered his eyes to follow the motion of her finger.

"I came straight from work. I'm a little…breathless."

He lifted his gaze then and fixed it on her. "You're wearing clingy dresses in your therapy sessions these days? For which client?"

She gave a throaty laugh. "Don't be silly. I changed into my thong and dress in the bathroom before I drove over here."

Jordan sucked in a breath. "You're playing with me, aren't you?"

Yes, she was enjoying turning the tables.

"I don't know what's put you in this mood—"

"Well, it's been a while since we've had sex. Now that I've had a taste, I want more."

He groaned, and she gave him a naughty smile.

Jordan thrust his crumpled napkin onto the table. "That's it. Let's go. I'll leave a big tip for the wine we ordered and for the meal we didn't."

"But we haven't had dinner."

His gaze was hot on her face. "We'll order in. After."

"Jordan," she murmured, "you look a little flushed. Are you hot?"

"Yeah, for you," he growled back, waving away an approaching waiter. "Great invitation, by the way. I accept."

She curved her lips and then shifted in her seat. She took a large swallow from her water glass to steady herself and then regarded him over the rim.

"Sera." There was an edge to his voice. "We need to leave now. Otherwise I won't be able to without—"

"Mmm. Wouldn't want your teammates to see that, would we?"

"Exactly."

"After all, you're the one who's supposed to make me melt."

Jordan stilled and then groaned again. Except this time, the sound was self-deprecating.

Sera tilted her head and regarded him.

"I can explain."

"I'm sure. I can't wait to hear it."

"Who told you? Dante?" he said on an exhale. "Sera, it was a ridiculous bet—"

"At my expense."

"And a flippant remark—"

"To uphold the great and mighty Jordan Serenghetti reputation?"

"Damn it."

"Amen."

"Are you going to make me grovel?"

"Or at least work for it," she replied teasingly. "Let me help you out here. 'I was just being one of the guys.'"

"Check."

"'We don't wear emotion well.'"

"Check."

"'It was false male bravado. Psych 101.'"

"Check again." He took her hand. "I'll take it from here. I'm frustrated about not being on the ice. Getting grief about you from my teammates was heaping—"

"Insult onto injury?" she asked drolly.

He looked sheepish. "Yeah. I didn't want to go there with them…about you. Because it was you, and you're special."

"I'm going to have to get tough with the Razors crew."

Jordan smiled. "They already know you can kick ass on TV."

"Mmm-hmm."

He lifted her hand and kissed her knuckles. "Forgiven?"

"I ought to make you take cooking lessons live for a season."

Jordan shuddered. "Please. The last episode nearly did me in." Then he sobered. "Anyway, this isn't about some asinine bet or tit for tat. The truth is I've lost track of which one of us owes a favor to the other. Because somewhere along the way, I stopped caring. Except about being with you."

Wow. She wanted to believe those words. His bet had cast doubt on what she'd thought was something genuine and true and beautiful. She still had faith in him, but it had been nicked. But then, she hadn't expected him to crack open with emotional honesty tonight.

"I had this germ of a plan to make a major donation to Welsdale Children's Hospital," Jordan went on after a pause. "Thanks to you, I might still have a career that'll make that possible."

She blinked.

"It'll be a hospital addition for rehabilitation facilities. Because I understand how important physical therapy is."

Sera parted her lips on an indrawn breath. She'd started out annoyed and ready to teach him a lesson, but somehow they'd ended up in a place where he held her heart.

Jordan caressed the back of her hand with his thumb. "I have a meeting with hospital management in the next few weeks. I'd like you to be there."

She blinked again. It wasn't a marriage proposal, but this was heady stuff. He was asking her to weigh in on a major life decision—one that would involve millions of dollars. "Why?"

"You'll have a perspective on things that I won't. I value your opinion." He gave a lopsided smile. "You're important to me."

His words were sexier than any underwear billboard. On impulse, she cupped his face and kissed him, heedless of the other diners scattered through the dim restaurant.

When she sat back, Jordan laughed.

"Hey," he said, "I wasn't joking earlier when I said we needed to get out of here fast. Any more PDAs and—"

"—we'll be putting on an R-rated performance?"

"Anyone ever tell you that you have a knack for finishing my sentences?"

"We're on the same wavelength."

"That's not all I'd like to be," Jordan growled.

"Get the check, Serenghetti."

Twelve

By the time he and Sera arrived back at his place, it was all Jordan could do to hold himself in check until they stepped off the elevator inside his apartment.

"This place is different than I remember," she remarked. "But then, I was a little shaken up after the accident and maybe not picking up the same details."

He was shaken up *now*. He kissed the back of her neck and let his hands roam up her body.

He wanted to make love to her again. It was a need he hadn't experienced this sharply…ever.

She'd surprised him with her reaction to the ridiculous challenge he'd taken up with Marc. Another woman might have given him the silent treatment and left him to guess why.

But Sera had…attitude. She drove him crazy and made him ache with need.

Even in his sleep, he could taste her and inhale her scent. And ever since their encounter after the wedding, he's been itching to get her alone. He'd meant it when he said all he could think about these days was being with her.

When they got to his bedroom, he turned her around to face him and kissed her. She met him with a longing of her own, her mouth tangling with his.

He pulled at the tie at her waist and her dress fell open. He drank her in with his eyes. "You're a fantasy come true, Sera."

They kissed again, and he inched her in the direction of his bed. Within a few steps, her dress fell to the floor, followed by his shirt.

He cupped her breasts, feeling their luxurious weight and letting his thumbs move over the twin peaks covered by the thin fabric of her bra.

"Do you like my hands on you?" he murmured.

"Yesss." Her breath was shallow and rapid, her pupils dilated.

He wanted her to feel the depth of his need and reciprocate it. He wanted to bring her pleasure.

Sliding his hands under her arms, he unhooked her bra at the back and watched those glorious breasts spill against him.

Then holding her gaze, he bent and gave attention to each breast with his mouth.

She moaned, and her fingers tangled in his hair. "Jordan…"

He closed his eyes, focusing on drawing one peak into his mouth and then the other.

Sera's knees bent, and she leaned in to him.

Yes. He told her all the things he wanted to do with her, until her breath came in rapid rasps. Her skin tasted flowery, making him want her all the more.

When he straightened, his hand went to the juncture of her thighs. "You are so ready for me, Angel."

She had a half-lidded look, her color heightened, her lips red.

"It's going to be so good. I've been waiting for days for a repeat."

She wet her lips and then stroked her hand up and down his erection. "Please."

He breathed deep. "What do you want?"

In response, she surprised him by undoing his belt and stripping him out of his pants. She pressed kisses to his bare chest, making him groan. And then she stroked him with a sure hand, bringing him ever closer to the brink.

"Ah, Sera."

She bent before him and took him in her mouth, loving him.

Jordan's eyes closed on a wave of pleasure. When he couldn't take anymore—knowing he was unbearably close—he tugged her up and stripped her underwear from her.

She lay back on the beige comforter covering his bed, her hair splayed around her.

Jordan fumbled with some protection from a nearby dresser drawer and then braced himself over her.

Holding her gaze as her legs came around him, he sheathed himself inside her, and they both sighed.

Jordan gritted his teeth. "You're so damn hot and tight. So good."

He began to move, and she met him stroke for stroke. Jordan closed his eyes, intent on drawing out the interlude. Within minutes, however, it was too much for both of them.

Sera lifted her hips and arched her back with her climax, and watching her glorious reaction, Jordan came apart himself, his hoarse groan a testament to reaching a new peak.

Afterward, he slumped against her and gathered her to him, and they were both content to let sleep claim them.

* * *

Sera reflected that the only word that could sum up the past week or so was *idyllic*. She and Jordan had snuck away to spend a weekend at a cozy bungalow he had on Cape Cod, taking a balloon ride over the wooded fields and overall enjoying living in their own new and kaleidoscopic little world.

Now as she and Jordan arrived hand in hand at a local movie theater near Welsdale, Sera found herself both content to enjoy the evening and bursting with plans for their burgeoning relationship. Jordan's recovery was going so well, soon they'd be able to head to the boxing gym together. And in future outings to Cape Cod, they could water-ski, take a boat out on the water and even go parasailing. Jordan had dared her to try the last.

"Jordan, Jordan!"

The paparazzo came out of nowhere, camera flashing like a firearm. Sera bent her head down as she and Jordan headed toward the doors of the theater. So far, they'd been able to duck photographers despite his celebrity. Probably the fact that it was the off-season and he'd been convalescing helped.

Sera didn't delude herself, however, that their honeymoon would last forever. Jordan was too well-known. And while they'd been able to keep their relationship under wraps until recently even from their families, this photographer meant she'd have to figure out fast how to deal with being outed. The fact that she and Jordan were holding hands was a giveaway that they were more than casual acquaintances.

As the photographer snapped away, he also jogged to catch up to them. "Any comment on the news report?"

"Whatever it is, the answer is no," Jordan tossed back.

"Are you denying that you're the father of Lauren Zummen's child?"

Sera stiffened and swung her gaze to Jordan, whose expression had turned grim.

"Anything you want to say?"

"Again, no."

In the next moment, Jordan changed course and was hustling her back to his car—obviously trying to shake the paparazzo.

"No denial?" the photographer called out after them.

"How did you know where we were?" Jordan asked, not looking behind him.

"I have my sources." The paparazzo sounded cheery.

Stunned, Sera silently followed Jordan. Suddenly, what their families might think of their relationship was the least of her problems. And her concern about the stupid bet he'd made with his teammates seemed laughable in comparison.

They both said nothing as they got into the car and Jordan pulled away from the curb, leaving their pursuer far behind them. Obviously, a night out couldn't happen now. They'd be sitting ducks for more unwanted attention.

Sera felt a roaring in her ears. Finally, she forced herself to say, "Do you know what he was talking about?"

She could tell from Jordan's face that he had some inkling at least—and he'd chosen to say nothing to her about it.

"There are rumors…"

She gripped her handbag, pressing her knuckles into the folds. She could've heard those rumors at any time and would have been unprepared to deal with them. She was unprepared to deal with them *now*. "Where are we going?"

"Back to your place because it's closer, so we can talk. Privately."

She took his words as confirmation of her worst suspicions and briefly closed her eyes. "So there's a baby?"

Jordan nodded, not taking his eyes off the road.

"Did you know the mother?" She felt as if she was chewing sawdust as she said it.

"The first time I heard her last name attached to the rumors is when the photographer just said it. Yes, I knew her. But once and for a short time."

"Once is all it takes, isn't it?" she retorted.

This time, he did glance at her. "There's no proof that I'm the father."

"And there's nothing to say you're not."

Jordan hit his palm against the steering wheel. "You're asking me to prove a negative when I haven't even taken a paternity test."

How could this be happening to her again? Was she a marked woman? She'd now dated *two* men who'd had families—children—she hadn't known about. For the second time, she'd experienced the most brutal deception.

"Sera, those kinds of accusations are not that uncommon for professional athletes."

She knew what he was saying. Sports stars were targets for fortune hunters. Her own cousin Marisa was the product of a pro athlete's short-term liaison, though Aunt Donna hadn't asked for or received a penny from Marisa's father, whose minor-league baseball dreams had died along with him in a freak accident.

"The story is that the girl is two and a half," Jordan said quietly.

"When are you going to take a paternity test?"

He didn't take his eyes off the road—didn't glance at her. "This allegation has come out of the blue. I need to have Marv, my agent, arrange to investigate it."

"Why didn't you tell me?"

"I figured it was baseless gossip until now. I want to have the facts first."

Right. Time to figure out how to spin this story for her,

perhaps? There was always a reason—an explanation. Neil had had one, too.

When they arrived at her apartment, she popped out of the car and shot for the door. She heard his car door slam and then Jordan rushing to catch up to her.

"Sera!"

She didn't want to talk about this right now. How could she be so stupid? *Again.*

She must be giving some kind of signal to men: *this one is easy to dupe.*

Jordan touched her arm, and she spun toward him. "Leave me alone."

"We need to talk. Listen—"

"No, you listen." She stabbed a finger in the direction of his chest. "I don't like being had."

He had the indecency to appear surprised. "Neither do I."

"There's a lot about you I apparently didn't know."

"Let's talk somewhere more private."

"I don't think so." No way was she continuing this…*discussion*. Especially inside her apartment. So he could work his *charm* on her and *gaslight* her. There'd be nowhere to run if she was completely broken.

Neil had played with her mind, too. And her feelings—and her heart. *You've got it all wrong, Sera… My marriage isn't real… I adore you.* Afterward, she'd discovered at the bar where she'd first met him that he'd been a longtime customer, and she hadn't been the first woman he'd dallied with. And there'd been a baby, all right—or at least a toddler. A two-year-old who'd lived with his wife in Boston.

Jordan remained silent but sighed and shoved his hands in his pockets.

"What? Nothing to say? This news didn't come as a complete surprise to you."

"I told you what I know. It was sudden, and I just learned the mother's last name. I'm still processing it."

"How stupid do you think I am? These types of scandals are usually percolating for a while before they grab a lot of headlines. And you—" she sucked in a deep breath "—didn't tell me."

"I didn't think you'd be this upset that I'd waited."

"What?" She stared at him. "I wouldn't be upset that you're a father, and I didn't know it?"

"Alleged father. And I recently found out myself."

"But you knew before tonight." She made a strangled sound and then muttered, "I should have learned my lesson with Neil."

"Who's Neil?"

"The guy I had the misfortune to date after he walked into my bar." She paused. "Until I discovered he was married and had a wife and toddler daughter squirreled away in Boston." Her voice dripped sarcasm. "Conveniently far but not too far away from Welsdale, where he traveled frequently on business."

Jordan swore.

Sera gave a humorless laugh. "To think that I thought my biggest problem with you was some ridiculous bet that you'd made with Marc Bellitti about—" she waved her hand "—making me melt. I guess we all know who the fool is, don't we?"

Jordan looked solemn. "Sera… I'm sorry."

"Yes, I guess there's nothing else to say, is there?" she replied flippantly, feeling traitorous tears welling. "Except sometimes *I'm sorry* isn't enough. Goodbye, Jordan."

Jordan stared broodingly at his apartment wall from his spot on the sofa.

When he'd reluctantly driven off earlier without settling things with Sera, he realized that he needed the truth first before he could convince her. Had he really fathered a child he hadn't known about? He'd always been careful. In this case, more than three years ago, he'd been intimate with Lauren once, and he'd used protection. Sure, such measures weren't foolproof, but it gave him reason to question the veracity of the claims here.

He'd met Lauren at a party, and she'd come on strong. She'd had a summer-vacation share on Cape Cod with a bunch of twentysomethings—and his house had been nearby. He'd quickly realized they didn't have much in common, so he'd let her down easy and had never seen or heard from her again. Until now.

Sure, those minimal facts would be small consolation to Sera. But he also wasn't the same person he'd been three years ago. These days, an aspiring groupie held little appeal for him.

He knew what he had to do. If he was already being stalked by paparazzi, the story was spreading quickly. He couldn't afford to wait, even if his agent had flagged the story for him just yesterday—as he often did when his name popped up online, associated with good or negative articles. He'd have to tell his family before they read about it. *Before they had a reaction of shock and disappoint akin to Sera's.*

He winced inwardly. First, though, he had to marshal his resources.

Picking up the phone, he called Marv.

His agent answered on the third ring, sounding sleepy.

"Early bedtime these days, Marv?" Jordan couldn't resist teasing.

"What's up?" Marvin replied in a gravelly voice.

Jordan sobered. "I need you to follow up on the recent gossip story about the baby I allegedly fathered. I can't afford to wait, and we need to move up the timeline about how we react."

"What happened?"

"A paparazzo caught up with me tonight, and the story is gaining traction." He paused, tightening his jaw. "He blurted the woman's last name, and I just discovered that this Lauren is someone I may have known."

He didn't need to spell things out for Marv. Lauren was a common enough name that it had been easy for both him and his agent to initially dismiss this story. But now he was admitting to Marv that this was a woman from his past. And Jordan knew he had to face the consequences, one way or another. "I'm willing to take a paternity test if necessary."

What if he was the father? He weighed the idea. Sure, he figured he'd have kids someday. He liked kids. He loved being the newly minted uncle to his brothers' babies. He cared enough to fund-raise with Once upon a Dream and want to sponsor new facilities at Children's Hospital. But having children of his own wasn't something he'd seriously contemplated up to now given his lifestyle; he was at the peak of his career. Plus, if he was honest, he'd say he'd never met a woman he wanted to have kids with.

An image of Sera flashed through his mind, and he started to smile. His baby and Sera's would be a firecracker, no question.

Marv sighed. "You know, a scandal on top of everything else won't be good for the revenue stream or your contract-negotiating position. I gotta put that out there."

"We're living in the era of reality-TV stars. Don't be too sure," Jordan responded drily. "Anyway, I want the truth—whatever it is."

"Of course."

"I want you to hire a private investigator and find out all you can. I need as much background as possible fast."

He trusted Marv and considered him more than an agent because of their long-standing working relationship. That was why he was asking him to be the point person and hire whomever and do whatever it took.

"You got it," his agent said. "And Jordan?"

"Yeah?"

"No matter what the truth is, you can handle it."

"Thanks for the vote of confidence, Marv."

His life had been turned upside down, but he'd been in worse situations before.

Thirteen

"Bernice, I need to be reassigned."

Sera stood in the doorway of her manager's office, not looking at Bernice but focused on the bobblehead dolls on the shelves. Frankly, she felt a bit like a bobblehead herself lately.

It wasn't every day that a woman had to deal with being outed as a couple in the press and a private breakup *at the same time*. From some angles, it would seem that she and Jordan had the shortest relationship on record. They were the local version of a Las Vegas wedding *and* divorce.

Plus, the juiciness of Jordan being outed as a baby daddy while dating another woman at the same time was making the press slaver.

The twin headlines ran through her head: "Jordan Serenghetti's Secret Love Child." "Jordan Serenghetti's New Mystery Woman."

Bernice swiveled her chair so that she faced Sera more

fully. "You want to be reassigned? Because Jordan may have fathered a child?"

"You know already?"

"Honey, everyone knows. It's Jordan Serenghetti. The news is hard to avoid, especially around here, and I'm not a good gossip-dodger."

Sera wasn't ashamed to admit she'd cried last night. The pain had been a dull throb in the region of her heart. If it had been sharp and awful but over and done within minutes, she might have been thankful. Instead, she had this agonizing aftermath.

It wasn't as if she'd be able to avoid Jordan for the rest of her life. Not unless she declined Marisa and Cole's future invites. And maybe not entirely even then. Welsdale wasn't that big a town, and she was bound to run into Jordan eventually, even if she ducked every event that Marisa and Cole planned for Dahlia or any other child they might have.

Which brought Sera back to the children she and Jordan would never have. Because he may have already plunged into parenthood with another woman, and had hidden it from her—just like Neil had.

Why hadn't she learned? Her inner voice wailed and raged, refusing to be silenced.

Bernice looked at her sympathetically.

"I know you said we need this contract with the Razors…" Sera trailed off and bit her trembling lip. Damn it. *She would not cry.* She'd thought she'd used up all her tears last night.

"Things got a little too cozy with Jordan?"

Sera nodded, still avoiding her manager's gaze. She'd behaved unprofessionally—she inwardly rolled her eyes—and with Jordan Serenghetti, of all people. He was an in-law and a sports celebrity.

"Feelings?"

"Yeah," she responded thickly.

She blamed Jordan—and herself. How had she fallen prey to his charm? She should have known better. She did know better. And even if she had to keep banging her head against a wall, she *would* do better next time.

Bernice sighed. "The smooth-as-honey jocks are always the ones that are hardest to resist."

"You know?" Sera raised her eyebrows. Bernice seemed to be speaking from experience.

"Remind me to tell you about Miguel another time."

Sera's eyes widened because her manager had been married for years. Had Bernice had an affair?

"He was pre-Keith," her manager added. "I learned my lesson."

Sera wished she had, too.

"Okay," Bernice said briskly. "When's your next appointment with the Razors' resident bad boy?"

"Wednesday at two."

"Let me look at my schedule and see who else on staff is available."

Sera relaxed her shoulders. "Thanks, Bernice."

"We can tell him you're unavailable this week and work from there, until this situation gets resolved."

As far as Sera was concerned, this situation was already resolved. She and Jordan were over and done. She shook her head. "This isn't a temporary squabble. There's no hope—"

Bernice waved her hand. "We'll see."

Sera sighed. At least she had a temporary reprieve. "Thanks, Bernice."

Sera did her best to focus on work for the rest of the day. On the way home, she stopped at Bellerose in order to pick up some groceries. She was either going to cook and bake her troubles away or indulge in some premade comfort food—maybe both.

On the way to the ice-cream section, she stopped

abruptly as she caught sight of her cousin Marisa—or rather, her cousin spotted her. She bit back a groan.

"We have to stop meeting this way," Marisa joked, maneuvering her cart out of the way.

Tell me about it. The last thing she needed right now was to run into her cousin. She wasn't sure she had time to put on her *brave face*. "Let me guess. With Dahlia around now, you mostly get to do the supermarket run only in the evenings when Cole gets home."

Her cousin smiled. "Bingo."

Unfortunately, Sera thought, it was also the time when she'd be getting out of work and maybe stopping for milk on the way home. Karma was against her these days in a major way.

Marisa searched her cousin's face and then glanced around them as if to be sure they had some privacy for the moment. "How are you doing?"

"As well as can be expected today," Sera responded noncommittally.

"I was going to call you later on, after I knew you'd be home from work. If you need someone to lend an ear or a shoulder…"

Sera blinked. "To cry on?" She shrugged. "Sorry, all my tears have been washed away."

Marisa sighed.

"How are the Serenghettis handling the news?" Sera damned herself for asking.

After she and Jordan had been ambushed by the photographer, she'd figured it was just a matter of time until the news became really public—though she hadn't expected it to find its way to Bernice so quickly. Perhaps Jordan had called to forewarn his family…a courtesy he hadn't extended to her. Maybe he'd learned something from her reaction to being caught by surprise and decided telling others himself was the better course.

"Jordan has told all of us that he doesn't know what's true yet."

Sera shrugged again. "Well, best of luck to him."

Marisa looked worried. "Oh, Sera, I know you care."

"Do you?"

"I thought, especially at the wedding, that there was a special spark between you and Jordan." Marisa searched her expression again. "Was I wrong?"

"Does it matter now? The only thing that does is that I was a fool. Again."

"Because Jordan may have a child?"

"Because he didn't tell me!" Sera waved a hand. "Like a certain lying ex-boyfriend. I seem to have a special gift for ferreting out impostors."

"Oh, I don't know, the feelings between you seemed very real to me."

As another customer turned into their aisle, they moved apart.

"I need to go," Sera said quickly. "Before someone recognizes me from the news."

"I'm here if you need me."

Sera just nodded as she moved down the aisle, but she mulled over Marisa's words.

Feelings. The magic word. First Bernice, now her cousin. She was hoping these *feelings* would go away soon. Far, far away.

Fool. Sera had called herself the dirty word more times than she could count in the past few days. What kind of pushover got taken for a ride twice by men singing the same tune? Would she ever learn?

She'd taken to the gym with a vengeance. Pilates, yoga, kickboxing, two-mile runs. There was no hurdle that she wouldn't surmount. But she couldn't overcome her fury. Okay, her pain.

Damn it.

And now she was facing Sunday dinner with her family at her mother's house. Not showing up wasn't an option. Her family would just take her absence as confirmation that something was amiss—and perhaps wonder and worry more than they already were. She had to face reality, and the sooner the better.

After serving the spaghetti and meatballs, her mother eyed her speculatively. "I heard the most outrageous story this week. I knew it couldn't possibly be true."

"Hmm." Sera didn't look up from her plate.

"Something about you and Jordan Serenghetti being an item," her mother went on. "I told my hairdresser that the press must have snapped you together because of some invite from your cousin Marisa. You're related by marriage these days, after all."

Yup, and bound to stay that way. It was a gloomy prospect. She was destined to see Jordan again and again. Some traitorous part of her longed to see him again—still—but at the same time, she knew it would be unbearable to maintain a brave front.

"So am I right?" her mother asked brightly, glancing from her to a studiously silent Dante, who'd arrived for the family meal only minutes before.

"It wasn't an event that Marisa was hosting," Sera mumbled.

"And then Natalie—that's my hairdresser—also said she'd heard that Jordan had fathered a child with some woman recently." Rosana Perini heaved a sigh. "Honestly, Natalie hears the worst gossip."

Sera's face grew hot. "Yes, I heard the same story."

Her mother paused and blinked. "You did?"

Sera played with her food. "The photographer who trailed me and Jordan to the movie theater mentioned it."

"Where the Serenghettis were having an outing and invited you. How nice."

Sera held her mother's gaze. "Where Jordan and I were going, just the two of us." *After spectacular sex.*

Dante coughed.

Rosana tilted her head, puzzlement drawing her brows together. "So the story is true? You and Jordan have been dating?"

"Yes."

"And now it turns out he's fathered a child with another woman?"

Sera felt her face heat again. Put that way, it sounded like just another scrape that, in her family's eyes, *poor Sera* would get herself into. "That's what the press is saying."

Her mother seemed to be floundering, unsure of how to process what she was hearing. "You didn't tell me that you and Jordan…were seeing each other."

Right. Precisely to avoid situations like this.

"But he's been injured…" Her mother's voice trailed off, as if shock had left her at a loss for words.

"I've been giving him physical therapy." *And more.*

An uncomfortable silence hung in the air so that every tinkle of a fork sounded loud and clear.

Dante cleared his throat. "Sera got mixed up with Jordan because she was helping me out."

Rosana's bewildered expression swung to her son.

"I asked Sera to take on Jordan as a client so I could look better at work." Dante shrugged. "You know, new job and all."

Sera threw her brother a grateful look. For a long time, she'd been out to stake her independence and competence, and these days her family—or at least one of them—seemed ready to acknowledge her help.

"I don't know what to say," her mother said after a pause.

"Don't worry, Mom," Sera said quickly, because old

habits died hard and she still felt the need to reassure her mother. "Jordan and I are no longer seeing each other."

"Because of the story that's circulating?" Rosana asked.

"That was part of it. More because it took me by surprise. *He didn't feel the need to tell me.*"

Her mother sighed.

Dante helped himself to some more meatballs from the serving bowl. "Well, the world has tilted on its axis," he joked. "Sera is bailing me out these days, and Mom has a beau."

"What?" It was Sera's turn to look surprised.

Her mother suddenly looked flustered.

Dante cracked a smile. "Mom's not the only one who has her sources among the town gossips. The gentleman caller is alleged to be a mild-mannered accountant by day, and one mean parlor cardplayer by night."

Sera tilted her head. "Let me guess. You ran into one of Mom's friends from her monthly card-playing posse?"

"Yeah," Dante said slyly. "One of them let it slip. In her defense—" her brother paused to throw their mother a significant look "—Mom's friend thought I already knew."

"Wow," Sera said slowly, her gaze roaming from her brother to her mother and back. "Anyone else have any secrets to share?"

Dante swallowed his food. "Not me. I play it straight."

Sera resisted rolling her eyes. And then, because her mother continued to look embarrassed, she added, "I'm happy for you, Mom. Really happy. It's about time."

"Thank you, Sera," her mother said composedly before raising her eyebrows at Dante. "We're taking things slowly, despite any rumors your brother may be spreading."

Dante just grinned cheekily.

Her mother then focused on Sera again, fixing her with a concerned look. "Are you okay? This must be a lot to deal with."

"I'm a grown-up, Mom. I can manage."

Rosana Perini suddenly smiled. "I know you are, but if you want to talk, I'm here." She waved a hand. "I realize Marisa has been your confidante, but ever since your father died, I think I know something about being the walking wounded."

Sera tried a smile, but to her surprise it wobbled a little. She couldn't help being touched. First Dante, now her mother. It seemed her family was finally able to give her space as an adult—as well as owning up to their own weaknesses. Her mother showed signs of moving on from her fears after the death of a child and, more recently, of a husband. "Thanks, Mom."

Her mother reached across to give her hand a reassuring squeeze and then stood to take some empty plates to the kitchen.

When their mother had departed, Dante threw Sera a curious look from across the table. "So, you and Jordan…"

"Yes?"

Dante leaned forward, keeping his voice low. "Let me know if I need to challenge Serenghetti to a duel. Job or no job, family comes first."

"Thanks, but I've got this."

"I thought…the bet."

"I know. We patched things up. He seemed to have real feelings for me." *Feelings* again. She was starting to sound like Bernice and Marisa.

"So things were getting real between you and Jordan, and then this happened." Dante cursed.

She leaned forward, too. "He said he doesn't know if he's the father."

Her brother sighed. "For what it's worth, celebrity sports stars are targets for gold diggers and fame seekers all the time. Don't believe everything you read. It might not be true."

Jordan had said as much—or tried to—but at the time, his argument had paled in significance to the parallels to Neil. Except the similarity to Neil wasn't exactly right. Because...because—

"So Jordan has feelings for you. How do you feel about him?"

I love him.

Sera's heart thudded in her chest. She finally admitted to herself what had lingered on the edges of her consciousness despite her pain. Jordan made her sad, mad and bad but vibrantly alive. Sexual tension had given way under her feet like thin ice once she'd gotten to know him.

Yes, she'd been hurt and angry about hearing the bombshell news from a stranger instead of Jordan himself. But unlike her former boyfriend, Jordan hadn't tried to cover up the fact of a secret family for months. And didn't she want to be part of his life, child or no child?

Seeming to read the emotions flitting across her face, Dante continued, "Ser, if you do care about him, you have to figure out what to do."

Sera stared at her brother, and then as their mother reentered the dining room, both she and Dante sat back.

She loved Jordan. The question was: What was she going to do about it?

Fourteen

"I've got news," Marv announced.

"No news is good news," Jordan joked, holding the phone to his ear, "but I'm prepared for anything you have to say. So what did you find, Marv?"

Despite his easygoing tone, Jordan tensed. He'd taken a break from his physical-therapy exercises in his home gym as soon as he'd noticed who was calling. Now the stillness in his apartment on this weekday morning enveloped him. His heart pounded hard against the walls of his chest. Marv's answer had the potential to change his life. If he were already a father, any future—with or without Sera—would be more complicated and a big departure from his life up to now.

He'd agreed to take a paternity test but had told Marv to hire a private investigator and get back to him once they had a fuller story. He could tell a moment of reckoning was upon him.

"I can say with certainty you're not the father. It's not

just the paternity test, but other information that's come to light."

Jordan took a deep breath and lowered his shoulders, the tension whooshing out of him like air from a punctured balloon. Then he silently cursed.

His life had been a roller coaster recently. On top of everything else, Lauren Zummen had given a salacious interview to *Gossipmonger* about their meeting and her subsequent pregnancy.

Jordan winced just thinking about Sera reading that piece. Not that he'd seen her. Bernice had reassigned him to another physical therapist, and he didn't have to ask why.

"Jordan?"

"Yeah, I'm here."

"Lauren wasn't pregnant."

Jordan paced around the gym, wandering aimlessly. "What? How can that be?"

"Her identical twin is the mother of the baby. It took some digging, but the private investigator checked records and talked to people in the small town near Albany that Lauren grew up in."

"What?" He was outraged. "How did they think they were going to get away with this?"

"They weren't. But maybe they'd get a lucrative payment or two from the gossip press for their story and some fame."

"I'm surprised they didn't go for the old-fashioned blackmail route," Jordan remarked drily, curbing another surge of anger. "You know, make me pay hush money."

"Too risky. They're smart enough to know you could have called their bluff and gotten law enforcement involved. The end result would have been a jail sentence."

Jordan tightened his hold on the receiver. "We've got to get the facts out there. At least the fact that I'm not the father."

"I know, I know."

"Wait until *Gossipmonger* finds out they may have paid for a false story."

"The women are identical twins. They can easily come up with some explanation for why they told the story that they did. Given the timing, you couldn't be ruled out as the father. And the women could claim that they swapped identities three years ago for some reason. That the one you met called herself Lauren but was actually her identical twin, and you didn't know it. The possibilities are endless." His agent paused. "Anything to keep the payments they might have received."

"You've got some insight into the criminal mind," Jordan joked.

"Well, I've been talking to the private investigator, and I've been in the business of representing famous people for a long time."

Jordan took a moment to compose himself. "Thanks, Marv. For everything."

The older man gave a dry chuckle. "It's what I do. A sports agent's work is never done. But for the record, you've been a lot easier to work with than some of my other clients. No secret plastic surgery, no sex tape, no drugs."

"Great for the endorsement deals and the contract that are coming up for negotiation."

"Yup."

"I'm a veritable angel."

Marv chuckled. "Go enjoy the rest of your life, Jordan. If your physical therapist keeps working wonders, we'll be in a good bargaining position."

After he hung up with his agent, Jordan reflected on Marv's last words.

Go enjoy the rest of your life. Marv's news today should have lifted the heavy cloud he'd been under, but somehow he still felt dejected and incomplete.

Jordan raked his hand through his hair and cast a glance

around the room. He hadn't bothered mentioning to Marv that Sera was no longer his physical therapist.

She'd worked wonders on him all right, though, and not just with his knee.

He was changed. *She'd* changed him.

Because he loved her.

With a cooler head, and without the issue of possible paternity clouding his judgment, he acknowledged that, given her past experience with men, Sera might easily have felt betrayed by his not initially sharing certain allegations with her. Instead, she'd found out the story from a paparazzo.

He was not that much better than Neil, whoever he was. And wherever the other guy was, Jordan wanted to plant his fist in his face.

Jordan figured his own playboy past hadn't helped him in gaining Sera's trust. He hadn't even remembered their spring-break encounter at the beach, though she definitely had. But he wasn't the same guy he'd been in his twenties or at the beginning of his relationship with Sera—or even a few weeks ago when he'd been brushing off Marc Bellitti's teasing at the Puck & Shoot.

He'd closed himself off from deep involvement—wanting to have fun at the height of his fame and fortune. But Sera was different. She'd challenged him and made him think about the man he was behind the facade of the well-known professional athlete—until his only choice had been to kiss her and fall all the way in love with her.

Crap. His long-standing rule of keeping to casual relationships hadn't protected him—from a gold digger, a paternity claim or anything else. And now, with Sera, he hadn't just *broken* his rule, he'd exploded it with dynamite. By falling in love with a woman who currently wanted nothing to do with him.

He had to do something about that.

*　*　*

The Puck & Shoot was familiar territory, so it was ridiculous to be tense. She knew that booth two had a rip in its seat cushion and that table four had a chip on its corner. She'd been here a million times.

Except she'd agreed to help out Angus again—and Jordan Serenghetti had just parked himself at table four. Alone.

He looked healthier and stronger than ever. Firm jaw, perfect profile, dark hair that she'd run her fingers through while moaning with desire…

Damn it.

She'd underestimated the power of his appeal. The time that they'd spent apart had either dulled her memory or whetted her appetite.

Still, she tried to draw strength from the crowded environment. At least they weren't completely by themselves.

Sure, she'd been doing some thinking since that night at the movie theater, but seeing him here now was sudden and she wasn't prepared. She expected him to be keeping a low profile with the gossip in the press, and Angus had assured her that he hadn't seen Jordan in a while.

Jordan turned, and his gaze locked with hers.

Steeling herself, notepad at the ready, she approached. "Are you ready to order?"

Her voice sounded rusty to her own ears. This was beyond awkward. Only the fact that she had a job to do kept her moving forward. When they'd parted, accusations had flown and feelings had been hurt. She'd nursed a bruised heart.

"Sera."

Not Angel. Why was he sitting alone when a few of his teammates were at the bar? "What do you want?"

The words fell between them, full of meaning. Then recovering, she nodded at the menu.

"I want to explain."

Flustered, she looked around them. "This isn't the time or place."

"It's beyond time, and it's the perfect place." One side of his mouth lifted in a smile. "And unless you conk me on the head with a menu, I'm in great shape."

She perused him. Unfortunately for her, he was as attractive as ever. Square jaw, laughing eyes, hot body. And Bernice had mentioned that he was continuing to recover well—though Sera had made a point of not asking.

"Fortunately for you," she sniffed, "I'd hate for my hard work in whipping you into shape to be undone."

Jordan laughed, and Sera crossed her arms.

"You have made me better," he said softly. "In more ways than one."

Sera swallowed and dropped her arms. *Ugh.* He could make her mad one minute and want to cry the next.

She glanced around, making sure they weren't drawing attention. "I wish you the best of luck sorting things out with…" She didn't know what to say. *Your baby mama? Ex-lover? Former one-night stand?*

Her heart squeezed, and she felt short of air. All she could manage were shallow breaths.

"I have."

She blinked. "What?"

He looked at her steadily. "I have sorted things out."

"Oh?"

He nodded. "I should have told you right away about the rumors." He paused. "I'm sorry."

She waved an arm dismissively, suddenly emotional and looking anywhere but at him. "Oh…"

He reached into the pocket of his jeans. "The results of the paternity test came back."

She looked down at the papers in his hand uncomprehendingly, her brain frozen.

"The child isn't mine."

Her gaze flew up to his.

"Lauren isn't even the mother."

Beyond the roaring in her ears, she barely made out Jordan's explanation.

"Thanks to Marv, the press should be posting corrected news stories as we speak." He smiled ruefully. "The gossip sites love a story with unexpected twists and turns."

"How can Lauren not even be the mother?" she asked, dumbfounded.

"Her twin sister is."

"How did they think they'd get away with this?"

Jordan's expression darkened. "That was my question. They had to know they'd eventually be found out, but maybe not before they received a fat payment or two to print a juicy story."

Feeling a tremor, she dropped her notepad on the table. "For the record, it doesn't matter. I already made up my mind that whether you were a father already or not was beside the point."

"Sera, I love you."

What? She'd pitched a revelation at him, and he'd hit it right back. And then, because it was all too much and she couldn't think of what else to say, she blurted, "Why should I believe you?"

Jordan stood up and moved closer. "Because you love me, too."

He said it so casually, she almost didn't process the words.

She blinked against a well of emotion and lifted her chin. "Does it matter? You're still…who you are, and I'm who I am."

"And who am I?" he queried, his voice low. "I'm a changed man—"

She opened her mouth.

"—especially since my casual remarks here to Marc Bellitti." He looked contrite.

They both knew which remarks he was referring to.

"At the time, it still seemed safer to play the game, or try to, rather than acknowledge the truth."

"Which is?"

"I love you." He glanced around them and then signaled the bartender.

Sera's eyes grew round. Now they were really creating a scene. "What are you doing? I have to take the order at my next table."

A slight smile curved Jordan's lips. "Already taken care of." He signaled again to someone across the room. "Angus has you covered with another waiter."

"He's short-staffed!"

"Not anymore he isn't. Another employee just stepped out of the back room."

Sera snapped her mouth shut. "You planned—"

"Let's just say Angus is a romantic at heart who's happy to lend a helping hand."

"He called me in when he didn't need me."

"I need you," Jordan said, looking into her eyes. "I've had a chance to sort out my priorities lately. And I've figured out what's important to me besides the career and whether I recover from my injury."

After he gave a sign to the bartender, the music was turned off, and everyone stopped talking. In the sudden stillness, Jordan raised his voice. "I'd like everyone's attention."

Bewildered and worried for him—was it fever? A momentary bout of insanity?—Sera leaned close and whispered, "What are you doing?"

He gave his trademark devilish smile. "In lieu of a jumbotron or big screen…"

OMG.

"I'm making a public declaration—"

Some people hooted.

"—that I think my teammates never thought they'd hear from me."

There was scattered laughter.

"This should be good," someone called out.

"I'm declaring my undying love for—"

Jordan took her hand and kissed it.

"The Puck & Shoot?" someone else wisecracked.

"Hey, maybe it's Angus or his beer." One patron elbowed another.

"Nah, Angus has been married for ages," Vince Tedeschi put in.

"—Serafina Perini," Jordan finished.

"Aww."

"Makes my heart flutter." Marc Bellitti clutched his chest dramatically.

Several women gave audible sighs.

Jordan turned to the peanut gallery lining the far side of the bar, including Vince and Marc. "Hey, guys, knock it off. This is difficult enough. Wearing my heart on my sleeve with no clue about my chances…"

Sera swallowed hard because she'd been getting choked up. Jordan was putting it all on the line for her—in public. She could spurn him, make him pay…or confess that she loved him, too.

Jordan opened his mouth to say more, and Sera impulsively leaned forward and shushed him with a kiss. She could feel his surprise, and then he relaxed, his lips going pliant beneath hers as he let her kiss him.

"Aw."

There were a few laughs, and some women gave audible sighs again.

When she broke the kiss, her gaze connected with Jordan's.

"Is that a yes?" he asked.

She nodded and then slid her arms around his neck. "Yes, yes…yes to everything. I'm all in with you." She looked into his eyes. "I love you, Jordan."

"I think I have a new lease on life in professional hockey thanks to you, and with your help, there are going to be new facilities at the hospital, too."

Sera felt her eyes glisten, so to make up for it, she teased, "They're going to name it the Serenghetti Pavilion?"

"Let's talk. Maybe we should name it after our first-born."

"You've got big plans, Serenghetti."

"Yup."

"Our families will go nuts over the news. And our kids would be double cousins with Dahlia."

He pulled her in for another kiss.

There was a smattering of applause around them.

"I love a happy ending," a woman in the crowd commented.

"Hey, who's going to be the most eligible New England Razor now that Serenghetti has retired?"

"Angus is going to start changing the TV channels from hockey to the feel-good drama of the week," a guy at the bar grumbled.

"What's wrong with that?" a woman beside him demanded.

As they ended their kiss, Sera laughed against Jordan's mouth. *Nothing, nothing at all.*

Epilogue

If someone had told her a year ago that she'd be planning her wedding to Jordan Serenghetti, Sera would never have believed them. Life was good in unexpected ways...

As she stood next to Jordan, Sera surveyed the assorted Serenghettis mingling in Serg and Camilla's Mediterranean-style mansion before the engagement party began. Soon, she'd be one of them. Serafina Perini Serenghetti, or SPS for short. She'd tried out the name numerous times already in her mind, and it always made her heart thrill. It felt right...like she was exactly where she should be.

Of course, the Serenghettis already treated her as one of them. She was Marisa's cousin, but they'd also embraced her as Jordan's fiancée. In fact, they'd been thrilled with news of the engagement months after she and Jordan had reconciled at the Puck & Shoot.

Camilla had exclaimed that she'd known all along that Sera would be a perfect match for her youngest son. Serg had congratulated Jordan on making a wise decision. Cole and Rick had called their brother a lucky man and joked that he'd soon be joining them in the ranks of fatherhood—making Sera flush. And Marisa had been thrilled that she and Sera would be sisters-in-law as well as cousins.

Mia Serenghetti came up and gave Sera's arm a quick squeeze. "Congratulations. I just wanted to say that again before your family and the other guests get here."

"Thanks, Mia."

Glancing at Jordan, Mia added, "You've made my brother very happy…and he'd better behave himself."

"Now that I'm engaged, you're next," Jordan teased.

His sister feigned offense. "How can you say that, after I kept your and Sera's secret at Constance and Oliver's wedding?"

"Simple. Mom. She's ready for her next starring role. Mother of the bride."

Mia rolled her eyes. "Don't jinx me. I'm married to my fledgling design business."

Sera nudged Jordan. "Good luck, Mia. I'll prolong Jordan's wedding planning as long as I can."

Mia threw her a grateful look. "Thanks. I'm glad I'm gaining an additional ally in this family." She gave her brother a baleful look. "It's been rough going."

As Camilla called Mia over with a question, Jordan glanced at his watch. "Your family should be here soon."

Sera squeezed her hands together. Not out of nervousness but excitement. "Yup. And Mom is bringing a date."

Her mother's *male friend*, as Rosana Perini referred to him, had turned out to be a mild-mannered, middle-aged guy with glasses and a quiet sense of humor. Sera had liked him instantly and was glad her mother was taking the next step by inviting him to be her date today.

Dante, of course, wouldn't miss today, either. Once he and their mother had understood that Sera and Jordan had worked out things between them, and how in love they were, they'd been just as excited as the Serenghettis about the relationship. And Dante naturally had been thrilled about becoming the brother-in-law of the Razors' star player.

Sera hooked her arm through Jordan's and beamed at him.

He was having his best season yet with the Razors. And as a result, Marv had had a great negotiating position. In fact, Jordan's new contract with the Razors had exceeded expectations, and his endorsement deals had so far been renewed for impressive sums. The result was that Jordan's plans to fund the rehabilitation facility at Welsdale Children's Hospital were right on track. Even Bernice was happy with all the new sports-team business that Astra Therapeutics was getting after their success with Jordan.

He leaned down to whisper in her ear. "Have I told you recently that I love you?"

"Not in a few hours."

"Maybe it's time to find another cloakroom."

Sera half laughed, half gasped. "We're at our own engagement party."

Jordan straightened and his eyes gleamed. "It wouldn't surprise anyone. And Mia might even be expecting it."

"Something tells me we'll be searching for a cloakroom for the rest of our lives."

Jordan leaned in for a kiss. "I'm counting on it."

* * * * *

REFORMING THE PLAYBOY

KARIN BAINE

This book is for my sisters, Heather and Jemma, who first got me hooked on ice hockey and encouraged my stalking of No. 28! Also for Jaime and Lucy, the next generation of Giants fans.

Thanks must go to Andrew, because without his help I never would've been able to write this book. Or so he would tell you. And to Ricky so he doesn't feel left out!

It's been a rough few years for all of us and, though I never say it, I love you all. xx

Finally, to fellow author Annie O'Neil. You've been an angel, and although we've yet to meet you've become such a lovely friend.

Listen to the rhythm

CHAPTER ONE

IF ALIENS HAD landed in the middle of this rural Northern Irish town and declared her their new supreme leader, Charlotte Michaels couldn't have been any more surprised than she was now.

'Hunter Torrance? *The* Hunter Torrance is the new team physiotherapist?'

Although he was standing there, casting a shadow over her, she didn't quite believe it. Didn't want to believe it. The Ballydolan Demons was *her* team, *her* responsibility, and having ice hockey's most infamous bad boy on board wasn't going to dig them out of the hole they were in.

'Yes. Deal with it, Charlie. We need him.' Gray Sinclair, the head coach, delivered the news and strode away, leaving her face-to-face with the new signing in the arena corridor. She'd been on her way to watch the team train when the pair had ambushed her and literally stopped her in her tracks.

'Hunter Torrance, the new physio. For now. I guess my future employment will be dependent on results.' The latest addition to the team held out his hand as he introduced himself but she wasn't inclined to shake it until someone convinced her this wasn't some sort of sick joke.

'Like everything around here,' she muttered. He wasn't the only one on trial. This was her first season as team doctor, and so far, with the list of injuries they had, a run of poor results and the last physiotherapist quitting on short notice, it could be her last too.

With a build more like a willow tree than the mighty oaks usually associated with the sport, she'd worked hard to be taken seriously but now they'd landed her with a sidekick who still held the UK Ice Hockey League record for most time spent in the sin bin she was worried the professionalism of the medical staff would be in jeopardy. The ex-Demons player had undermined the team's position in the league once before and she wouldn't sit back and let him do it again. In any capacity.

He smiled at her then, even as she ignored his offer of friendship. It was a slow, lazy grin, revealing the boyish dimples which had made him a pin-up for many a girl around here. Her included. If someone had told her at eighteen she'd be working alongside this one-time NHL hunk some day she would've died with happiness. Now the sight of him here was liable to make her forget she was a strong, independent career woman and not that same vulnerable teen. Something she had no time for nine years on.

He hadn't changed much in that time, at least not physically. Although this was probably the closest she'd ever been to him without the Perspex partition separating the players from the fans. He was still as handsome as ever, only now the pretty boy-band looks had morphed into the age-appropriate man-band version. Those green eyes still sparkled beneath long, sooty lashes, his dark hair was thick and wavy, if longer than she remembered, and he was dressed in a black wool coat, tailored blue shirt and jeans rather than the familiar black and red Demons kit. Damn but he'd aged well; the mature look suited him. It was a shame she could barely look at him without the abject humiliation of her past feelings for him spoiling the view.

'It's good to be back,' he said, and continued walking towards the rink as though he was returning to an idyllic childhood home and not the scene of his past misdemeanours.

For a moment Charlotte contemplated walking back in the other direction and locking herself in a nice quiet room somewhere until he'd gone away. He'd appeared from the shadows as if he were a bad dream. Or a good one, depending on which Charlotte was having the fantasy—the young infatuated girl or the cynical woman who knew bad boys weren't exciting or glamorous, they just screwed people over.

She didn't. Instead, she followed him towards the ice. Hunter wasn't to know she'd been enamoured with him to the point of obsession the last time he'd been on Northern Irish soil but he had cost her beloved Demons the championship with his antics. Even if she hadn't been embarrassed by her teen fantasies she still wasn't convinced he was up to the job and simply didn't trust him to do it effectively.

'Why are you here?' Her forthright attitude obviously wasn't something he was used to, or expecting. She could see him tensing next to her and she didn't like it. To her, the guarded reaction meant he had something to hide. The very nature of his defensive body language said he was fighting to keep his secrets contained but she wouldn't be fobbed off easily when it came to work matters.

'No offence but you're an *ex*-player for a reason. The drinking, the fighting, the generally bad attitude…they're not qualities I look for in a co-worker either.' His last appearance here had been a coup for the Demons to have him on board when no other team would have him. A big name for a budget price. Unfortunately, even this easy-going community hadn't been enough to tame his wild ways. He'd become a liability in the end, his playing time down to single figures for his last matches, as opposed to the many minutes he'd spent in the penalty box. Eventually people had given up on him. Charlotte too, once she'd realised he wasn't the man she'd thought he was when he'd snatched success away from the team. There'd been a collective sigh of relief when he'd flown back to Canada and she couldn't say she was happy to work alongside someone prone to such unpredictability now either.

'Ah, so you witnessed that particular phase of my life? In which case I can't expect you to be performing cartwheels on my return but I can assure you I'm here to work, not to raise hell.' Something dark flitted across his features that said he was deadly serious about being here, and sent chilly fingers reaching out to grab Charlotte by the back of the neck. She wanted desperately to believe that having him here would benefit the team, not hinder it, but she needed more proof than his word.

'I don't understand. Why would you want to come back to a team that holds memories of what I imagine was a very dark time for you? Especially to work off the ice rather than on it?' She made no apology for her blunt line of questioning. It didn't make sense to her and she'd made it a rule a long time ago to question anything she deemed suspect. She'd learned to follow her gut feeling rather than blindly take people at face value. It prevented a lot of pain and time-wasting further down the road.

'Despite…everything, I like the place. I want to make this my home again. There's also the matter of laying a few personal demons to rest and proving to you, and everyone else, I'm not that same hothead I was nine years ago.' It had taken Hunter some time to answer her but when he did he held eye contact so she was inclined to believe what he was saying, even though she doubted it was the whole truth.

'I trust you have all the relevant qualifications and experience?' Although she expected his appointment was more to do with his connections here and last-minute availability than actually being the best man for the job, she couldn't stop herself from asking. She needed someone who knew what he was doing on the medical staff with her.

'All my papers are in order if you'd like to see them.' He was teasing her now, the slight curve of his mouth telling her he wasn't intimidated by her interrogation technique.

'That won't be necessary,' she said, folding her arms across her chest as a defence against the dimples. This so wasn't fair.

'Look, I'm the first one to admit I was a screw-up. Not everyone will be happy to see me back but I'm sure we're all different people now compared to who we were back then.' He leaned back against the barrier, his coat falling open for a full-length view of the apparently new and improved Hunter.

That giddy, infatuated fan who shared Charlotte's DNA insisted on taking a good, long look. Who was to say that Mr Sophistication here wouldn't someday regress back to his rebellious alter ego too?

She'd never been a fan of that particular side of him. The young girl she'd been then had enjoyed the macho displays of the defenceman body-checking his opponents into the hoardings or dropping his gloves in a challenge fight. There was something primitive in watching that, even now, and there'd been times she'd wanted someone to defend her the way he had his teammates. He'd definitely been a crowd- and a Charlotte-pleaser for a time. But those later months when he'd fought with his own coach and smashed equipment in bad temper had made for uncomfortable viewing. It had felt like watching someone unravel in public and had come as no surprise to anyone when the Demons, or any team, had refused to renew his contract. He'd slunk back to Canada in disgrace, never to be heard of again. Until today.

'Clearly Gray thinks you've changed since this was his doing and he's the man in charge, not me. Well, I mean, if I was in charge I'd be a woman, not a man...'

'Obviously.' Hunter dropped his gaze to her feet and she followed it all the way back up to her eyes. He may as well have had X-ray vision the way he'd studied her form so carefully, smiling whilst she burned everywhere his eyes had lit upon her.

No, no, no, no, no! This wouldn't do at all. Behind the scenes of an ice-hockey team was not an appropriate place to suddenly become self-aware and he certainly wasn't an appropriate male to be the cause of it. These men were out of bounds. All of them.

Hunter mightn't be a player, or one of her patients, but he was a colleague. Given their past history, albeit a one-sided affair, his presence here complicated matters even more for her. With the team languishing in the bottom half of the league her position was already a tad precarious, without him in the picture too. Especially when he kept looking at her as though he was trying to pick her up in a seedy bar.

'Well, I'm sure you'll want to meet the team...' She backed away, reminding herself this wasn't about her, Hunter or any ridiculous crush. They were both here to do a job and a team of sweaty, macho hockey players should be a good distraction from any residual teenage nonsense.

'Maybe later. I wouldn't want to disrupt training. We should probably use the time to get to know each other better so I can convince you I'm not here as some sort of punishment.'

'That's really not necessary.' Charlotte gave a shudder. She knew all she needed to know about Hunter Torrance.

Probably more than most due to her teenage obsession and enough for her to want to keep a little distance between them.

'Hey, we're both on the same team, right?'

'Not by choice,' she muttered under her breath.

It was no wonder the powers that be had kept this snippet of information from her until it was too late to do anything about it. She'd been surprised they'd found a replacement physiotherapist willing to see out the last few games of the season and hadn't asked any questions, simply glad to have help getting the team back to fighting strength for the play-off qualifiers. Now she knew the good news had come with a catch.

'Well, I'll do my best not to get in your way. Actually, I wasn't even expecting you to be here today. I thought team doctors practically only made appearances on match days with the slew of outside commitments and specialist clinics you all usually have to boost your salaries. I know this is a different league from the NHL in terms of rules, technical terms, profile and especially finances. Or are you the official welcome committee?'

She knew he was deliberately being facetious as he took a little payback for the hard time she'd given him so far. His sneer earned him her narrow-eyed stare, which usually had the power to wither a man at fifty paces, but the bad boy of the tabloids took it all in his stride. What was a dirty look in the grand scheme of things when she supposed his whole past would probably be raked over again in the national press when they got wind of his return?

'Clearly, I didn't get the memo we'd have a VIP joining us otherwise I would have dusted off my pom-poms.'

Hunter opened his mouth to say something then seemed to think better of it and simply shook his head. It was probably a good idea. She wasn't in the mood for innuendo-based banter in the workplace, even if she had left the door wide open for it.

'In answer to your question, I'm here for the play-off matches. I schedule my sports and musculoskeletal clinics around my time here so I don't miss anything.' It wasn't easy but she used her personal leave to make sure she was here for the most important dates on the hockey calendar.

'I'm sure there aren't many who have such commitment.' He seemed impressed that she took her role here seriously but that only made her blood boil a fraction more. If he'd ever been as dedicated as she was to the game he would understand the sacrifices she made. Experience had taught her Hunter wasn't the team player the Demons needed.

'This is my team. I want to see them win and I'll do what I can to help realise that dream, but we do have our work cut out for us at the minute. Carter has a meniscus tear, Jensen has bursitis, Dempsey a groin strain, and Anderson, our star player, needs a serious attitude adjustment.' She listed those battling injury who were already causing concern for the upcoming matches. He needed to understand the workload was substantial and this job wasn't simply a position with a title.

'I'm sure we can manage between us. After all, that's what I'm here for. Not to make your life more difficult or to cause trouble. Those days are long gone. What do you say we start over with a clean slate and work together to get this team back on its feet?' He held out his hand in truce, asking that she forgive whatever sins he might've committed in her eyes.

Perhaps she was overstepping the mark here when she wasn't in any position of authority but she'd thought someone should have the Demons' best interests at heart when Gray's judgement seemed clouded by sentiment, or sympathy, or something that had no business in his team decisions. Still, the deed was done now and as a professional she knew better than to let her personal feelings get in the way of doing her job.

'Fine.' She hesitantly reached out towards him and shook on the new partnership. Her hand tingled where Hunter's gripped it so confidently and it wasn't simply because of the sheer size and power of him, making her fingers seem doll-like compared to his. There was also the moment of fantasy and reality colliding in that touch. Hunter Torrance was *actually* in her life now.

She inhaled the fresh, citrus scent of his aftershave so deeply she made herself dizzy. An entirely primal reaction that probably would've happened whether she'd known who he was or not.

For most single women he'd be the perfect package. If tall, dark, handsome and Canadian did it for you. Which it did. Why else would she be sniffing him as if he were made of chocolate and she wanted a taste? He was wrong for her on so many levels so she'd simply have to resist licking his face.

She'd done her best to fit in here as one of the crew, and making doe eyes at the new recruit wasn't very professional, it was asking for trouble. And it had definitely found her in the shape of a six-foot-four, two-hundred-pound ex-hockey-player.

Okay, so she still had stats memorised, it didn't mean anything other than she'd once been a girl with way too much time on her hands. An unhappy girl from a suddenly broken home who'd sat in her room like some fairy-tale princess in a tower, waiting for her knight in shining armour to come and rescue her. Except her hockey-playing knight had turned out to be an immature mess who had stolen the chance of that championship title from her beloved Demons and fuelled the theory all men had the ability to inflict mortal wounds to the heart. Not so much galloping off into the sunset as a life sentence distrusting anyone who dared come too close.

She knew her hostility towards him would seem uncalled for, petty even. That didn't stop her from hoping his past might catch up with him and send him back to the land of snow and ice. He'd shown he wasn't a man to be relied on when his team needed him. Surely she wouldn't be the only one to hold a grudge?

In his short time here he'd insulted and fought with many, had damaged the reputation of the club and generally been a pain in the backside to all those around him. Not everyone would be glad to see him return and she was kind of hoping those with a legitimate reason to give him a hard time would, to save her blushes and her position on staff.

Gray, the coward, had apparently left it to her to break the news to the others. It had taken all of her inner strength *not* to protest, *You were on that team he decimated, you should know better than anyone why I think he's a liability.*

She hadn't because she did her best to keep her passion for the game and her job separate. There was no fair reason he shouldn't be here if he had all the relevant experience needed for this job.

'Guys? Can we have a quick word?'

The team trooped off the ice and lined up, waiting for the news. Charlotte swallowed hard. There was definitely no going back now.

'We just wanted to tell you there's a new addition to the medical staff. Hunter Torrance will be your new physiotherapist for the rest of the season.' She didn't sugar-coat it. They could come to their own conclusions about what this meant. Her only job had been to relay the message and she'd done that as quickly and as bluntly as she could so this was over soon and she could go home to lick her wounds.

'What?'

'*The* Hunter Torrance?'

'You're kidding!'

There was a stand-off moment as they stood looking blankly at each other, no one knowing what to do with that information, including Hunter. He was frozen beside her, probably trying to decide on the fight-or-flight method of defence. She knew which one she'd prefer and would happily book him a one-way ticket back to Canada.

The first stick hit the ground with a heavy thud, then another, and another, until he'd received a round of applause hockey-style.

Floret, the captain, stepped forward and shook Hunter's hand first. 'Good to have you on board.'

Charlotte figured the move was because he was a fellow countryman but he was soon followed by the rest of the multinational squad.

'You're a legend, man.'

'Dude, I'm sure you have stories to tell.'

Charlotte rolled her eyes as they surrounded their new physio as if he was some sort of rock star. The last thing she needed was the players taking their cue from him that bad behaviour would ultimately be rewarded.

At least Hunter had the good grace to look slightly embarrassed by the positive attention. In her opinion he didn't deserve it and by the way his cheeks had reddened and he was trying to back away from the crowd she guessed he didn't think so either. Too bad. They were both stuck in this hell now.

'They're all yours,' she muttered as she walked away unnoticed and left him at the mercy of his adoring fan club.

After all, he'd insisted he could handle them and she was done for the afternoon. With the play-off matches looming, which could see them knocked out of the Final Four Weekend in Nottingham, they'd soon find out if the ex-rebel had turned over that new leaf and could justify his new place with the team.

The fan in her wanted him to work some magic and help get them match fit to fight their rivals for that place in the finals but she was a cynic at heart. She'd rather not take the chance of getting her hopes up, only to be disappointed at the last moment.

Hunter hadn't come to ruffle any more feathers. He had enough old enemies without making new ones and he certainly hadn't intended on upsetting the resident doctor. Gray had called in too many favours for him, none of which he deserved, to screw this up now. His old teammate was the one person who knew what he'd been through and had been willing to give him a chance. One he was grabbing with both hands.

Those selfish, heady days were far behind him now. There was only one reason he was back in this County Antrim town and that was for his son.

Hunter Torrance, the responsible father. It was the punchline to a very sick joke. A disgraced hockey player who'd barely been able to take care of himself now found he was the sole parent to an eight-year-old boy who'd just lost his mother in a car crash. He'd only had a few months to get used to the idea of being a father and to grieve for the relationship he could have had with Sara, the ex-girlfriend who'd hid the huge secret from him. Perhaps if he'd been in the right head space back then, able to love her, they could've been the family he'd always dreamed of having.

Instead, he'd walked away from her, consumed by his own self-pity, and returned to Edmonton.

For as unreliable as the old Hunter had been, the new one was as determined for his son to have the stable upbringing he'd never had. So he'd given up everything he'd worked hard to rebuild back home to do it. Now all he had to do was convince Sara's parents, Alfie's grandparents, and everyone else here he was up to the job.

He'd expected an initial backlash over his appointment here from the players and fans but not from the rest of the medical staff. This doctor probably knew nothing of him beyond his reputation yet it seemed enough to warrant her displeasure at the prospect of having to work alongside him. Not that he could blame her. The back-slapping welcome he'd received had come as a surprise to him too. Tales of his hockey days were probably a novelty to young, up-and-coming players still caught up in the thrill of the game.

For those who'd been personally affected by his behaviour, himself included, he'd prefer to confine his exploits to the past, and he'd told them so. After he'd confirmed or denied several of the urban legends attributed to his name and number.

'Is it true you spent longer in the penalty box than on the rink for the last month of your career?'

'Yes.' He wasn't proud of it. He hadn't been trying to play the villain or even defend his own players. The issues from his childhood that he'd tried to suppress had finally come to the surface in an explosion of misdirected rage. Years of therapy had taught him that but it wasn't information he was willing to share, or a time of his life he was keen to revisit. He was a different man now. Hopefully one more at peace with his past and himself.

'Did you really punch a linesman and knock out his teeth?'

Hunter sighed. He'd long since apologised to the unfortunate man whose offside decision he'd so violently opposed. 'One tooth, but I'm afraid to say I did.'

He didn't want any impressionable young talent to think his past behaviour was an advertisement for anything other than career suicide. 'It cost me my place on the team, my life here, everything.'

By that stage he'd been completely out of control, drinking too much, lashing out and acting out the role of a child in pain seeking the attention of a family that didn't want him. Ironically it was that behaviour that had made Sara turn her back on him and deny him a chance of a family of his own.

'I imagine tales of my debauchery have been greatly exaggerated in my absence. It's probably best you don't believe everything you've heard about me and form your own opinion. Which mightn't be any more favourable when you see the new programme I've devised for you…'

Whilst a new, intensive regime wouldn't endear him to his new buddies, it was his way of proving he was serious about his job here. He hadn't moved halfway across the world to be one of the guys; he was here to make a difference to the team and secure a future for him and Alfie. Gray had clued him in on the challenges he was up against and it was possibly the reason he'd secured the job against the odds—no one else was willing to take on the responsibility of a struggling team at such short notice. Hunter had done his homework and he knew exactly what he was up against but he'd been training for this ever since he'd hit rock bottom and had decided he wanted his life back in whatever capacity was available to him. After years of therapy and retraining he certainly wasn't going to be put off by the thought of some hard graft.

If only Charlotte had stuck around she would've seen the adoration had been short-lived. He'd come prepared with notes and ideas on strengthening and stability exercises for the guys. As a player he knew how much stress the joints and muscles went through. The mechanics of the game and the repetitive actions left the body vulnerable to injury and even a slight strain could easily become a nagging injury, refusing to heal. It was his job to prevent more serious problems further down the line as well as treat them. Regardless of her departure, he'd forged ahead in implementing his new exercise regime, strapped up those who'd needed a bit of extra muscle support and massaged any problem areas in preparation for these next important games.

He'd gone on to treat Colton's groin strain with a myofascial release of the muscles involved, manipulating the connective tissue with a sustained, gentle pressure to help regain function again.

Murray's torn meniscus, caused by the trauma of the knee joint being forcefully twisted, thankfully wasn't severe enough to warrant surgery. Hunter worked to strengthen the muscle surrounding the knee and add to the stability of the joint. The excess swelling and pain were treated with anti-inflammatory medication.

He was sorry Charlotte hadn't been here to witness his switch back into business mode. His commitment should make her job a little easier too. After all, the medical team was supposed to work together to get the most from the players. It wasn't an in-house competition to decide who deserved their place here over the other.

The noise of the crowd and the smell of the crisp, clean ice took Hunter back to his own game nights, and gave him the same adrenaline rush it always had. His first match tonight wasn't so much about that final score for him but about his personal performance. He wanted to make a good impression and shoot down all the naysayers who still believed he was a liability in any capacity here.

He filed down the players' tunnel with the rest of the game crew. It was odd being part of the team without being *part* of the team. He was almost anonymous, standing here in the shadows. The way he preferred it. It was circumstance that had dragged him back into the outer edges of the spotlight.

He ventured out far enough to glance around the arena, trying to pick out those present who'd brought this sudden and dramatic change to his way of life.

'Are you looking for someone?' Charlotte appeared beside him.

'Er...no one in particular.' The seats he'd arranged for Alfie and his grandparents were still empty but he wasn't going to share that information with anyone. He'd learned the hard way to keep details of his personal life out of the public domain and he wasn't about to jeopardise his chances of getting custody of his son for anybody. Even if it might take that look of disgust off her face.

The intense reaction he was able to draw from her with minimal goading fascinated him and he didn't know why, beyond wondering what he'd done to deserve it. She wasn't his usual type, at least not the old Hunter who'd enjoyed the company of more...appearance-obsessed ladies who'd revelled in their sexuality. Sara hadn't been bold or brash but she'd certainly given her feminine attributes a boost with beauty treatments and figure-hugging outfits.

Charlotte was a natural beauty, shining brightly through her attempts to disguise it. Even wearing her game crew red fleece and with her chestnut-brown hair swept to one side in a messy braid, she was as pretty as a picture. He wouldn't deny it but neither would he act on it even if she didn't treat him as if he was the devil incarnate. They were co-workers and all women were off limits for the foreseeable future. For once he had to think about someone other than himself and Alfie's well-being came before hockey or his love life.

'Well, if you can drag yourself away from whatever has caught your interest, the game is being played in *that* direction.' She nodded towards the ice, obviously mistaking his keenness to see his son for something more lascivious.

Given his reputation, it wasn't a huge stretch of the imagination that she should jump to that conclusion but he did wonder if she would ever give him the benefit of the doubt when it came to questioning his commitment to the job. Especially since he had no intention of correcting her or making her aware of Alfie's existence. They weren't close enough for him to share such personal information and as first impressions went he didn't think they were going to be best buds any time soon.

Still, he did take a certain pleasure in her *tut* and the roll of her eyes before she stomped away in temper. It was good that she took her work seriously but she really needed to loosen up. He wasn't the enemy, even if it was fun playing the part now and again.

Hunter's smile died on his lips as he wrenched his gaze away from his colleague's denim-clad derriere and back to the crowd. Sara's parents were in their seats, watching him with disapproval etched across their faces. Whilst he'd been busy with Charlotte he'd missed their arrival and had fallen at the first hurdle by ignoring his son in favour of a woman. It had taken a while simply to get them to tell Alfie he was his father and this was the first time he'd been allowed to see him outside their home.

They didn't want Alfie's parentage to be public knowledge any more than he did until things were settled a bit more. Their caution was understandable when he'd already left their daughter in the lurch and probably ruined her life. Unfortunately he couldn't do anything to make amends for their loss but he could try to be the parent Alfie needed him to be.

He gave a wave, his eyes now only for his son, and the swell of love that rose in his chest for the excited little boy waving back put everything into perspective once more. It didn't matter what anyone else thought of him as long as his son loved him, trusted him enough to be with him.

The O'Reillys weren't against the idea of him having custody as long as it was in the best interests of their grandson. All he had to do was make sure he was match fit for the parenting game and leave the old Hunter back on the ice. Along with any wayward thoughts towards his fiery new colleague.

CHAPTER TWO

THE ATMOSPHERE AROUND the arena was electric, everyone buoyed up for the game against the Coleraine Cobras and the chance of getting one step closer to the play-off finals. The Demons were the underdogs at present and to secure their place they needed to come out on top after playing one home and one away match to the Cobras, who were sitting at the top of the league table. It was a tall order but Charlotte kept faith along with all the other fans.

She could hardly believe she was now part of the action instead of a mere spectator sitting in the stands with everyone else. It was a privilege to be on the ground floor of the establishment but she'd also worked damned hard to get here. There was no way she would let everything she'd achieved slip through her fingers for the sake of one man's ego. Whatever, or whoever, had brought him back to town needed to take a back seat for the team's sake.

She'd had to swallow her pride and come out to stand alongside Hunter in the tunnel because that's where she needed to be—on site and focused on the players. It didn't stop her unobtrusively watching him as the lights dimmed and the crowd was whipped into a frenzy with roving spotlights and blaring sirens hailing the arrival of the home team.

Each time the lights fell on his face for a split second

she could see his eyes trained on the ice waiting, watching for that puck to drop. As intense as he'd always been.

A shiver danced its way along her spine as she recalled those past games when she'd found it difficult to watch anything other than him on the ice. It wouldn't do to regress to that sort of infatuation again and for once she should follow his example and get her head in the game. Although he perhaps wasn't as single-minded about tonight as he'd led her to believe. She'd caught sight of him waving to someone in the crowd. Someone who'd made him smile. Not that she was jealous. She pitied him really that he couldn't be alone in his own company for five minutes without the need to hook up with a woman.

The single life suited her and she believed she was stronger without a partner to fret over. Between her and the apparently lovestruck Hunter she knew she'd be the one giving her all to the team without distractions. Not everyone would put the Demons first in their life the way she did, but it was concerning he had other priorities already. They didn't need any more drama behind the scenes and if he really was serious about being part of the squad he ought to be focusing somewhere other than the contents of his trousers. It gave credence to the notion he was only back here for Hunter Torrance's benefit, not the Demons'. She doubted he'd be willing to put in the overtime or go the extra mile the way she did if he had other pursuits outside working hours.

The first two periods of play were relatively uneventful, with both sides playing it safe and focusing on defence, so there were high hopes and expectations for the third period. Especially when the Demons had several near misses, with more attempts on goal than their opponents.

'Come on, guys.' Hunter's booming voice and the thump of his hands clapping as he willed the Demons to score didn't make it easy for Charlotte to concentrate on what was going on inside the rink instead of the decoration around it.

'You must miss this.' She hadn't meant to say it aloud when they'd seen the rest of the game out in virtual silence but he was so involved, animated on behalf of the team, it occurred to her how hard it probably was to no longer be part of the action. He'd skated on this very ice, played for this very team, and seen out the last days of his career here. She'd only been a fan so her position was akin to a lottery win in some aspects while his could be seen as a demotion, standing on the sidelines now.

The roar of outrage from around the arena after a high stick incident against one of their players drowned out her observation.

'What's that?' Hunter didn't take his eyes off the play but leaned down so he could hear her better.

She swallowed. This wasn't supposed to be a *thing*, it was simply her mouth opening before she'd realised. Now he was standing so close to her she could almost feel the rasp of his stubble against her cheek.

'I…er…was just saying you must miss this.' It sounded so feeble the second time around it really wasn't worth repeating.

Of course he missed it. Hockey had been his career, his life at one time. It had been a stupid thing to say, right up there with the people who asked her if she missed her mother. Duh. Generally not unless someone brought her up and made Charlotte realise how incomplete her life was without her in it. Now she'd done the same thing to him.

'Sorry. I should be following the game too, not chatting.'

For the first time since face-off he focused his full attention on her, his eyes bright and his smile wide. Enough to make her stop breathing.

'I do miss it. However, as has been pointed out to me, I'm probably more of a hindrance than an asset to the team these days.' His mischief-making brought the heat to her cheeks, and everywhere else.

To all intents and purposes he was the team's new signing, doing his best to fit in, and she'd acted the superior know-it-all, making life difficult for him. She didn't know this man yet she'd made preconceived judgements and behaved accordingly when he'd been nothing but friendly in the face of her childishness. For someone who was all about equal rights in the workplace she knew she wouldn't have been so forgiving if a colleague had been so awful to her for no apparent reason. A little teasing in return wasn't something she should complain about.

For a second she thought about apologising. The truth was, he *was* an asset. He'd treated all those on the injury list the way any experienced physiotherapist would have. She'd checked. It was her, letting her personal embarrassment over an old crush get in the way of a harmonious working relationship.

In the end she kept her mouth shut because she didn't trust herself not to blab about her past devotion for him when she was looking into those eyes that had once stared at her from her bedroom wall. Worse, she might go the other way and insult him again so he didn't realise she was having inappropriate thoughts about him.

She had to block him out of her sight and focus back on the game, something she'd never had any trouble doing before. Usually it was more a case of not losing herself in the match and making sure she was watching the players for signs of injury. Sometimes separating Dr Michaels from fan-girl Charlie took a great deal of effort.

The dizzying pace of the players covering the ice was as heart-pumping as it got for her. The hard-hitting alpha males and the danger of the sport had always been like catnip to a girl whose life had become so troubled and lonely. That was probably why she'd been instantly drawn to Hunter the first time she'd attended a game. Everything about him had said danger and excitement.

It still did.

The hairs prickled on the back of her neck and she knew Hunter was close again before he even spoke.

'Is there something wrong with Anderson I should know about?'

The object of his concern was already on her radar, a bit more sluggish than usual, which was worrying when he was their star player.

'He has missed a few training sessions lately, which would account for him being more breathless than usual. His fitness needs working on. I'll put a word in with Gray, if he hasn't already picked up on it himself.' She doubted she'd have to point anything out. Anderson was popping up on everyone's radar lately with his diva attitude. As top goal scorer they'd let his stroppy behaviour slide but now it was affecting his performance someone was going to have to take him to task.

'Hmm. It looks more serious than that to me.'

Anderson had been making rookie mistakes all night, getting caught offside and hooking the opposition with his stick in full view of the ref.

'I assure you he'll get a full physical after the game and if I find any areas for referral I will let you know.' This was her jurisdiction and it didn't matter who the new physio was, she was still the medical lead.

They watched Anderson shoulder-charge everyone out of his path. With the giant chip perched there these days it wasn't difficult to do.

'And if the problem's mental, not physical?' Hunter

crossed his arms, his shirt tightening and vacuum-packing his biceps in white cotton.

'Well, it would also be down to me to make that judgement call.'

Not you. Back off.

He smirked and shook his head. Charlotte tried to ignore it but he was so far under her skin he'd burrowed right into her bones.

'What?' she finally snapped, the thought of her past infatuation sneering at her too much to take.

'I get it. You're the sheriff in this here town and I'm merely your deputy.' He tipped his imaginary Stetson and she conceded a small smile. Well, it was better than swooning after that image and a Southern drawl double whammy.

'And don't you forget it.'

They locked eyes for a second too long, the laughter giving way to something more...serious. She looked away first and let the background game noise fill in the gaps in conversation. Just when it seemed as if they were starting to bond, stupid chemistry, or stupid rejuvenated teenage hormones, tried to turn it into something she didn't want, or need, in her life.

Before she was tempted to take another peek at him, a face was mashed into the Perspex in front of her, the violent thud shaking the very ground beneath her feet. The distorted features of a Cobra player slid down the glass, making her wince. She was always conflicted when it came to such territorial displays of male aggression. As a fan, it was a barbaric form of entertainment, watching your team dominate the other. As a medical professional, she understood the physical ramifications of such an impact and as the on-site doctor she'd be called on to treat any injuries caused to the opposition too. That was why she was standing here with her first-aid bag by her feet, for those players who couldn't shake it off and get back on their feet.

The shrill peep of the ref's whistle pierced the air.

'What was that for?' Charlotte demanded to know, along with most of the crowd rising from their seats as Anderson was reprimanded.

Hunter flinched. 'He checked him from behind. That's gonna cost him time in the penalty box.'

'Oh. I didn't see that,' she said, cowed by her own mistake. She knew it was an illegal move because it carried a risk of serious injury but she couldn't tell him she'd missed it because she'd been busy gawping at him.

'I'm guessing he hoped everyone else had missed it too. Now what's he doing? He messed up. He should own it and do the time.' Hunter threw his hands up in despair as Anderson remonstrated with virtually everyone in authority as he made his way to the penalty box.

His gestures imitated that of a clearly frustrated Gray too as he yelled at his star player from the bench. The coach was a disturbing shade of purple as he fought to control his temper and she made a mental note to check his blood pressure.

Anderson's penalty left the Demons short-handed for the dying minutes of the game and Charlotte held her breath with every other fan desperate to keep the dream alive. There were so many bodies in the goal crease as they fought for a victory it was difficult to make out who had possession. Until the klaxon sounded and the red light behind the net flashed, signalling a goal.

The Demons had defied the odds and claimed a win, sending the crowd into a furore, but Anderson's mood didn't improve when the game was over and he left the ice. He stripped off his kit and threw it piece by piece down the tunnel in temper as he clunked past Hunter and

Charlotte, unleashing a string of expletives directed at no one in particular.

Despite his public celebration with the team on the ice after their narrow win, Gray's demeanour changed too when he approached them. 'I don't know what the hell is wrong with Anderson but he needs sorting out before the next game. You two are supposed to be the experts around here. Find out what's eating him and fix it, or don't expect to be signing new contracts any time soon.'

'Gray—' Hunter tried to put a hand on his shoulder in an apparent attempt to calm him down but he shrugged it off.

'I pulled a lot of strings to get you here, Hunter, and I expect a lot in return. I don't care if you talk to him as an ex-pro, sports physician or a fellow maniac, it's your job to get him match fit and right now he's following in your footsteps to career suicide.'

She could almost hear Hunter's heart fall into his shiny shoes with a thud as his so-called ally cut him down with a few cruel words. The hand of friendship fell slowly to his side, the pain of rejection chiselled into his furrowed forehead. Her previous disparaging comments aside, she kind of felt sorry for him. His past misdemeanours were always going to be thrown back in his face regardless of his subsequent achievements and acts of repentance.

'There's really no need for that, Gray.' She put herself in Hunter's position for the first time and thought how it might feel to have someone cast up the naivety of her youth. Horrendous. Soul-destroying. Unfair.

She'd spent a lifetime distancing herself from that person and if he was to be believed, so had Hunter. Switching careers from hockey pro to qualified sports therapist wasn't something that would've happened on a whim. It would've taken years of dedication and determination. All of which was being cast aside as if it was nothing because someone was in a bad mood. Or because someone was deflecting the shame of their own past.

Gray held his hand up to stop her. 'It goes for you too, Charlie. Fair or not, I need results. I'm sure you can come up with a diagnosis and treatment plan between the two of you. After all, that's what you're here for.' With that, he spun on his heel and powered towards the changing room.

She lifted an abandoned puck from the ground and tossed it in her hand, tempted to lob it in his general direction. Two could let temper get the better of them.

Hunter caught it in mid-air. 'You don't want to do anything you might live to regret, Charlotte.' That serious face said he was speaking from painful experience. One he'd never be allowed to forget.

She let her aggression subside with a sigh, partly due to his voice of reason and perhaps because he'd used her name for the first time. Everyone here called her Charlie, in keeping with her efforts to remain one of the guys. Her full name, in that accent, made her feel positively girly. Even in her game night layers of fleece and comfort.

'He'd no right to say any of those things. At least, not the personal stuff. I guess he's kind of right about the reason we're here. He just didn't have to be so rude about it,' she huffed on his behalf, since he seemed determined not to rise to it. Not so long ago she imagined he wouldn't have thought twice about charging down there after him and duking it out.

Perhaps he had changed. Perhaps he did deserve to have someone give him the benefit of the doubt. Then again, if his one friend here couldn't let go of the past and fully trust him, why should she?

Hunter shrugged, those broad shoulders refusing to carry any more baggage upon them. 'He's right. He did call in a lot of favours for me. I owe him big time.' Either he had really matured or he was putting on an award-winning performance to dupe her into thinking he had. Especially when she was the one chomping at the bit to retaliate.

She had to remind herself he didn't owe her anything personally; there was nothing to be gained in convincing her he was anyone but himself, except to prove his commitment to the job.

'So what do we do?' Stitches and concussion she could deal with. A burly hockey player with his finger on the self-destruct button was out of her comfort zone.

'I wouldn't want to step on your toes…' He held up his hands in mock surrender to her self-appointed superiority.

'Okay, okay. If I have to tackle an irate man twice my size, I could use the backup.'

And because Gray had said so.

'We can't do anything until we've seen to everyone else. We're going to have our work cut out for us back there, after that last scrum especially.'

'Then what? The chances Anderson is waiting patiently back there for counselling, treatment or another rollicking are slim to none.'

They had no clue what was ailing him and from her experience thus far, hockey players were stubborn about admitting any weakness. There was definitely more of an 'I can tough it out' attitude to injury than she was used to from other athletes. It made her job that much more difficult when those niggling pains turned into something more serious left untreated.

If it was some sort of chronic or traumatic acute injury sometimes it could mean the end of a career. In which case, Anderson would be even less inclined to admit there was a problem. Male pride could be a terrible affliction if left unchecked.

'You heard Gray. *We* have to find him.'

She let out her breath in a huff, which may or may not have had to do with his continual glances into the crowd.

'Unless the Demons have taken to tracking their players, how on earth are we going to do that?' By the time they finished up here he could be anywhere. It would be dark, and she would be more than a bit cheesed off with the whole drama. Especially when she was expected to do it with Mr Torrance and that brought him much too close for comfort.

'If I know my hockey players, and the heart of any Northern Irish town, there's only one place Anderson will be sitting his time out. Let's hit the pub.'

If she didn't love her job so much she would've left him to it but these were still her players, her patients, her team, and she wasn't afraid of dropping the gloves herself to fight. It wasn't only the Demons' honour at stake here.

Not only was Gray frothing at the mouth despite the result but Hunter was struggling to find those feel-good endorphins too. It was his son's first match, the first time he'd seen his father's team in action, if not playing himself, and he hadn't been able to share it with him.

'Sorry I couldn't sit with you tonight, bud.' He managed to catch Alfie and his grandparents before they disappeared out of the arena and into the night.

'That's okay. Maybe we can come again?' He glanced up at his guardians with the same hope Hunter was still clinging to.

'We're coming to the end of the season now but perhaps I could bring Alfie for a tour behind the scenes some time?' It was a big ask, he knew, but if he was to win over his son he had to start fighting for time alone with him.

Alfie's face lit up but his grandmother shut down the notion of any unauthorised trips with a stern 'We'll see'.

The light began to dim again before flaring back to life. 'Maybe Dad could come back with us for supper?'

It was the first time Alfie had called him Dad and it choked Hunter up that he was even starting to think of him in that role. It killed him to have to let him down.

'It's getting late and I still have some work to do here. Another night, bud.' He knelt down and Alfie rushed towards him, hugged him so tightly it brought tears to his eyes. He didn't care he could barely breathe because he'd never been as happy as he was in this second. This was the beginning of the family he'd never had and the pieces were finally slotting into place.

'Come on, Alfie. It's bedtime.'

Although Hunter was thankful for the opportunities afforded him to get to know his son, he was looking forward to the days when there wouldn't be a time limit set on their relationship.

He slowly and reluctantly peeled Alfie from around his neck. 'I'll see you again soon. You be good.'

The kiss he dropped on his son's head inadequately expressed the love he felt for this child he'd been without for too long but it was all he had to give for now.

Someday they'd be watching the games and eating popcorn together before going home to their own house. Until then they'd have to snatch whatever time was granted by those who thought they knew what was best.

''Night, Dad.'

''Night, son.' He waved the trio off, watching them safely across the road until he was too misty-eyed to make them out.

He sucked in a deep breath of the cool night air to fortify his aching heart and blinked away his sentimentality. It was time to focus on the positives. Alfie was happy and safe and he had a job to do. He'd prefer to keep it that way.

It was close to midnight before they were able to leave the arena. His, or Anderson's, personal problems had to wait until the players who actually hung around after the game were properly cooled down. Ice baths and stretches were equally as important as the warm-up to keep the muscles in prime condition. He knew Charlotte had a few nicks and grazes to treat on both teams but nothing serious or unusual for men in close contact with sharp blades every day of the week. He came to knock on her door just as she was lecturing her last patient.

'Remember: RICE. Rest, ice, compression—'

'And elevation. I got it, Doc,' a weary Evenshaw replied as she strapped up his ankle.

Hunter gave him a hand down off the bed and watched him limp away. 'I hope that's nothing serious.'

'A slight sprain,' she said as she packed away the dressings and other bits and bobs she'd used to patch players together again.

Now she'd ditched her zip-up outer layer he could see she was wearing a white round-neck T-shirt. It wasn't a particularly remarkable piece of clothing, forgettable, if it wasn't for the fact she'd unwittingly exposed her toned midriff as she'd yawned and stretched.

He coughed away the sudden surge of awareness heading south of the border. It had been a long time since he'd had the pleasure of seeing a female body who wasn't a patient, otherwise he wouldn't be responding like a virgin seeing a naked woman for the first time.

'I hope you're not too tired to go Anderson-hunting?'

Although it might be better if she was. Regardless of Gray's insistence and the prospect this could somehow improve working relations between him and Charlotte, he was beginning to have doubts this was a good idea.

He kept losing focus when he was around her, not concentrating on the game or the arrival of his VIPs but watching spots of colour rise in her cheeks as he baited her. There'd also been that moment when she'd stood up for him against Gray. That had been unexpected. From both sides.

Clearly he and his one and only friend still had unresolved issues. Although Hunter knew Gray had said those things in the heat of the moment, there was truth behind them. He'd let him down in the past and though the words had hurt, he'd deserved them and Gray had needed to say them. He just hoped now he'd got it off his chest they could move on again. He wouldn't dwell on it when he knew how much more pain could be caused by letting a grudge fester out of control. It had already ended one career and he didn't think he had it in him to start over again if this didn't work out.

No, it was Charlotte's attitude that had been most surprising when she'd been the most outspoken about his reputation so far. Perhaps they were starting to make progress after all and she was no longer seeing him as the Ballydolan Demon come to life. Whatever it was, it had felt good to have someone on his side after all this time. Someone whose opinion of him appeared to be turning and she wasn't afraid of saying it out loud.

'Of course I'm not too tired,' she snapped.

'Of course you're not,' he replied. For a woman who appeared so delicate on the outside she wasn't afraid of much. He got the impression she'd trawl the whole of Ireland even if she was dead on her feet if it meant sticking two fingers up at the doubters.

'Where do we start?' Charlotte was back at his side, refusing to let him forget her.

'Wherever's within walking distance.' He set off at a brisk pace, determined to get this over with and get back to his bachelor pad as soon as possible. Minus company.

'How do you know he hasn't just gone home or taken a six pack off into the woods?' Charlotte was almost running to catch up with him as she struggled back into that hideous jacket but he didn't slow down for her. With any luck she'd get fed up and go home.

That was as likely as Anderson being tucked up in bed.

'I know we Canadians are a hardy lot but we're not stupid. That would mean having to go into the bar to buy booze and take it away. Dark woods might appeal to a brooding romantic hero but he's a hockey player, he needs to blow off steam fast.'

'He could have gone home like any other disgruntled employee after a hard day at work,' she grumbled under her breath, but she didn't know hockey players the way he did.

It was much easier to understand Anderson's state of mind when you'd been there yourself. If he was anything close to following the same pattern he himself had, not only would he be somewhere, getting drunk quickly, he'd be spoiling for a fight to unleash some more of that aggression they'd witnessed earlier.

'It's possible but if we're thinking logically, there are about six bars on the route back towards his house.' He'd asked around for details, not that there were many forthcoming. Although he knew where Anderson resided there was little information about his personal life. It wasn't because the players were reluctant to share with him—in that respect they seemed quite open to him, probably because of his hockey background. No, it seemed no one knew much about Anderson outside the team or alcohol-fuelled nights out. That in itself was dangerous. Hunter understood only too well how isolating it could be out here with no family around to catch you when you fell and pull you up by the scruff of the neck. Perhaps if he'd had someone do that for him he might've salvaged something of his sports career.

'I don't know why they need so many pubs in such a small space anyway,' she bristled, every inch the reluctant partygoer, and he was beginning to wonder why she was so against the idea of calling in at the local establishments when it was the obvious place to start their search.

Maybe she was teetotal, although that seemed as farfetched out here as leprechauns and their crock of gold.

'So you have somewhere to go when you get kicked out of the last one?' Well, that's how he'd treated the place when he'd done his fair share of drinking and brawling here. Strangely, it had only seemed to ingratiate him more with the locals. Until he'd taken it too far, of course, and cost them the championship.

There was a very unladylike grunt behind him but he refrained from continuing the argument. Anderson was close by, he'd put money on it. The sound of the *craic* coming from behind the doors and the draw of the liquor would be too much to resist.

They started their bar crawl at The Ballydolan Inn, the first dingy building no bigger than one of the nearby cottages at the bottom of the hill. Once they made their way past the smokers outside they were hit with a wall of noise as the doors swung open. The deafening roar soon died down to a curious silence as the locals eyed them suspiciously. If this had been a Western his trigger finger would be itching, waiting for someone to make their move.

Voices rumbled low but Hunter caught the mutterings about 'that hockey player'.

He scoured the interior, imagining an angry, drunk, Canadian forward would stand out in this crowd of regulars. When he saw nothing but curious Irish eyes staring back, he was ready to leave too. He wasn't up for another round of twenty questions about his personal life after leaving this place under a dark cloud and turned to chivvy his companion back out onto the street. 'Let's try the next one.'

They received much the same welcome there at The Hillside Tavern.

'Isn't that the big hockey fella who went nuts a few years back?'

'Aye.'

'Thought he'd be dead by now.'

'Used to play hockey. No longer *nuts*. Definitely not dead but very much older and wiser.'

Hunter tackled the rumours head on as they flew around him.

There was much more back-slapping after that, propelling them both towards the bar.

'Glad to hear it.'

'Sure you'll have a wee drink for old times' sake.'

It wasn't long before a space was cleared at the bar for them.

'Your local drinking establishment?' Charlotte mocked with a raised eyebrow, finding difficulty imagining him partying in here during his time with the Demons. In her head he'd been living it up in the clubs in Belfast or exclusive house parties for the rich and famous. If she'd known he was only down the street she might have socialised a bit more herself.

'Once upon a time. It hasn't changed much.'

'I doubt it's changed at all in the last century.' It still had the dark wood interior she remembered, permeated with the smell of the peat fire and sweat.

'I suppose we should really find out if there's more

than one hockey player they've been doling out booze to tonight.' She was beginning to see how easy it would be to fall into the drinking culture here. Honestly, there wasn't much else to do at night. When the game had first come here over a decade ago it had been a godsend to the young inhabitants like her, giving them somewhere fun and exciting to go without getting into trouble.

He shook hands with the landlord. 'Sorry, not tonight, Michael, I'm still on the clock. Have you seen one of ours in here? Anderson?'

'There was a big, blond fella who talks like you in here earlier but he was a bit worse for wear. He made a nuisance of himself, to be honest. Spilt a few drinks, broke a few glasses. I had to chuck him out. Sorry, if I'd known he was with you—'

'I'm sure he'll not be too far away. How long ago was this?'

'A good hour ago, I'd say.'

'Thanks.' Hunter grabbed her hand and bolted out the door with a renewed sense of urgency. The electric touch of his strong fingers clasping hers sent her pulse racing as they stole back out into the night.

He let go of her long after they had an excuse to be holding hands.

She absent-mindedly rubbed the palm of her hand where his had crossed it, mourning the loss of his touch already.

'Do you really think we're going to catch up with him?' She was a little on edge, spending so much time with Hunter. Every minute together altered her perception of the man she'd loved and hated in equal measure without ever knowing him beyond his public image. It was unsettling to find out he was as normal as anyone else. She'd moved past her crush a long time ago but she was worried it might take her somewhere more dangerous than a shallow physical attraction if she wasn't careful.

'Oh, aye.' His attempt at the local accent couldn't fail to make her laugh and she was rewarded with a toothy grin.

She'd always thought him attractive—that was a no-brainer. What teenage girl wouldn't have had her head turned by a handsome sportsman from a distant land? Finding out Hunter hadn't the hero she'd imagined him to be had been the biggest betrayal of all. Her mistake had been compounded by watching him fall apart before her eyes in those last matches until he'd convinced her there wasn't actually anything more than good looks and bad attitude there.

His short time back in the country was already beginning to change that opinion when he was doing whatever was asked for him to aid the team. That eye-opener spurred her on over the crest of the hill towards the old brick building with the faded green 'Kelly's' sign.

She was saved from further personal revelations as a rather large, unkempt figure came barrelling out of the pub door to land at their feet on the pavement. It didn't take a genius to work out what the cheer from inside and the sight of a burly barman dusting off his hands at the door meant.

'Anderson?' Hunter hunched down and brushed the dirty, bloody mop of hair out of the face of the unfortunate who'd been swiftly tossed from the premises.

'That's me,' he said with a slur. 'Gus Anderson. Man of the match. The crowd go wild.'

He was cheering now, swaying from side to side and pumping his fist in the air.

'Someone's got a high opinion of himself.' Charlotte was having second thoughts about helping if he really was this deluded. He'd almost cost them the match, the play-offs and their very jobs tonight.

'He's wasted. He doesn't know what he's saying.' Hunter struggled to get him onto his feet and although he didn't ask her to, Charlotte felt compelled to help.

She ducked under one arm of their patient, bolstering his left side. He weighed a ton, even though she knew Hunter was probably shouldering most of the weight.

'Er…now what? How are we supposed to fix *this*?'

'We can take him back to my place.' Hunter was already a bit breathless bench-pressing the man mountain so she hoped he lived somewhere close before all three of them ended up in a ditch by the side of the road.

They half dragged, half carried their wayward charge until they came to a cottage down the lane past Kelly's.

'This is your house?' The pretty chocolate-box cottage and garden didn't seem very *him*.

'Here, hold him until I get the door open.' He deposited most of Anderson's bulk around her shoulders and stopped her asking any of the questions flooding her head as she fought to stop her body being concertinaed into the ground.

Are you renting? Did you inherit? Does your girlfriend live here with you?

In hindsight she suspected that was the very reason he'd been so ungentlemanly in the first place. Whatever the secret, he wanted to keep it to himself. Thankfully, once he opened the door and found the light switch, he shared the burden with her until they were able to dump Anderson into a nearby chair.

'We'll need to get him cleaned and sobered up.' Gray would be expecting results and now under the glare of the living-room light she could see Anderson was a bit battered and bruised.

'Let's see if we can get him up to the bathroom.' Hunter steered them towards a narrow staircase and they somehow managed to manoeuvre him into the shower cubicle, still fully clothed.

A grinning Hunter switched on the water and closed the bathroom door on Anderson's shrieks as he underwent some sobering cold-water therapy. He backed out of the room, bumping into Charlotte in the cramped hallway. She stumbled back, tripping over the upturned edge of the faded hallway carpet. There was that helpless moment when she felt herself overbalance and tip over the edge of the staircase. All she could do was brace herself for the hard, painful landing she knew was coming.

Hunter shot out an arm around her waist, catching her before she fell off that top step and pulling her roughly against his chest, knocking the breath out of her.

'Sorry. I thought we should get out while he's cooling off. I didn't mean to nearly break your neck in the process.'

Her adrenaline was pumping as much from the near miss as being pressed against his hard body.

'You're forgiven.' She aimed for a friendly smile to hide the fact he'd unnerved her by being so close but her heart was pounding so hard she could no longer hear anything but the rush of blood in her ears.

For an instant their eyes locked, this intimate moment between the two of them frozen in time. His eyes darkened as they lit on her smiling lips and the conspiratorial joviality seemed to fade. He was watching her with such hunger, such focus there was no denying what it was he wanted, what he wanted to do to her. Just as before, she felt herself submit helplessly to gravity, only this time it was pulling her ever closer to his lips.

'Hey, you guys are too cruel. What, are you like SAS trainers or something?' Anderson yanked the door open and exploded the fantasy.

Hunter wrenched away from her so quickly he'd probably left friction burns in the carpet.

Charlotte was more appalled by her own behaviour. They'd almost kissed. Totally inappropriate with a work colleague, especially when there was every chance he was involved with someone else. So they hadn't actually made lip contact but she was pretty sure the intention had been there on both sides and that was bad news all around. Clearly she hadn't yet reached her lifetime's worth of humiliation where this man was concerned.

'I'll get some coffee on the go.' Hunter took the stairs two at a time in his obvious haste to get away.

She waited until she heard him banging about in the kitchen before she dared follow. At least Anderson, who'd ditched his sodden clothes for a bath towel, made for a distraction from the sudden atmosphere in the house.

She reached for her trusty first-aid bag, which she'd been carrying all night, predicting it would end in some sort of medical emergency, and pulled out an alcohol wipe to cleanse the deepest scratch on his face.

'Ouch!' He drew in a quick breath as if she'd poured salt into an open wound.

'Seriously?' She'd barely touched him and, with the stench of alcohol emanating through his very pores, she'd imagined he was probably numb from the scalp down.

'It stings, man.'

'Sorry. I'll be as gentle as I can.' Perhaps she'd been a tad more abrasive than she should have when she was angry at herself for the incident at the top of the stairs. She should know better than to let her personal feelings leak into her professional manner. Although Anderson was the reason she'd been thrown together with Hunter tonight, it wasn't his fault she'd thrown herself *at* him.

'What happened back there anyway?' She tried to turn

her thoughts back to her patient's current predicament, not her own, but it was easier said than done when she could still imagine Hunter's arms wrapped around her.

'At a rough guess I'd say a disagreement with some Cobra fans. Am I right? That's where the opposition hang out when they're in town.' Hunter handed him a mug of black coffee and offered her one without any indication this was in any way awkward for him after what had just occurred.

She declined. A nightcap of any description here wasn't going to happen. Once she had her big, brave soldier patched up she was packing up and running back to the safety of her own house, where she could analyse the reasons behind that almost-kiss.

Her patient took a sip of the strong-smelling brew and winced. 'Just some friendly rivalry.'

'Hmm. Well, it looks like one of your new friends took serious offence to something you either said or did. That cut on your cheek is going to need stitching.'

He was fortunate it wasn't closer to his eye but she'd lecture him tomorrow when he would remember it. It was too bad she wouldn't forget the events of tonight as easily because she knew they were going to change everything between her and Hunter at work. If she wasn't careful things were going to get even more complicated than they already were.

CHAPTER THREE

CHARLOTTE WENT TO wash up and proceeded to suture the deep cut. Hunter knew it was saving them all a hospital trip but the longer she spent in his house, the antsier he was becoming. They'd had one close call already. Only an irate Canadian water rat had pulled the brakes on that near-kiss that had come from nowhere and yet had seemed so natural. That was a direct contravention of his new dad regulations. He hadn't figured romance into his future plans at all.

As Charlotte tended to her patient, whose massive frame was wedged into the floral old-lady furniture, it struck Hunter how odd the set-up here must've appeared to her. At the time of renting the place he'd thought only of being close to Alfie. The owner had been keen to sell if he decided to stay permanently since this had been his late mother's house. One day Hunter imagined he and Alfie would put their own stamp on the décor. Until then he'd have to put up with the crocheted blankets and rocking chairs.

'All finished.' Charlotte had done a neat job, even in these unusual circumstances. Not that he was surprised when he'd seen and heard exactly how passionate she was about her work. The Demons were lucky to have her, yet Anderson hadn't even bothered to thank her.

He had an inkling they were all in for a very long night.

In the old days Hunter's first reaction to dealing with the stresses of the evening would've been to head straight to the bar. Whilst he was sorely tempted, it wouldn't solve any of their problems, so he served himself a shot of caffeine and took his position in the therapist chair.

'Do you want to talk about what happened tonight?' It would be easier than having him tear up the house in another rage-filled rampage.

Anderson eyed Charlotte sideways through his mop of wet, straggly blond hair.

'Surely you're not suddenly shy now? Charlotte's seen all of your antics tonight, don't forget.' Regardless of their personal faux pas, he didn't think she'd walk out if they were about to make a breakthrough here. As far as he'd seen, she always put her job first and wouldn't be sidelined when it came to the players' treatment on anyone's account.

'Anything you say in front of us is strictly confidential. We just want to help, Gus.' She took a seat next to Hunter on the couch, confirming that she wasn't going anywhere.

Anderson sighed. 'These Irish chicks…it's like they bewitch you or something.'

He was shaking his head but there was a ghost of a smile in there somewhere behind all that hair. It was a start, an opening to what was going on beyond the Hulkish façade. Hunter would've agreed except he didn't want his captivating companion beside him knowing that's exactly what she was doing to him. That was the only explanation of why he was veering so dangerously off track from common sense.

If there was one thing guaranteed to make a man want to smash stuff in a testosterone-fuelled rage it was woman trouble. Make that two things. Parents who wished you'd never been born had the same effect.

The big guy was on his feet, pacing. Hunter scanned the room for valuable antiques he should probably remove before he was charged for breakages but he was sure he could afford to lose the ugly owl ornament on the mantelpiece made from seashells and the tears of frightened children.

'This place was only supposed to be a stopgap, somewhere I could make a name for myself and move on.'

The opposite of Hunter's career slide into oblivion here. It had been the beginning of the end for him when he'd been shipped out here but a young, up-and-coming star like Anderson had a future in the UK league, maybe even the NHL, if he didn't screw it up too.

'Unless there's something you're not telling us, the only one putting that in jeopardy is you. Trust me, that temper is gonna get you attention for all the wrong reasons. Whatever you've got going on, deal with it now before your name is one no team wants attached to them.' It was true for him almost a decade later, even with a change of career. If it wasn't for Gray throwing him a lifeline he'd be stacking shelves in the local supermarket.

Gus flopped back into the chair and Hunter waited quietly so he didn't spook his unpredictable companion. Charlotte seemed to be of the same thinking as she remained quiet too. Neither of them would benefit from him kicking off again. Instead of forcing the issue, they let silence dominate.

He'd learned a lot from his own counselling sessions where the onus had been on him to fill the gaps in conversation. In the end the uncomfortable lack of interaction had forced him to verbalise the feelings he'd been avoiding since seeking out his birth family, and confront the crushing damage their rejection had caused to his self-esteem and self-worth.

It had taken him years to tackle the subject and understand he wasn't the one who'd done anything wrong. By which time it had been too late and he'd lost everything and everyone else. If he could prevent the same thing happening to his friend here, he would.

Whether there was a physical or emotional issue behind his behaviour, he needed to ask for help, instead of hiding behind the villain mask and pushing everyone away. He might've processed what had happened to him in his past, apportioned blame to the right people now and finally moved on, but that didn't mean there wasn't lingering frustration at having blown his hockey career along the way.

'Maggie's pregnant.' Anderson finally punctuated the silence with his shoulder-slumping admission.

Charlotte let out a long breath beside him. So it wasn't a serious injury he was battling but it was potentially a mess. At least he was opening up. It was progress; the first step towards salvaging the man and the player.

'And Maggie is?' Hunter wasn't assuming anything. She could be a fan, a one-night stand or a married woman for all the anguish this situation was apparently causing.

'We've been seeing each other for a few months. I mean, I like her. I really like her but I'm not ready for this.'

'Okay. This isn't the end of the world. I mean, I know it's a big shock but it happens to people every day and they live through it.' Charlotte attempted to reassure him and Hunter could almost see her mind ticking over, trying to figure out how they could help him come to terms with impending fatherhood.

He resisted a lecture on contraception when it wasn't going to make any difference now but he might suggest to Charlotte that they provide some literature on the subject to try and prevent more unwanted pregnancies or STDs among the players in the future. Although it did make him a feel a bit of a hypocrite when he'd made the same mistake at this guy's age. The only difference between him and Anderson was he hadn't known about Sara's pregnancy.

Perhaps that had been for the best. He hadn't been in the right frame of mind to be a father to Alfie then, or a supportive partner to Sara. By all accounts, they'd had a happier life without him and it had taken reaching rock bottom alone for him to finally get the help he'd needed to be the best dad he could be for Alfie.

'How does Maggie feel about it?' Of course it was Charlotte who remembered there was someone else's feelings in the equation here.

Gus looked at her as though it was the first time he'd even considered the effect it would have on his probably equally young girlfriend. The arrogance of youth.

'She's scared about how her parents are going to react to the news. I'm sure a hockey player wouldn't be their first choice for their daughter's baby daddy.'

'I hear ya.' Even without the drinking, fighting and generally acting like a jerk, he suspected Sara's parents would always have disapproved of him. Everyone, including him, had known he wasn't good enough. Sara and Alfie should have had a stable, reliable guy with a steady job to support them. He was doing his best to be that man for Alfie now. That's why the idea of getting together with anyone, even Charlotte, was dangerous.

He didn't miss Charlotte's raised eyebrows as he sympathised but he wasn't ready to share his own surprise baby story with anyone just yet. 'Do you have any family of your own here, Gus?'

He shook his head. 'We keep in touch from time to time but I haven't seen them for a while.'

It was too easy to distance yourself from family when living abroad, even if they did care about you, and they were the very people who could save a person from total despair. Unfortunately his hadn't.

'I would really make the effort to talk to your parents about this. You and Maggie both need the support. As someone who was effectively stranded here without any sort of emotional backup I would advise making the most of it so you don't end up making the catastrophic decisions I did.' So he'd shared a little personal info but it would be worth it to stop someone else making those same mistakes and throwing away the chance of a happy family.

Charlotte shifted in the seat next to him but he couldn't bear to look at her and see any hint of pity there. This wasn't supposed to be a group therapy session, he genuinely just wanted to help and the best way to do that was by showing some solidarity.

Anderson frowned. 'I really couldn't deal with their disappointment on top of everything else.'

'I know it's going to be a difficult conversation to have but, trust me, you don't want to go through this alone. Right now you're reacting on an emotional level. You need that grounding. Someone to give you a kick up the backside to start thinking clearly. If I'd had parents who'd given a damn, who I could've turned to for help when I needed it, I might never have left here in the first place.' Even now it was hard not to be bitter about the hand he'd been dealt: two sets of parents who'd happily sat back and watched him self-destruct. The only person who'd been there for him had been Sara but he'd been in too much pain to even let her get close emotionally.

'Hunter's right. This is too big to keep to yourself. If you're still on good terms with your mum and dad, swallow your pride and at least pick up the phone to talk to them if you can't visit in person. Make the most of having them in your life because you'll miss them when they're gone.' Charlotte was leaning forward in her seat, her arms wrapped around her waist, and he recognised that self-protecting gesture of someone who'd experienced that same isolation and loneliness, even if her experience of family sounded vastly different from his.

'You've both lost your parents?' The roles were reversed as Anderson took over the role of therapist.

'Mine aren't dead. They just wish I was. Neither my adoptive nor birth parents are in my life. Their choice, not mine.' There was no point dancing around the facts but it did make for an awkward silence as the blunt statement made an impact and he wondered if he had overshared after all.

'I...er...did lose my mum a few years ago. My dad, much like Hunter's family, has decided he'd rather not be part of my life.'

Hunter wanted to lean over and give her a hug but she probably wouldn't appreciate the public display of solidarity. Feckless parents were the worst. Which was why he worried so much about getting it right himself. His actions now would affect Alfie for the rest of his life and that was a huge responsibility, one not to be taken lightly or disregarded without a second thought.

'Listen, this isn't about us or our absent parents but you can see for yourself that the decisions you make as a parent from here on in will have long, far-reaching consequences.'

'No pressure, then,' Anderson grumbled, his immaturity stubbornly shining through despite the pep talk.

'Which is why you don't want to be hasty, acting out without giving thought to the consequences of your actions.'

Where had Charlotte been when he'd needed to hear that straight talking? If he'd had someone like her on his team during those dark times, things could've been so very different. Maybe, just maybe he wouldn't have treated Sara and everyone else here with such reckless abandon.

'I don't want to spend the rest of my days here changing diapers. I want to go places.'

'The two aren't mutually exclusive, you know. There are plenty of dads on the team whose families are quite happy to move wherever the opportunities arise. Have you had a talk about the future, or what either of you want?' It seemed hypocritical to be dishing out advice on relationships when he'd never had a successful one of any kind himself but Hunter believed his failure made him the best person for the job. He'd been that idiot incapable of dealing with his emotions and was still dealing with the repercussions. A living example of what not to do.

At least Anderson had the grace to look ashamed. 'No. I guess I didn't take the news very well when she first told me and she isn't replying to any of my messages.'

Hunter groaned at the idiocy as history repeated itself. He might not have known Sara was pregnant but it was that same lack of communication that had killed their chances of being a family. That and his descent into the red mist that had consumed him and was now beckoning Anderson to the dark side.

Had he really been this self-absorbed when Sara had been making decisions about her future and that of their baby? Probably, and it was too late to apologise. He knew now the reason behind his own meltdown but it didn't excuse his behaviour and he took full responsibility for those he'd hurt. He bore many regrets but that one hurt the most.

Thankfully it wasn't too late for Gus and Maggie.

'Here's an idea, why don't you go and see her in person, prove you're taking this seriously and stop acting like a spoilt brat?' Insulting him was a risky move but there was no time for tiptoeing around him any more.

The slight nod in agreement enabled Hunter to speak freely without worrying he might lose a couple of teeth for his trouble.

'Do you love her?'

'Yes.' There was no hesitation, which gave some hope for the parents-to-be.

'Good. That's the foundation you need to start from. Concentrate on that for now. Find out if she feels the same and work together on taking that next step. A little word from the wise, you might want to quit the temper tantrums on ice too. You don't want her to think she has two babies to deal with and getting fired isn't going to help you, Maggie or the baby. Been there, lost my shirt and the girl. Don't recommend it.'

'You're right. I need to step up and be there for her.' He made to get out of the chair and it dawned on Hunter he meant now, wearing only a towel and still slightly slurring his words. Not the best impression to give if he wanted Maggie to forgive him and understand he was taking the matter seriously.

Hunter was quicker getting to his feet. He put a hand on Anderson's shoulder and firmly guided him back into his seat.

'It's late. She's probably asleep. I have a spare room you can stay the night in. Go see her tomorrow after you've sobered up.'

'I can probably give you some coaching in effective grovelling techniques before you see her, if it'll help?' Charlotte added her weight behind the campaign to get him back into Maggie's good books. They were turning out to be quite a team after all.

'It can't hurt. Thanks for all your help, guys.' Anderson threw his arms around Hunter, catching him around the waist in an awkward man hug.

'No problem. Just remember, we're your family too.' He took the hit so Charlotte wouldn't have to, hoping Gus would go to bed before he entered the 'I love you' stage of drunkenness.

Hunter knew he was in for a long sleepless night himself. Not only was he going to have to make frequent checks on his intoxicated patient but he had a lot of thinking to do about his own life. He couldn't very well preach the importance of communication one minute and pretend there hadn't been a shift between him and Charlotte the next.

If he followed his own advice and admitted he liked her, that there was a powerful attraction pulling them towards each other, then they'd have to discuss their next step too. The problem was if he let her into his life he was going to have to be honest about Alfie. Her reaction to that bombshell would determine what happened next.

Just as he'd told his fellow new dad, the time for playing games was over. They both had some growing up to do. These days a kiss meant much more than a kiss when it could potentially put the custody of his son at risk.

'Right, well, it's getting late. I should probably go home.' Charlotte waited until Hunter had safely ensconced his new lodger in the spare room before she made her excuses to leave.

There was no reason to hang around any longer than was necessary now her professional obligations had been fulfilled for the night and they appeared to be making progress with Gus. The biggest breakthrough for her, though, had been the sensitivity with which Hunter had handled everything. He'd given so much of himself tonight in the effort to get through to their teammate he'd really touched her heart. So much so she'd thought it a good idea to kiss him. Thank goodness for Anderson's intervention, which had averted the looming disaster.

If they had given in to whatever attraction had flickered in the moment there was no limit to the amount of damage it could have done, crossing the line of all her boundaries. She didn't want an atmosphere at work other than a professional one and didn't need any more complications that could impact on the team. It was a moment of madness she couldn't let happen again for her sake and everyone else's. That feeling of being out of control wasn't something she wanted to get used to.

'I'll walk you back to the arena so you can get your car.' Hunter was already holding the front door open for her, keen for her to hit the road.

'That's really not necessary. I'm a big girl. I can look after myself.' She'd been doing it for years and she couldn't afford to look any weaker than she already had tonight after almost kissing him.

He leaned against the door, arms folded. 'I know you can but do I really seem the sort of guy that'll stand here and watch a woman walk off into the darkness alone?'

No, he didn't. He was the perfect gentleman.

She didn't know when exactly she'd realised that after the low expectations she'd had about him. Probably around the time she'd been closing her eyes and waiting for him to kiss her.

He'd surprised her tonight with his level head and calm handling of the situation. Whilst that could only mean good things for his position with the Demons, it brought more concerns for her on a personal level. She was beginning to understand who he was beyond that hot-headed hunk who'd caught her eye and broken her teen heart. More so now he'd shared those deeply personal circumstances and given an insight as to what had been going on behind the scenes in the midst of his public meltdown.

She stepped out into the darkness and Hunter pulled the door shut behind them.

'What about Anderson? We shouldn't really leave him—' She tried one last time to put some distance between them so she had some space to put her feelings back in order. It didn't matter if Hunter Torrance was still a loose cannon or he'd turned out to be the nicest guy in the world, he had to remain off limits.

If only she could get her treacherous pounding heart to remember that every time he was near.

'He's snoring the house down already. I'm sure he won't miss me for ten minutes,' her escort insisted as he followed her down the path.

Even if she hadn't heard his heavy footsteps in the darkness, the hairs standing on the back of her neck alerted her to his presence as he caught up with her. She was doomed now to be at the mercy of her attraction whenever he was near. Not the best conditions to be working under. Together.

'I...er...think I have an apology to make. I judged you unfairly. If I'd known about your family situation... anyway, I shouldn't have been so horrible to you.' Although this being nice to each other didn't seem to be doing her any favours either. If anything, it was creating more problems for her.

'Don't worry about it. I'm used to it.'

That only increased her self-loathing for falling into line with all the other people who'd given him a hard time without just cause. She'd been there as that abandoned child and could easily have gone off the rails too. Perhaps having that one parent who'd loved her had been enough to save her from a complete breakdown when everything had gone wrong in her life. At least her mother had been there as a shoulder to cry on when she'd deemed herself unlovable, and had insisted it wasn't true. Hunter hadn't had anyone to allay his fears, only enforce them. With that little knowledge of his upbringing, it was amazing he'd ever been able to find his way back from the darkness, not that he'd ever succumbed to it.

'I know how much it hurts to be cast aside as if you're nothing. You should be proud of where you got to on your own.' She knew she was, whether her father cared or not.

'I am and ditto. If you don't mind me saying so, your dad sounds as much of a tool as mine.'

That made her laugh out loud, even though it was a sad state of affairs for them both. 'Yes, well, I try not to think about him too often.'

'Me either. Not any more. I'm all about the future these days and trying to leave the past behind.' They were walking into the car park now so she was able to see the determined set of his jaw under the arena lights. It was only natural she should wonder what, or who, that future should include.

They reached her vehicle and she found herself reluctant to end their chat, regardless of her subconscious urging her to jump in the car and hightail it out of there.

'That's definitely the healthier way to live, instead of letting old mistakes haunt you.' She'd been guilty of that on so many levels and she wasn't sure she'd ever really be free of her old ghosts. She had a growing admiration for Hunter, and his strength, if he'd truly been able to break free from his.

'Who would ever have imagined Hunter Torrance would become the spokesperson for common sense?' There was that self-deprecating smile, which almost had her sliding down the driver's door in hormonal appreciation. That mixture of handsome male and genuine good guy was too much for a girl to handle. It was usually one or the other and she didn't know how to defend against that kind of superpower combo.

'I think it did Anderson a world of good to hear it tonight. Hopefully it'll help him think clearly about his next step.' She appreciated the fact Hunter had shared those painful personal details in the hope their troubled friend would take something useful away from it. Not many would have, probably not even her unless he'd taken the lead first. It showed a real connection to the team on a personal level, which she'd doubted would ever happen.

'We made a good tag team tonight.'

'We did, didn't we?' She was smiling, proud of their joint achievement, as she made the mistake of looking up into his eyes. Her breath caught in her throat. In the aftermath of that last encounter she'd hoped she'd imagined that hunger but there it was again, flaring back to life and throwing her equilibrium into a death spiral.

'Perfect.' Hunter was focused on her soft lips tilted up towards him, beckoning him to find some comfort there after opening up old wounds. They'd both been hurt, they were both survivors and he was drawn to her more than ever before.

In that moment he was totally consumed by the need to kiss her and seal that connection once and for all. He watched her eyes close in anticipation and acceptance of his intention. There was no interruption this time, no one to prevent him from doing what came naturally.

It seemed to take for ever to close those few inches between them, as if he was moving in slow motion and preserving the memory of this first kiss for all time.

That soft cushion of her lips against his was a relief; a

pleasure he'd been denying himself for some time, but soon even that wasn't enough. He wanted more, he wanted to taste her, to lose himself in her, and that's when he knew he was in trouble. If they'd stood here until daybreak, the kissing lasting until morning dew glistened in their hair, it would've ended too soon. There was a red flag waving somewhere in the distance, making sure he didn't stray too far into deep waters. That future he was so determined to get right for him and his boy didn't include anyone else in the picture.

He broke away and swivelled around to glance back in the direction of his house. 'I should probably get back to my house guest.'

Kissing Charlotte had given him that same rush of testosterone that accounted for every minute of his time in the penalty box. It was that feeling of doing what he needed to do in that moment, of being true to the man he was, and stuff the rules. He'd worked hard to regain his self-control and this set a dangerous precedent. Especially when he couldn't bring himself to regret a second of it. His whole future here was based on his repentance for similar rash decisions.

He was sure Charlotte was as confused as he was about what was happening. Regardless of her initial hurry to get away, she'd been into that kiss as much as he had. A woman like her didn't need a complication like him messing up her orderly life but there was no denying the chemistry. They'd tried doing that and it had landed them here, making out in the middle of the car park, but anything more than this would be bad news for both of them.

She nodded, probably coming to the same conclusion.

He only got a few steps away before she called after him. 'Hunter? You don't have a girlfriend, do you?'

'No, I don't have a girlfriend, Charlotte.'

'I...er...saw you waving to someone in the stands tonight. I thought maybe—'

'I'm not with anyone. I'm not in the habit of cheating.'

There was an edge to his tone but it felt like a step backwards to be accused of two-timing already.

'Right. A friend, then?'

'Goodnight, Charlotte.'

It was all he was giving her for tonight. So far he wasn't doing a very good job of resisting temptation and prioritising his son over his love life. In his defence, he hadn't planned any of this but that didn't mean he was sorry, or that he would follow it up.

Alfie was his personal business. Tonight's journey to find Anderson had been a matter of professional survival. At first. Somewhere in between those chats Charlotte had created a whole new section of his life to worry about.

She was smart, funny, beautiful, not afraid to show her emotions and up until tonight he'd been darned sure she'd hated his guts. He'd never expected her to be responsive to his advances unless it came in the form of a fist to his face. Although the impact had been pretty much the same.

Charlotte wasn't like other women he'd known. She didn't care for the man who'd played in the NHL or spent longer in the penalty box than the entire national team. Now she'd taken the time to get to know him, or as much as he'd allow, it was certainly an ego boost to find someone who liked him without the fame or notoriety. However, there was the worry that one kiss had just blown apart all the careful planning of his new life when all he could think about as he walked away was recapturing the moment.

Indeed, it was probably a small blessing he'd been lumbered with the Demons' resident troublemaker for the night or they might never have left his place. The next few hours on vomit watch would give him the space to think about what he'd done and what he was going to do about it, if anything.

He wasn't ready to share Alfie with her. It was too early to say, *Oh, yeah, here's my kid. I'm trying to get custody. I'm sure you'll make a great stand-in mom.* That wasn't fair to anyone on the back of one kiss. Neither did he want to jeopardise his chances of getting custody by flaunting a new relationship in front of the grieving O'Reillys or upsetting Alfie. He was going to have to tread very carefully now he was no longer free to behave however it suited him. Everything he did had consequences for those around him—he'd learned that the hard way and he wasn't about to make the same mistakes over again.

CHAPTER FOUR

CHARLOTTE WAS AT the rink bright and early and long before any training was due to start, with her own skates slung over her shoulder. She hadn't cut it as a hockey player herself but she could skate. The lessons had been her weekly escape from the rows and the tears of her unhappy home life.

The first skate of the day on unsullied ice always helped her unwind and unclutter her mind and she needed that more than ever this morning. There was so much to process and a lot more she needed to work through with Hunter. Despite pulling rank yesterday, they'd worked better in a partnership to get to the bottom of Anderson's diva fever and there was still a long way to go to get him back on top form. A child was supposed to be a lifelong commitment, not a problem that could, or should, be *fixed* overnight. He would need sustained support as he came to terms with the big changes in his life.

Then, of course, there was also the whole kissing Hunter thing. She was trying to work out if it had been a one-off, caused by working too closely outside office hours, or if the fire would still burn inside them both in the cold light of day. Hence the early start and restless legs. There were all sorts of implications in getting involved with a co-worker and there were risks involved she wasn't yet sure she wanted to take, no matter how tender his touch or how much she wanted more.

Unfortunately, as she made her way towards the ice it seemed she wasn't the only one to arrive early. Shouts echoed around the arena along with the sound of blades cutting through her fresh ice. She stashed her skates away until she could manage some alone time here again. This wasn't the start to the day she'd anticipated, especially as she realised the two men who'd gatecrashed her quiet morning were the same ones who'd kept her up late last night. Hunter and Anderson were so focused on their drills they didn't appear to notice they had a spectator.

Even the sight of the man with whom she'd been in a passionate clinch only hours ago gave her system a jolt to rival her early shot of caffeine. A shiver danced a merry jig along her spine at the memory of his hands there whilst his lips had caressed hers. He was a man of many fine skills.

Although he was no longer a professional player he'd certainly maintained his fitness level and she was sure he had the body to show for it. Damn it if she couldn't stop thinking about that image as her eyes followed him powering along the full length of the rink.

It took a lot of self-discipline to stay in that great a shape, even if his past antics had caused her to question it. He was still that mesmerising figure she'd never been able to take her eyes off during a game.

Hunter dropped his stick to the ice and rounded up the pucks littered around him. One by one he and his partner whacked them into the back of the net with such ferocity Charlotte was convinced they'd lodge in the advertising hoardings. It wasn't until he was skating back towards the centre that he caught sight of her on the sideline.

'Hey. I didn't see you come in.' He seemed pleased to see her if the bone-melting grin was any indication.

It was a sign that he might have seen last night as more than a spur-of-the-moment mistake and while that felt good, it meant she might have to make some decisions on what it was she wanted to happen next. She'd sworn she wouldn't cross that line with him, only to find herself entwined with him moments later. A physical attraction was one thing but working alongside him, getting to know him, took any further shenanigans into the realms of a relationship. That was something she didn't jump into easily when too-vivid visions of her parents' messy divorce made her wary of getting in too deep with anyone, never mind a man known for his unreliability in the past. Still, she was a woman who knew how to protect her heart. She just didn't let anyone in.

'Slaying some demons, are we?' She tipped her head towards his training partner, who was more focused than he'd been when she'd seen him last time. He'd barely been able to walk then, never mind balance the weight of his bulk on two sharp blades.

'One or two. What about you? Are you up for an early morning session?'

It was an entirely innocent remark. If he'd meant to conjure up a picture of the two of them lolling around in bed on a lazy Sunday morning he would've said it with a wink and an intention to make her blush.

'I'm, uh, just here to get a few things from the office.' Skating was something she did for herself and not something she was ready to share with him. It was her private pleasure, and no longer a team pursuit. After witnessing Hunter's drills, she wasn't sure he'd understand that distinction.

Anderson acknowledged her with a nod. 'I think I'll hit the showers. I have a lot to do today.'

Left alone with Hunter in his old Demons shirt she

wasn't prepared for the memories it brought back of him at his best, including last night when he'd had her in his arms. It was too early in the morning to be dealing with raging hormones, too scary to start examining what the hell was happening and definitely too public to find out what came next.

'That's one way to get Anderson to work out his frustrations but I don't want him to think brute strength is the answer to all his problems.' It might work in hockey but he was going to need to adopt a gentler, more methodical approach to his personal life.

He cocked his head to one side, a smirk playing across his lips. 'Are you calling me a brute?'

Charlotte gulped. *Brute* conjured up all sorts of primitive connotations she certainly didn't need to associate with him when she was already having trouble controlling herself around him.

'With the penalty minutes you've clocked up over the years, some might say *brute* was appropriate.'

'Ouch.'

It was a low blow but she'd do whatever it took to put an end to this apparent flirting. She couldn't cope with it. Wobbly knees would destroy the illusion she was confident about what she was doing here and turn her into Bambi on ice instead.

'I see Anderson's almost human today.' She changed the subject, using Anderson as a buffer for this unresolved sexual tension between them. He was the poster child for bad judgement and rash decisions. She was probably one more Hunter clinch away from an epic breakdown of equipment-smashing proportions and she didn't even know it.

Once she'd pulled the brakes on the hot and meaningful exchanged glances, Hunter followed suit and put a bit more space between them.

'I think we've made some progress. He has some work to do but it was his decision to get started early and make up some ground today. I do know he's serious about getting back on track with the club.'

'Gray will be happy.'

'That might be overstating it but at least there's a chance he'll think again about getting people fired.'

'That's a win all round, then. It's good to start the day on a high. I'll check in with Anderson later and see how he's getting on. I need to take a look at those stitches again anyway.' It wasn't that she didn't trust Hunter's word but she wanted to see, and speak to, Anderson herself to gauge his mood. She wanted to be optimistic about his future as well as her own but she was also a realist. That sort of behaviour wasn't often cured overnight and she, along with Gray, would still be watching him with a careful eye.

'Be my guest.'

'Right, I have a few things to sort out for Nottingham so I should go.' She was already making her way towards the exit and away from trouble.

'You're being hopeful. We still have an away match to win before we get there.'

'I like to be organised.' It wasn't that she was overly optimistic about their chances. A hockey fan through and through, she'd booked her flights for the Final Four Weekend long before Hunter had come on the scene. She would be there no matter who made it to the finals and if the Demons were there it would be all the sweeter.

The doctor didn't usually travel with the team but she'd be happy to combine work with pleasure. Except now it would mean she and Hunter would be spending more time together in close proximity. If they carried on from where they'd left off last night there was a danger it would all burn out of control and she knew better than to let her heart overrule her head.

He didn't try to stop her leaving, for which she was grateful. One more romantic recall into his arms and she knew they'd be melting the very ground they were standing on. She'd used up her quota of bravado in walking away and she would make sure she left enough time for Mr Torrance to have packed up his kit before she ventured out of the office again and risked another pulse-racing encounter. He was just too much excitement for this sleepy town and always had been.

She grabbed what she needed from the filing cabinet and was ready to leave when the sound of running water coming from somewhere nearby alerted her to the fact she wasn't alone.

'Anderson, is that you?' she called out before she entered the changing room, as she always did so anyone who wished to preserve their modesty could do so. Not that they were usually shy about parading in the buff. She was sure they'd done it on purpose in those early days just to get her flustered but she was used to it now. Men's naked bodies were part of the fixtures around here.

The shower shut off and she hoped to goodness he covered up before he came out to speak to her. A serious conversation about his state of mind would go more smoothly if she wasn't worried about a lapse in eye contact.

'I…uh…just wanted to see you…er…to make sure you were all right after last night.'

'Do you make a habit of dropping in on the players when they're in the showers?' A bemused Hunter, not Anderson, padded out barefoot and double-towelled, with one around his waist and another in his hand, drying his hair.

Holy six pack!

She was sure her mouth was dropping open and closed

like a sea creature stranded on the shore, fighting for survival. Eventually she forced herself to speak before he felt it his duty to come and give her mouth to mouth.

'I don't get my kicks spying on naked hockey players, thank you very much.' Only ex-hockey players.

'Oh, yes, we're much too *brutish* for you, aren't we?' He tossed the hair-drying towel aside and she was finding difficulty coming up with an argument, or even why she wanted one as he walked towards her.

'If we're talking sexy Canadian stereotypes I'm more a Gilbert Blythe kind of girl,' she lied, wanting to focus on someone the opposite of the muscle-bound hunk advancing on her. It would be dangerous to admit to the attraction here, alone in a small room with Hunter naked except for a scrap of white fabric.

'I'll start calling you Carrots, then, shall I?' He had every right to look pleased with himself when he'd just scored extra hottie points.

'You know *Anne of Green Gables*?' Now she came to think of it, he did resemble her other teenage fantasy boyfriend with his dark wavy hair and that accent that made every *Sorry* impossible to forgive.

'Read it, and watched the mini-series as an essential part of getting inside the female psyche at an early age. I even wore a flat cap for a while.' He smiled bashfully at the memory and Charlotte couldn't help but sigh out loud.

'Yes, well, we're all older, wiser and much more cynical these days.'

'Perhaps, but there's always room for a little romance, don't you think?' He was doing it again, staring at her with such naked lust it took her breath away.

She was doing her best to remain strong and avoid falling too quickly under his spell again but her mouth was dry with want. A droplet of water fell from the ends of his tousled hair and she watched it with the thirst of a traveller lost in the desert, searching for that life-giving oasis. It splashed onto his shoulder and trickled over the muscular planes of his chest, its journey gaining momentum over the smooth skin, unimpeded until it reached that trail of dark hair from navel to...

Oh. He'd caught her staring.

'Do you shave?' It was the first thing that popped into her head so she said it to divert her thoughts from where they were headed. Except she hadn't given any thought to where her gaze was lingering.

His taut belly moved with his laughter. 'No. Do you?'

She frowned, not quite understanding his meaning. Did he think she had a hairy chest? Then the penny dropped and she wished the ground would too.

'I didn't mean... I was talking about your chest. I wasn't staring at your...'

She so was.

He cleared his throat, clearly as embarrassed as she was by her staring. She would've imagined someone with his history would've been used to it and that lack of arrogance only added to his appeal for her. There was nothing more off-putting than a man who was fully aware of his looks and used them to his advantage.

'About last night—'

'I'll leave you to get dressed. I only came in to get a few things.' She could tell he was gearing up to give her the brush-off. If he'd wanted anything more they wouldn't be standing here, making small talk, while he was dressed in nothing but a towel. Until this second she hadn't realised it was her who didn't want this to be over already.

'Wait.' He grabbed hold of her arm, pulled her back so they were almost nose to nose, his hot breath mingling with hers. His freshly soaped skin was warm and wet against hers, reminding her he was *au naturel* below that towel.

'What are we doing, Hunter?' This was her chance to reclaim control. If she truly wanted to prevent this from happening she should've been pushing him away, not welcoming his touch as though she'd been waiting for it all her life.

'Probably something really, really stupid.' At least Hunter was acknowledging that he was also powerless against this attraction as he took her in his arms.

Any fight left her at that first contact and she surrendered to the next. There was something more urgent in his kiss this time, matching her need to make up for lost time. As if the pressure of fighting these feelings had finally been too much and had exploded in a frenzy of body parts desperate to connect.

His tongue courted hers and with his two hands planted firmly on her backside, he pulled her closer, leaving her in no doubt about how much he wanted her. He was as hard for her as she was wet for him, their mutual appreciation reaching critical levels.

Her carefully layered shirt and sweater combo, chosen to keep her body temperature regulated for skating purposes, now seemed excessive for this increasingly hot interlude. Arousal coursed through her veins, reaching her every nerve ending until she was nothing but a mass of erogenous zones.

He was the only man capable of making her act this recklessly but she wasn't so far gone she was prepared to lose her inhibitions in public. It definitely wouldn't aid her career if the team doctor was to be discovered getting passionate with the half-naked physio in the locker room.

'This is a mistake. Someone could walk in at any time. You were right. This is a stupid idea.'

'Charlotte, wait!' Hunter could only watch as she bolted from the building. It would only cause more of a scene if he ran after her, his towel at half-mast around his waist.

He did, however, dress as quickly, and as cautiously, as he could without causing serious injury to himself as he waited for the after-effects of their unexpected, extremely hot tryst to wear off.

So much for careful planning and taking things slowly. Apparently his impulsive side hadn't left him altogether, although he would deny any man not to respond as primitively as he had to the hungry way she'd stared at his body. Her emotions were as easy to read now as they had been that first day they'd met and she'd made no attempt to disguise her contempt for him.

After Sara and the years he'd missed of Alfie's life he preferred knowing where he stood. No good came of secrets and that went for him too. He'd deliberated telling her about Alfie's existence when he'd been unsure last night had been anything other than a moment of weakness. Given this morning's events and the persistent frequency of the tightness in his jeans, the chemistry with Charlotte was rapidly invading all areas of his life.

He might be wary of inviting someone to share his most personal, private secrets but if her hasty exit was anything to go by, so was Charlotte. It was important she knew they were braving this strange new land together.

She didn't seem the type to engage in passionate embraces on a whim; she wasn't one of the puck bunnies who'd kill to be in that position with a player in the locker room. If she was he would've heard about it by now. Players weren't known for their discretion on such matters. Then again, until recently he hadn't been the settling-down type whose only goal was a steady cheque to pay a mortgage. People weren't always who they appeared to be but he trusted his instincts. She was the first woman he'd had time for since finding out about his son and that had to mean something, something he was keen to explore.

He chased her down to the car park and called after her. 'Can we at least talk about this?'

Apparently not as her little silver hatchback screeched away from the arena.

For someone who spent most of her spare time at the arena, Charlotte did a good job of eluding Hunter until the night of their away match and even then she'd driven rather than taken a seat on the team bus. Something that hadn't gone unnoticed by the others, who'd wondered what had caused her to forsake her free ride when she normally insisted on travelling, despite the away team providing their own medical support. Hunter had simply kept his head down and muttered something about her having other errands to run. It wasn't as if he could put his hands up and say it was his fault she wanted to be on her own. That he'd made her act as irresponsibly as he once had and now she regretted it.

He felt the need to apologise the minute he cast his eyes on her, even though they hadn't done anything wrong. Under the fluorescent lights of a jam-packed concourse probably wasn't the ideal spot to confront what had happened but she hadn't left him much option when she kept dodging him.

'Charlotte, you have to talk to me at some point. I'm sorry if I made you uncomfortable but we still have to work together.' There wasn't much hope for more than that since a couple of kisses had sent her scurrying into the shadows.

They were jostled by the stampeding crowds keen to get their pre-game snacks and drinks from the nearby concession stands. Hunter took her by the elbow and gently led her to a corner where there was considerably less footfall and noise going on around them.

'Did anyone see us? In the changing room, I mean.' The events had clearly been at the forefront of her mind when she launched into her fears immediately, rather than continuing to dance around the subject.

'No. Our secret's safe.' He only managed a half-smile at the thought of being someone's dirty little secret. For her sake he wanted to laugh it off, pretend the matter wasn't of any great significance so they could move on past it. In reality, though, he would rather be someone Charlotte was proud to be seen with regardless of what people thought. Not being reminded that he was still the man no one wished to be associated with.

'Good.' A delicate blush stained her skin but it was difficult to tell if it was through embarrassment or heat at the memory. He knew which one would be easier for him to stomach.

'Charlotte—'

'Hunter—'

They stumbled over each other attempting to address the chasm that had opened up between them after their latest indiscretion. In ordinary circumstances making out should have spelled the beginning of a relationship, not the end of one. It might be wishful thinking on his part but he was holding onto the small hope it was circumstance alone that had caused Charlotte's sudden retreat from him.

'I'm sorry if I put you in a compromising position at work but, for the record, we haven't done anything wrong.' They'd only done what had come naturally, albeit at the wrong time and in the wrong place.

She glanced around, obviously still skittish about getting caught even when the passers-by were more interested in getting to their seats before the puck dropped than two people freaked out by their attraction to one another. 'I know... It's just... I wasn't expecting this.'

He understood her fears, he had reservations himself, but for altogether different reasons. Whilst she might be concerned she'd be nothing more than a notch on his bedpost, he feared the opposite.

'Neither was I. We can take things at whatever pace you want.' One thing was for sure, it was impossible to walk away and pretend nothing was happening.

She studied him closely, as if she was trying to work out if he was spinning her a line or he was being genuine. That hurt more than she could ever have imagined.

'It's not only what nearly happened, or could happen between us that I'm worried about. I don't know you, not really.' This was a very different woman from the one who'd been in his arms not long ago, a cautious Charlotte who probably didn't make a habit of the sort of behaviour he'd been famous for.

He couldn't blame her. They'd taken a risk of being spotted, of being ridiculed or, worse, sacked on the spot. Sara's parents would've had a field day with the news and then he'd have had to explain to his son why he'd screwed up their future together for a woman he'd just met. Only he knew he wouldn't have put either his or Charlotte's livelihoods at risk for something trivial and it was frustrating he couldn't get that point across.

'Now, how can we rectify that if you won't be in the same room as me? Hmm?' He tilted his head to one side and gave her his best hound dog impression so she'd stop seeing him as some sort of threat.

That earned him a soft, sweet laugh. 'So you found the flaw in my total avoidance ploy, huh?'

Hunter sucked a breath in through his teeth. 'Not the most practical tactic when we do play for the same team.'

'Always thinking about the long game and not the interim strategy, that's me.' The skin at the corners of her eyes creased with laughter, a most welcome sight after an anxious few days of silence.

'Sometimes it does you good to act on impulse and not worry about what happens further down the line.'

'And how did that work out for you?'

He'd been talking about letting their attraction win out over common sense but Charlotte's raised eyebrow suggested another nod back at his hockey days.

'I said sometimes. Not as a lifestyle choice. Sometimes the most spontaneous moments can bring the greatest pleasure.' He lowered his voice so his next words were for her ears only. 'I have many regrets, Charlotte, but kissing you will never be one of them.'

If it wasn't for the constant stream of people nudging past he would be tempted to do it again.

He was running the risk of scaring her off again by being so blatant about his desires but it was going to take at least one of them being honest if there was a chance of repeating the experience.

'Hunter... I...'

He watched her gulp and swallow, struggling to form a reply, and waited patiently for the verdict on his gamble.

The klaxon sounded from deep inside the arena, signalling the end of the pre-game warm-up and penetrating their bubble. The teams would be making their way off the ice after their drills and stretches to prepare for the game behind the scenes. Where he and Charlotte should be.

'We really need to hustle our backsides down there before Gray starts on the warpath.' She turned away from him, timing, as ever, against them.

Hunter mused over whether or not to force this conversation to its conclusion so he would know once and for all where he stood with her. She was driving him crazy. Since it had taken this long to pin her down he figured it wouldn't help matters to put her job in jeopardy again by making her tardy.

'We wouldn't want that but, believe me, I'm still keen on that getting to know each other idea.'

Charlotte almost fell down the steps at Hunter's insistence they pick up where they'd left off. Especially when his hand was at her back, escorting her towards the changing rooms and heating her skin with the warmth of his touch. She'd been stupid to think a few days and some distance from him would put any lustful thoughts out of her head. One glimpse of him, a promise of more of the same and her willpower had dissolved.

It had been all too tempting to ignore her duty to the players and the team in favour of spending time with him again. The very reason she'd beaten herself up over the last time they'd lost track of where, and who, they were. When she was with him nothing else seemed to matter and that was dangerous when she was putting her job at risk for a man she barely knew beyond how good his lips felt on hers. She didn't know where they went from here and she certainly didn't want to have to commit to anything if it left her position on the team vulnerable, so she was glad she'd been buzzed out of her reverie in the nick of time.

They were lucky that Gray hadn't missed them either and they were able to merge back into the team preparations as if nothing had happened. On the outside at least. Her insides were having difficulty catching up with her logical brain, still fluttering and unsettled by being so close to Hunter.

At least being squashed in behind the bench as a stowaway on the away side meant they were most definitely in a crowd and close enough to the action to keep their minds where they were supposed to be—on the ice.

'Anderson seems to have recovered form. Good job, you two.' There was a brief nod from Gray as the player stretched his legs, skating rings around the opposition in the opening minutes of the game.

He didn't ask what was behind the transformation, more concerned with results than the journey, and neither Charlotte nor Hunter volunteered the information. She knew from her subsequent conversations with him that he and Maggie were trying to work things out and that in itself had improved his mood and his play, but Anderson's private life was exactly that and unless he chose to share the details of his recent troubles, they would remain confidential.

She and Hunter exchanged smiles over the pat on the back from their leader before he went back to discussing tactics with the rest of his men. Their joint effort with Anderson certainly appeared to have yielded favourable results and she could see Hunter stood a little taller with the recognition. She couldn't help but wonder how long it had been since someone had actually congratulated him on a job well done.

For a long time he'd probably endured nothing but negativity and scepticism over his work ethic and she was as guilty as everyone else who'd refused to give him a break. So wrapped up in her own thoughts and feelings about how she'd been affected by his presence here, she'd given virtually no thought to the positive addition he'd *actually* been to the team. Perhaps it was self-preservation. She didn't need any more reason to like him when he was already sidestepping around those work-colleague boundaries.

The volume levels of the crowd rose around her at a skirmish out by the Demons' goal as they went all out to defend. It was hard to see what was going on through the throng of bodies vying for prominence. Suddenly there was a cry for the medic. As the crowd parted and anxious players called for help, it became obvious there was something seriously wrong. One body remained prone on the ice, the area around him rapidly turning scarlet with blood. It was Colton, the Demons' winger.

Hunter swore, grabbed a towel and had vaulted over the bench before she'd even taken her first step onto the rink. Two Demons players arrived either side of her and escorted her quickly over to the scene so she didn't slip on the ice.

'Ambulance. Now!' she shouted to the Cobras' medical staff, who were making their way over too. The amount of blood spurting from Colton's leg told of the severity of the injury and this was no time for territory marking.

'It's an artery.' Hunter dropped to his knees and held the towel to the deep gash across the thigh, probably caused by the blade of someone's skate in the melee.

'Keep applying the pressure. Colton? We need to try and elevate this leg.' In such circumstances there was always a chance of a patient bleeding to death as the blood was pumping so quickly from the heart and a cut artery was a time-critical wound. Everything she and Hunter did now to stem the flow of blood could determine whether or not he survived.

'Charlotte?' Hunter directed her attention to the once-white towel, which was now a bright red, infused with their patient's blood. It would only take losing two pints of blood before he went into shock. There was no more time to waste.

'Give me your belt.' She didn't even wait for a response and simply helped herself. Despite the adrenaline pumping in her own veins and the struggle to keep her breathing regulated in the midst of the drama, her fingers worked nimbly to unbuckle his belt.

She tugged him roughly towards her and whipped the strip of leather from around his waist. All the time he kept pressure on the wound without blinking an eye at her, as if having bossy women strip him was an everyday occurrence. Or he knew exactly what she was doing. The belt made a perfect tourniquet around the thigh and she pulled it just tight enough to hopefully slow the bleeding but not cut off total supply to the limb.

'Nicely done, Doctor.' Hunter offered his support with a smile and a wink. He was the one grounding source for her in the midst of the drama. It was a comfort knowing that she wasn't in this alone.

'You too, Mr Torrance. Now let's get you to hospital, Colton.'

It was only as they rushed off the ice towards the waiting ambulance that the uneasy silence around the arena became noticeable. Everyone had been waiting with bated breath to see the fate of the injured player. It didn't matter what side he was on when there was a life at stake. She was glad she hadn't felt that weight of expectation on her shoulders as she'd worked and that had been down to Hunter's assistance. It wasn't that she couldn't treat this sort of injury solo—after all, that was the nature of her job here. No, it was simply...reassuring for someone to have her back.

She relayed all the relevant information to the paramedics so they could radio ahead to the hospital and prep for surgery. With Hunter still taking charge of wound pressure, they both climbed into the vehicle alongside their patient.

'We need oxygen, double cannula and get fluids started.' She was talking to herself as much as anyone else in the vicinity so she had all bases covered.

The back of an ambulance made for a small workspace

and she couldn't help but brush against Hunter with every bump in the road as she inserted the cannulas into Colton's hands.

'Sorry,' she said as they went around a corner and she was forced to brace herself against Hunter's frame to steady herself. It was more important to get the IV and much-needed pain relief up and running than continue her ill-conceived avoid-body-contact-with-Hunter plan.

'No problem.'

She didn't take her eyes off her patient but she could feel the warmth of Hunter's slow grin on her back. It made her shiver all the same.

'Will I make it back for the final period, Doc?' The pale Colton was trying to sit up and displaying that hockey-player spirit that demanded to see the game out, no matter what. On this occasion she was definitely going to have to disappoint him.

'I'm afraid not. You're going to have to go straight into Theatre to have that artery stitched.' She wasn't even sure if they'd finish the match after that scare.

'Even Gray should understand you missing the rest of the game. I don't think he'll be docking your wages this once.' Hunter attempted to soften the blow and she appreciated it. It probably aided Colton's compliance to have a kindred spirit on board, someone who knew from personal experience how it felt to be left on the sidelines.

'But I'll be okay to play in the finals?' The pleading eyes were begging for reassurance but Charlotte didn't have it in her to lie, even to a seriously injured man.

'Don't worry about that for now. First things first. We need to get you into Theatre. We're almost at the hospital now.' They'd done as much as they could for Colton but her mind would be much more at ease when she knew the surgeon was doing his bit to save his life too.

'I'll phone Gray as soon as we arrive and let him know you're keen to get back ASAP.' Hunter wasn't making him any promises other than to relay a progress report but he was providing that extra reassurance she was beginning to realise she could count on. Even though they both knew Colton was probably finished for the season, there was no need to give him more reason to worry before he went into surgery.

It wasn't until they'd handed over their patient into the hands of the hospital staff that Charlotte was able to take time for some deep fortifying breaths. She could only watch, her stomach in knots, as he was stretchered away down the corridor at high speed, her part in ensuring his survival over for now.

'Wow. That was a rush.'

It seemed she wasn't the only one coming down from the adrenaline high as Hunter let out an unsteady breath next to her.

'Not one I'm in a hurry to experience again, thanks.' Now she had time and space to think about events, the enormity of the undertaking was beginning to hit home.

A chill penetrated her bones and set her knees trembling. She practically fell into one of the chairs lining the corridor.

'Your first life-or-death emergency?' Hunter landed in the seat next to her with a heavy thud and she could see he wasn't unaffected by the drama either. It was a comfort to see her reaction was totally normal.

She nodded. Her eyes were already beginning to well up as emotion built inside her and she didn't trust herself to talk without her voice cracking. They'd very nearly lost one of their own tonight and the responsibility of keeping him alive had rested heavily on her shoulders. It was the nature of the path she'd chosen but her work in sports therapy tended more towards joint and muscle problems than life-threatening crises. Tonight had been a sobering reminder of the serious commitment she'd made to her career and the team.

'Mine too.' He reached across and squeezed her hand. It was the closest she'd get to the hug she needed right now.

She swallowed the unprofessional tears away since she was the one who'd actually trained for this and focused on the fact Colton was alive.

'You certainly seemed to know what you were doing back there.' As she recalled, he'd applied pressure to the wound area before she'd even told him to.

'Well, I do have some training in the field. I was at medical school briefly before I decided to toss it all in for hockey.'

Her eyes widened at that new information. 'Ah. So the physiotherapy didn't totally come out of left field? You could easily have been Dr Hunter Torrance?'

'Medicine was definitely something I was interested in pursuing. Actually, I'm not sure which career was more about rebelling against my parents.'

'Your relationship with them was that strained?'

He nodded solemnly. 'I was adopted and always made very aware of the fact. Told I should be grateful they'd taken me on. At eighteen I decided to find my birth parents, only to be rejected again. They didn't want me any more then than when I was born. Becoming a doctor would've stuck it to those who thought I would never amount to anything but the idea of being a hockey player… well, it was glamorous and exciting and something I knew they'd envy. Until I screwed it all up, of course.'

It was her turn to squeeze back. 'Don't be so hard on yourself. We've all had our struggles. Yours just happened to be very public.'

Her heart broke for his younger self who'd so obviously been hurting and searching for acceptance. She was able to see that explosive behaviour in a different light now she knew it had been more than bad temper at play and forgave him every wrong he'd done in her eyes. Not only had he been dealing with that loneliness and isolation of his personal circumstances but he'd been demonised by the press and disappointed fans. Even when he'd shown up, full of remorse, she'd clung onto her own grudge and dismissed his claims. It only added to the injustice done to him and to the guilt she was feeling as a result.

If she imagined her trials and tribulations with her parents playing out in arenas around the country she doubted she would have recovered as effectively as he had. When he'd turned up professing to have changed his life she'd assumed sports medicine was second best, the closest he could get to the ice without playing again. That the Demons' medical staff was the consolation prize when it had been the jackpot to her. To find out he had that calling to help others ingrained in him after all challenged her preconceived ideas about his character and stripped away some of those fears about getting involved with him.

She was fast running out of excuses to avoid her feelings, leaving only the outright terror at the thought of putting her heart on the line again. What if she gave it away only to find it cast aside like an unwanted toy when something, someone better came along? She hadn't been enough for her father to stick around and she didn't want to put herself in the position again of letting someone else have so much control over her emotions or her life.

The only certainty she had with Hunter tonight was there would be no escape from these growing feelings for him until they knew for sure Colton had pulled through.

CHAPTER FIVE

HUNTER WASN'T USED to being the one receiving pats on the back or hand squeezes and he couldn't decide if the squirming in his seat was because he was uneasy over it or *too* comfortable with it. It seemed as though he was finally finding his feet as part of the team. More than that, he and Charlotte had formed their own partnership. Not so long ago professional courtesy would've been all he'd wanted from her but they'd gone way beyond that point. He wouldn't have shared details of his personal life with the same woman who'd turned her nose up at him when they'd first met. There had definitely been a shift in their dynamic and it wasn't only down to the random bouts of kissing.

'You didn't do so badly under the spotlight tonight. Actually, you were kind of amazing out there.' The way she'd handled the situation so calmly and efficiently had shown everyone this was so much more than a job to her. She was dedicated to the team but also a medical professional whom any man could trust with his life. Maybe even with the knowledge of his son.

'We're good together.' Her coy smile suggested she was thinking about more than their time in the cramped confines of the ambulance.

'That we are, and if I recall there was a promise made

about getting to know each other a little better.' It was as important to him to be upfront and honest about what this was as it was for her. A relationship for him now was always going to include someone else and he was done with secrets.

'Well, we've made a start. I had no idea about your time in medical school.'

'That makes it your turn for the Q and A. Let's start with an easy one. Why the Demons? What made you join the team?' He wanted to know everything that made her tick so he could work out what it was that kept putting obstacles in their path. Even if he ignored the comings and goings of the staff and patients flooding through the emergency department and stole another kiss from her, he knew she'd be running again by tomorrow.

'I've been into hockey since the arena opened.'

'A real fan, then?' He knew she enjoyed hockey nights, he'd seen it, but he hadn't realised her love of the game had come before her role on the team.

'You could say that,' she muttered under her breath, but he could see no reason why she'd be embarrassed by it.

At a time when most young girls would've been more interested in fashion and make-up, she'd committed her time to a sport that wasn't for the faint-hearted. It explained so much about her character.

'That must've been around the time I played here?' He did the mental calculations. The chances were he'd seen her in passing at one time or another.

'Yeah.' Her embarrassment continued to flare a crimson contrast to her porcelain skin, the same flushed look she had every time he kissed her.

'It's kinda hot, knowing you're a *real* hockey fan.' He wanted to reach out and tilt her chin up to look at him and make that connection again but he didn't. An invisible barrier had been hastily erected since their last moment of weakness but he thought he could break it down again with a hit of honesty. Hockey had been his life and it was a new experience having someone who understood that commitment and passion.

He'd screwed up his own career but his love of the game had never diminished. That was why he'd jumped at the chance Gray had given him to work here. He could've come over, set up his own practice and eventually built up a client list, but as the Demons' physio he got a chance to recapture that passion. Now he could do that with Charlotte too if she would only let him.

'I'm a Demon through and through.' She sighed as if it was a bad thing when he'd seen her loyalty as a positive. It gave them more common ground other than this mutual attraction they were having difficulty with.

'Good. I'm sure Gray's glad he'll never have to worry about losing you to a rival team.'

'You don't understand,' she said, her downcast gaze giving him sudden reason for concern. He wasn't used to her being so cagey with him. Usually she was very vocal with her opinion.

'So why don't you tell me what it is that's bothering you?' He wanted to understand so they could move past whatever was causing this stumbling block between them. If she couldn't share this obviously personal problem with him, it was going to be very difficult to confide in her about his son. Trust was a two-way street for him.

She took a deep breath, refilling her lungs and doing nothing to allay his worries that there was a serious problem here. 'I'll admit I wasn't the *kindest* person to you on meeting for the first time but I, uh, might've held a bit of a grudge against you.'

'Oh?' It didn't come as any great surprise but he was interested to know the reasons behind it.

'Well...you kinda ruined my life.'

They were the words Hunter had always expected to hear from someone but they still hit hard. He didn't know what he'd done to Charlotte to deserve them but he wasn't in any doubt that he did. After all, ruining people's lives was what he'd done best before he'd turned his own around.

He was staring at her as if she'd gone stark raving mad. Maybe she finally had. It would explain why she was about to spill her biggest, most humiliating secret but it was now or never. She couldn't avoid this any more when he was opening up to her and showing he was just as human and flawed as she was. Perhaps after this confession, whatever the outcome, she'd finally be able to move on from that chapter of her life. As long as he kept the story to himself and saved her from prolonged mortification.

She gulped in another breath and prepared to unload her greatest shame. In the middle of a busy hospital, waiting for news on the fate of one of their players for goodness' sake. She was beginning to think she should've told the whole sorry story from the outset and saved herself a whole heap of trouble. After this bombshell he wouldn't be so keen to get up close and personal with her.

'It might sound dramatic but teenage girls are, and when the one thing they love falls apart their whole world collapses. You have to realise ice hockey coming here was a big deal. When they built the arena, drafted in all of these handsome Canadians and Americans to play in that first team, it was like a hurricane sweeping in through our town. It was dangerous and exciting and turned everything upside down. I needed something to cling to while my home life was in freefall. In the lead-up to their divorce my parents were constantly fighting and hockey became my escape.'

'Did I do something to hurt you? It was a difficult period for me. I wronged a lot of people and I'm doing my best to make it up.' There was genuine confusion creasing his brow into a frown but how could she clear this up without coming across as the pathetic, sad case she'd been?

'We only met in passing at fan events, signings and such. Nothing you'd remember.' Why should she, a gangly wallflower, have stuck out in his mind when there'd been so many confident, beautiful women tugging at his jersey?

'Sorry,' he said, the need to apologise for his past so deeply ingrained he wouldn't even know what he was saying it for.

Charlotte ached for the young boy who, like her, had probably grown up taking his parents' disinterest to heart, believing he'd been at fault. It put a different perspective on the rebellious player he'd been, whose misdemeanours now seemed so obviously a cry for help from someone suffering tremendous pain. His return here, facing up to those he'd hurt, had taken a lot of courage and she hadn't given him enough credit for it.

'It's not your fault. Really. I invested a lot in the team. Some might say too much. When you got tossed out of the championship match and we lost, I took it personally. A decade later and I guess I still couldn't shake off that disappointment when we were first introduced. I was afraid you might let us down again.' That wasn't half the story behind her initial resistance but it was the least humiliating half.

'It's understandable. I was a mixed-up kid and I let a lot of people down during that time. All I can do is apologise and hope you'll forgive me.' With that lopsided smile, that resignation as he accepted any blame that could be apportioned to him, it was impossible not to forgive him anything.

'I'll hold my hands up and say you're not the person I feared you were. I've seen what you've done for the team already, how you've handled Anderson and, of course, tonight when we fought to save Colton. There's no question of your commitment.'

'But there's obviously something else going on I don't know about when you keep running out on me.' He took her other hand, forced her to turn around in her seat to face him. Close enough for him to see through any lies.

She swallowed hard. This was where things got tricky. 'You were a big name in a small pond when you came here the first time. Exotic. Irresistible to a vulnerable teenage girl whose life seemed like it was falling apart. I might've developed a bit of a crush.'

That was putting it mildly but even that admission managed to raise his eyebrows and widen his grin.

He rested his hand on his heart. 'I'm flattered.'

'Don't get carried away. I *had* a crush. Past tense. There's no need to get all big-headed about it.' His ego didn't need to know adult Charlotte was beginning to develop more mature feelings on the subject. He'd probably worked that out for himself by now anyway.

'We never met or went on a date?'

'No. I just invested a lot of faith in you and let myself get carried away. I was genuinely devastated when you got thrown out of that game and we lost the championship.' With hindsight she was able to see that her lonely teen self had been dealing with so many intense emotions at the time she'd probably transferred some of that onto his shoulders, believing that he'd failed her too.

It was a relief knowing he didn't think she had a screw

loose, that he was on her side, but that didn't make the situation any easier for her to come to terms with.

'Do you see now why I gave you such a hard time in the beginning?'

'I do. All I can do is say sorry. Again.'

'I guess seeing you back here awakened all of those old feelings. It didn't help that I'd got it into my head you were hiding the real reason for your return. As I said, my issues.'

The colour slowly drained from his face. He edged back in his seat, regaining his personal space, and it was then she realised then she'd touched a nerve, that she might be on the verge of unravelling the truth behind his sudden reappearance. She instantly regretted this whole honesty thing. Whatever he was hiding, she had a feeling she wasn't going to like it.

Hunter was so overwhelmed with the information, so conflicted about how he should react, he was beginning to wish he'd waited until they were off the premises for the emotional edition of show and tell. If at all.

The line of this conversation deserved a dark, quiet corner somewhere with a stiff drink for both of them.

He hadn't suspected there was a history of anything other than his damaged reputation and it was almost worse, knowing the truth. It wasn't only the possibility of him failing her that had made her wary, it was the fact he already had. There was nothing he could do to rectify that except be honest about who he was now. He couldn't go on letting her think it was solely her paranoia keeping them from making any sort of commitment to each other.

That brought him right back to the subject he'd been avoiding. Alfie.

'I haven't told you the real reason I came back.'

She flinched, preparing herself for the worst and making him feel as though he was about to throw away that game all over again.

'I knew it.'

He could already see the barricades shutting down around her. Usually she had no problem telling him what she thought of him.

That defensive stance she'd taken instead might've been a better course of action for him than lashing out or self-medicating with alcohol. It could've saved his hockey career. Then again, it wasn't good to keep things bottled inside and isolate yourself, letting everything build up until some day it exploded and caused chaos, or slowly killed you from the inside out. He didn't want either for Charlotte, only for her to be happy.

'It's nothing bad. At least, I don't think so.'

Any earlier playfulness had vanished, any hint of a smile now evened out to a harsh thin line across her lips, and Hunter knew he should've found the courage to tell her about Alfie earlier. It didn't matter whether she minded if he was a father or not now, the damage had been done with the omission.

'I have a son, Alfie. I came back for him.'

He waited for a response but she said nothing.

'I didn't know he existed until a few months ago. My ex, Sara, was pregnant when I went back to Canada and didn't tell me. We all know what a mess I was back then so I can't blame her for not wanting me around. She died in a road accident last year and her parents got in touch. They thought Alfie should have one parent in his life at least. Although they aren't keen for me to have custody until they're one hundred percent sure it's best for him. Hence the move back to Northern Ireland and the need for a steady job.'

'I'm sorry to hear about Sara. I'm sure it all came as

a great shock to you.' The news he had a son had all but rendered her mute so she could only imagine how floored he'd been on finding out. It took any sort of relationship between them to a different level, one she wasn't sure she was ready for. Although Hunter hadn't been given a choice in the matter either by the sound of it.

He would have had every right to be angry about being denied the opportunity of that father role all this time only to have the responsibility dropped on him without a moment's notice. It showed the true strength of his character that he was trying to do the best thing for his son and put him first.

Discovering this new side of him had its pros and cons. It made her warm to him even more when the circumstances had just become even more complex.

'This was supposed to be a chance for me to make amends with all the people I hurt.'

'You seem to be doing pretty well with that as far as I can see.'

'I'm sorry I didn't tell you this up front but let's face it, we didn't exactly hit it off at the start. I understand why now, of course, but at the time there didn't seem the need to get involved in each other's personal lives.' He held his hands up but she knew that first day must have been akin to walking into the lions' den for him, with the lioness fiercely defending her territory.

'I understand.' She really did. If he'd announced he'd come back for his illegitimate son she probably would've imagined it was some sort of ploy to gain sympathy during those first days when she'd still believed the very worst about him. Actually spending time with him had taught her he was the new man he'd proclaimed to be after all.

'It's still early days for me and Alfie. I'm struggling to bond with him as it is without bringing someone else into his life. It was never my intention to get involved with anyone whilst I'm working towards gaining custody, and his trust. Despite the ridiculous urban myths, I'm not some sort of Lothario who'll welcome a string of *aunties* into his life.'

'No?'

'No. I'm deadly serious about all of my responsibilities these days.' He held eye contact with her until she saw the sincerity of his words reflected there.

She gave a tiny shiver, realising the significance of his decision to tell her about Alfie if he didn't invite just anyone into his son's life.

'It's my eternal shame Sara decided it was better to raise Alfie alone in secret than have his reckless, volatile father in his life. A decision I'm sure was very difficult for her to make and I don't want to hurt anyone to that extent again.'

'So, what's the problem between you and Alfie now? Is he having trouble coming to terms with having you in his life?' Charlotte understood that his ex had been trying to protect her son from the kind of questionable parenting she'd been subjected to but the very idea Hunter was considering other people's feelings already made him a better father than hers had ever been.

'Quite the opposite. I think I'm a bit of a novelty given he's never had a father figure in his life before. Not something I'm proud of and I desperately want to make up for lost time but I am a bit out of my depth. It's not helped by his overprotective grandparents who daren't let him out of their sight.'

'Okay, so he likes you, he wants to spend time with you… Surely they wouldn't mind if the two of you spent the afternoon together? Maybe somewhere local so they don't worry too much?' It wasn't fair that he should still be made to keep something of a distance when he genuinely wanted to be part of his child's life. She would've been devastated to find out her father had been kept from spending time with her. Unfortunately the opposite had been true for her. Her father had wanted to forget she'd ever been born so he could pretend he was still young, free and single.

'This is all new to me too. I'm not sure what kids' activities are age-appropriate for an eight-year-old. I don't have any experience of adventure playgrounds or family days out. At that age I was already practically living at the skating rink.'

'Can Alfie skate?' That sense of escape on the ice was something they definitely shared. As the son of a hockey player she would've imagined Alfie would've had that desire tenfold too.

'I don't think so. I don't know for sure. Sara wasn't into hockey and I doubt I did anything to persuade her otherwise.'

'Why don't you bring him to the rink? If he can't skate, I'm sure you could teach him. What eight-year-old boy wouldn't want to do that with his dad?' She put forward the suggestion with a shrug. It was all she'd ever wanted to do, with or without adult supervision.

'You're right. I'd have done anything to have had someone take me by the hand and lead me around the rink, showing some sort of affection, or even interest. Like all those other childhood skills, I taught myself how to do it because my parents hadn't had the time to spare. You know, I think they regretted my adoption because I got in the way of their self-indulgent lifestyle. They probably hadn't meant for me to be much more than a cute accessory, when I'd been a living, breathing little boy in desperate need of a loving home. That's why it's so important to me to get this right for Alfie.'

'I get it. We have neglectful fathers in common. Mine seemed to think divorcing my mum meant ending his relationship with me too. He threw nineteen years of marriage and family away for a fling with someone half his age. The one person I thought would always be there to protect me was the same person who broke my heart, and my mum's. I guess I was too much of a reminder of his failure as a so-called family man but he just walked away, leaving me confused about what I'd done wrong and why we weren't enough to make him happy. That betrayal of trust is hard to get past.'

'It is. I don't think I ever truly gave myself to Sara because I was always waiting for that final kick in the teeth. I needed to hold part of me back. Just in case.'

She nodded. 'I understand. I didn't even date until university because I was so cynical about the idea of love after the divorce. I missed out on those silly things young girls do at that age. There was no snogging in the back row of the cinema or hanging out in the local park in the dark for me because I didn't want to get close to anyone again. I couldn't go through that trauma a second time.' She shrugged. So much time had passed it shouldn't really hurt as much as it still did.

'See, this is why I want to be the best parent I can be for my son. I don't want to be the cause of him suffering that same uncertainty and fear. We need time together but just the two of us in the middle of that arena seems a bit intense. There's no distractions, you know, unlike the cinema or something. Maybe I should take him there instead then there's no pressure to talk. I don't even know if we've got anything in common other than our DNA.'

'You need to talk, to get to know each other the way we are.' She nudged his elbow to stop him fretting even more than he had been about the situation.

'It will help you bond much quicker than sitting in silence in a dark cinema. Listen, if it would help I could pop by and say hello, see how you're getting on. If all else fails we can break out a DVD at your place or something.'

Hunter was trying to do the right thing. All he needed was a little push in the right direction and if it meant one family could be saved some heartache she was happy to help. He deserved to have someone fighting in his corner and it might salve her conscience a fraction about her initial treatment of him.

'I'd really appreciate that, Charlotte. Exactly when did you get so good at dishing out advice to new fathers? Did you take a parenting class or something?'

She snorted at that. 'Definitely not. It's come from years of experience in how not to raise a child.'

'I'm sorry you had to go through it to be able to help me now but I am grateful to have a wingman for my first dad date with my son.'

'I'll pass on your thanks to the man who made it all possible if I ever see him again.' It was highly unlikely. Last she'd heard he'd started a new family and the last thing he'd want would be his adult daughter turning up and spoiling the doting dad illusion.

'So, as far as keeping secrets are concerned, am I forgiven?'

'You're forgiven.' How could he not be when he'd welcomed her into that sacred circle of trust?

This should've been the moment she'd wished him good luck and backed away. He and Alfie were a package deal and accepting that meant leaning towards the kind of commitment she'd always tried to avoid. She preferred her life uncomplicated but now there was a child involved it would change everything. She couldn't imagine the range of emotion he must've gone through on finding out he had an eight-year-old son he'd been denied all knowledge of but he'd accepted the role without blame or recriminations and had shown a maturity he'd been lacking during his last days here. Family hadn't worked out well for her in the past and this had bad idea written all over it. Except his determination to make a better life for his son made him the noble, loving sort of man she wanted to be around more.

All she could do was try and keep whatever emotional detachment she could from Hunter and Hunter junior and let them make that connection without becoming a part of it.

It was a long night waiting for news on Colton. Not to mention uncomfortable. Hunter had stretched his legs, making several trips to the vending machine for something calling itself coffee, and Charlotte had made several attempts to garner some information, to no avail. In the end the only way they were able to make themselves in any way comfortable was to lean their bodies against each other.

On a personal level they had taken baby steps forward but it would be inappropriate to take advantage of that when they were technically still on the clock and waiting for an update on their friend. That didn't mean it wasn't killing him, having her resting her head on his shoulder and not be able to pull her closer.

His cell buzzed in his pocket and he had to read the text from Gray twice before the contents sank in. He gave Charlotte a gentle shake.

'Hmm?' The sleepy response and the nuzzling further into his neck made a direct call to the side of him that had a tendency to forget the need for discretion.

'I've had a message from Gray. Look. We won.'

'What?' She blinked at the screen.

'They finished the match. We're in the finals.' He

couldn't quite believe it himself. The pride in the men who'd played out the game and won despite the awful circumstances swelled so deeply inside him he was fit to bust.

Charlotte stared at him then back at the screen and suddenly launched herself at him. Her arms wound around his neck in a tight hug.

'We're in the finals,' she said, and he couldn't help but laugh with sheer relief. It was the best news they'd heard all night.

'Dr Michaels? Sorry to keep you waiting but I just wanted to let you know Mr Colton is out of Theatre. The surgery went as well as we hoped for. We had to open up the thigh in order to operate so there is a significant wound that will be at risk of infection but he's out of immediate danger. We'll be keeping a close eye on him over the next forty-eight hours.' The surgeon who'd met them on admittance delivered another helping of good news with that same relieved grin he was sure they were all sporting.

'Can we see him?' Charlotte was wide awake now, on her feet, and would probably be in the room, checking on him, if she knew which ward he was on.

'He's sleeping now. I don't want to disturb him and it might be best if you change before you do see him.' There was a nod towards their crumpled attire and Hunter saw Charlotte tense next to him but it wasn't something she should take offence at.

'Of course. It wouldn't do much to aid his recovery to see us covered in his blood. Would it, Charlotte?'

He saw the penny drop as she gazed first at his crimson-stained shirt then her own. They'd scrubbed their hands clean since their arrival in the building but the evidence of the evening's battle for Colton's survival was in the very fabric of their clothes.

'No. It wouldn't be very nice to be reminded. We'll

come back in the morning to see how he is. Thank you for everything you've done tonight.' She shook hands with the man in green scrubs first and Hunter did the same.

'I think you two played a huge part here too. Now go get some rest.'

Hunter waited until the surgeon was out of sight before he took Charlotte's hand and marched her out of the building.

'What are you doing? Where are we going?' She was digging her heels in as they rounded the corner but they both needed to blow off some steam after the night they'd had.

'We need to celebrate. Do you really think the rest of the team aren't out partying now they know Colton's okay and they've bagged a place in the finals? We'll be lucky if they've recovered from their hangovers in time for the trip to Nottingham.'

'Look at the state of us.'

'It's getting dark. No one will see.' It was that time just before complete darkness moved in when everything was a muted shade of grey. The perfect camouflage for them to venture out in public without someone thinking they were two criminals escaping the scene of a brutal crime.

'Yeah, outdoors.' She didn't sound convinced but she followed him nonetheless.

That small sign of trust was a bigger prize to him than tonight's win over the Cobras. Now he was under pressure to produce something to deserve it. In the middle of nowhere. The gas station he'd set his sights on at the end of the road might not appear to be the ideal venue for first-class entertaining but he was determined to make this night memorable for the right reasons. He wanted to do something for her after she'd been there for him tonight, listening and advising on how to connect with his son.

'Wait here. I'll only be a few minutes.'

'What are you up to, Hunter?'

'Shopping,' he said vaguely, before leaving her on the other side of the automatic door. In truth he had no idea himself what he was doing but he'd improvise. They deserved some down time and a little fun following the stresses of the day. He for one wasn't ready to go home alone and attempt sleep when he knew his mind would be running over the alternative outcomes of their medical intervention and what could have happened out there on the ice.

Distraction filled two carrier bags and he hoped there was enough there to persuade his companion to remain in his company for a while longer.

'We all need to go through those silly teenage rites of passage and although there's no back row for us to mess around in, I'm sure I saw a forest park somewhere nearby.' He began his march again, thankful that the spring weather was being kind for once. It was mild enough for them to sit outdoors without hypothermia claiming them and that was unusual for this place. He'd been here when the first daffodils had been poking their heads through a layer of snow at this time of year. It was positively balmy here in comparison.

'Surely you're not being serious?' Her laugh rang through the darkness like musical wind chimes, bringing life to the still night.

He could just about make out the dull edges of the nearby picnic tables against the linear forms of the trees in the background.

'Always. Which is exactly why we both need a time out from being adults. I thought we could combine dinner, celebrating our win and Colton's recovery and pretend we're still teenagers all at the same time,' he said as he deposited his purchases on the wooden bench.

'In a picnic? Here? At this time of the night?' She wasn't more than a dark smudge now in the fading light but she did take her place at the table, waiting to see what he had planned. He had her engaged in something other than hockey or painful childhood memories at least.

'Never let it be said Hunter Torrance doesn't know how to party.' He unpacked a plaid travel rug he'd picked up at the cash register and laid it out.

'I don't think that was ever in doubt, was it?'

'Well, I've never done it *sober*. This was the closest I could get to alcohol.' He produced two small bottles of non-alcoholic sparkling white grape juice.

'I'm sure if I could see it I'd be impressed all the same.'

'Aha!' He rummaged in the bottom of the bag for the two glass candle holders and set one at either end of the bench before lighting them with the small box of matches he'd purchased too.

Charlotte sniffed the air. 'That smells very, uh, sweet.'

'Vanilla ice-cream, I think it said on the box.'

They flickered to life and cast a small pool of light over the scene. Charlotte's smiling face was revealed in the glow of the small flames and made all this effort worth it.

'It's making me hungry.'

'Good. Now, I'm afraid they didn't have a fine dining section because you know I would totally have shopped there. You'll just have to make do with chicken salad sandwiches and if you're good I might even let you have a cookie.'

There were many *oohs* and *aahs* as he laid out their makeshift dinner, both pretending this was some kind of grandiose feast. It could have been a three-course gourmet dinner as they wolfed it down with the same gusto.

'Do you woo all the ladies in your life with moonlit picnics in the park?' Charlotte surprised him with the question just as he was taking a mouthful of not-champagne fizz. Tears sprang to his eyes as he gulped it down the wrong way.

'I can honestly say this is another first. There have been no other picnics and very few ladies since Sara.' He couldn't even remember the last time he'd been this relaxed. These past years he'd been working his backside off, trying to rectify the mistakes he'd made, with no time for frivolity. Cutting loose with Charlotte showed him it didn't have to have negative connotations. The only thing that would make this perfect would be if Alfie was here too. It was all so easy when he was with Charlotte and he wished his rapport with his son could evolve as naturally too.

'Well, thank you. You've made me feel very special tonight.' She couldn't believe he had done this for her and had tried not to get too carried away with the romance if it was simply part of his usual seduction technique.

He'd come halfway across the world, given up his life there to come and be a proper father to Alfie, and she knew his son was his priority. Not that she would expect him to put someone he'd just met above that but they did seem to keep gravitating back towards one another.

'That's because you are. Didn't I say I'd share my cookies with you? I don't do that with just anyone.' He grinned and offered her the packet of chocolate-chip heaven.

She snacked on the crumbly biscuit and watched with fascination as he tidied the rubbish into the bin and laid the rug down on a patch of grass with the candles either side. 'Have I just sold my soul for a cookie? Is this where you sacrifice me to appease the hockey gods?'

'We could do that or, you know, just chill with some star-gazing.' He made himself as comfortable as he could, trying to fit his large frame onto half of the small rug, with his knees bent and his hands behind his head.

She had nothing to lose by joining him. Except perhaps all feeling in her backside when she tried to get up off the cold ground again.

'This is what you did as a teenager? I imagined something more rock and roll.'

'It might've involved a beer or two I'd sneaked out of the house but, yeah, I liked to lie in the quiet and just look at the stars. I used to imagine what was out there in the universe waiting for me, prayed there was more to life than the one I had.'

'You and me both.' Although she'd chosen hockey games as her fantasy landscape.

'Those three bright stars in a row are Orion's belt and that right there is the Big Dipper.' He pointed up at the constellation of seven stars.

'I think we call that The Plough over here but I've never taken much interest, to be honest.' There'd been nothing there to capture her imagination until tonight when Hunter had been so transfixed and the most relaxed she'd seen him to date. He looked just like the naïve kid they'd probably both been before real life had crept in and made them so jaded.

'I'm a bit of a nerd about it, I guess. I could bore you with the names of all those stars if I had a mind to but we're supposed to be having fun.'

'I *am* having fun. I didn't know you were into astronomy. I'm finding out so much about you tonight.' She knew every time she looked up at the sky from now on she'd always think of him and this night together. This gesture to recapture the childhood ripped from her was something she'd never forget.

He turned his head to look at her. 'Isn't that what you wanted?'

They were lying so close together she could see the twinkle in his eye. He hadn't planned this, she was pretty sure, but it had done the job. Hunter had told her everything she needed to know in order for her to let him into her heart. It didn't make it any less scary about taking that chance on him.

She reached across him so her face was only millimetres from his, her chest brushing against his, and watched his throat bob as he swallowed. As quick as a flash she grabbed the cookie from his hand and stole back to her own side of the blanket.

'This is what I wanted,' she said, and took a bite of her ill-gotten gains. It would do him good to be kept on his toes now she'd laid herself bare emotionally.

'Yeah? Are you sure that's all you have a craving for?' He rolled over and pinned her to the ground with one arm either side of her body and began kissing his way along her neck. It was so damn hot the much-sought-after cookie slid from her hand into the grass, now totally forgotten.

'Uh...maybe not.' She threaded her fingers through his hair as every blast of hot breath on her skin sent her into raptures. It was true. Ever since that first kiss she'd craved more of this, more of him, and tonight had taught her that life was so fragile you just had to grab the good times where you could.

'Good,' he murmured as he closed his mouth around hers and sealed her fate. She was lost to him now, whatever the consequences.

They ignored the first drops of rain as they fell, so wrapped up in each other they didn't care. Even when the candles fizzled out and Charlotte could feel the dampness on Hunter's skin she was reluctant to break away from him again. She was content where she was with his body pressed against hers and passion keeping them both warm. Unfortunately it couldn't keep them dry when the heavens opened and doused the flames.

She let out a shriek as they scrambled to their feet, the rain so heavy it was dripping off the ends of their noses and their clothes were sticking to their skin. It would've been romantic if not for the sudden drop in temperature and the very real possibility of pneumonia. They snatched up their waterlogged belongings and headed straight for shelter in the wooden hut where the forest route map was displayed.

'I'll phone for a taxi back to the arena so you can get your car.' Hunter wrapped her in the blanket, which was slightly less sodden than her clothes, and pulled out his phone.

Charlotte chattered her thanks through her teeth. As much as she didn't want this night to end, she needed a hot shower and a warm pair of pyjamas to get her body temperature back out of the danger zone. Sharing a bed naked with Hunter would undoubtedly have the same effect but sleeping with him wasn't going to make things any less complicated.

'I'd say that was a successful first date, wouldn't you?' Hunter tucked his phone back in his pocket and huddled in beside her.

'Is that what it was?'

'We're together outside of work commitments... Good food, great company... I'd call that a date.' He nodded his head, pretending that he'd planned the whole thing all along. If that had been the case he might've added an umbrella or a hot-water bottle to his purchases.

'You're a smooth operator, Mr Torrance, I'll give you that.' It had been her best first date ever.

A car approached from the main road and dazzled them in the headlights. Their ride back to reality.

'So, my place or yours?' Hunter leaned in and made her very tempted to carry on the impulsive nature of the evening but she was a woman who didn't give any part of herself so easily.

'It's a first date, isn't it? I'm afraid I'm just not that kind of girl.' She dropped a kiss on his cheek and walked nonchalantly towards the taxi, hoping their next dates would live up to the high standard of this one.

CHAPTER SIX

HUNTER WONDERED IF Charlotte might've had second thoughts about getting involved with a father and son when there was no sign of her at the rink. Now she'd had time to think about the implications of his tangled personal life there was a possibility she'd back out of the offer to support him today. They'd had fun in the park together but she hadn't signed on for a third party. Neither had he.

The strong connection he'd made with Charlotte hadn't figured in his plans when he'd moved out here but he couldn't imagine not having her in his life now. He didn't want anything to affect his relationship with Alfie but she was good for him and surely his happiness would filter through to his son too? A dad who'd found someone he enjoyed spending time with and could really talk with had to be better for him than a man still locked in his own world of guilt and regret.

His day was made with the sight of her walking in and giving him a tentative wave, as if she didn't really know if this was a good idea either. Hunter waved back, careful not to let go of Alfie as he took his first wobbly steps on the ice. This was an exercise in trust and if he let him fall it would be difficult to get him to have faith in him again.

He'd had to get Sara's parents to agree to this unsupervised afternoon out with Alfie and it did feel a little as though he was betraying their trust by inviting Charlotte along too. They hadn't been thrilled about the prospect of their grandson pulling on his first skates and Charlotte had been right about treading softly, not rushing things, when his relationship with the O'Reillys was still fragile, to say the least, but her presence meant a lot to him.

He tried to convince himself that this *chance* meeting wasn't deceiving anyone. It was more about having a friendly face around, someone to help fill the long silences with his son when he couldn't quite find the words himself. After their impromptu picnic in the park he was also happy to see her on a more personal level. He wanted that chance to reconnect and maybe even advance their relationship a little further too.

'I've got you. Don't worry.' He grabbed Alfie's arm to steady him as he began to lose his balance. One heavy fall could be all it took for him to lose interest in the idea of skating altogether and he wanted this to be the one thing he could do for his son that no one else could.

Alfie was still getting his bearings, clinging onto the barrier with one hand and Hunter with the other, as he tottered around the rink.

'Hi. I just thought I'd call in and let you know I've been up to the hospital to see Colton. He's doing well, all things considered, though he's not happy about missing Nottingham.' Charlotte skated out to meet them halfway around.

'That's good. I'll try and get up to see him myself at some point.' For some reason he felt as skittish as a boy on his first date. He was glad to hear his teammate was on the mend but he couldn't get past the worry over this meeting to truly relax. He'd spent more hours lying awake fretting over this than he'd ever had before a big game.

There weren't many women he imagined would've been willing to take on a hockey reject and his grieving son with such understanding. He was almost afraid to think his luck might be changing for the better since moving back here. Now he'd made amends for his past misdeeds perhaps karma had decided to give him a break after all.

'Hi!' Alfie too greeted her, giving Hunter the opening for an introduction.

To his credit, the boy wasn't shy about meeting new people, not even with the man who'd turned up after eight years, claiming to be his father.

'Alfie, this is Charlotte. She's the doctor for the Demons. Charlotte, this is Alfie, my son.' It still choked him up to say it out loud and held such significance the words deserved a choir of angels and light splitting the heavens to accompany them.

There was pride in being able to claim this beautiful boy as his own. The best thing he'd ever accomplished in his life was being his father, albeit a recent surprise. It also made him question his parents' behaviour more than ever. By blood, or through adoption, being a parent was a privilege, not a right, and those who'd professed to be his guardians had taken it for granted, abused that position.

After being declined the role and the chance of being there for Alfie's milestones, he couldn't imagine treating a child with the disdain he'd been subjected to. He hated all of those involved, or not, in his upbringing yet there was still a morsel of sympathy to be found in the situation. They'd never experienced the love and special bond between parent and child, and never would. More than that, they'd never know their grandson. He'd let them all know about Alfie's existence because there had been too many secrets to date but their selfishness would never let them accept another child into their lives. It was better for Alfie, and him, that it remain that way. He was just so afraid of making the same mistakes he was literally tongue-tied around him.

'Cool. Hi, Charlotte.' Alfie reached out to shake her hand and Hunter was pleasantly surprised that Sara and her parents had raised such a well-mannered young man. It made life easier for him and gave him more reason to be proud, even though he didn't deserve any credit for how he'd turned out. All he could do was continue to raise him in a manner of which Sara would've approved.

'Well, hello, Alfie.' Charlotte too appeared completely bowled over by his charm, which boded well for the afternoon ahead.

Hunter didn't know what he would've done if Alfie had blanked her or taken umbrage to her being here with them because he was sure as hell glad to have her here.

Unfortunately, Alfie's gesture left him off balance since he'd let go of the barrier. His blades slid from underneath him and Hunter had a job keeping him upright.

'Whoa, there.' Luckily Charlotte was there too to take his other arm and help steady him.

'I'm not very good at this.' Alfie's head went down and Hunter was afraid this wasn't as much fun for him as they'd both anticipated.

'It's all about balance. If you hold your arms out straight and bend your knees a little, you shouldn't need to hold onto anything.'

'Like this?' He recognised that stubborn tilt of the chin as his son gradually let go of his hand. That independent streak had definitely made its way into the next generation.

'You're a natural. Now just push off with one foot and follow it with the other. Good lad.' Hunter thought he would literally burst with pride at how quickly his boy was learning and following in his footsteps.

'I'm doing it!' The over-exuberance at his success set

Alfie off kilter again and the wobble was enough to bring Hunter and Charlotte back to catch hold of him again.

'This is your first time, right? Well, you're already doing better than I did. The first time I stepped onto the ice I ended up flat on my backside, with a bruise the size of a dinner plate.' Charlotte moved in before his confidence was too dented with one of her own painful tales.

'Well, they do say the most important thing to learn is how to fall properly. If you do feel yourself falling, bend your knees and sort of squat. Put your hands out to break your fall but make sure you clench your fingers into fists first.' He demonstrated the safest way to fall because it was a key part of the learning experience.

'Do you know something? I was able to skate by the end of that first lesson. All it takes is a bit of courage. Something I'm sure you have oodles of. Then someday you might even be able to play your dad at hockey.' She gave Hunter a wink and he almost lost his own footing. He'd been right to take her up on her offer today. If it was possible he could have both of these fantastic people in his life he would find a way to do it. As much as Alfie demanded he fulfil his responsibilities as a father, Charlotte was there to remind him he was still a man with his own wants and needs. He was able to be himself here today in their company, a whole person and not just someone playing the role he thought people wanted.

'And beat him?' Alfie's eyes were wide at the prospect, as if it was the coolest thing he'd ever heard.

'Probably.' Hunter wouldn't care. It would mean the world to him simply to be able to play hockey with his son.

'Can I try again on my own?'

'Sure.'

He happily stepped aside to let burgeoning confidence take flight, every shaky step bringing him closer to his son.

The three of them began to make their way slowly around the ice, he and Charlotte on standby to catch their student if he fell, but it wasn't long before Alfie was striking out on his own. Watching his son skate out onto centre ice could've been a scene straight out of Hunter's dreams about the future come true. A future which he was hoping Charlotte might become a part of.

He did what he always did to distract his mind and grabbed an abandoned stick left from practice and lined up an attempt on goal. There was nothing like smashing pucks into the net to prevent him from getting soppy about finding someone who really understood and accepted him, chequered history and all.

Before his stick made contact with the rubber disc, Charlotte appeared from nowhere with another hockey stick and intercepted the puck from him. She took off behind the net to slot in a wraparound goal herself.

'Easy,' she taunted, skating backwards down the ice, leaving him with his mouth hanging open and Alfie cheering.

'Where did you learn to skate like that?' He was impressed. She had proper hockey skills that went beyond the remit of the team doctor. Usually, all that was required for that position was an ability not to fall over if and when they attended casualties on the ice, and even then that was with assistance.

Just when he thought he knew everything about her, she went and surprised him again.

'I took some lessons when I was a teenager.' Things had been getting a bit too cosy for Charlotte, too much like a family day out, and she'd decided to break out a few of her moves to shake things up. She wanted Hunter and Alfie to bond but she was worried she was becoming too involved.

Goodness knew why she'd volunteered to crash this

father-son bonding session. It wasn't as if she had any more experience than Hunter did in these matters. She just knew by making the effort he was a good dad and she wanted to encourage the sort of relationship she'd always dreamed of with her own father. This waver in Hunter's confidence over his parenting made him all the more human and less of that two-dimensional pin-up on her wall with no real feelings or worth.

In the space of a few days he'd become so much more to so many people. The team needed him as their physio and friend, Alfie needed him as a father and, well, she just needed him. He'd invaded all areas of her life and suddenly she couldn't imagine not having him there to talk to, to have fun with, and to kiss when the urge took her. Yet meeting Alfie today represented a commitment of sorts on both sides and that terrified the hell out of her.

Today was simply about being emotional support for Hunter. By all accounts, it was the first time anyone had stepped up for him in that way. She was keen to make a good impression on Alfie too. The fact Hunter had kept him a secret told her exactly how much he meant to him.

She'd never contemplated having a child of her own, much less someone else's. That responsibility for another's well-being wasn't something she was prepared to take on when this thing with Hunter would probably fade before it got serious anyway. He had his son, she had her career, and those were totally conflicting priorities that could never gel long term.

No, she'd let this attraction play out until it became obvious they were still a world apart. That's why it was probably best for this informal meeting with Alfie here at the rink where there was no pressure. She didn't want him confused into thinking she was going to be a potential mother figure. That would be too much, too soon, for all of them. He'd end up hating her before getting to know her if he thought she was staking a claim on his father when he'd only just found him. It was a minefield already.

With a flick of the wrist she scooped up another puck and tapped it from side to side, daring him to take it from her. Okay, she was showing off but she could see Alfie was enjoying the sparring. He'd even picked up a stick himself and she knew there was nothing father and son would love more than to face each other on the ice. Leaving her out of it.

Hunter suddenly set off down the ice towards her, and she gave an inward yelp whilst briefly thinking about making a run for it. Face on, he made an intimidating opponent, shoulders broad even without the padding of his kit, and thickly muscled thighs driving his every move. It was no wonder he'd struck fear into the opposition and love hearts into the eyes of his fans.

In this game you couldn't show any weakness, even when a powerhouse was headed straight for you. She stood her ground, hands clenched around the stick, bracing herself for the hit. At the last second before inevitable impact, he pivoted his hips and came to a slow stop, scooting ice over her skates.

'Just remember, us *brutes* have skills of our own,' he said, easily reclaiming the puck now she'd been rendered immobile.

Some men might have been miffed at getting challenged by a girl, many had in various aspects of her life when they'd underestimated her abilities. Not Hunter. That oh-so-kissable mouth was turned up at the corners as he squared up to her. Charlotte tried to come up with a smart comment to get him to back out of her personal space but he was so close, giving her that tachycardia-inducing smoulder, she could barely think straight.

'I think it's Alfie's turn to take a few shots.' She turned away from Hunter so she was no longer under his thrall. This exercise was supposed to cool things down, not turn her and the ice into a puddle with the heat they were generating.

'Sure.' Hunter adopted the goalie position, almost filling the net with his broad frame, whilst she skated back to find him a new challenger.

'I'm not sure I can…' Alfie was managing to balance with his stick resting on the ice but they all knew it would be a different story if he took a swing at a puck.

'Don't worry, I'll help you.' This was about him and his father having fun together and she wouldn't let this time end on anything but a high. She wanted him to make the memories she'd never had with her dad so he always had something to look back on fondly.

She skated behind Alfie and placed her hands either side of his waist. 'You keep your feet on the ice and I'll push. When we get close enough to the net you slide that puck in wherever you think you can get it past your dad.'

'Got it.' Alfie leaned over, knees bent and hockey stick in hand.

'We're coming for ya, Hunter!' she bellowed, getting caught up in Alfie's determination to show off his new skills.

'Bring it on.' The Demons' sexy substitute goalie grinned, urging his opponents to take their best shot.

She steered Alfie on a steady course to meet him and as soon as they reached the goal crease, he guided the puck to the tiny space uncovered to Hunter's left. Hunter stretched too late to prevent it from going in and Charlotte wasn't sure if she or Alfie cheered loudest.

In their race for a goal, no one managed to think about how they were going to stop and they collided with Hunter, all three tumbling into a heap. He took the brunt of the fall so they landed on top of him, laughing, in the back of the net.

'This is the best day ever!' Alfie took turns to hug them, the unsolicited affection taking her by surprise. She was like a rabbit in the headlights, unsure how to proceed for her own safety in case one wrong move spelled the end of life as she knew it. This was supposed to bring Hunter and his son closer, not pull her into the relationship. Yet she couldn't seem to help herself hugging him back, her heart melted by the gesture.

Hunter mouthed a *thank you* over the head of his son and she found she no longer noticed the cold seeping in through her clothes. The duo of Torrance smiles was more than enough to keep her warm. She was sure it was Hunter who'd become suddenly misty-eyed, not her, but the ball of emotion almost blocking her airway told a different story.

This was how a father was supposed to love his child and it highlighted even more what she'd missed out on all of these years. Parenting wasn't something that could be done from a distance. These two needed each other to feel complete and it was a revelation to someone who, up until now, had been content in her own company.

Family time was much more fun than she remembered.

Hunter couldn't remember his life ever being so full, or being so at ease with everything in it. It had been a busy few days and not solely because they were preparing for the play-offs. The afternoon he'd spent with Alfie had been such a success he'd been granted more access by the O'Reillys. It was all down to Charlotte. She'd had more faith in his abilities as a father than he'd had and simply having her there had helped put him at ease. That skating session had almost been like watching Alfie walk for the first time in hockey terms and as close to those missed milestones as he'd ever get. He'd be grateful to her for ever for facilitating that special day. It just wouldn't have been the same without her.

Since then he'd been able to pick his son up from school, take him out for pizza and generally do all the other things dads took for granted. As cautious as the O'Reillys were about his credentials as a reliable adult, he got the impression they were glad to have someone to share the childcare with and get some of their freedom back too.

The only downside of the whole situation was that he hadn't been able to spend as much time with Charlotte alone as he'd expected. It would be a balancing act of his time, trying to make sure neither was too freaked out by the other's presence in his life, but if Charlotte was going to be in his life she'd have to understand that Alfie came first. He was wary of letting things get too serious when he couldn't fully commit to her. Experience had taught him a very harsh lesson—a romantic relationship impacted on more than just him.

It was one thing to risk his heart again but he was a dad now. He'd hurt Sara by being so cavalier with her emotions and he wasn't about to do that to his son too. Unlike his parents, he cared about the damage he could inflict with a careless attitude towards his charge. He just hoped Charlotte was on board with his parenting approach too. Especially since he'd had to cancel their date tonight at short notice to babysit Alfie so the O'Reillys could visit a friend in hospital.

'Can we watch this one, Dad?' His companion for the evening selected a movie for them to watch together, a hugely popular animation that ordinarily would have seen him reaching for the remote control. Not tonight. He'd be content to sit on the couch with his son even if there was nothing but a blank screen in front of them.

'Anything you want, bud. Your choice.'

'Did you watch this when you were my age?' Alfie tilted his head to one side with that quizzical look Hunter had come to recognise. He'd become increasingly curious about his father's background, and whilst it was heartwarming that he had an interest in getting to know him better, Hunter didn't want him to delve too deeply. If possible, he'd prefer to avoid conversations about his family as long as possible.

'No. This wasn't out when I was a kid.'

'But you had cartoons in Canada, right?'

'Sure. Although the graphics are better these days.' And not the billion-dollar merchandise factory they were now. At least, he'd never had any expensive movie franchise toys but that could've been entirely down to his adoptive parents' refusal to spend that kind of money on a son they barely cared existed.

On the flip side, if he and Alfie enjoyed watching this together, Santa Claus would be raiding the workshop for every related item he could find this Christmas.

'Does it snow all the time in Canada? We only get it here sometimes and then the rain washes it away.'

'It depends on the time of year. We have seasons like everyone else.'

Alfie thought for a moment and Hunter was on tenterhooks waiting to hear what would come out of his mouth next. The boy was clearly trying to process their different backgrounds and try to relate better to his father.

'Can we go someday? To Canada? Together?'

Hunter had been so consumed with getting his life set up here it had never occurred to him that Alfie might want to visit his homeland in return. It might be kind of cool to take him back, show him the sights and make some happier memories there. Some closure would be good.

'We'll have to talk to your grandparents about that but a vacation would be nice. Someday.' He wouldn't make any promises he couldn't keep but he would have the summer relatively free…

Alfie jumped up on the couch next to him, close enough for Hunter to know he was after something else. 'Maybe we could visit your mum and dad too? Do they know about me?'

They'd done it again. Somehow his parents still managed to ruin the good times without even trying.

'Yes, they know about you, Alfie, but I'm afraid I'm not really in contact with them any more. I'm sure we wouldn't find the time to see them anyway with all the cool things there are to do out there. You know Canada's the home of the Stanley Cup, the championship trophy for the winner of the NHL play-offs? I'd really love to take you to a hockey game over there if I could.' It was difficult to be diplomatic and avoid hurting Alfie's feelings at the same time. He could rage about his parents and what terrible people they were but there was no point in them being a black cloud in his son's life too.

'Oh. Okay.'

Not even the prospect of an NHL game was able to lift his spirits again and Hunter knew the kid just wanted to get to know his family. It was better for him in the end to keep his distance but he knew that heart-sinking realisation that wishing for something simply wasn't enough to make to happen.

'Don't worry. You've got me and your grandparents here to love you and we're not going anywhere.' He wrapped an arm around his son and gave him a reassuring hug. It was important in these circumstances that Alfie learned to focus on the positives, who and what he did have around him. It had taken years for Hunter to do that.

'And Charlotte?' Alfie looked up at him with hope in his eyes and Hunter was afraid he was going to have to disappoint him even more.

'Well, uh...' He didn't want to lie but neither did he know what the future held for him and Charlotte or how long she would be in their lives.

The doorbell rang and saved him from having to explain his complicated love life to an eight-year-old. He jumped up and practically sprinted to the front door to avoid that conversation.

'Hi, Charlotte.'

It had been Alfie's idea to invite her along too and Hunter had worried it was asking too much of her. Her last involvement with Alfie had been as a favour to him in an effort to get to know his son. A cosy family night in might be taking things too far, too quickly. Then he saw the bag of popcorn and the huge bar of chocolate in her hands and he realised she was in this with him.

'Are you sure this is okay? I mean, this is your time together. I wouldn't have come except he was so insistent on the phone...' She was already turning back before she'd given him the chance to invite her inside and he could see the debate going on in her head about whether or not this was a good idea.

The significance of her coming here tonight wasn't lost on either of them. She wanted to be part of this tonight, part of their lives and, regardless of the long-term implications, Hunter couldn't have wished for a better addition to the evening.

He threw the door open wide. 'Come in. You're more than welcome.'

The only thing that stopped Charlotte from throwing

the movie night treats at Hunter and beating a hasty retreat was the sound of Alfie laughing in the next room. He was the reason she was there, gatecrashing their father-son time again, simply because she didn't want to let him down. Hunter had been very apologetic with the last-minute change of plans and his son's plea for her to come over, and she had the impression he wasn't any more comfortable with the set-up than she was. It was natural for him to protect Alfie by keeping her at a distance—after all, she'd had the same worries about getting involved when there was a child in the picture—but she and Alfie already seemed to have formed a bond of their own. Goodness knew, she'd missed seeing both of them these past couple of days.

'Thanks. If I'd been left alone with all this junk food in the house I might have been tempted to pig out.'

'I'm sure I can find someone to help you out with that. I'll get a bowl.' He took the bag of popcorn from her, leaned in close until his cheek was touching hers and whispered, 'I'm really glad you're here.'

With those words of acceptance she was able to walk into the house knowing she'd made the right decision in the end by taking the risk.

'Hey, Alfie.' She peeked into the living room to say hello and make sure he was still on board with her being there.

'Charlotte! Guess what? My dad's going to take me to Canada and we're going to see someone called Stanley and an ice hockey match.'

She needn't have worried as Alfie launched himself at her, fit to bust with his news.

'Really? That sounds amazing.' Relations really had improved if they were thinking about taking an unsupervised holiday and she was pleased they were getting on so well.

Hunter walked in armed with the sugary treats and rolled his eyes. 'Now, Alfie, what did I say?'

'Maybe. Someday,' he muttered into his shoes.

Those same words made Charlotte's stomach sink for him. She'd heard them over and over again when she'd asked her father if they could spend time together in the early days of her parents' separation. In his case they had always meant never but she knew Hunter was different. He was trying to build his relationship with his child, not walk away from it.

He set the snacks on the coffee table as he huffed out a breath. 'Well, I guess it won't hurt to price the flights in the meantime.'

His solid confirmation as one of the good guys immediately lifted the mood in the room and by the time the credits rolled and they'd scoffed their fill, Alfie was sound asleep in her lap and she was cuddled up against Hunter. The perfect night in.

'You two really seem to be hitting it off,' she whispered, so as not to wake the sleeping boy.

'You too. I'm really glad you came. The only reason I didn't suggest it myself was because I didn't think it would match up to the evening I'd originally planned for us.' He stroked her arm with the back of his hand, raising goosebumps with every stroke.

'Oh? And what did that include?' Whatever it was, it would be hard to top this right now, but he was being so playful it was impossible to resist finding out exactly what he'd had in mind.

'Dinner, music, a little wine…' His phone buzzed on the coffee table next to the empty popcorn bowl and robbed her from finding out what the rest of that evening entailed.

'I guess that means time's up?'

He nodded, already moving away from her. 'They're home from the hospital and keen to get Alfie to bed.'

'It's a shame they won't let him spend the night when he seems so at home here.' It seemed the most obvious thing in the world to someone on the outside, looking in, but she knew Hunter wouldn't do anything to rock the boat with Alfie's grandparents. He was being more patient than she would ever have expected given his strong emotions when it came to his son. During his playing days it would've taken a lot less for him to lash out and turn any precarious situation into complete chaos. She believed he'd changed from those days and she prayed Alfie's guardians would recognise it soon too.

He simply shrugged and gave a half-smile as he rose from his seat. 'Maybe. Someday.'

From him that was an optimistic outlook on what had to be an increasingly infuriating acquiescence to their wishes.

She eased Alfie's head onto a cushion so she was free again and reached for her shoes, which she'd kicked off at Hunter's request to make herself comfortable.

'What are you doing?' he demanded with a glare, arms folded across his chest.

'Getting ready to go home.' She was under no illusion she'd be part of Alfie's bedtime routine. It wouldn't do Hunter's cause any good if she rocked up at the O'Reillys' with the two of them. They were grieving for their daughter, about to hand over custody of their grandson, and she doubted having a strange woman on the scene would instil their confidence in Hunter any further.

'Is that what you want?' He was still frowning at her and for the life of her she couldn't figure out what she'd done wrong.

'I'm not going to insist on accompanying you back with Alfie, if that's what you mean. You can rest easy on that account. I'm done gatecrashing for the night.' She really didn't want him to be under the misapprehension she was going to wedge herself into both of their lives at every given opportunity. This was a one-off. Probably.

'That's not what I meant. I just thought you might wait here until I came back.'

Charlotte sank back into her seat. It might've been a swoon if she'd been standing up, like a regency heroine who'd been propositioned by an infamous rake.

'Oh? Now, why would I do that?' She couldn't help herself. Every time he alluded to spending some alone time she wanted him to spell out in graphic detail what he imagined that would include. It was as close as they got to dirty talk with a child in the room.

Hunter leaned down and whispered in her ear. 'I think we're past the dinner stage but there's always time for music, a little wine...'

In the end it was his unspoken intentions that had her bunching the upholstery in her hands as she fought arousal from completely taking control of her body. She was still sitting there, clutching the furniture, as he scooped Alfie up and took him home.

There was no mistaking what would happen if she waited for him to come back and she had to admit the idea of spending the rest of the night with him, in bed, sounded delicious. If it wasn't for the implications tomorrow morning. Then there would be no confusion about what was going on between her and Hunter. A few kisses here and there and they could still keep up the pretence there wasn't something serious going on that could alter the course of their lives.

Yet her feet still refused to move and her heart wouldn't quit yearning for the chance to truly be with him. Even for one night. It was a risk when every step forward with him brought her closer to that family commitment she didn't want, but tonight had shown her some risks were worth taking.

Not for the first time Hunter was glad he'd found a house close to Alfie. As much as he wanted to get back to Charlotte as quickly as possible, he was still able to take his time putting his son to bed. He was sure the grandparents hadn't approved of tonight's snack choices but he reckoned he had eight years of treats to make up to his son and a little junk food was fine in moderation. After all, someday these sorts of decisions would be entirely down to him. The consolation for their disapproval was Alfie's sleepy smile as he tucked the covers around him, which said he'd enjoyed the evening every bit as Hunter had.

Alfie had treated Charlotte more as a friend than a threat, or someone trying to replace his mother, and that was all he could ask for. In turn, she'd been her warm, kind, funny self and not once had she patronised or treated him with anything other than affection.

He hadn't even known he'd wanted her there until she'd been in front of him, but it meant everything to him that she'd wanted to spend time with them just for fun. There'd been no obligation, no plea from him to be a conversation starter this time, but she'd voluntarily pitched up to see them anyway. To him that proved she saw Alfie as more than an inconvenience or someone she was simply forced to endure. She genuinely cared. There weren't too many women who would've taken a last-minute date cancellation so well, never mind brought treats for her replacement. He was a lucky guy. One who desperately wanted to believe he could have it all.

The lights were still on in the cottage when he pulled up outside and he hoped that meant she was still inside, waiting for him. He hadn't planned any of tonight's events, they'd pretty much happened organically, but he did know he wanted to spend the rest of the night with Charlotte.

He let himself into the house to find her in the kitchen, pouring two glasses of wine. The hypnotic swing of her hips as she danced along to the radio drew him straight to her. Just like the earlier cosy family scene on the couch, it was too easy to forget this welcome-home sight was a one-off. But it was fun to play make believe every once in a while. He wrapped his arms around her waist and kissed the back of her neck.

'I found a bottle of white in your fridge. I hope that's all right?' She turned around to hand him a glass and took a sip from her own. He watched the liquid coat her lips and a sudden thirst came upon him that had nothing to do with alcohol.

'Was tonight that bad you couldn't wait for me to get back?' he teased, and took a sip before placing the glass back on the kitchen counter.

'I thought it would get the wine and music out of the way quicker so I could see what else you had planned.' She bit the inside of her cheek as she teased him right back.

He slowly and silently took the glass from her and set it down. Somewhere in the distance the saxophone sounds of nineties power ballads set the mood for seduction as he moved in. 'Nothing's planned. I thought we'd just see where the night takes us again.'

It took him straight to her parted lips to indulge in the tangy taste of wine and temptation. He inhaled the scent of her sweet perfume as he bunched her hair in his hands and deepened the kiss. She was most definitely real and his for as long as she wanted.

Over these past days she'd given him everything he could ever have asked for, joining forces to help him at work and at home, and trusting him not to let her down. That was a big deal given her past history and he wanted more than anything to prove he'd been worth the risk.

He cupped her breast through her grey sweater but the bulky fabric was too big a barrier between them for his liking. He loved her urban look, especially the tight black jeans that were showcasing her pert backside and long legs tonight, but the top layers left too much to the imagination.

'Take it off,' he demanded, his desire to see her, feel her turning his voice to a growl.

She leaned back and did as he asked, revealing a decidedly feminine silky black bra. He brushed his thumb over one nipple until it tented under the silk covering. Charlotte arched her back and primal instinct took over as he latched his mouth around the suckable point, taking fabric and all into his warm mouth. He flicked his tongue over the covered tip but it wasn't enough to satisfy either of them. He yanked the straps of her bra down her arms to free those perky nipples for his full attention. She fitted perfectly into the palms of his hands and he lapped his tongue over the soft mounds of flesh, lingering on the sensitive rosy peaks until her groans of pleasure were filling his head.

He skated his hand down her flat midriff, popped open the button on her jeans and made her gasp as he slowly unzipped her. Beneath her silky underwear he sought her moist heat with his fingers, sliding inside her so easily his breath caught in his throat. She was ready and waiting for him, yet he wanted to do this for her, give her some of the pleasure she'd already given him.

He made small lazy circles at first, opening her up to him, exploring her, with the slow, intimate rub. Those ever-increasing circles soon picked up pace to match her desire, stimulating that little nub of nerve endings that had his body at its mercy too. When he pushed his thumb into her she clutched at his shirt and he knew she was close. Her body tensed around him and his excitement reached critical levels right along with her.

She buried her face into his chest to muffle her groans, panting as he pushed deep inside her and that final burst of climax claimed her.

He was having trouble breathing himself and rested his head against her shoulder. 'Next time, I want to hear you scream, Charlotte.'

'Next time?' she said through hiccupping breaths as she adjusted her underwear.

'The night's still young and so are we.' Every muscle in his body was trembling with restraint but he didn't want this to be the end.

He took her by the hand and led her up to his bedroom, every creaking stair beneath their feet making this feel more illicit by the second when he'd never been more certain he wanted to be with someone in his life. This wasn't some random hook-up or a habit he'd simply fallen into and hadn't had the courage to break. He was emotionally involved with Charlotte and that made this virgin territory for him. Once he gave himself to her he knew there was no taking it back. It was a step into the unknown he was willing to take.

Charlotte's heart was about to force its way out of her ribcage if this man insisted on more of the same. This much arousal couldn't be good for a person. He'd brought her to orgasm without even getting naked and she was afraid once he did she'd end up needing a resus team. Not that it was stopping her from stepping into his bedroom. She'd always longed to see the wonders of the world.

She gave a shiver once the door closed and it wasn't only because she was still only half-dressed. Caught in the undercurrent of their passion, she walked towards him, being pulled ever deeper until she was in danger of drowning. Hunter undid the top buttons of his navy piqué shirt, which was stretched so tightly across his broad chest she couldn't wait for him to take it off. She lifted the hem and ensured he stripped off in double quick time to reveal a body that deserved its own social media account.

Sleeping with Hunter was a bigger event than she could ever imagine for who he was now, not who he *had* been. This wasn't about a teen fantasy come true, this was a real desire to be together, a connection between two adults who needed to get this attraction out of their system so they could get back to who they were outside it.

Okay, so she was trying to have her cake and eat it but she had a very sweet tooth and a libido that apparently wouldn't quit around him. Except every second she spent with him claimed a bigger piece of her heart with his name on it.

She mightn't be ready to be part of a family, or want to get hurt again, but it didn't mean she was made of stone. In these few moments of peace there was no talk of work, family or the future, only the silent acceptance of attraction. Here, away from the messy reality of getting involved, it seemed possible they could be together without causing some sort of cosmic fallout to rip the universe apart.

Watching each other undress was somehow as erotic as tearing their clothes off in haste. Perhaps it was because they never broke eye contact, the moment more significant than simply getting naked. They were stripping away the layers of their past, the outside influences they had no need for in the bedroom and concentrating on what it was they wanted here and now. Each other.

That didn't mean she couldn't see the impressive evidence of his arousal. It was difficult to miss.

She was only self-conscious about standing here stripped

bare before him for a few seconds because when he started kissing her she didn't care about anything else. He guided her towards the bed and she took him with her down onto the mattress, body to body, mouth to mouth, heart to heart.

With his finger and thumb he pinched her pebbled nipple and made her gasp with delight. Now he was aware that was her weak spot, he latched on tightly, sucking her into his mouth until she was bucking against him with unbridled lust.

She reached down and gripped his erection, sliding her hand along his shaft until she made him equally as breathless.

'As much as I don't want you to stop what you're doing, we need some protection.'

It was understandable he'd be more careful after having one unplanned pregnancy but she was restless against the sheets, waiting for him to grab the condom from his nightstand.

He lowered himself between her thighs and kissed her on the mouth as he joined his body to hers. Their breath mingled with a mutual gasp of relief now the veil had fallen. There was no more pretence that this wasn't what they'd been waiting for, regardless of all the obstacles in their way.

Charlotte hitched her knees up to her waist, drew him deeper inside and lost all inhibitions in favour of revisiting that place of utter bliss he'd taken her to earlier. She was close to the edge again already when she should have been exhausted after the last time, not coiled and waiting for more.

So far Hunter had been a gentleman. If that gentleman was a sexy stud acting out all of her very grown-up fantasies at once. She wanted him hard and fast, slow and steady, every which way he would oblige.

He filled her, stretched her with every stroke, and she rode with him, watching the intensity of the moment play across his features. The way he looked deep into her eyes every time he joined his body to hers, the breathy sound of her name as he buried his head in her neck and the tender kisses he placed on her skin said this was more than sex for him too.

If that was all this had ever been about they could have ended this in the kitchen or on the stairs, but he'd taken his time to make this right. It was as perfect as she could ever have hoped, except for one tiny flaw. She didn't want it to be over.

This feeling of completion was to be cherished, not thrown away because she was afraid of being hurt again. Regardless of the lectures to herself on the contrary, she'd fallen for him, again, and she wondered if she was hurting herself more by denying them a future together if there could be one waiting.

Hunter panted close to her ear and prevented her from over-thinking when it was far more enjoyable just to feel. She clenched her inner muscles as another wave of arousal crashed over her and clung tighter to him, her groans matching his as they reached breaking point together. Her cry filled the room as he fulfilled the promise to make her scream and she surrendered her body, her heart, once and for all.

After what they'd just shared it was going to be harder than ever to maintain that emotional distance she'd been clinging to desperately since he'd appeared in her life. She'd given him everything of herself now and she was trusting him not to fail her when she was taking the greatest risk of them all. Her heart.

CHAPTER SEVEN

Hunter fought consciousness because that meant leaving the warm, comfy confines of his bed and he wasn't ready to tear himself away just yet. He was happy where he was, thank you very much, with Charlotte's naked body draped across his, her hair splayed over his chest keeping him warm since the covers had hit the floor long ago. Probably some time in the early hours of the morning when his amorous companion had given him the best early-morning wake-up call he could ever remember.

If rendering him immobile with exhaustion was her ploy to keep him here as her sex slave he wouldn't have a problem with it.

Last night had been amazing on so many different levels. He was making such great progress with Alfie he'd been afraid to push for more time in case he upset Sara's parents, but Charlotte's support had given him the courage to move things forward and it was beginning to pay off. His dream of being a proper, twenty-four-hour father to Alfie was within reaching distance. What part in that picture Charlotte was going to play he wasn't certain but their time together recently had convinced him it could be a possibility.

'I suppose we should really get up,' Charlotte mumbled

into his chest, letting him know she was awake too and they had responsibilities other than their libidos.

He grunted his displeasure at the idea because talking took energy that could be better spent with one last period of play. Charlotte reached across him to turn the alarm clock around, her breasts squashing against him and re-awakening a certain part of his body.

He ran his hand over her pert backside, wondering if he could manoeuvre her into another performance of her cowgirl routine.

'I wanted to check in on Anderson today and see how things were between him and Maggie before he's shipped off to Nottingham.'

'You're thinking about another man already? You really are insatiable,' he teased. It was unsurprising she was starting the day with work at the forefront of her mind when she was so emotionally attached to the team. Her dedication was just one more thing to admire in her. Even if it did come at the cost of his comfort.

She smacked his chest. 'As much as I would love to lie here with you all day, we have jobs to do and people who need our help. You need to get up.'

'I'm nearly there,' he grumbled, knowing she was right even if his idea of how to spend these last moments alone sounded more fun.

'You can stay here if you want or meet me over at Anderson's in about an hour. I need to go home and get changed. It'll only cause a stir if I turn up in last night's clothes.'

Hunter watched with growing admiration as she walked around the room, still naked, collecting their discarded clothes from the floor. He propped himself up on his elbows to better enjoy the scenery.

'I think you missed something down here.'

His shirt, followed by his trousers, landed on his head, obscuring the view, but he could hear her tutting nearby.

'As soon as I put my mind to rest that everyone is match fit for the play-offs, I'm all yours. In the meantime, you need to be a big boy and get yourself dressed.'

'Spoilsport.' Though he hated to agree and deny himself these remaining moments with her, he had a few last-minute tasks to do himself, including saying goodbye to his son. Which he wasn't looking forward to. Even a couple of days apart was going to be quite a wrench for him.

By the time he'd taken his blindfold off, she'd wrapped the smooth curves of her body in the bulky quilt off the bed. Playtime was over.

He was aware her job and her reputation were everything to her but that didn't mean he'd go quietly. Sleeping together marked a change in their relationship and not something they should simply walk away from without acknowledging it. She clutched her quilted modesty tighter as he crossed the room towards her.

'I had a good time last night.'

'Me too.' She watched him through lowered lashes, surprisingly coy after everything they'd done together, to each other.

He wanted to tell her that he didn't want it to be over between them, that they should make a go of this, but those past mistakes haunted him still. Sara had had to deal with the mess he'd left behind for years and he didn't want to do the same thing to Charlotte if he wasn't one hundred per cent certain this was going to work out. The only definite commitment he was able to make was to his son.

'I guess we should face the outside world, though. I'll grab a shower and meet you at Anderson's. You can let yourself out, right?' He walked out of the bedroom towards the bathroom because he was having serious thoughts about throwing her over his shoulder and carrying her back to bed, pretending there was nothing to keep them from being together.

'Right. I'll see you there, then.'

Hunter didn't want to think about how small her voice seemed as he shut the bathroom door on her because he knew whatever happened next someone was bound to get hurt.

Charlotte was almost praying Hunter wouldn't be at Anderson's house as she walked the short distance from her place to his. It wasn't that she still wanted proof he didn't have her commitment to the job, she needed a time out when she could think clearly without their naked bodies getting involved. After last night she was risking her peace of mind more than ever by continuing to be with him. This wasn't just about him now, he came with an Alfie attachment, and she was fast falling for them both.

'Good morning, Dr Michaels.' Hunter joined her on the doorstep, waiting to be permitted entry to Anderson's personal life.

'Morning, Mr Torrance.' Pretending they hadn't just spent the last twelve hours naked together was going to be tough when her insides were already dancing with glee at the sound of his voice.

'Thank goodness you're here, Doc. There's something wrong with Maggie.' Anderson opened the door so quickly they were almost sucked inside by the vacuum he'd created.

'Where is she?' Charlotte pushed past him in search of the patient.

'On the couch. We were just talking and she collapsed.' Anderson and Hunter followed her into the living room where the red-headed Maggie was slumped in her chair.

Charlotte hunched down beside her as she started to come around. 'Maggie? My name's Charlotte. I'm a doctor. Gus said you aren't feeling too well.'

'Just a little woozy.'

Charlotte checked her pulse and felt her forehead but there were no obvious signs of anything serious.

Anderson appeared at her side, clutching at Maggie's hand. 'Is she okay? Is the baby going to be all right?'

'How far gone are you, Maggie?' There was already a small bump visible under her tight tank top but she wanted confirmation.

'Coming up on three months now but I only found out a few weeks ago.'

Which coincided with Anderson's descent into madness.

'How have you been feeling generally? Any nausea? Tiredness?'

Maggie nodded. 'Morning sickness, although it seems to go on for most of the day. I can't seem to keep anything down.'

'The first trimester is generally the hardest. It should start to get better from here on.' Not that she knew, or had ever intended to find out.

Hunter appeared at her side with a glass of water. 'I hear ginger biscuits can help with that.'

She couldn't help staring at him. That definitely wasn't information generally found in anatomy textbooks.

He shrugged. 'Internet forums. You know...'

She did know. Without a doubt he'd researched every aspect of parenthood the minute he'd found out about Alfie because that's the sort of man he was now. A wonderful, caring father who wouldn't leave anything to chance.

'I'll get some today,' Anderson assured Maggie, still refusing to let go of her hand. At least they appeared to have patched up their differences and that was good news for everyone.

'Have you had your scan yet?' It would probably put their minds at rest if they could see their baby was all right and might help Anderson get used to the idea of becoming a father. Make it real.

Maggie checked her watch. 'We were just on our way to the hospital for the appointment. We can still make it if we try.'

'You need to take it easy. Tell her, Doc.'

'Gus is right, you do need to take it easy, but I don't think there's anything serious going on. You're probably a little dehydrated. Make sure you mention everything at your appointment. You are going too, aren't you, Gus?' Charlotte would be happier if Maggie was checked over at the hospital where they could run any necessary tests to rule out anything more sinister and it would be better if Maggie had his support.

'I wouldn't miss it for the world.' He rested his hand protectively on Maggie's burgeoning bump, every inch the proud father-to-be.

Whatever had happened between the couple since Charlotte and Hunter's chat, he appeared to have grown up overnight and accepted his responsibilities. It seemed some men were capable of changing and maturing when they became family men, even if her father hadn't been one of them.

'I have to make another house call but I can give you a lift to the hospital if it would help? Trust me, you don't want to miss a minute of this pregnancy.' There was sadness in Hunter's voice and Charlotte knew all too well the reasons behind it. He'd been denied these early moments—the scans, the first kick and the anticipation of the birth. He was a good father and he deserved to have that chance all over again. That was exactly why this romance was never going to work long term. She wasn't the woman he needed to complete his family.

'That would be great, thanks. Are you okay to walk, sweetheart?' Gus was on his feet immediately, clearly keen to see his baby and get the all-clear as soon as possible.

She knew very well the difference a couple of days could make when it came to relationships when her uncomplicated singleton life now seemed a long way away.

'I'm fine.' Maggie smiled at him, the look of a woman in love that said they'd worked on those communication issues.

Hunter chivvied them all outside to his car. 'Are you coming too? I thought we could make that last house call together. We can both say goodbye before we leave for the play-offs.'

'If that's what you want…'

She knew exactly who and what he was talking about and damn if she wasn't a little choked up. It was a step further into his life, and into Alfie's, by taking her with him to say goodbye. That made this more than a casual affair. She knew he wouldn't risk hurting his son with such a move unless it really meant something and it suddenly made her want to take a step back.

Perhaps the intensity of last night had made her too carefree with her heart because now she felt as though she was standing on a trapdoor, just waiting for the drop to certain doom. She wasn't part of this family and that left even more chance she'd be the one left behind if things went wrong. As much as she wanted to be with Hunter, her self-preservation meant more.

They dropped Anderson and Maggie off at the hospital before they picked Alfie up for a spot of lunch since he was still on half-term holidays for school. If he hadn't already phoned ahead and told him they were coming, Charlotte would've backed out there and then.

She remained in the car at the O'Reillys' rather than cause any controversy by showing up on the doorstep and making any sort of claim on their grandson. In contrast, Alfie had bounced up as pleased as Punch to see her, and at any other time she would've been put at ease about joining them.

They called into the local fast-food place where the Torrance men devoured burgers the size of dinner plates before Hunter broached the subject of their trip.

'You know I have to go away for a few days?'

'With the team?' Alfie asked through a mouthful of fries.

'That's right. It's play-off season and we have to go to Nottingham for the weekend. I'll phone you every morning,' he promised, and Charlotte imagined it was as much for his own peace of mind as his son's.

Alfie paused in mid-chew and flicked a glance between Hunter and Charlotte before he swallowed. 'Is Charlotte going too?'

'Hmm-mmm.' She nodded then made a well-timed exit towards the bathroom, leaving Hunter to have that particularly delicate conversation with his son.

It was awkward on so many levels, not least because they hadn't discussed this weekend away as a couple. They'd be travelling for work purposes but it would be naïve for either of them to think things would remain strictly professional between them for the duration of the trip now. At best she was hoping they could have a what-happens-at-the-play-offs-stays-at-the-play-offs attitude to save her from getting involved any deeper and still get to enjoy the physical side. Not that they could explain that to an eight-year-old boy and she wasn't even going to attempt it. That was Hunter's call and nobody would thank her for interfering.

Unfortunately there was a queue for the one bathroom on the premises and she was forced to stand in the hallway around the corner, where she could hear the conversation she'd tried to avoid.

'She's the doctor for the team so, yes, she'll be travelling too.'

'Is she your girlfriend?'

Charlotte had to smile at the forthright Canadian side of the gene pool. Why dance around a subject you wanted a straight answer to?

'I guess... We've been spending a lot of time together. Would that be a problem?'

Alfie was worryingly silent, and Charlotte's heart was in her throat, waiting for the answer. It must be so much worse for Hunter. If his son didn't want her to be in their lives she knew he wouldn't force the issue, and where would that leave her? Time ticked by like treacle as they both waited for Alfie's verdict.

'I like her.'

'Me too.'

'Is she going to be my new mum?'

'I...er...it's too soon to be thinking about that. I don't know. Would you want her to be?'

'Well, she wouldn't be my *real* mum but she is cool.'

Charlotte's heart stuttered right along with Hunter's voice and she was unsure whether to duck back into the bathroom or leave the premises altogether. She couldn't breathe. The last thing she wanted was for Alfie to rely on her being around. The boy had only just found his father, found a stable influence, and it wasn't fair she should be included when she knew nothing of how to parent. She couldn't bear the pressure of that expectation if she and

Hunter didn't work out. Didn't want to be the cause of more pain and loss for him when she knew all too well how devastating that could be to a child.

There was no way she was lining herself up to be Alfie's mum, or anyone else's, and if that was what Hunter was looking for it was definitely time to back off. She'd already let herself get too involved, permitting her heart to take over from common sense.

Hunter and Alfie were still too raw to include her as anything but a passing acquaintance in their lives, even if they couldn't see it. If she was going to risk her heart and her dignity again, she needed some chance of a happy ending too. The wicked stepmother never got hers. It usually comprised a grisly death or a lifetime of misery.

She waited until they broke apart before she re-joined them. It would've been insensitive to interrupt them and immature to walk out without saying a word. In Alfie's eyes she didn't want to be anything more than a friend. A non-threatening, nothing-serious female friend. It was probably best if it stayed that way.

She plastered a big smile over her slowly breaking heart. 'Who wants some ice cream?'

It was her prerogative to eat her body weight in chocolate fudge ice cream to console herself when she was going to have to put a stop to this runaway affair.

'Me!' Hunter and Alfie chorused with their hands in the air.

She was honestly delighted for them that they'd built the foundation for a lovely life together. It just shouldn't include her in it.

By the time they'd polished off their desserts it was nearly curfew time for Hunter and Alfie. She'd seen him anxiously checking his watch, not wanting his allotted time with his son to end but unwilling to get on the wrong side of Alfie's gatekeepers. It was difficult for him and she wouldn't purposely make things any more complicated for either of them.

'Could you drop me home before you take Alfie back?' She ignored Hunter's startled reaction to her request, knowing full well he'd avoid a scene in front of Alfie by asking why.

In his head it probably made more sense for her to wait here or in his car until he'd dropped him off, so they could continue their quality time together. However, for her, that time had passed. If she made the decision to break up with him now before anything else happened it would be kinder in the long run. He got to keep his son and she got custody of her dignity.

They travelled the short distance back with Hunter quietly seething in the driver's seat next to her, hunched over the steering wheel, jaw clenched, forbidding a conversation he didn't want to have in front of his son.

'Thanks for lunch.' She was already unbuckling her seat belt and opening the car door before either of them had a chance to respond.

Unfortunately Hunter's quick reflexes hadn't waned since his hockey-playing days. She heard the engine being turned off and the car door open and close before she even had her house keys in her hand.

'Why the sudden rush to get away? I know I've been a bit preoccupied with Alfie but I promise I'll devote my full attention to you for the rest of the evening.' The growl in his voice and the sudden darkening in his eyes was promise enough of a good time.

Charlotte's libido insisted she abandon the moral high ground to taste the delights he was offering her. A night of passion from the man who could turn her insides to mush with innuendo alone was almost too hot to even contemplate. Every time he looked at her that way her body shivered in anticipation, but the fantasy was over.

'I would never deny you that time with your son. I know every second is precious after missing so much. That's why I'm taking a step back, Hunter. It's too much, too soon for me. I have enough to worry about with the play-offs. I'm sorry, this simply isn't going to work.'

There, she was letting him off the hook. He should be grateful she was making this easy for him, not frowning as though someone had confiscated his skates. Fatherhood had to be about more than his ego.

'I don't understand.'

He wouldn't because she wasn't going to tell him she'd overheard their heart to heart and make him feel any guiltier than he already did.

'Of course you're going to need to spend time with your son, it's only natural. What kind of person would I be if I didn't understand that? You two are making great progress and with Anderson back on track too we should probably quit while we're ahead. If you think about it, neither of us are in the right place to start anything just now.' She forced brightness into her eyes and smile to hide the shadow suddenly cast over her heart.

She was being honest in that she wouldn't deny them their time together—this was a child who needed his father, and vice versa. This situation simply highlighted the need for all the defence mechanisms she'd somehow forgotten in the chaos of getting to know them both.

It just proved how much you had to sacrifice for the greater good where kids were concerned, even when they weren't yours.

He stood there, forcing her to watch the pain and confusion burrow into his handsome features. So this was how it felt to hurt someone? How did her father or Hunter's parents ever live with themselves when her stomach was churning with self-loathing and a sudden urge to whip herself with birch branches?

'We've got the play-offs. We should concentrate on that and put this all behind us.'

'And you'll find that easy to do?'

'Yes.'

The intensity of his stare burning a hole into her soul, searching for the truth, made her breath catch on the lie. At least at the end of the season they'd be able to concentrate on their other priorities, away from each other.

'Right.'

It was a body-check to his ego but he'd get over it, over her, in no time at all. Really, they'd only known each other for a few short days. Not enough to expect him to spend the night crying wrapped in a comfy duvet, the way she'd probably spend her night. That was totally her prerogative. As was trying to be altruistic here.

'So I guess I'll see you at the airport.' She didn't hang around so she could feel any worse. This wasn't going to be a clean break when she'd be flying off soon for a weekend away with the very man she should be avoiding at all costs. There was a very strong chance she'd discover breaking up with him was the last thing she wanted to do.

CHAPTER EIGHT

ORDINARILY THE PLAY-OFFS were the high point of the season and this one should have been especially sweet for Hunter. He was back with the Demons and they'd made it to the finals. However, he seemed to have built an immunity to play-off fever. He was excited for the guys but it was no longer the most important thing in his life.

It had been harder than he'd imagined leaving Northern Ireland, leaving Alfie, even for a few days. He missed his son already. There was a hole in his chest, a void in his day and that awful sick feeling that something was missing. Not even his numerous phone calls home had helped improve his general mood.

In the end he'd had to concede it wasn't only his newly forged role of father that had him propping up the bar, staring into his drink, while the rest of the team was getting an early night.

He was missing Charlotte too. It didn't matter they'd shared the plane, the bus and the workload getting here, the emotional ties had disintegrated. Worse still, he didn't even know why it had happened or why it was bothering him so much.

He'd taken the grilling from the O'Reillys over Charlotte because naturally they'd wanted to know who she was. Regardless of the fact she'd cooled significantly towards him since their night together he'd defended his right to see her and had stood up to them when apparently having her in his, or Alfie's, life was no longer an issue. Somewhere deep down he'd believed Charlotte was worth taking the stand.

Ultimately it had been Alfie himself who'd put the argument to bed with a simple 'I like Charlotte. She's not my mum but she's Daddy's friend. And mine?' he'd added hopefully.

Hunter had nodded, only wishing Charlotte could've seen their situation in such simple terms too. He hadn't been actively searching for a mother for his son if that's what had scared her off. They'd been getting along well, so well perhaps he'd gotten too carried away with the idea of becoming a cosy threesome and she'd picked up on it. It was difficult not to let his hopes and dreams for the future shine through when he'd had everything he'd ever wanted as they'd skated around the rink hand in hand.

Charlotte would never take Sara's place in Hunter's heart because she'd given him Alfie but she did hold a much bigger part of it. Damn it if he hadn't gone and fallen for her. Now he was actually capable of loving himself and his son, it had left the door open for a wonderful woman just like her. Only her.

In trying to do right by everyone he'd messed everything up. He'd upset the O'Reillys and lost Charlotte, none of which was going to help his relationship with Alfie. This do-over had simply been a repeat of his past mistakes. Compounded this time because his son was old enough to witness his foul-ups and experience the consequences.

As he stared down at the murky depths of his pint he considered downing it and ordering some shots. A few years ago that's exactly how he would've coped with this—by blanking it all out so he didn't feel anything. Only the image of the disappointed faces of those close to him wouldn't let him flush everything he'd worked so hard for down the toilet. He'd done that once before and it had been too damned hard to get back to where he was now to go down that same dead end.

'Hunter Torrance. I'd heard you were back in town.'

He almost had the self-pity knocked out of him as a meaty palm slapped him squarely between the shoulder blades. His hand clenched in a fist in an automatic response and released again when he saw who it was. Chris Cooper, CC to his teammates, had spent a couple of seasons at the Demons before he'd moved to England to play.

Now he was assured it wasn't someone here in Nottingham wanting to settle an old score, Hunter happily shook hands and ordered his old friend a drink.

'Yeah. I'm the physio for the Demons these days.'

'I'd heard that.' CC nodded sympathetically, as many did on hearing about the career change. It didn't bother Hunter any more.

'And you? Still involved in the game?' He hadn't kept in touch with anyone, too busy trying to sort his own life out to keep track of anyone else's.

'You could say that.' CC grinned and took a mouthful of lager.

Hunter did the same, his mouth suddenly dry with that awful sensation he'd missed something big. Most of the guys he'd played alongside were retired these days and he hadn't seen any familiar names on the coach roster apart from Gray. That only left 'Management?'

'I made a few property investments along the way, made my name there after I retired and was able to buy my way back into the game. I'm part owner of the London Lasers now.' There was no boasting there, more of an I-know-I'm-a-lucky-son-of-a-gun vibe from him, but to have that sort of clout in the industry took more than a well-timed gamble.

'Impressive. So I take it you're settled in London, then? Wife? Kids?' CC had been a blow-in, just like him, so there would've been some reason for him to stick around after his playing days were over. Perhaps if Hunter had known about Alfie he wouldn't have left either.

'Married to Lenora for five years and we have two girls, Lily and Daisy.' He was beaming now, his already ruddy complexion shining with pride, and Hunter was alarmed to find he envied his marital status more than his bank balance.

Precisely when had he become the settling-down type, yearning for a wife and two point four children? Probably around the time Alfie and Charlotte had crashed into his life and turned it inside out. He'd had his days of partying and reckless behaviour. Now he found more pleasure in simply being in the company of those he loved. He didn't have to chase the good times any more when they came so easily. At least they had done until recently. He took another gulp of beer.

'What about you? Who, or what, brought you back?'

It was a simple question, an obvious one between two old friends catching up, yet Hunter took his time replying. His circumstances weren't wrapped up as succinctly as his new drinking buddy's but he was done with keeping secrets.

'I have a son, Alfie. Things didn't work out between me and his mum. As I'm sure you're aware, I…er…had a few problems back in the day.'

'Kudos to you for getting back on your feet.' CC held his glass up to toast him before a split second of panic hit. 'This is okay, isn't it? I mean, I'm not enabling your fall off the wagon here or anything?'

That was always going to be a worry for everyone who'd witnessed his overindulgence, and something he made sure to keep in check himself, but he wasn't that same hurting, out-of-control kid any more.

He clinked his glass to CC's. 'Those days are long gone. I'll be tucked up in bed after this one. I've turned into something of a bore since becoming a dad.'

'Some might call it being responsible. There's nothing like having kids to curtail the partying. So, you're settled for good in Ireland?'

'That's where Alfie is.' He'd never really considered being anywhere else.

'And you have a permanent position with the Demons? It's all set in stone?' CC was digging even deeper than Charlotte had in the beginning but Hunter had no more skeletons lurking in his closet. At least, none he was aware of.

'Well, no. Not as yet. I was drafted in on a handshake. I'd like to stay on but I'll be working on building up my own practice too once I'm settled.' That had been his original plan but reaching out to Gray had given him his lucky break and enabled him to make the move sooner than expected. It might've been a trial run but it was also a pay cheque whilst he got to know his son.

'Hmm.' CC twirled the cardboard beer mat between his fingers, his mind working overtime somewhere else.

'Hmm, what?'

'We could do with a stand-up guy like you with the Lasers. We've built up quite a medical team focused on strengthening our players. It would be good to have you on board next season.' The steely set of his jaw said this was a serious offer, not a throw-away comment over drinks.

'Are you serious? I mean, the last time we saw each other I was a bit worse for wear.' Whilst the job offer had damn near knocked him off his bar stool, he didn't want CC to be mixing him up with someone else.

'I think tossing the entire team's collection of sticks across the ice was a particular highlight but, yes, I'm serious.' He rested his elbow on the bar top and leaned in. 'Look, everyone deserves a second chance. I've been there myself. Let's just say there was a dark period in between hockey and the property empire. I know what it takes to start over and that's the kind of strength and determination I like to see on a résumé. Besides, who's in a better position to know what hockey players' bodies go through than an ex-pro?'

This had come so out of the blue Hunter couldn't process it and found himself having to break it down in simple terms to get his head around it. 'You're *actually* offering me a job? In London? Wow!'

CC nodded and his belief in Hunter's abilities on face value made it tempting to latch onto the exciting opportunity. A job in London could set him up financially for some time to come and offer so many opportunities for him and Alfie. A new city, new team might finally help him put the past behind him for good. He'd only been in the dad role for a short time and he'd already fallen back into old habits by getting involved with someone without properly thinking it through. He still had to find a way to break it to Alfie that Charlotte would no longer be in their lives and the last thing he wanted to do was let his son get hurt in the crossfire of his love life.

A new start away from the everyday reminders of his failures might be just what they needed to start healing. It wouldn't hurt to find out a bit more about it at least.

'Come see me tomorrow before the game. We can have a proper discussion in private.' CC pulled a business card from his wallet and gave it to Hunter.

CC downed his pint and shook Hunter's hand as he got up to leave. 'Oh, and good luck for the finals. You're gonna need it.' Even here and now between old teammates the competitive spirit was alive and kicking.

'We don't need luck when we've got skills, bro.' Hunter popped the sophisticated silver and black calling card into the back of his wallet along with the picture of his son.

As he'd discovered, life never panned out the way he often expected and he had to make the most of opportunities like this where he could. It wasn't every day he found people who still had faith in him. Charlotte had been the first person in a very long time to show that belief in him as a father and a medical professional and he'd lost her. Perhaps it was time to start over with a clean slate somewhere new.

The atmosphere between Charlotte and Hunter since that afternoon with Alfie felt as though someone had run the Zamboni right through it, coating the surface with fresh ice. It seemed to her they were both afraid to take the first step out and be responsible for leaving deep grooves in the calm, crisp surface.

Things had been as cool as could be since they'd boarded the plane to Nottingham. They hadn't moved on from small talk about the team injury list. It was probably for the best. If they ventured into more personal matters she might actually break and tell him she'd overheard his conversation with Alfie and panicked and she didn't want him to talk her around, tell her things would work out. She was getting in way too deep.

Hunter Torrance, her colleague as well as a single father, was more heartbreak waiting to happen. More than she was going through now. She could just about bear the broken glass stabbing pain in her chest every time she saw him, every time she imagined his lips on hers. Another afternoon spent playing happy families only to have it torn apart again would shatter what was left of her soul.

If she'd let herself get drawn any further into their developing relationship it would've meant opening her heart up for two, double the potential sense of loss when it didn't work out. It couldn't work out. Hunter was a family man now and she was a career woman. One successful season with the Demons and her client list would be a mile long at her own clinic. Her job was her baby and it wouldn't hurt anyone but her if she failed at it. Not that she had any intention of that now it would be receiving her full attention again.

'Anderson certainly seems to be back on form. He showed me the baby scan. I guess fatherhood really does change a man.' Even with the sound of the crowd ringing in her ears she couldn't bear the silence between her and Hunter as they stood and watched the game, or the noise of her own thoughts.

The Demons had five minutes left in the third and final period of play in their match with the Glasgow Braves. They were one nil down and to her amazement Anderson hadn't lost his cool once, even after a dodgy offside decision. He'd taken it on the chin and got straight back into the game without wasting a second of play. A week ago he'd probably have been in danger of being prosecuted for GBH.

'Maggie's here, supporting him, and I know they've told their folks about the baby so I guess it all worked out. It's amazing what simple communication can do for a couple.' The barbed comment said he was still miffed by the way she'd ended things.

Okay, she mightn't have handled it perfectly but she'd been in a panic. She didn't respond well when cornered and that's how she'd felt, trapped, listening to his heart to heart with his son. Over these past years she'd learned to run rather than walk away when things started to get serious and they didn't get more serious than having a kid in the picture.

'Hunter, I—' Her lame apology and explanation was cut off by a deafening cheer as Anderson scored an unassisted goal.

He didn't hear her attempt to build bridges, celebrating the equaliser with his own 'Yes!' as he punched the air.

That unexpected surge of vocal passion gave her chills beneath her fleecy jacket, pinching her nipples into little beads of need begging to experience that passion again for herself.

She would've failed to snag his interest again even if she had figured out what to say as tempers began to fray on the ice. With everything to lose in this semi-final both teams were involved in a bit of pushing and shoving, trying to reclaim possession of the puck. One of the Glasgow players received a two-minute penalty for roughing, giving the Demons a power play, an extra man on the ice, in the dying moments of the game.

Shot after shot was launched at the opposition's net with the one-player advantage, each successfully blocked by the net minder as the seconds ticked down on the scoreboard,

Ten. Nine. Eight...

The sound of sticks hitting rubber echoed around the arena as players valiantly fought for victory and fans held their breath for that last burst of emotion, be it joy or sorrow.

Time seemed to stand still, players moving in slow motion as they made their final attack. The battery of Demons launched themselves down the ice in a fearsome display of gladiatorial determination to survive the battle.

Seven. Six. Five...

The puck passed from player to player, taking the game towards the opposition. Both teams crowded into the penalty area, a scrum ensuing in the goalmouth. The Demons' captain, Floret, claimed the last shot with a mighty thwack.

Goal!

The Demons were play-off finalists.

The arena erupted and as ecstatic as Charlotte was about the win, she knew she and Hunter wouldn't have a chance to reconnect for the rest of the evening. Tonight's success and preparation for tomorrow's battle would keep them otherwise engaged. She should've been glad there was less chance she'd have to explore that idea of communication he was keen on but tomorrow officially ended the season, and with it this period of her life with Hunter. Even if they both returned next season, this break sounded the death knell of their relationship.

Instead of making her feel light and carefree, the thought of no longer being part of Hunter's or Alfie's lives left her feeling numb.

It was difficult to get the players to sit still long enough for a post-game check-up. They were still buzzing behind the scenes long after that final klaxon sounded their win.

'You need that hand seen to.' She practically had to drag Evenshaw into the room so she could treat him.

'Don't fuss. It's only a scratch,' he said, wiping the blood down his shorts.

Men, why did they have to be so damn stubborn?

Take Hunter, for example. She'd ended their relationship and yet he wouldn't stop staring at her as if he had a right to.

As the visiting side at the arena, they didn't have the luxury of the space they had at home to treat their patients. She was currently sharing the small box room with Hunter, acutely aware of his eyes on her regardless of the sweaty players swarming in and out.

With an antiseptic wipe she cleaned the blood away from her patient's palm and watched him wince despite his protestations anything was wrong. It was a clean slice, probably from someone's blade, which thankfully wasn't too deep. She'd seen a lot worse recently. It was a sport where speed, sharp skates and rivalry definitely didn't mix well.

'You'll be pleased to know you don't need stitches.'

'See. I told you.' He attempted to get up to join the rowdy celebrations next door.

'Sit.' She pushed him back down into the chair so she could dress the wound properly.

'Yes, ma'am! I do like a woman in charge.' His toothless grin and flirty wink got him nothing except a cuff on the shoulder.

It was a joke, something she didn't take too seriously, but one look at Hunter and she was worried he might wade in and try to protect her honour.

'Ouch. Not so hard.' The unfortunate player on the massage table took the brunt of his apparent rage. Some might have said kneading muscles a tad too roughly was an improvement on smashing up equipment but Charlotte doubted his current patient would agree.

'Sorry.' Hunter returned his gaze from Charlotte back to the burly thighs of the net-minder who'd overstretched during his heroic saves.

'So…can I go now?' Her patient's impatience drew Hunter's attention once more.

'Er…yes. Try to keep that dressing dry and stay away from sharp objects.'

'Yes, ma'am.' He didn't need to be told twice and bolted towards the ruckus going on in the locker room.

'You're finished too.' Hunter gave his permission for the net-minder to go and join the celebrations too as he went to wash his hands.

Within seconds Charlotte and Hunter were alone for the first time since she'd called things off and she tried to get out as quickly as possible to avoid a scene.

'I'm looking forward to the team dinner. It's the most important meal for staff as well as players. I think we all need to replenish our energy stores with protein and slow-acting carbs. I'm starving.' It was a lie. Food was the last thing on her mind but if they were going to have to talk she wanted to keep it neutral.

'What happened to us, Charlotte?' Hunter seemed to see straight through her bluster, his calm, measured voice a contrast to her erratic rambling. It made her question who was actually having more trouble accepting the break-up.

'It doesn't matter, it's over.'

'Just tell me why and I'll walk away. I won't bother you again.'

She knew she couldn't keep lying to him because he'd torture himself about what he'd done wrong when in truth he'd only ever done right by his son.

'I overheard you and Alfie talking and I... I couldn't have him thinking that I'm going to be part of this new life you have planned together. It would only end in tears. His and mine if we'd carried on believing in the fairy-tale. I'm sorry.'

He stared at her, unblinking, probably trying to rewind back to that supposedly private conversation. 'Charlotte, he's a frightened eight-year-old boy still mourning the loss of his mother. You think I should've put him right and said we're just having a fling? I was trying to protect his feelings, to reassure him there isn't going to be any more disruption in his life. I wasn't asking you to be his replacement mother. All I wanted was for you to give us a chance. I'm trying to be careful about saying and doing the right thing so I don't hurt anyone again the way I did his mother.' Hunter's sincerity climbed along the back of her neck and stood the hairs there to attention.

'I guess it doesn't matter now.' If only they'd managed to leave emotions other than rampant lust out of the equation she might still be with him. Except she knew her feelings for him had gone way past merely the physical aspects of being together and distance was no longer a safety net for her fragile heart.

'I guess not.'

'We'll chalk it up as another one of those teenage impulses we needed to get out of our system.' She forced a smile but she felt sick to the stomach pretending that was all it had been to her, and to him. A part of her wanted him to fight for her and salvage something of what they'd had but he remained silent, unmoved by the suggestion.

There was a sharp knock on the door, calling time on their heated confessional. 'Let's go, people. The party bus is here.'

'We should really try and catch up with everyone before they leave without us.' She turned towards the door, unable to look at him any more without tears filling her eyes. It really was over.

Hunter needed to go along with Charlotte's decision to end things because it had become impossible to ignore the growing feelings he had for her. She was much more than a friend to him. Generally, his buddies were a lot hairier, missing a few teeth, and only good company over a beer or two. He didn't spend every waking moment thinking about kissing them or wanting to knock out one of their players for coming onto her.

After everything she'd told him about her past he could see why she was wary about getting too close but that chemistry between them wouldn't simply dissipate because they deemed it inconvenient. It made London seem more appealing by the second if Charlotte was never going to be part of the family he wanted for himself and Alfie. He couldn't see her day after day at work, pining for her yet knowing she didn't feel about him the way he did about her. She was right—it wasn't fair for Alfie either to watch him develop an attachment to someone who wasn't in this for the long haul. There didn't seem any point in fighting for someone who clearly didn't want them in her life.

They made their way back out the maze of corridors to find the team bus but a familiar meaty hand on his back soon stopped him in his steps.

'Good game, eh? I suppose it doesn't matter to you who wins or loses now. After today I do expect your loyalties to lie with the Lasers. Glad to have you on board, bud.' Another back-slap Hunter could've done without forced a strained smile on his face. CC wasn't to know his timing was completely off. It was no one else's fault but his own that he hadn't mentioned their conversation with Charlotte yet.

'What's he talking about?' She was staring at him, not seeing CC's departure, only his revelation.

'I've been offered a permanent position with the Lasers.'

'You're leaving?' Her brow knitted into an ever-deepening wound.

'I agreed to a meeting. That's all.'

'What about Alfie?'

'It was Alfie I was thinking about when I said I might be interested. I thought it could be a new start for both of us in London.'

'What about the team?'

'It was only meant to be a temporary position. I'm sure Gray would understand if it came down to it.'

'What about me?' Her voice was small, almost impossible to hear even in the relative quiet of the arena as the Zamboni trundled out to begin cleaning the ice. If only life was as easy to start afresh, leaving no trace of past traumas, people would be a lot happier with their lot.

'You said you didn't want to be part of us.' Yet he could see the hurt etched in her furrowed brow and her soulful brown eyes.

'So the first sign of trouble and you're running away again? I thought you were the kind of man who fought for the things that mattered? I guess that really doesn't include me.' She folded her arms across her chest as if she was protecting her heart. He knew his was breaking with every painful second he spent with her, unable to touch her or tell her how he really felt about her because there was no room for second thoughts when it came to Alfie's future.

'I'm not running from anything. You were the one who didn't want commitment, remember? I was just—'

'Keeping your options open? I said I didn't want to commit to you and Alfie because I was afraid I'd get hurt. Turned out I was right all along. There is no room for me in your life. Not really. I'll always be the one you leave behind if a better offer comes along.'

'I'm a washed-up hockey player in the back of beyond. Of course I'm going to jump at the chance of a better life for my boy. He is always going to come first.' He couldn't care less about the money or social status, that stuff had stopped being important a long time ago. The truth was, the idea of him, Alfie and Charlotte cosied up in his cottage would be bliss if it were possible. Recent events had shown him it wasn't. It was selfish of him to have believed he could have everything he wanted, someone was always going to suffer as a result.

Ten years ago this would've been much easier. That cavalier attitude to other people's feelings wouldn't have given him this stabbing pain in his gut. At times such as this he missed the old Hunter who hadn't cared about anything except making time to wallow in liquor or his own self-pity.

'Of course he is. Well, good luck in London, then.' Charlotte turned her back on him and walked away, her refusal to lose her cool and get emotional harder to watch than if she'd burst into tears. It signalled her retreat back to where she'd been when they'd first met. She'd been right in trying to protect herself from him all along. He was still making those same mistakes, hurting people he loved and walking away from the devastation.

This was the last time and it was for the right reasons. From now on he was completely devoted to Alfie. As he should've been from the start.

CHAPTER NINE

DINNER HAD BEEN an awkward affair. At least between him and Charlotte. Much like having to live under the same roof after a break-up. An impossible situation that couldn't be avoided and made for a very frosty atmosphere. It wasn't helped now they were back on the team coach on the way back to the hotel with darkness falling outside. She'd taken the aisle seat across from his rather than the empty one beside him. Close enough to prevent any questions being asked about why they were avoiding each other but also putting that significant distance between them. If there'd been no other available seats it wouldn't have come as a surprise if she'd chosen to sit on the floor rather than next to him again.

He didn't blame her. All he'd done lately was confirm both of their fears he would always be the same flaky guy he'd always been, no matter how hard he tried.

'Right, guys. Can I have your attention front and centre, please?' Gray stood at the front of the coach, clapping his hands for attention, diverting it from poker games, cellphones or the very attractive team doctor.

The bus lurched over a pothole, jogging everyone in their seats except Gray, who was undeterred from his motivational speech at the front. He simply planted his feet on either side of the aisle and gripped the headrests of the front seats. 'I know I've already said it—'

'Yeah. Probably at the last speech you gave about ten minutes ago.' The brave heckler at the back prompted a chorus of whoops and whistles.

Gray raised his hand to calm the noise back to an acceptable level. One where his voice was the only one getting airtime.

'Let's not get too cocky. As I was going to say, congratulations on tonight's win. You deserved it and I know we were all thinking of Colton out there.' He started a round of applause for the performance, which Hunter and Charlotte enthusiastically joined.

Getting to the final was a big deal. The season tended to be pretty flat if it ended before they made it to Nottingham so the fact they'd made it all this way had left most of them on a high. With any luck they'd be taking the trip back home with some silverware so they didn't have to come back down to earth too soon.

Gray motioned for silence again. 'That being said…'

There was a collective groan as they waited for the kicker.

'Tomorrow is another day, another game, and there's no time for resting on our laurels. I want you all up bright and early for drill practice.'

Another groan went up. Although Gray didn't linger on sentiment too long, pride was there in his grin. Somehow he managed to make Hunter feel a part of it all. That sense of belonging was something he'd been searching for a long time but he was afraid to embrace it. Nothing in his life had ever been secure for long and he wanted to change that for Alfie as well as himself.

Suddenly, there was a loud bang, followed by the

screech of tyres as the bus jolted from side to side and the driver tried to regain control.

This wasn't good.

Gray, who was still out of his seat, was flung to the floor but he was too far out of reach for Hunter to make a grab for him.

They seemed to gather speed, the confused shouts in the dark adding to the sense of disorientation. The coach veered off down some sort of embankment, branches clawing at the windows failing to slow them down. Glass smashed all around as gnarly limbs reached in and grabbed at the passengers inside.

He glanced over at Charlotte, who was hanging on to the armrest so hard her knuckles were white. He hated being this helpless, pinned by his seat belt as they hurtled at speed and unable to protect her. The driver was hitting the brakes and doing his best to swerve through the trees threatening their survival.

After what seemed an eternity of pinballing between obstacles in their path, there was another loud crash. Even Hunter was lifted out of his seat with the force of the impact as the vehicle hit its final resting place, wedged into a tree trunk.

For a few stunned seconds the only sound was the dying breath of the engine and the flickering headlights before they gave up the ghost and plunged them into complete darkness. He fumbled in his pocket for his cellphone to call for help but there was no signal. At least it came in handy as a torch if nothing else. Some of the others had had the same idea and fireflies of light began to appear in the shadows. He undid his seat belt and went to Charlotte first.

'Are you okay?' He shone the light in her face, forcing her to blink. She was pale but conscious and the relief was so overwhelming it was all he could do not to gather her up into his arms and hug her tight.

'I'm fine. You?'

'I'm good.' Now he knew she wasn't badly hurt.

'Can you smell smoke?'

Hunter sniffed the air and swore. There was no mistaking that acrid odour slowly filling the bus and his lungs.

'We need to see who's been hurt.' She unclipped her seat belt, her thoughts firmly on the welfare of everyone else.

'We've got to get them as far from here as possible.' From the front of the bus he could see the smoke curling out from beneath the crumpled hood and there was no time to waste.

The electrics were shot so he was forced to use brute strength to prise the doors open and let some much-needed air into the vehicle. He helped the driver stagger outside into the night first and went back to assist those who needed it.

'Gray? Can you hear me?' Charlotte was kneeling by Gray, checking his pulse. He was lying face down in the aisle, unmoving, and blocking the exit route for everyone else.

Hunter went cold at the thought of the injuries he could've sustained, tossed around like a ragdoll. Unlike everyone else, he'd been on his feet, unsecured and unprotected, as they'd bumped and smashed their way down the embankment. While Charlotte took care of Gray, he quickly checked the bus for other casualties but luckily everyone else seemed okay.

'Guys, can you make your way out of the emergency exit at the back and get as far from the bus as you can, please?' he shouted to those moving about at the back so they weren't putting themselves in more danger by waiting here if there was a chance of fire on board.

He crouched down beside Charlotte, holding his own breath and waiting desperately to hear any sound of life coming from his friend on the floor.

There was a moan as Gray came to and let Hunter breathe again.

'We have to get him out of here.'

'We really shouldn't move him until we know the extent of his injuries. He took quite a knock back there.' The doctor in Charlotte protested about the proposed evacuation and he understood why—she didn't want to exacerbate any injuries he'd already received, but they were fast running out of options.

'Charlotte, we have to move. Now.'

She followed his gaze outside, where flames were already beginning to lick at the windscreen.

'Okay, but we need to be careful.'

'On the count of three we'll roll him over onto his back. One...'

'Two...'

'Three.'

Charlotte cradled Gray's head so he wasn't jarred too much and Hunter eased him into a better position for them to help him. He was breathing at least and there was no sign of blood. That didn't mean there weren't any internal injuries but they couldn't leave him here. Charlotte was already coughing violently and Hunter's eyes were streaming from the effects of the smoke. If they left him here he'd die from smoke inhalation alone.

'You come down this end and take his feet and I'll do the heavy lifting.' It was going to be awkward trying to get him off this bus in one piece but he knew neither of them were leaving without him.

With another count of three they managed to lift him off the floor. Charlotte backed down the aisle, steering

Hunter towards the door with Gray's full weight resting in his arms. His lungs burned with the effort as they stumbled their way down the couple of steps. They didn't stop even when they got outside just in case there was a fuel leak that could see them all blown sky high.

'Careful setting him down,' Charlotte reminded him as they reached the road, where the rest of the guys were. A few of them bundled their jackets together to pull together a makeshift bed so at least they weren't laying him directly on the cold, wet tarmac.

Hunter had never been as glad in his life to hear Gray groan as they set him down and he knew his stubborn friend would be okay.

'Is everyone else here?' Hunter yelled to the crowd standing at the side of the road.

'We'll do a head count.' Charlotte made sure Gray was comfortable before she was back on her feet, giving everyone a provisional check-over and singling out those she suspected needed medical treatment. 'You have some cuts on your face. There could be some glass left in there. Take a seat on that tree stump over there. Has anyone phoned for an ambulance?'

'Wait, where's Scotty?' As far as Hunter could see at first glance the team was all here but their kit man was noticeably absent.

'I thought he was behind us.' Floret confirmed he'd been on the bus but there was no sign of him in this current line-up.

'I'll go back and look for him.' He wouldn't be able to live with himself if he'd left someone behind in the wreckage.

'Hunter, you can't.' He felt Charlotte's hand on his arm but even her touch wasn't enough to deter him from doing what was right. Scotty had family too and he knew if he'd been in the same position he'd want someone looking out for him.

'I have to. I promise I'll be careful.'

'In that case, I'm coming with you.' Charlotte stubbornly strode alongside him and he knew he was wasting time fighting a losing battle.

'Scotty? Are you here?' he bellowed as they reached the clearing where the bus was barely recognisable as anything other than a cloud of smoke.

'Over there.' Charlotte pointed towards a flash of colour in the midst of the grey, a small figure sitting huddled on the ground at the back of the bus.

'Scotty? You can't stay here. The bus is on fire.' He hooked a hand under his elbow and helped him to his feet but the stunned kit man didn't seem to grasp the severity of the situation.

'Let's go.' Charlotte was there as always when he needed a hand and took Scotty's other arm so they were able to hurry him away from the scene. As they climbed the embankment towards safety there was a loud bang and the sound of smashing glass as the fire took hold and blew out what was left of the windows. It had been a close call, as his pulse rate would attest to.

'Scotty, are you all right? Talk to me.'

He heard the concern in Charlotte's voice a fraction of a second before their patient's legs went from beneath him and he collapsed, a deadweight in their arms. They had no choice but to fall to the ground with him only metres away from the road.

Charlotte felt his forehead. 'His skin is clammy.'

She took his wrist. 'His pulse is rapid and faint. I think he's going into shock.'

Hunter positioned him on the ground so his head was low and his legs were raised and supported to increase the flow of blood to his head. Charlotte loosened the collar of his shirt to make it easier for him to breathe.

The distant sound of sirens filtered through the night.

'We need to keep him warm.' Charlotte whipped her jacket from around her shoulders and tucked it in around him. 'The ambulance is on the way, Scotty. Give me a nod that you understand what's happening.'

There was a small acknowledgement.

Charlotte was working hard to keep him engaged, checking his level of response, and Hunter knew it was because there was a danger this was more than emotional shock after the accident. It could also be a life-threatening medical condition as a result of insufficient blood flow through the body, leading to a heart attack or organ damage.

'Hello?' The crunch of forest debris underfoot and sweeping torch beams dancing in the distance signalled the arrival of the emergency services, guided by a few of the players.

'We're over here!' Hunter shouted, and waved them over.

Charlotte gave the rundown of injuries, the most serious ones being Gray's and Scotty's. The paramedics ably took over, checking Scotty's vitals and wrapping him in a warm blanket. As Hunter and Charlotte got up from the damp earth, she began shivering uncontrollably. He held her close, trying to transfer some body heat.

'We should get you seen too.'

'I'll be all right. I just have to make sure the others get checked over at the hospital and I'll go back to the hotel for a bath and bed. You should probably let Alfie know we're okay in case the press gets hold of the news we've had an accident.'

'I will as soon as I know you're going to be okay.' He

was a little taken aback she was thinking about Alfie when she'd been so sure she didn't want to be part of their family. That instinct to reassure him, the knowledge his welfare was the uppermost thought in her mind, said she was already invested in them both. It was a revelation that changed his own ideas about what was best for all of them. If there was a chance they could be together and work this out, he wanted to cling to it.

'I can't believe you followed me down here.'

'I wasn't just going to sit back and watch you get hurt, now, was I?' She'd put herself at risk for him and Hunter struggled with the urge to kiss her. In that moment all that mattered was that she was safe. He brushed away bits of leaves and twigs that had become tangled in her hair along the way and the movement revealed a small cut on her forehead he'd missed up until now.

'You're hurt.' He reached out and sticky blood coated his fingers.

'I banged my head on the seat in front when we hit that tree. I'll probably have an egg-shaped reminder in the morning.' She moved her hair back over her face to hide it, as if that would somehow solve the problem.

'You could have whiplash or concussion even. You know what could happen if that's left untreated. Do you have any pain? Blurred vision?' Head injuries, especially those caused by a high-impact crash, could lead to serious complications, ones he wasn't going to risk.

'Hey, who's the doctor here? I think you've a tendency to overstep your jurisdiction, Mr Torrance.' Her defences were back up as she stepped back from him and out of his hold.

Unfortunately, it was in that second her knees buckled and belied that she wasn't as indestructible as she made out. Hunter made a grab for her before she could hit the ground and scooped her up into his arms. Despite her huge personality, she weighed virtually nothing and he was reminded of how vulnerable she really was despite her insistence otherwise. He wasn't prepared to take any risks where her health was concerned.

She might claim she didn't want him in her life but that didn't mean he'd simply stop caring about her. She'd made an impression on his heart that could never be erased, even if he did move to London.

'Let's get you into the ambulance with the others.' He carried her up through the trees himself, with no intention of leaving her until he knew she was safe.

Charlotte's head was in a whirl and it wasn't entirely down to the knock she'd taken in last night's crash. Hunter's words and actions towards her simply didn't marry. One minute she was finding out he was planning a move to London with no thought for her, the next he was refusing to leave her hospital bedside, playing the role of a concerned partner. It wasn't fair when she was supposed to be getting used to not having him around. How could she remain aloof and disinterested in someone who was so clearly passionate about helping others, and about her?

He'd stayed with her until she'd been discharged in the early hours of the morning when she'd assured the medical staff she'd return if any other symptoms of concussion occurred. Gray had been kept in for observation and apparently they'd run a battery of tests on Scotty too. When she'd begged the nurses for information they'd told her he was on an IV for fluid resuscitation to raise his blood pressure again and they were looking at an ECG and bloods to determine any underlying heart problems. A bump on the head seemed minor in comparison but Hunter had insisted she get checked over too.

He'd even offered to stay with her back at the hotel—on the floor, of course—in case she needed him during the night. She hadn't accepted his offer because one night simply wasn't enough any more. She wanted for ever. For too long she'd been denying she was in love with the man because she'd known it would bring her nothing but heartache, and she'd been right. When she'd found out about the job in London the sense of betrayal, the knowledge he would happily abandon her in pursuit of his ego, had turned her into that wounded, lonely girl again.

In the end she hadn't even had breakfast with him. He'd been a complete no-show for the meal with the team, and was still missing here at training. Uneasiness settled heavily in her stomach along with the few bites of toast she'd managed. She knew where he was, he was off making great plans for his future in London without her.

Last night had proved to her how far she'd fallen for him because she'd never been as scared in her life as she'd been when he'd said he was going back to that bus. She didn't want to imagine her life without him in it if something had happened to him. It didn't matter because she hadn't fought any harder than he had to save the relationship and he'd taken that as her acceptance of his choice to leave.

If she'd only told him she was in love with him, that she wanted to spend every day with him and Alfie, he might've stayed, but she'd been too scared to take that risk and she'd lost him anyway. She didn't know whether to laugh or cry at her own stupidity, continuing to let the past overshadow the good things in her life now, and in the early hours of the morning it had been a hideous combination of both.

There was one familiar face waiting at the arena for practice but it wasn't the one she'd hoped to see.

'Gray? What on earth are you doing here?'

'The same as everyone else, I expect,' he said, coming to watch the drills out on the ice alongside her.

She rolled her eyes at him. 'You know very well what I mean. What are you doing out of hospital?'

'They sent me home so someone who actually needed a bed could have one.' He folded down one of the seats and gingerly sat down, clutching his right side.

'Hmm. Well, if they *actually* discharged you I'm sure they told you to rest.' She doubted his version of events. If nothing else, they were supposed to notify her when he was released to avoid this very situation.

'Nothing's broken, just a couple of badly bruised ribs.' He adjusted his position and sucked in a breath even with that minimal effort.

'I'm sure it's still painful though.' It didn't take a doctor to know that sitting all day in an uncomfortable chair in a cold arena wasn't going to help a rib injury.

He patted his jacket pocket. 'I've got my painkillers right here. It'll take more than a few bruised ribs for me to miss this game.'

'Well, take it as easy as you can.' Which was akin to asking a lion not to roar, but she was well aware nothing she said would persuade him to rest and aid healing.

'How are the rest of the guys? Are they fit enough to win?'

'They're a bit shaken up, battered and bruised, but there's nothing to rule them out of playing. Scotty got the all-clear too but he's doing the sensible thing and staying in bed, like he was told.'

It might be harder to keep their minds on the game after the shock of the crash. Although now Gray was here it would be a relief for them to see him and he'd certainly be a motivator to get them going. That only left one of their party MIA.

'Good.'

'Did, uh, Hunter pick you up from the hospital?' She was grasping for a rational, painless explanation for his absence. If Gray had discharged himself, as she suspected, he would've sworn any accomplice to secrecy until the deed was done.

'I phoned a cab. Where is he anyway?' He turned his head as much as his injury would allow to scour the building.

'He had to…er…take care of something. I said I would manage here until he got back.' The lie burned her tongue as well as her cheeks in the knowledge he hadn't trusted her with any such courtesy.

As it turned out, Hunter didn't make an appearance until training was over, and then without a hint of urgency in his swagger.

'You do know the season isn't over yet?' Gray arched an eyebrow at him, clearly not amused by his sudden unreliability.

Hunter shrugged off his jacket and rolled up his sleeves. 'I do know and I'm here with plenty of time to spare before the big game.'

'I hope so, for your sake.'

'Uh, Gray? I need to have a word with you. In private.' He flicked a glance at Charlotte, sufficient to justify her paranoia.

Only a few hours ago he hadn't wanted to leave her side. Now it appeared she was somehow in the way, a nuisance he couldn't wait to be rid of.

'Don't mind me. I'm only here to do a job after all.' She bristled past the two men before her anguish at her dismissal manifested in not very professional tears of self-pity.

When it came to Hunter choosing between her and, well, anything, she knew she'd lose every time.

'I do hope your personal problems aren't leaking into your career prospects again,' Gray said as they both watched Charlotte storm off.

There was no point in pretending he had the wrong idea about their relationship when she showed her emotions so clearly for everyone to see. Right now, they could both see she was royally ticked off at him.

'That's exactly what I'm trying to avoid and why I wanted to talk to you.' He inhaled a lungful of air to fortify himself. It wasn't going to be an easy conversation with any of those affected by his future plans.

Gray fixed him with a steely stare. 'You've been given a second chance here.'

'For which I'll be eternally in your debt. I don't want to mess things up with Alfie, that's why I've had to make a few tough decisions.'

'That doesn't sound good. You do know I'm recovering from my injuries here and my team, which has just been in a road accident, is about to play in the final? Couldn't this wait?'

Hunter understood Gray's frustration. It was bad timing, like every other major event in his life. The difference was that he was taking control this time, not simply letting events carry him along.

Work got in the way of the talk he so desperately needed to have with Charlotte. Although they'd been given the all-clear last night, a lot of the guys were suffering from more aches and pains than usual as a result of the accident. The trauma and exposure had kept him up to his elbows in deep-tissue massages for most of the morning. He was running out of time to set the record straight with her but he couldn't let the team down now. This was the last time he'd have the opportunity to show Gray he'd been worth the risk. If he got the Demons fighting fit to win this final they might forgive him for trying to walk out on them. Even if Charlotte couldn't.

They kept missing each other, with players coming and going between them, and having to grab breaks where they could. Not that this conversation was ever going to be one they could squeeze in between patients.

It wasn't until near the end of the game she ventured down into the tunnel, away from the bench and a mass audience.

'About this morning...' This wasn't the time or place he'd been hoping to have this conversation, with the soundtrack of bodies slamming into the hoardings playing in the background, but he needed to explain what had happened.

'Is it a done deal?'

'Pardon?' Her need to get straight to the point always threw him. That's why it had made her reluctance to talk through the end of their relationship so hard to come to terms with.

'Is it too late?'

'For what?'

'Us.'

It took a moment for the line of her questioning to register and when it did it felt as though a weight had been lifted off his chest. That didn't mean he was happy to be left guessing exactly what it was she wanted this time.

'What are you saying, Charlotte? It was only yesterday you were telling me there was no way this could work, that you didn't want to be part of my and Alfie's lives.' He still had to be careful that she meant this—that she knew exactly what she was getting into and didn't run out on him again when it hit home.

'I was scared, Hunter, afraid to get close in case I'm not

enough to keep you happy. Last night when I thought you might get hurt…it made me realise it doesn't matter how much I fight it, I'm already in love with you. I'm sorry I let my fears get in the way of what we had, what we could have if you'll still have me. I should've been prepared to take a risk, the way you did in letting me into your life with Alfie. Is there still a chance? Do you love me?' She barely took a breath and left Hunter dizzy with the rapid speed of her admissions, but there was only one thing that mattered at the end of all this. She loved him.

'Of course I love you!' When she'd been hurt last night it had become very clear to him how much she meant to him. He would've swapped places with her himself if he'd been able to and taken away even the slightest discomfort for her. He loved her and it was time to stop running away from the fact.

When she'd had doubts about being part of his family he'd snatched hold of that excuse and used it to justify a move to London. She was right, the first sign of trouble and his instinct was to run. Not any more. This time he was prepared to stay and fight.

Last night had made him see everything in a different light. She hadn't given a thought for her own safety in the chaos, following him back to the accident site to ensure his. Then there'd been her concern for Alfie, the boy she'd tried to convince herself and him she could never get close to. They were meant to be together, to be a family, if only they could face their fears instead of being overwhelmed by them.

She took a deep breath. 'That's all I needed to know… If London is where you're going to be, I'll come too. I'm sure I can set up my practice there just as easily. I'll do whatever it takes for us to make a real go of this. You and Alfie are worth the risk.' Her smile as she handed her heart to him on a plate just about broke him. He'd never imagined anyone could love him enough to give up everything for him.

'You would really do that?'

'I'll go and hand my resignation in to Gray as soon as the match is over.'

'You don't have to, Charlotte. I'm not going to London. I met with CC this morning to tell him I'm staying put. Everything I want is in Ireland and right here.' When he'd sat at that desk across from his prospective new boss and the life he'd laid out before him it had all seemed so cold and impersonal without Charlotte in it. He'd almost had the perfect family he'd always wanted and had been close to throwing it all away. He'd been willing to crawl to the ends of the earth to retrieve that final missing piece of the puzzle. Charlotte had simply got there first. 'Perhaps I was keeping you at a bit of a distance because I was worried I'd hurt you the way I hurt Sara. There's one glaringly obvious difference between then and now. I never loved her the way I love you.'

'But—but what about Gray? Have you handed in your resignation already?'

'That's why I wanted to speak to him, for confirmation I would still have a job with the Demons next season so I know I have something to offer you other than another dead-in-the-water career.' He'd been honest with Gray about what had happened, risking their friendship over the betrayal, but he was a father too and he'd understood his motives. Right before he'd told him to move his butt and get back to work before face-off.

Goal!

As they turned to face each other and confront the situation, the celebrations around the arena stalled the response he'd been waiting to hear all day. They were so locked in that moment, intent on finally resolving their status, neither even turned to see who'd scored. Although they did share a smile when the announcement came that Anderson had put the Demons ahead.

'I guess our jobs are safe for another season, huh?' He cracked a joke because he was afraid those three words he'd waited a lifetime to say had come too late. This wasn't Hollywood, there was no guarantee they'd just run titles and walk off into the sunset because he'd broken out the 'I love you' speech.

Charlotte was stunned by the news that he'd given up a new job and a move to London all for her. 'You really mean it?'

'I really mean it.'

He grabbed her hand and placed it on his chest. A definite ploy to stop her from thinking straight when that solid muscle beneath her fingers brought back memories of their night together, exploring each other's bodies until she'd known every inch of him.

'Do you feel that? My heart is pumping with adrenaline, waiting for you to tell me that you want to be with me and Alfie.'

'You were, are, the best thing to ever happen to me. I didn't know what living was until you two came along.'

She could tell how much he'd struggled, trying to combine parenthood with everything else. The worry lines were etched deeply on his brow and she dared to move closer to test the theory this wasn't the same man who'd planned to run away from her when the going got tough.

'I love you, Charlotte. I still want that fresh start but this time I want it with you. No secrets, no pretending I know what's best for everyone else, just open and honest discussion about what we want, or where we go, as a family.'

'A family?' She needed someone to pinch her and prove this was real, not a dream conjured up by her broken heart.

'You. Me. Alfie. Together. For ever.'

'I couldn't think of anything more perfect.' She wound her arms around his neck and snuggled in close, willing to risk everything she had for a chance of happiness.

Somewhere far away the final klaxon sounded and declared the Demons play-off champions, but it was Charlotte who felt like the real winner now they'd both shaken off the shadows of the past for a future together.

EPILOGUE

'How did it go?' Charlotte hadn't been able to settle all afternoon, waiting to hear how Hunter's meeting had gone with Alfie's teacher.

It had been a whirlwind of a year for all of them and she hoped it hadn't affected his schoolwork. There'd been the move into the cottage and getting used to living together as a family and the rushed wedding when they'd decided life was too short to waste any more time. It was a lot for a young boy to deal with all at once.

And her.

That parental guilt she'd worried about all along had well and truly kicked in but she wouldn't be without either of them for the world.

Hunter sat on the end of her desk. 'It went great. Mrs Patterson said he's top of the class for reading and maths.'

She could stop sweating now she'd been reassured his new stepmother wasn't responsible for a decline in his grades. He didn't appear unhappy with the new arrangement, he was as good as gold for her. She simply worried constantly about his well-being. It was taking a lot of willpower not to become a helicopter parent. Especially when she might be in danger of upsetting the family dynamic again.

'I'm so glad. He's been through a lot.'

'To quote his favourite teacher, "He's a happy, well-adjusted little boy."'

Hearing that made her well up because it was so important to her. Plus she was a tad hormonal these days.

'I'm sorry I couldn't make it in time. My appointment overran, otherwise I would've been there too.'

'I know, sweetheart. It's fine. You were there for his school play when I couldn't make it. That's part of the reason we make such a good team. There will always be at least one of us there waving pom-poms for him.'

It was true, they were a great team in all aspects of their lives. Gray had been only too happy to sign them both on for the new season and when the office next door to hers came onto the market Hunter had been able to set his own private practice up too. They shared the parenting as much as they could, with a little help from the O'Reillys every now and then.

'Where is he?'

'With his grandparents. They suggested we might like to go out to dinner or something while they babysit tonight.'

'Or something?' She hadn't missed the fact he'd locked the door on his way in. A clear indication they wouldn't make it out in time for dinner.

His cheeky grin said he had more than food on his mind too. 'Are you finished here?'

'For now. I need to write up a few progress reports for Gray but I can do that before the next match.'

'I can't believe it's play-off season already. That means a certain one-year anniversary. Perhaps we should celebrate?' He waggled his eyebrows. As if she needed reminding what they'd got up to this time last year. They'd done a lot more since.

'We can celebrate but it'll have to be minus the alcohol.' The news she'd been hiding was bubbling to the surface.

'You're not feeling sick again, are you?' He reached out to feel her forehead.

'I have a confession to make. I had an appointment today but as a patient, not a doctor.'

'You're scaring me now. Why didn't you tell me there was something wrong?' He scrambled off the desk and took her hand, his concern touching.

'I wanted to confirm my own diagnosis first. I think we're on our way to starting our own little hockey team.' She moved his hand to her belly, which was apparently full of more than Hunter's maple syrup pancakes.

'You're pregnant?' His eyes were like saucers as his slack jaw gradually widened into the happiest, sexiest smile she'd ever seen. She hadn't known men could get the pregnancy bloom too but he was beaming from the inside out.

'*We're* pregnant. I expect you to be with me in this every step of the way.' As happy as she was at the news too, there was a little trepidation at what the next few months had in store.

'Don't worry, there's nowhere I'd rather be than right here.' He placed a soft kiss on her belly to confirm they were in this together.

This baby was a new beginning for all of them. One they all deserved.

* * * * *

PLAYING TO WIN

TARYN LEIGH TAYLOR

This one's for my Women's Hockey Network cohost, and the best amanuensis in the business. Cool Crystal, I owe you a slab of cake with a cupcake on top.

To Adrienne, who always makes my stories better. I don't have the words to thank you enough. (But editors like irony, right?)

My love forever to Uncle Don and Auntie Shirl for keeping it real and staying true to the home team amidst a sea of red.

Mimsy, Dadoo and the man behind Grammataco – I'm so lucky to have you guys in my corner. High-fives and secret handshakes all around.

And to my Palisades Crew: Michele, Michelle, Lori, Carolyne, Marilyn and Laura. The kind of women, and writers, who inspire me even now.

1

"Quit squirming, Hol. You look totally porn-hot."

Holly Evans glared at her friend and cameraman. "Well, thanks, Jay. I feel so much better now. After all, 'porn-hot' is just what we professional sportscasters aspire to, right, Corey?"

She immediately regretted throwing the question to the reporter setting up a few feet down the rubber-floored hallway. Corey Baniuk was Portland's favorite on-the-scene sports authority...at least for now.

Rumor had it that Jim Purcell, the longtime sports anchor at *Portland News Now*, was contemplating retirement and that Corey had a lock on the in-studio position. That meant Holly's dream job might soon be up for grabs—and Holly intended to do the grabbing. Provided she hadn't screwed up all her credibility by playing Sports Reporter Barbie for the next three months, of course.

"Sure." Corey shot her the familiar, good-natured grin that was a staple of both the six and eleven o'clock news. "Someone will be by to oil my chest any minute."

His camera guy chuckled and heat prickled up Holly's

cheeks, no doubt rivaling the fire-engine-red color of her outfit. She forced a wan smile—small thanks for him taking the high road, but it was all she could muster. God, she envied him his conservative gray pinstripe suit. And he was even wearing a shirt under his jacket. She would give up her firstborn for a shirt.

"How did this happen?" she lamented in Jay Buchanan's general direction. "I am an intelligent, educated woman who is passionate about all things sports." She glanced down at her brazen skirt suit, but with her boobs pushed up to her chin, not much of it was visible to her.

Damn Victoria and all her secrets.

"When did I become the Hooters girl of broadcasting?"

Jay rolled his eyes. "Hey, you knew what you were signing up for. Hell, I'll bet Lougheed had dollar signs circling his head when he saw your audition tape."

Holly cringed at her friend's choice of words. "It wasn't an audition tape," she protested weakly. "It was a favor for you. And a fight against injustice."

When she'd agreed to shoot the joke video with Jay's fledgling production company, she was aiming for satire, intending it to be biting commentary on how female sports reporters were perceived. It was an attempt to show people the stereotypes she fought against every day in pursuit of her dream. Instead, she was now the star of a bona fide viral video, sporting a teased-out helmet of blond hair and freezing her butt off while she pretended to be hockey-impaired.

It had caught the attention of Ron Lougheed, the GM of Portland's professional hockey team, and the ditzy routine was now, sadly, the best on-camera experience she'd been offered since she'd graduated broadcasting school.

"No one cares what it *was*. What the Women's Hockey Network *is*, is a YouTube sensation! People are eating it up and coming back for seconds. To the suits, you're the living, breathing, high-heel-wearing crowbar they're gonna use to pry into the coveted female demographic."

"And they somehow figure short skirts are going to help me accomplish that lofty goal?" she asked snidely, tugging said skirt back down her thighs.

"Hell, no! That's to keep the guys interested while you're talking about girly stuff like player hairdos."

With a deep breath of arena—rubber and concrete and sweat and ice—Holly called upon the stupid yoga class she'd suffered through two years ago at her best friend Paige's behest. Something about a mind/body connection, and inner peace, and deep breaths, and—ah, screw it.

Time to suck it up, Princess.

Jay was right. She'd accepted the job as the Portland Storm's web reporter for the duration of their play-off run, and if dressing like someone's too-slutty-to-acknowledge cousin was the price of breaking into her dream career, then that's what she'd do. She gave a determined nod at the thought, slamming a mental door on the last remnants of her doubt.

The buzzer sounded to hail the end of the game, and Holly's newly minted courage took a nosedive. This was it. Her debut.

She watched with mounting nerves as twenty massive men in skates and full equipment stalked toward her.

And speaking of porn-hot...

There he was: Luke Maguire, team captain, number eighteen, a premier left-winger with a career-best thirty-seven goals in the regular season this year. Not to mention sexy as hell and in possession of all of his teeth—no rare feat after six years in professional hockey. The man looked incredible, all tall and sweaty and pissed off over the loss of their first play-off game against Colorado.

When she caught his eye, she was torn somewhere between lust and duty. Then his gaze dropped to the straining top button of her suit jacket, and she felt extreme mortification enter the mix. He slowed his pace, lifted his beautiful blue eyes from her cleavage to her face and stepped out of the single-file line of burly hockey players to take a question. *From her.*

This was it. Her big moment. Thirty seconds with one of the elite players of the game. But instead of being able to ask something pertinent, like his thoughts on the lackluster performance of the Storm's players, or his musings on the unprecedented twenty penalty minutes they'd accrued, she was contractually obligated to say:

"This is Holly Evans of the Women's Hockey Network, and with me tonight is the captain of the Portland Storm, Luke Maguire! Luke, it's play-off season, a time when superstitions run rampant and hockey players all over the league stop shaving, even though a recent study shows that women prefer the clean-shaven look to a full beard by a margin of almost four to one. Do you think tonight's loss had anything to do with the fact that you chose to shave today, and do you plan on reconsidering your stance on facial hair as the play-offs progress?"

One straight, brown eyebrow crooked up, the only indication he'd even heard her "question." (She was willing to concede that she was using the term loosely.)

Then he grabbed the logoed towel some *Sports Nation* lackey had slung on his shoulder, wiped the sweat from his face and turned and walked away.

"Buck up, Cap. Why so down?"

Luke took a deep breath and started pulling off the tape wound around his socks and shin pads. "You mean aside from getting shut out in our own building, setting a franchise record in penalty minutes and the looming press conference I have to spend assuring reporters that we know we sucked out there?"

As far as Luke was concerned, the only upside to their spectacular 5–0 loss to Colorado was that Coach Taggert had been so pissed that he'd refused post-game media access to the dressing room. At least they could shower, change and lick their wounds in relative peace.

Brett Sillinger, the Storm's eighth-round draft pick, ran a hand through his sweaty curls. "Well, sure. When you put it that way. But look at the bright side! We're loaded, and women throw themselves at us! We've got the best goddamn job in the world, bar none. And we're in the play-offs, baby!"

Luke's stomach lurched. "Trust me, rookie, I know we're in the play-offs."

Did he ever. It was a pretty big deal to some very rich people in some very high places, people who were...*eager* to see the team perform well in the franchise's first run for the cup since joining the league five years ago. That fact had been made abundantly—and repeatedly—clear to him in the month since they'd clinched their play-off spot.

It was also Luke's first time in the play-offs since the worst night of his life. Three years had passed, but the wound was still as fresh as ever.

He shoved the nightmarish memory back into the mental penalty box where it belonged, barely aware he'd reached for his helmet until he caught himself brushing his thumb across the number ten sticker he'd placed inside it—a talisman to keep him focused. With a sigh, he reached up and set his helmet on the shelf above his head.

He was the team captain now, he reminded himself. He had a job to do and he couldn't afford to wallow in personal issues. You couldn't lead a team to victory if they didn't trust you to take care of business. And yet he didn't seem to be leading the team anywhere but to an early play-off exit. They all needed to get their heads out of their asses.

"We won't be in the play-offs for long if we keep playing like we just did. I know there are some nerves in the room. This franchise has never been in the play-offs before, and no one here has ever won a championship. None of that matters. We need to play our game, stay hungry and determined.

"And we can't get sidetracked by the increased media scrutiny. Especially now that even the non-sports media are hunting for stories and interviews. The blonde out there actually asked me if I thought we lost because I'm not growing a play-off beard."

The entire dressing room went silent as Luke untied his skate. He glanced around at his eerily quiet teammates. "What?"

"Well, we *did* lose..."

Luke's face twisted with disgust. "Are you kidding me? It's the first game! None of you even have beards yet. You guys really buy into this 'no shaving' bull?"

The rookie stroked his pitiful day's worth of stubble.

"All I know is that I'm in this to win this, and if sportin' a Grizzly Adams gets me closer to a championship, then I'm on it like STDs on a hooker."

"You realize that three out of four women hate beards, right?" Luke pulled his skate off, hating that he'd actually reduced himself to quoting stats from that reporter.

Sillinger got a philosophical look on his face. "Shave and you get laid for a night. Do what it takes to score a championship ring, and you'll be up to your balls in puck bunnies for the rest of your life. I mean, seriously, Mags. A woman with a body like that reporter's names me her 'hockey hottie of the month,' and I'll answer any stupid question she asks."

Luke paused in the act of loosening his other skate. "What are you talking about?"

"Are you serious?" Sillinger's surprise was obvious. "Holly Evans? The Women's Hockey Network?"

Luke gave a bewildered shrug.

"Dude, she's all over YouTube! She does this girly hockey-analysis show that's gone viral. And in it, she named *you* the hottest hockey player in the league. The top brass practically begged her to be our web reporter during the play-offs! Do you guys believe this? Hot Stuff here doesn't even know who Holly Evans is!"

The announcement set off a round of catcalls and ribbing. Luke turned to his linemate, Eric Jacobs. The stoic centerman gave a shrug of his big shoulders and shook his head. Luke was relieved he wasn't the only one out of the loop on this.

"Okay, okay." Luke waited for the dressing room to quiet. "Let's stay focused, guys. The game might be over, but we've still got work to do."

Work that involved hours of ripping apart the carcass

of the worst game they'd played all year. The assembled jackals—uh, *reporters*—were going to eat him alive, Luke thought soberly. He shed the rest of his equipment and headed for the showers.

But that was the price of the *C* on his jersey. The price of earning a living doing what he loved. Which was an honor and a privilege, considering some people never got that chance. And others had it stolen from them. Luke sighed.

At least the evisceration wouldn't have anything to do with beard statistics and superstitious nonsense. And yet somehow Luke sensed that Holly Evans was a bigger threat than all the other sports reporters combined…

2

"The Storm essentially played an entire period short-handed, which, given the dismal play of your PK unit, definitely contributed to tonight's loss. Can you give us any insight as to what led to this unprecedented number of penalties for the Storm?"

Holly hit the pause button on last night's broadcast and whirled on the couch to face her best friend, Paige Hallett. "Did you hear that? That was my question. Corey Baniuk just asked Luke Maguire *my* question. And did the dumb jock walk away without a word? No. He stood there and answered it, the jerk!"

"You asked him that question and he ignored you?" Paige looked offended on her behalf.

"Well, no. I asked him if he thought he might grow a play-off beard—then he ignored me. But that's the question I *wanted* to ask him. That was a great question!"

Paige turned back to the magazine she was perusing. "I'll take your word for it. He lost me when he started talking about China. Besides, why would the Storm play a whole period shorthanded? Seems kind of counterproductive to me."

Holly sighed and set the remote on her coffee table. "They didn't play an actual period shorthanded, they got twenty penalty minutes, so over the course of the game, they essentially played a man short for the length of a period. And he didn't say Peking, he said *PK* unit. When a team gets a penalty, they put out their best penalty killers, their *penalty kill* unit."

"Oh. Well, why didn't he just say that?"

"He did! He *did* say that, and Luke Maguire answered him, because it was a relevant question asked by a serious sports reporter."

Paige shot her a sympathetic look. "*You're* a serious sports reporter."

"No, *I'm* a traitor to my gender. Last night I wore a tiny suit and high shoes and made a mockery of everything I love."

"Would you cut yourself some slack? Those were some seriously great shoes I picked out for you to wear. Besides, the only way you're truly a traitor to your gender is the complete lack of readable magazines in your house." Paige held up the *Sports Illustrated* she was flipping through as proof. "Seriously. If these guys weren't shirtless, I'd throw this across the room in protest. Oh, wow." A dreamy smile spread across Paige's pretty face. "Who is *that*? Come to momma."

Holly glanced over at the glossy, two-page spread featuring a certain hot, shirtless hockey player. His brown hair was the perfect length between shorn and shaggy, his blue eyes intense as ever. He was sitting in the dressing room, kitted out in hockey gear from the waist down—pants, socks and skates—and all muscle and beautiful bronzed skin from the waist up. Behind him, his last name and a big number 18 gleamed white against the navy of his Storm jersey.

"That's *Luke Maguire*. The topic of my diatribe for the last twenty minutes? The man currently paused on my television?" Holly gestured at his stupid handsome face in HD.

"Well, why didn't you tell me he was so yummy? I would have paid better attention." She glanced at the television, presumably for the first time since her arrival. "*Mmm*. Maybe you were right. I should watch more hockey."

Holly couldn't help but smile. She had been trying to open Paige up to the wonders of sports for the better part of a decade now. How had Holly not realized the best way to turn Paige on to sports was to *turn Paige on*? "You're incorrigible, you know that?"

Paige smiled sweetly. "I'm a divorcée with no serious relationship prospects on the horizon. I have to take my thrills where I can get them." She flicked her gaze back to the TV. "And that man looks like he gives good thrill."

Holly couldn't argue. Irrationally, it made her even angrier at him. At one of her favorite hockey players. One day of playing dress-up and her view of the sports world was already starting to become skewed. So far, a steady paycheck was the only thing she enjoyed about this gig. Especially after such a mortifying first night. She'd taken the job because it was her chance to get on camera. One step closer to her big dream of talking sports on TV. But now...

"I'm wondering if taking this job was a mistake," she confessed.

Since she'd graduated, she'd been plugging away,

ghostwriting sports pieces for a bunch of online sports blogs. Hockey, basketball, baseball, football, golf…you name it, she wrote it. Not that anyone knew, since all her painstaking work was credited to "staff writer." But it was the only way she could continue to write for enough outlets to make a living. She spent what little free time she had busting her butt trying to get one of her sports op-eds picked up.

That was the kind of writing she really loved—not spewing facts and stats and scores, but interpreting them, putting them in context, figuring out what was making a team successful, suggesting what they could do to become more so, having a go at dumb managerial decisions and underperforming athletes.

That sort of in-depth analysis was the key to getting where she really belonged—on television, just like her mom used to be. She wanted to read her pieces aloud, share them with people who loved sports as much as she did. Anyone could read a teleprompter; Holly wanted to make an impact.

"I mean, Jay and I made the Women's Hockey Network video as a joke. And now it's gotten me closer to my goal of being on camera than any article I've ever written." Holly looked down, picking at the red lacquer Paige had insisted on slicking over her stubby nails. "But instead of feeling great about that, I feel like I've sold out. I'm a joke. I mean, can you even imagine what my mom would think of all this?"

"Woah. Back up the pity bus. I will not let you go down the mom road. She loved you and she would want what's best for you. But Hols, even if your mom was still alive, what's best for you would be your choice, not hers."

Holly flopped onto the couch. "I know. But I still worry about letting her down. When I accepted this gig, I thought it was going to be a case of 'all publicity is good publicity.' Now I'm not so sure."

She ran her hands down her face. "Luke Maguire believes I'm a total idiot! How can I ever do an in-depth interview with him now? And I don't even get to travel with the team! That's how dumb the questions I ask are supposed to be. I'm not worth a seat on a chartered plane that's already been paid for."

Paige glanced up from a picture featuring a shirtless LA Laker. "Lighten up, would you? It's been one day. This job is a stepping-stone—one with over a hundred thousand hits on YouTube so far. You never know where this opportunity could take you. Besides, what do you think the rest of your former sports broadcasting classmates are doing right now? Interviewing team mascots and reporting on who scored the most baskets in soccer games played by twelve-year-olds? I'll bet you're closer to a real gig than any of them." Paige shut the magazine and tossed it onto the coffee table. "You're working with a real hockey team, interviewing some of the best players in the game. And yeah, it's not perfect, but it could be a hell of a lot worse. So to quote a good friend of mine—" Paige arched one perfectly winged eyebrow "—*suck it up, Princess*. Go out there and do the job."

Holly sighed. "I hate it when you're right."

"Then you must hate me all the time," her friend lamented with a grin. It faded after a moment. "Was that enough of a pep talk? Because I'll bail on my date and we can go out for a drink if you want to talk this out some more."

"Oh, right! You have a date." Holly shook her head. "I keep forgetting since you've been so secretive about this mystery man of yours."

"It's new. We're still feeling each other out. Once we start feeling each other *up*, then I'll have some details to share." Paige was the only person in the world Holly knew who could pull off a wink with such aplomb.

"Of that I have no doubt. Now go and have fun. Besides, I'm already in the middle of a sports-related crisis. There's no way I can muster the fortitude and patience it would take to teach you that you don't score baskets in soccer right now."

Paige laughed at the jab.

Holly squared her shoulders. "Like you said, I made this choice. I'm going to honor this contract. Maybe I can even convince them to let me do some real reporting. Wow 'em so they give me a chance to document the Storm's first time in the play-offs with the gravitas and seriousness that it deserves."

"That's the spirit! You show those men who's boss." The phone rang just as Paige stood to leave. "See? That's probably some titan of the hockey world, impressed with your journalistic integrity and calling to poach you for his own team."

"Who else could it be?" Holly agreed drolly. "Say hi to your date for me."

"No way. Get your own man, which I hope you do soon. You're in desperate need of some hunky distraction in your life," Paige advised, heading for the door. "At the very least, this job will be great for that."

Holly rolled her eyes in a silent goodbye as she grabbed the handset of her phone, recognizing Jay's number on call display. Paige didn't like him very much, but Holly and Jay had hit it off immediately in broadcasting school.

When the Storm offered to let her pick her own cameraman, she'd eagerly snatched Jay away from filming weddings and local stories. It was a relief not to have to fake sports stupidity with at least one person.

"Hey. The footage looks great." Embarrassing as it might be for her personally, she had to admit that Jay had edited her interviews with Luke and the rest of the team into a professional-looking comedic montage that could now be viewed by the world at portlandstorm.com.

"I'm glad you think so, because the boss man agrees."

"What?"

"That's why I'm calling. Check your texts."

"Or you could just tell me since we're, you know, *on the phone*," she pointed out.

"Okay, smart-ass. It seems your big-haired alter ego can do no wrong. Hits on the Storm's website have increased twenty percent since your interview was posted last night. Usually after a loss, website traffic goes down. They've decided to give us an extra assignment."

"Oh, God." Holly cringed. She couldn't help it. A twenty percent uptick? That did not bode well for Operation: Journalistic Integrity. She'd be stuck asking about favorite childhood breakfast cereals for the rest of her career while important stories, like Luke Maguire's scoring drought that had now entered its twelfth game, went unmentioned.

On the upside, at least the team captain was so annoyed with her about the play-off beard thing that she could focus her insipid questions on the rest of the players. "What do they want us to film?"

"Some fluffy pregame interviews with the guys, tomorrow after their morning skate. The brass plans to air them as teasers between periods to help drive up website traffic. We're starting with the big three, then we'll try to fit in as much of the rest of the team as we can manage."

The big three: goaltender Jean-Claude LaCroix, centerman Eric Jacobs, and, because sometimes life sucked with a vengeance, captain and left-winger Luke Maguire. Holly couldn't bring herself to speak through the impending sense of doom.

THWACK.

Luke's slap shot missed the net completely.

God—*thwack*—damn—*thwack*—mother—*thwack*—fuc—

"Mags!"

Luke looked up from the line of pucks he was systematically assaulting to see Jean-Claude LaCroix—J.C. to his teammates—standing in the players' box. He was dressed in a navy T-shirt that mimicked the Storm's home jersey, this year's standard issue for doing press.

With another muttered curse, Luke skated over to the bench.

"I just finished with the reporter, and Eric's in the hot seat right now. Someone can cover for you with her if you want to grab a shower, but to avoid the wrath of the higher-ups, I'd suggest you get a move on."

Luke pulled off one of his gloves so he could remove his helmet and set them both on the boards. "Yeah, I'll be there in a minute."

"You okay, man?"

He ran a hand over his sweaty hair. "Sure. What could be wrong?"

J.C. gave him a look. "You're the one who snapped two sticks in practice and is still out here pounding the boards. You tell me."

Luke appreciated his friend's tact. It wasn't like his problem wasn't obvious.

He couldn't hit the net.

It had been twelve games since he'd scored a goal—the longest dry spell of his hockey career. But no matter how hard he practiced, how much extra time he logged out here working on his shot, when he was in the game, he froze up. And people were noticing. He'd read the grumblings in the paper, heard the callouts on television. Hell, people were even tweeting him to say he sucked. If he didn't get his act together soon, he'd be headed for some obligatory couch time with the sports psychologist. And that meant talking about Ethan, a fate he tried to avoid at all costs.

"It's nothing." Luke brushed it off, hoping his buddy would let it go.

J.C. shook his head, rejecting the lie. Luke should have known he would. They'd been playing hockey together on and off since they were fourteen years old. At this point, his goaltender could read him just as well off the ice as on.

"It's *not* nothing, man. Don't overthink it. Besides, scoring isn't the only way to help the team."

"Easy for you to say. Your save percentage was .916 this season. You're doing your part, but we won't win if we don't put pucks in the other guys' net." Luke's shoulders tightened under the weight of expectation—from management, the fans, his teammates… "I haven't scored in over a month. What am I supposed to do about that?"

"Just relax and play the game."

Luke rolled his eyes at the Zen advice. "This is the reason people hate goalies, you know? You're all a bunch of pretentious assholes."

J.C. just grinned. "I'll see you up there, okay?"

With a nod, Luke grabbed his helmet and glove and headed to the dressing room to shower and change, hoping he could clear his head before he faced Holly Evans. His brain conjured the memory of the curvy blonde in the siren-red outfit. Yet another complication he didn't need right now. Because last night, he'd done something stupid.

With a self-directed curse, he'd opened a new browser window and typed "The Women's Hockey Network" into the search field on YouTube.

And there she was, Holly Evans, all big blond hair and big brown eyes and big, beautiful breasts. In fact, she was damn near perfect...until she got to the Hockey Hunk of the Month segment.

He wanted to be pissed.

Instead, he was oddly flattered.

Sure, he wasn't wild about the fact she'd used that damned shirtless picture of him from last month's *Sports Illustrated*, but after his on-ice struggles over the last month, he found his battered self-esteem had sort of appreciated the boost from those pouty, shiny lips of hers.

She'd even managed to make the award about more than his pectorals, citing his work with his pet charity, Kids on Wheels, and explaining its focus on providing wheelchairs and wheelchair-friendly sports programs for kids in need. Hell, she'd even brought up his role as a goodwill ambassador for ice sledge hockey, a cause near and dear to his heart.

If he wasn't so firmly anti-reporter, he might have approved of the way she'd so beautifully shifted the focus from the nonsensical to something that actually mattered. But in the end, what mattered most was winning, and ogling the pretty reporter wasn't going to help him put the puck in the net.

Now, Luke stood outside the dressing room, temporarily set aside this morning so that she could make a mockery of the sport he loved, willing himself to man up and walk in.

He scratched his chin self-consciously, wishing to hell that he'd shaved this morning. He didn't want to give her the satisfaction of assuming his decision not to shave had anything to do with her. If he'd been given any kind of heads-up about being locked in a room with Little Miss Play-off Beard today, he definitely would've given a big middle finger to all the doubts she and his teammates had planted about their loss. But there'd been no warning until just before practice. No doubt about it, karma was a stone-cold bitch.

With a deep breath, he stepped through the door to find his linemate was just finishing up his interview.

"That was great, Eric." Holly's voice, warm and sexy, called to mind the drizzle of honey on cream. Luke subconsciously turned toward it.

God*damn*, the woman was gorgeous. She was rocking the painted-on suit again, but this time the color was the same teal as the stripes and the cresting wave on the Storm jersey. (A color which, according to the Women's Hockey Network color chart, indicated a driven personality whose inner turmoil was often masked by an outward appearance of calm.)

She was sporting mile-high heels, a barely there skirt, plenty of cleavage and that big, tousled hair that probably felt like a helmet of straw in real life, but always managed to look kinda sexy on TV. And yet, now that she wasn't just a caricature on his computer screen, but a living, breathing woman, smiling and putting the notoriously shy Eric Jacobs at ease as they finished up their interview, he found himself wondering what she'd look like in jeans and a T-shirt.

The thought irritated him. He just wanted to get this whole thing over with so he could concentrate on the important stuff. Like winning hockey games. He made himself take a step forward. "So I guess that means I'm up?"

With obvious relief, Jacobs flashed him a thankful smile, said a quick goodbye and fled the scene.

Holly whirled around, tugging at her skirt as though willing more fabric to appear. "Luke! Uh, Mr. Maguire, I—"

"Luke's fine."

They lapsed into an awkward silence.

She bit her lip.

Damn, her mouth is amazing. And he really needed to stop noticing that.

He pulled a frustrated hand down his face, cursing inwardly as he realized his mistake. Satisfaction sparked in those coffee-brown eyes of hers—he and his day's worth of stubble were busted. But to his surprise, her dawning smile was more teasing than mocking, and it made him want to wipe it off her face in a way that would be pleasurable for them both.

"You guys want to get started, or what?"

The cameraman's sudden intrusion jerked Luke out of a mental image in which he and Holly were long past "started" and well on their way to "finished."

What a hypocrite! He kept telling his guys to focus and here he was, distracted by a pretty face.

Except he sensed she was more than that. Something about her ditzy act wasn't quite right. There was more going on underneath the glossy surface she presented to the world, he just knew it. He trusted his instincts—his livelihood depended on them. His shot might be off, but his gut wasn't. And if Holly Evans had another agenda, she was a danger to him and his team. Then again, just the sight of her in that outfit was dangerous.

"What? Yes! Of course, Jay, thanks!" Holly's voice was about an octave too high and a six-pack of Red Bull too perky. She gave Jay an overly bright smile and snatched her interview cards from the stool. "Luke, if you'll take a seat?"

Like a good little soldier, Luke walked over and sat down.

"We'll start with a quick Q and A with just you on camera, and then I've got a couple of more in-depth questions that we'll shoot with the two of us on-screen."

"Yeah, sure." He tried to appear casual and nonchalant.

She gave Jay a nod and waited until the little red light on the camera flicked on and the boom was in place. Then she turned back to Luke, fixed him with a look of professional interest and got down to business.

"What's the last thing you watched on YouTube?"

The question was like being cross-checked from behind, leaving him momentarily stunned. No way in hell he was going to admit he spent his evening re-inflating his ego by watching her call him hot.

"Are you serious?" He'd meant to sound casually mocking, but was afraid it had come out somewhat closer to defensive. "That's the hard-hitting lead issue? You've got to have something better than that. What's the next question?"

She looked flustered by his outburst, and he hated the fact that he felt badly about it. He should be out on the ice, working on his slap shot, not in here trying to hide his guilt. She glanced down at her note card and closed her eyes, just for a second, before opening them and meeting his gaze. She looked focused, determined and a little defiant, if he wasn't mistaken. She cleared her throat.

"Boxers or briefs?"

All his composure deserted him. He held up a hand and glanced over at the camera. "Turn that off."

He waited until Jay lowered the boom mic and stepped toward the tripod before he rounded on the woman who had the singular ability to distract and frustrate him beyond measure.

"Look, I get that you have a job to do, but what's going on here, it's a big deal. This team is in the play-offs for the first time in its five-year history. Not a single player on our roster has ever won a championship. We've got a chance to do something great."

He took a deep breath and unclenched his fist.

"The problem is, two nights ago we handed Colorado a shutout victory on a silver platter. This team is now skating on thin ice, and if we're going to get out of the first round intact, I need my guys focused on winning hockey games, not talking about their underwear and eyeing your cleavage. Everyone else thinks you're cute and harmless and charming, but I don't buy it. So if you're just using us to make a name for yourself, then you've picked the wrong team. We don't have time for distractions right now. I'm done here."

With that, Luke stalked away from her. Again.

3

"Luke! How did it go? I was just going to stop in and get a behind-the-scenes peek at the interviews."

Luke pulled up short at the familiar booming voice. You didn't stalk past Ron Lougheed, general manager of the Portland Storm, no matter how frustrated you might be. Besides, this was the perfect opportunity to bring up his concerns.

"Yeah, about that, sir… As team captain, it's my job to make sure that my guys are centered, that hockey is the top priority. We've been through a lot this season and now it seems we're finally gelling at the right time. I'm worried that Holly Evans is a distraction we can't afford right now."

"Nonsense! Holly Evans and her delightful brand of infotainment is exactly what the franchise needs in order to make some headway into the hearts and minds of hockey fans."

Ron Lougheed was a heavyset giant of a man and despite his gregarious demeanor, everyone in the hockey world knew that when he made up his mind, there was no changing it.

Still, Luke had to try. "But sir, our time is better spent if we—"

"Let me tell you a little something about the business of hockey, Mr. Maguire. For the last five years, our merchandising and ticket sales have consistently ranked in the bottom third of the league's teams. Since we made the play-offs, we've seen a fifteen percent jump in merchandise revenue and we've almost sold out tonight's game. That's after *one* post-season game. We need to ride this wave, and the Women's Hockey Network is helping us do that. That clip of you walking away from her the other night has half a million likes. I'm not exactly sure what that means, but it's good."

Luke nodded. Shut his mouth. Braced for impact.

"I trust I don't need to tell you how *eager* we are to see results in the postseason?"

"No, sir."

"Excellent. Now, what were you saying about concerns?"

A headshake was the best Luke could muster. "Nothing, sir. Nothing at all."

"That's what I thought. I'm looking forward to watching your interview footage from this morning. After all, a captain sets the tone for his team, and I know I picked the right man to keep these boys on track. And put a couple of pucks in the net, while you're at it. Understood?"

"Perfectly."

Ten minutes of fuming and a chicken and pasta lunch later, Luke was back in front of the doors emblazoned with the stylized cresting wave of the team's logo. The doors burst open just as he reached for them, but instead of revealing his sexy, skirt-suited nemesis, he came face-to-face with the rookie.

"Dude, you up next?"

"Yeah." He glanced over the kid's shoulder, but the doors swooped shut before he could catch even a glimpse of teal. "Yeah, I'm up next."

"Cool. Word of advice? If you stand close enough during the part where she's on-screen with you, you can see all the way down her shirt."

When his tip failed to elicit any reaction from Luke, Sillinger's cocky grin faded. "Look, Cap, I want to apologize for what I said after the game the other day. Cubs explained why you're so tense and everything."

The kid glanced away as he said it, so he missed Luke's look of surprise at the mention of Eric Jacobs, or Cubs, as everyone on the team referred to him. "Exactly what did he tell you?"

"Oh, you know. All the pressure you're under from the higher-ups. And dealing with the media. And about your shot being off and stuff."

Luke exhaled. He should have known Jacobs would have picked up on all of Luke's behind-the-scenes crap. The guy was eerily intuitive—it was what made him so great out there on the ice.

"Um, you ever consider that maybe your shot's off because, um…" The kid leaned conspiratorially close and murmured, "I'm just sayin', maybe it would help if you changed the oil."

Luke stared blankly at the right-winger. He didn't like where this conversation was going, mostly because he'd been thinking about it a lot since he'd watched that damn video last night. Holly Evans was beautiful, and she'd made him think about something other than hockey for the first time in a long while. And she could certainly get him riled up. Not to mention she didn't give a damn about hockey. All things he found way too appealing at this very moment.

"Sometimes things get rusty when the pipe's not clean, you understand? I mean, how long's it been, man? In my experience, a good lube job can really help work out the kinks. And lucky for you, right through that door is a smoking-hot woman who told the entire internet that she considers you a certified Grade-A cut of beef. Plus, when I made my move, she told me she's looking for a guy with more maturity. That's your in, dude! She totally wants someone *old*. You should hit that."

Luke was pretty sure he'd never felt more ancient than he did having this particular conversation and he was only twenty-six. "Thanks for the advice, rookie."

"Hey, no problem, Cap. I got your back." Brett glanced at the door to the interview room. "You need a wingman in there, or you good?"

"I think I got it," Luke assured him.

Their conversation was interrupted by the infamous "Charge" anthem, a staple of sporting events everywhere. The rookie yanked his phone out of his back pocket. He glanced at the screen and grinned like he was on the cover of *Hockey Digest*. "Yes! It's the car dealership. You are not even going to believe the sweet ride I just bought!"

He was bouncing up and down like a Chihuahua that was about to pee on the floor. "The guys won't be able to give me a hard time about my wheels anymore. I gotta take this, Cap. Good luck in there."

Luke waited until Brett disappeared around the corner before he stepped inside for his mandated face-off with Holly Evans, intrepid reporter.

"ARE YOU KIDDING ME, Jay? You took Salt Lake City over Vancouver in the first round? That's ridiculous. No wonder you always lose your hockey pool. I mean honestly. I expected better of you. Vancouver clearly has the edge and—Luke!" Holly bolted off the interview stool.

She hadn't been expecting *him*.

Like the rest of the team, he was wearing the navy T-shirt that mimicked his jersey, with the cresting wave on the front and his last name and number on the back. His T-shirt even had a white *C* on the front.

But unlike the rest of the team, the sight of Luke in his T-shirt and jeans did funny things to her hormones. *Seriously, is it hot in here?*

"I thought you were...not coming back...ever. How long have you been there?"

"Not long," he said, shoving his hands in his pockets as he sauntered farther into the room. His cocked eyebrow and smug half grin said otherwise. Holly worried that her attempt to appear innocent was failing miserably, because her thoughts were anything but G-rated.

"What are you guys talking about?"

"You know," she said, so brightly that she could have sworn he squinted a little. "This and that."

Luke nodded, glancing over at Jay, who avoided meeting his gaze. "Sounded like hockey talk to me."

"What? No."

"Yes," he countered, matching her wide-eyed tone. "It really did. I'm a bit of an expert on the subject. Salt Lake City, Vancouver, first round. Definite hockey talk."

Luke had already nailed the fact that she was using this job to angle for a promotion. If she confirmed it by dropping the shtick, he could have her fired before she even got started. The best way to reassure him that she was harmless was to *be* harmless.

Holly's laugh was both forced and slightly manic as she shooed his words away with the dainty flick of her hand. "Oh, that. I was just telling Jay about…uh—" *Think, Holly. Think!* "—the numerology class I took." She nodded, warming to the story. "Yeah, really interesting stuff. I was explaining how it can help you make decisions about important things. Like which handbag to buy. Or in Jay's case, he's doing some hockey thing with his friends and I was showing him how he could use it to pick teams."

"Cool. I'd love to see how it works." He raised an eyebrow to punctuate the challenge, and she couldn't quite hold back her frown. But she'd come this far. Might as well go all-in.

Holly could almost swear she saw something like respect in his blue eyes as she lifted her chin and squared her shoulders.

"Uh, yeah. I just added up the letters in Vancouver— A is one, B is two and so on, your typical cipher—and then you take whatever the sum is, add those numbers together if it's more than a single digit and you have it. And in this case, *it* was equal to nine. Jay's birthday is September ninth, so obviously Vancouver is the luckier team for him."

Luke smiled, but it didn't quite reach his eyes. "So it has nothing to do with the fact that Vancouver is a team with enough depth and experience that it's pretty much a foregone conclusion that they'll knock Salt Lake out of the first round?"

Holly shrugged. "What can I say? The numbers don't lie."

"Sorry to interrupt…whatever *this* is, but I gotta use the can," Jay announced. "Down the hall and to the left?" he confirmed, and Luke nodded. The members of the Portland Storm were so superstitious that she and Jay had been asked to trek all the way to the building's public washrooms because no one but the team was allowed in the dressing-room bathroom on game day.

The two of them watched Jay leave, and she used the silence to regroup. She felt much more formidable when her adversary's baby blues swung back in her direction.

Until he said, "What is your game?"

"Game?"

His laugh was derisive, but kind of sexy for all that. "You're not fooling anyone. I know something's up with you and I intend to figure out what it is."

Oh great. That was all she needed, this handsome bastard messing up the most real-life, on-camera experience on her résumé. She might not like this job, but it was good experience, and she certainly wasn't going to lose it by making him suspicious on the second day.

"Up to something?" She placed a hand on her chest like a Southern belle. "Me?"

His parry was a narrowing of his pretty blue eyes. "Something has been bugging me about your act since the moment we met."

"Oh, you mean that time you were so unchivalrous to walk away from me without answering my question?"

"So I asked myself," he continued, without missing

a beat, "why would someone who disliked sports so much that she asked about beards instead of the game bother to make a fake sports show? And the only answer I could come up with was, she wouldn't. The way I see it, you have your own agenda, and it's not going to do any of the members of this team any good."

Holly shook her head, eyes wide like an ingenue. "I don't know what you mean. The Women's Hockey Network is all about asking the kinds of questions we girls find important, such as what kind of cologne do you wear?"

He smelled so good she *was* actually a little curious.

"Oh, really? You're gonna keep up the act?"

Luke stepped closer. His big body sucked up all the oxygen, and her breath came faster to compensate. Who knew having a man accuse you of being smart was such a turn-on?

"That's the only question you want to ask me? I'll give you a free pass, on the record. Ask me anything. No holds barred. Nothing's off-limits. And I guarantee you a real answer. I promise not to say 'no comment.'"

Holly's hand clenched into a fist.

Any question. On the record. The reporting equivalent to winning the lottery.

She could ask about his brother's accident. Be the only reporter ever to get a statement on the one topic that was off-limits when interviewing Luke Maguire. Hear in his own words how it felt to be back in the play-offs for the first time since tragedy struck.

And she wanted to. She wanted to ask more than she wanted her next breath. But she wasn't supposed to know anything about hockey, so she restrained herself. Because if she took the bait, she would confirm that when given the opportunity, she'd put her ambition before the team. And she'd be done here. He could not only get her fired, but ruin her career. She had to keep her eye on the prize. She had to believe that one day, she would earn that story from him on her own merit, not as blackmail, and it would be worth the wait.

So she did what was best for her career and took a deep, centering breath. *Man, he really does smell amazing.* "Seriously, is that the new Hugo Boss fragrance?"

He narrowed his eyes and the crease between his brows deepened. It made him look even sexier, if that was possible.

"I've got my eye on you, Evans."

Not exactly the part of him she *wanted* on her just then, but probably the safest of the available options.

"I'm going to figure out what you're doing here and I'm going to expose you."

Geez. Everything sounded sexual when he was standing this close. She upped the ante and took a half step closer to him—she definitely wasn't going to let him intimidate her in this sexy game of cat and mouse they'd embarked on. If he thought she was going to let him be the cat, he was so very wrong. She'd been holding her own in a man's world for a long time.

"You can try, but there's nothing to expose. What you see is what you get."

"Oh, I very much doubt that, Ms. Evans. The truth is hiding somewhere behind that big hair and tiny suit."

"Look at me, Mr. Maguire. You honestly think there's room to hide anything under this suit?"

Her breath stuttered at the sudden fierceness in his eyes, the predatory gleam that pinned her in place. Were their lips getting closer because he was leaning in, or had she swayed toward him?

She was drawn to his body, hard as iron and just as magnetic. Her fingers brushed his biceps as his hands made first contact with her waist. She didn't want to stop looking at him, but her eyelids grew heavy as their breaths comingled and his lips moved closer, closer still...

"Okay, I'm back. What'd I miss?"

"Nothing!" Holly and Luke sprang apart at Jay's intrusion. Her heart thumped with a cocktail that was one part adrenaline and two parts unassuaged lust. She tugged at the bottom of her blazer, sneaking a quick glance in Luke's direction. He exhaled and rubbed a hand across the back of his neck.

Guilty. They looked as guilty as a couple of teenagers who'd been caught making out. Which they probably would have ended up doing if not for Jay's poor timing.

"Geez, Jay. You've been gone long enough. Let's get this interview going, shall we?" Her hand went to her hair—a classic Holly-ism that gave away her nerves. Good thing Luke didn't know that, she decided, dropping her hand. Luke lifted an eyebrow and Holly was sure she was blushing. Damn it.

"My pleasure," Luke said.

Jay, however, was not fooled in the least, and the look he shot her said she owed him an explanation. She waved him behind the camera and directed Luke back to the stool where their interview earlier had gone so wrong.

This one went a lot better. She had to hand it to him—he was as consummate a professional off the ice as he was on it. Charming, funny, quick with a witty answer. No one who saw this footage would dream for a minute that he believed her to be a threat to the team. In fact, the only question that tripped him up was "Do you have a secret talent?" She could have sworn he blushed a little before he stammered some nonsense about speaking a little French.

Then she sent him off to shoot some B-roll with Jay, which involved posing and puck tricks in the hallway.

For the first time all day, she was alone in the Storm's dressing room with a microphone in her hand. It was a pretty surreal experience, both as a hockey fan and as an aspiring sports reporter.

She'd watched it on television all her life, a reporter interviewing some member of the team or other, a bunch of bare-chested, sweaty-haired men talking about a big win or a battle-weary loss. The locker room looked different now, empty and quiet, all the jerseys clean and hanging number-side out, equipment neatly arranged on the shelves above each player's designated spot. Holly tried to just enjoy the moment, but her stupid heels were pinching her feet, reminding her that she was only living a fun-house version of her dream. But one day, she vowed. One day she'd be here, wearing pants and asking serious, in-depth questions.

And then Luke Maguire wouldn't be the only guy on the team who suspected that she was an expert on this stuff. Everyone on the roster would know she could hold her own.

She set the mic on the stool Luke had sat on for part of their interview and headed for the forbidden bathroom. Jay and Luke would be occupied with filming for at least five minutes. What harm would it do to sneak a peek?

It contained all the typical male bathroom accoutrements—urinals, stalls and a ginormous gang shower. But it was elevated to luxe standards by the details: gleaming navy and white tiles, stainless steel fixtures and enough accents of Portland Storm teal thrown in to pull it all together. Calculatedly masculine and very *go, team, go*!

Bracing a hand on either side of the sink, she stared into the mirror. She barely recognized herself. Gone were the usual blond ponytail and unadorned brown eyes. No T-shirt and jeans. She flexed her feet against the stiff leather of her heels—definitely no sneakers.

She wanted to splash some water on her face to assure herself the reflection in the mirror was just a mirage. But the sad reality was that the made-up, well-coiffed woman who was staring back at her now was the version of herself that had scored the biggest deal on her résumé by far.

This was the Holly Evans that was being invited to appear on local morning talk shows and well-respected podcasts. Hell, she'd even gotten a call about turning the Women's Hockey Network into a weekly comedy-sports show on satellite radio. And if fancy suits and a little lipstick were what it took to fulfill her dream of being a sports reporter, then it was a small price to pay. *Right?*

Holly sighed. This was who she was now, at least for the duration of the Storm's play-off run, and a splash of water wasn't going to change that. Besides, Paige had done such a lovely job with the goop on her face that she didn't dare. She settled for another sigh and tugged a few stray pieces of hair back into place before she headed for one of the navy stalls.

"Whatever it takes," she muttered to herself.

She'd just locked the stall door when the sound of footsteps made her freeze.

4

Aw, crap.

The footsteps were coming closer. Honestly. What were the odds? The bathroom had been deserted all day, and now someone decided to come in? Stupid hockey superstitions.

How could a bunch of grown men be this ridiculous? She was just wondering if perhaps there was a story in the naive belief wins and losses had anything to do with who used which freaking toilet, when her line of thought was interrupted by the "Charge" fanfare echoing off the tiled walls. The sudden burst of noise made her heart jump.

There was a muttered curse, followed by a hoarse, angry whisper: "Why are you calling me? It's game day. You know I'm not alone."

Her reporter instincts piqued, Holly abandoned all thoughts of superstitious nonsense and redirected her attention into eavesdropping.

"I'm very aware of that! But there's only so much I can do."

She frowned. She couldn't distinguish the voice, despite all the interviews she'd conducted today. All she could tell was that whoever had her trapped in a bathroom stall didn't have an accent. There were at least fourteen guys on the team proper who fit the bill. And that wasn't including coaching staff, cleaning staff, anyone who—

"I know we have a deal!"

Whoa. Holly flinched at the anger in his voice. She glanced down at her stilettos. Could she climb up on the toilet quietly enough to not blow her cover? Because from that height, she could peek over the top of the stall and see who the guy on the phone was. Not an ideal solution, but at least it would give her a lead.

Excitement brewed in the pit of her stomach. Now *this* was a story. Sure, she'd resigned herself to her fate of asking moronic questions and wearing short skirts, but maybe this was going to turn out to be a right place, right time kind of serendipity. She lifted her knee to test how high she'd need to hike up said skirt to make the big step.

"No. No! You can trust me. I've got it under control. You'll get your money's worth. We'll win tonight. Yes. By two. I got it."

There was another loud curse and the sound of shoes slapping tile as the man stormed out. Holly did an about-face in the stall and unlatched the door, hoping to catch a glimpse of the man, but she saw nothing. *Damn it, I missed him.*

But there, in the middle of the tile floor beside the sinks, was a folded piece of yellow legal paper. Holly rushed over and picked it up. It was a list of letters and numbers in stark black ink. L2+, W2+, W1, W1, W2 and on it went. And suddenly the cryptic conversation made a lot more sense.

Well, well, well. It looked like someone was partaking in a little over/under betting. But who was stupid enough to do that?

Not only was it illegal for someone affiliated with a professional sports team to bet on themselves, but it would get you banned for life from the sport, and that was on top of whatever criminal prosecution was handed down. And to risk all that on point-shaving? It was dicey at best, because no one player had full control over a hockey game. And yet, if you were favored to win anyway, there were subtle things you could do to make the game a little closer than it needed to be. Someone could have gotten cocky.

The Storm had already weathered a scandal earlier in the season, when the not-so-secret affair between captain Chris Powell and GM Ron Lougheed's trophy wife had become front page fodder. Lougheed and his soon-to-be-ex were currently fighting a pretty nasty custody battle in the courts—and in the media. This was the last thing the organization needed on its résumé, tainting its inaugural play-off run. But for Holly, it was perfect.

This was the windfall she'd been waiting for. Because breaking a story like this was the key to making herself the front-runner, not just for Corey Baniuk's position, but an on-air sports position at almost any station in the country. It was a first-class ticket to reporter legitimacy. All she had to do was figure out who the guilty party was.

She liberated her phone from her bra—she'd had to stow it there earlier because skirt suits like this one didn't come with pockets—and snapped a photo of the questionable list so she could inspect it more closely when she got home.

The key to a good investigation, her mother had told her once, was to let the action go on around you. If you disturbed things too early, you'd never get the answers you were looking for. To that end, she refolded the paper and placed it back where she'd found it.

It was the first time during this entire sham that Holly felt she might have made her mother proud.

Her head whipped around at the sound of a door swinging closed. Getting caught now would ruin everything.

She hurried back into the bathroom stall as quietly as her heels would allow. Was it her perp returning to the scene of the crime? Had he realized he'd dropped his list? Maybe this time she could catch a glimpse of whoever was striding into the bathroom.

She'd just pulled the stall door shut and was about to navigate her way up onto the toilet—no easy feat since there was only a toilet seat and no lid—when an indecipherable noise made her stop. There was a beat of dead silence, and then, "Holly, I know you're in there. I can see your shoes."

Busted.

She unlatched the door and did her best to appear sheepish. "Luke. Hey. I didn't hear you come in. You look nice. When did you get a chance to change? I thought you were filming puck tricks with Jay."

The surge of adrenaline at getting caught morphed into a surge of something else as she took in the sight of Luke Maguire looking big and handsome and powerful in the most beautifully tailored charcoal suit she'd ever seen. His silk tie was a deep plum and his blue eyes were flashing. "We finished up a while ago. I've already changed and done a pregame interview. Things move fast on game day. That's why I thought you were *gone*." He put particular stress on the last word.

Geez. How long had she been staring in that mirror? No wonder Paige was always late.

"Now maybe you can explain what the hell you're doing in here?"

She shot him a look that was all smart-ass. "It's a bathroom, Luke. Do I have to spell it out for you?"

He frowned at the joke, and she resisted the sudden urge to smooth his brow. Why was he so serious all the time?

"You need to get out of here, right now. Only the team can use the bathroom on game day." If she wasn't mistaken, he looked a little embarrassed when he explained. "It's a good luck thing."

"It's a stupid thing," she countered. "I'll never understand why elite athletes aren't more enlightened than medieval man."

"Well, you don't have to understand it. You just have to respect it. And keep your voice down! Guys are in and out of the dressing room this close to game time." He ran a hand through his close-cropped hair. "Jesus. Not even the cleaners are allowed in today. We've got to get you out of here before someone sees you. Come on." He reached out to cup her elbow, an old-fashioned gesture that took her by surprise. Holly was dismayed at the way her skin thrilled at the warmth of his fingers, even through the sleeve of her blazer.

She shrugged her arm from his grasp, an act of self-preservation.

Luke sighed, obviously interpreting it as an act of defiance.

"Holly, you remember all that stupid stuff you asked me earlier? I gave you the benefit of the doubt and I answered all your dumb questions because you were just doing your job. Now I'm trying to do mine, and part of me doing my job is making sure my guys are ready to play. Focused. And if maintaining a stupid superstition is what it takes to ensure we bring our A game tonight, then that's what I have to do. So do me a solid, okay? Even though it's silly, and inconvenient and probably makes no difference at all, *please* let's get out of here before anyone sees you?"

Holly had to look up at him, despite her four-inch heels and his lack of skates. When had he gotten so close? God, he was handsome, all tall and stubbly, his ocean-blue eyes pleading.

"Fine. Let's—"

"Shit. Someone's coming!"

Holly wasn't sure exactly how it had happened, but suddenly she was chest to chest with Luke inside the tiny bathroom stall, made positively miniscule by his large frame. She heard the telltale footsteps a moment later.

Luke scooped her into his arms, one hand around her back, his other forearm under her knees. He'd literally swept her off her feet, and the suddenness of it stole her breath. Her arms flew around his neck in self-preservation, and she was vividly aware of every inch of her body, especially the parts of her that were plastered against his broad chest.

She could feel his muscles beneath his suit jacket, enough to tell that they were barely straining under her weight. She shot him her best "what the hell?" glare through the onslaught of yum, and he gestured with his chin in the direction of her feet.

"Your shoes. That's how I knew you were in here."

He breathed the words quietly, his mouth so close that she could feel the exhalation against the sensitive skin beneath her ear. It tickled, and she turned her head to protect her neck. Suddenly there was nothing but a fraction of an inch's worth of air separating their lips.

His muscles flexed then, pulling her tighter to his chest and her breath came fast and shallow. Heat prickled over her skin and pooled in her belly. Her fingers clenched against the soft material of his jacket.

Holly had never experienced lust at first sight before, but man, Luke Maguire made her lust. She ran her hand up his chest, and he shifted his stance, but before their lips met, he banged his elbow against the stall. The thump reverberated through the bathroom, snapping them back into the present, and they froze, eyes wide.

They both cocked their heads toward the sink side of the stall, listening intently for any sign that they'd blown their cover.

After another moment of silence, Luke set her carefully on her feet. The lust hangover made Holly a little wobbly on her heels. He stepped forward and lifted onto his toes so he could see over the edge of the stall. "He's gone," he said, the words tinged with relief. They hadn't even heard him retreat.

Holly unlatched the door, and with a covert glance to assure herself they were, in fact, alone, took some tentative steps toward the sink. She paused for a moment, but the piece of paper wasn't on the floor, nor had it been kicked under the sink.

"No time for sightseeing, Evans." Luke's hand at the small of her back was warm and insistent. "Let's get out of here before you get caught."

They snuck back out to the dressing room, Holly letting Luke precede her so he could make sure the coast was clear. She wasn't four steps out of the bathroom before several members of the team strutted into the dressing room, bedecked in expensive suits and pregame gravitas. Luke sent her a "See? You really lucked out," kind of look.

Ass.

Then the "Charge" anthem sounded to her right. Holly's spine snapped straight as she watched Luke fish his iPhone out of the breast pocket of his suit jacket.

He glanced at the caller ID and that serious expression of his descended over his handsome face like a shutter. Holly decided she might prefer his pompous expression after all.

"I gotta take this," he said. She watched with interest as he turned away from her, shielding the call with his broad shoulders. "Why are you calling again? Seriously? Hold on." Was it her imagination, or did Luke glance in her direction. "Let me get somewhere I can talk."

The "Charge" fanfare? Why are you calling *again*? Pieces were falling into place and she didn't particularly like the picture they were forming.

Had it been Luke in the bathroom earlier? She'd just assumed that whoever had inadvertently held the two of them hostage had come back for his list. But now that she thought about it, Luke had definitely had enough time to pick up the wayward paper before he'd gone all foot fetishist on her and blown her hiding place.

That could be the reason he'd even noticed her shoes under the stall in the first place—he was bending over to pick up the list.

Holly strained to hear more of his conversation, but he pointedly disappeared back into the bathroom. To her dismay, there were too many team members in the swanky locker room now for her to follow. Still, the reporter buzz—that's what her mother used to call it—was zinging around her gut. She was on to something. Obviously Luke's regular deep baritone had sounded nothing like the whispered panic she'd heard earlier, but that ringtone was an indisputable clue, and one that she had to follow up on.

LUKE WALKED OVER to stand by the sinks, hating that his gaze went immediately to the stall he and Holly had hidden out in only moments ago.

But he couldn't afford to be distracted by sex right now. Harding Lowe was the kind of law firm that charged in the triple digits for phone calls like these, and with money as tight as it was, Luke had to pay close attention and cut to the chase. "What's so important?"

"I was going to wait until tomorrow to tell you this, but I'm worried it might hit the papers and I didn't want you to find out like that," Craig Harding informed him.

Luke's blood turned to ice. It was never good when someone started a phone call that way, but when it was your lawyer? Infinitely worse.

"What?" The word was flat, more demand than question.

"Brad Timmons is filing for bankruptcy."

Luke's face went numb. The asshole who'd put Ethan in a wheelchair, put his parents in debt, strained his family to the emotional breaking point time after time over the last three years, was going to screw them over again.

"Fuck."

The word echoed hollowly in the vast expanse of shiny white tile and empty navy stalls.

Luke wanted to punch something, but it wasn't worth the fine the Storm would levy against him if he did.

Jesus Christ, how had things come to this? He made almost two million dollars a year with his new contract and still it was all he could do to keep himself and the people he loved financially afloat.

Loans, renovations, lawyers, specialists, physio—it had all added up after the accident. His paycheck was all but spent before it got deposited. He was grateful he had the means to keep his family living a comfortably middle-class life despite their exorbitant bills, but the idea that the coward who'd put his little brother in a wheelchair wasn't going to have to contribute a dime to Ethan's recovery made Luke nauseous.

Timmons had already lucked out with his criminal charges. He'd been convicted of assault with a weapon for the crosscheck, but ended up with an eighteen-month conditional discharge, which meant he hadn't served any jail time and he wouldn't have a criminal record once his probation was complete. Now he'd found a way to punk out on financial restitution, too.

"Thanks for the heads-up, Craig. I'll take care of telling my family."

"Understood. I'll be in touch."

Luke hung up the phone. He would deal with the personal stuff later. Right now, he had to focus on his team. They were only two hours away from puck drop.

He reached into the inside breast pocket of his suit, exchanging his phone for a folded-up piece of yellow legal paper. He'd found it on the floor of the bathroom and recognized instantly what it was. That 5–0 loss had been brutal. The fact that it was predetermined made it cut even deeper. Luke shook his head against the proof clutched in his hand.

He couldn't believe any of his guys would do this. They'd battled too hard to get to where they were.

And yet…the entire premise of point-shaving and over/under betting was predicated on having an inside man, someone out there on the ice who could impact the game.

This was the last thing they needed right now. He'd only just put this team back together after losing their last captain in a blaze of scandal and lies. It had taken months of work to get all twenty-three players over the shake-up and focused on making the play-offs.

And look at them now.

The only bright spot in this rotten situation was that he'd been the one to find the betting sheet. At least this way he could deal with it internally—protect his team.

He didn't even want to think about how this would have played out if Holly had found it instead. She could've ruined their chance at winning the championship before it even began.

And he wanted that championship, not just for himself but for the team.

Each and every one of those guys deserved to hoist sports' greatest trophy above their heads, and he'd do whatever it took to make sure that happened.

For them. For himself. For his brother.

5

"We'll win tonight. Yes. By two."

The words still echoed in Holly's brain, hours after the final buzzer had sounded.

The Storm had handled their opponents with relative ease tonight, up 3–0 after two periods. Then at the start of the third, Sillinger had taken a bone-headed roughing penalty, Luke had fumbled the puck and failed to clear the zone, and seconds later, LaCroix had lost his chance for a shutout.

For a while, things settled down a bit, until Colorado scored to make it 3–2 with seven minutes left in the game. Things were looking grim for the list's prediction, and then Jacobs came out of nowhere, stripping one of his opponent's defensemen of the puck. He deked out the goaltender and put a wrister top-shelf to make the final score 4–2.

And the Storm won by two with eight seconds left in the game.

"You'll get your money's worth."

The eavesdropped whisper haunted her.

It could just be coincidence, she reminded herself. It

wasn't like 4–2 was an outlandish hockey score. And this was the first prediction on the list that had come true. She had nothing but suspicion at this point. Still, the words were on her mind as she conducted post-game interviews with the guys.

"Hi, everyone. This is Holly Evans of the Women's Hockey Network, reporting live from the Storm's dressing room after a big 4–2 win over Colorado tonight. I'm with Portland defenseman Doug Kowalchuk." She turned and held her mic in his direction.

"Doug, what do you think of the new jersey colors?"

On the ice, the burly D-man was a force to be reckoned with, but off ice, he reminded her of a big cartoon bear—imposing but nonthreatening. His grin was goofy and genuine. "They're great. Red and black is a really classic combination, you know?"

Holly couldn't quite mask the withering look on her face at his answer. She hoped Jay had zoomed in on the navy and teal jersey behind Doug instead of her face. *Seriously, this was her life now?*

"No, Doug. Not New Jersey's colors—I meant the Storm's redesigned jerseys."

"Oh right. Yeah. They're awesome. Go Storm!"

Holly forced a smile as she turned back to the camera. She could see Jay's shoulders shaking with laughter. "You heard it here, folks. Go Storm!"

When she was sure the camera was off, she let out a frustrated sigh.

"You're doing great," Jay assured her. "Who's next?"

Holly glanced around the scrum in the dressing room. She'd been hoping to sneak in an interview with anyone who'd made a direct contribution—be it positive or negative—to the final score tonight. She wanted to get an idea of their demeanors, a sense of their moods. But unfortunately, all four players that had risen to the top of her list—Eric, J.C., Luke and the rookie—were all big draws for reporters and had press queued up and waiting for them.

"I think we've got enough. Kowalchuk's was interview number five, and I'll do some highlight voice-overs later to cut with it. They only wanted a three-minute piece about the game, right?"

Jay nodded as he removed the camera from the tripod. "Yeah, that should be plenty."

"Okay. I'll catch you in about half an hour."

"Sure thing, Holly."

Now that she was off duty, she angled her way through the bustling dressing room toward the crowd around Eric Jacobs. He was known to be a little shy and incredibly humble considering the breadth of his talent, but he was always exceedingly polite to reporters and smiled easily. Holly hadn't seen him smile once tonight.

She listened in as Corey Baniuk asked Eric about his spectacular goal, but the handsome centerman seemed disinterested in the recap, a little tired maybe.

And though he made the Storm's PR department proud by saying all the right things—"Colorado played a great game and were worthy opponents," "I saw an opportunity and fortunately I was able to capitalize on it," "I couldn't have done it without my teammates"—there was none of the quiet intensity that he usually brought to an interview and his gaze wandered, like he was preoccupied.

Then the "Charge" anthem played, and panic flashed across Eric's handsome face. He turned away from the cameras and microphones being shoved in his direction and dug his phone out of the pocket of his jacket.

What the...? Eric and Luke have the same ringtone?

Eric's expression darkened when he glanced at the caller ID, as if he was expecting bad news from whomever was on the line. "Excuse me, please, I have to take this," he said to the group of reporters.

After Eric left, the reporters dissipated quickly, rushing off to grab quotes from other players before their allotted time in the dressing room was up.

Holly pulled out her phone and typed her observations into the memo she'd titled *SUSPECTS*. This investigation was the key to parlaying this farcical job into something she could be proud of, and every clue counted. To prove it, she added a note about the dark circles under Eric's eyes and the fact that his last-minute goal corresponded to the +2 win predicted by the list. And the ringtone, obviously.

"Texting or 'Candy Crush'?"

Holly started, almost dropping her phone at the sound of a voice so close behind her. "Oh, geez. Luke, you scared me!"

He jutted his chin in the direction of her phone. "Your thumbs were really burning up the keyboard."

She tucked the phone back in her bra, trying not to notice that his eyes tracked her hand, making the move feel far more suggestive than she'd meant it. "Oh, you know. Reporter notes," she said vaguely, hoping she was pulling off nonchalance. "So what's the story with the matching ringtones? You and Eric have some kind of 'linemates for life' pact or something?"

"Team building. Everyone on the team is using it,

kind of a 'keep hockey your top priority during the play-offs' type of thing."

"Your idea." It wasn't really a question so much as a statement. That was exactly the type of hands-on captaincy she expected from the man standing beside her. And also a huge hit to finding her guilty party, since it put everyone on the team back on the suspect list.

"Yes."

"That's great! Do you mind if I talk about that in the piece we're putting together? People love fun little details like that."

"Sure. I know you're all about the fun little details," he said pointedly.

Man, he was tenacious. Even after the sexually charged moment in the bathroom stall earlier, he wasn't about to let her off the hook. Holly had to admit, she liked that about him. And she really liked that this battle of wills they had going on made her feel as if he was talking to the real Holly Evans, not the persona she'd agreed to play. It restored her faith in men to see that Luke Maguire wasn't about to be derailed by some off-the-charts sexual tension. For the first time all evening, her smile was completely genuine.

"Well, I should probably go help Jay pack up. Good game tonight."

"No, it wasn't."

His candor stopped her.

It really hadn't been, but while she admired his honesty, she wasn't going to get tricked into revealing her cover. He might be a worthy opponent—his entire life was predicated on it—but when she put her mind to something, she wasn't to be underestimated.

Except in this case, she reminded herself, since her

entire goal was to convince him to underestimate her. To that end, she scrunched her face in a way she hoped might convey bewilderment. "What? But you guys won. Aren't you happy?"

"It'll do," he said simply.

"Well, I thought you guys were awesome." She couldn't tell if he was buying her enthusiasm.

Meanwhile, his big sweaty body and mussed-up helmet hair were making her remember those stolen moments in the bathroom earlier.

Focus, Holly! She made a point to slow her steps to a reasonable pace as she walked away, even though her thoughts continued to race.

Luke cared about his team. That was obvious. The question was, did he care enough about them to cheat? For some reason, Holly hoped that her investigation turned up nothing incriminating. At least, not on Luke Maguire.

LUKE WATCHED HOLLY walk away.

Normally, he would have been glad for the team's win, but since it had come at the price of the list being correct, he wasn't able to let himself enjoy it.

And Holly had sidled right up to Eric, the one who'd fulfilled the list's prophecy.

Luke had planned on talking to the centerman, too. Eric had seemed really down lately—quiet as ever, but in a different way. Like something was wrong. Like his heart wasn't in the game.

What were the odds that Holly "I'm not that into hockey" Evans had randomly chosen Eric to target... Luke didn't like the way their instincts were lining up. And her whole demeanor had changed when she thought no one was watching—the set of her shoulders, the look in her eye. It was as though she'd flipped the switch from bubbly to...almost predatory.

He recognized that look. It was the one reporters always gave him before they sank their teeth into him. The way they'd looked after Ethan got hurt. The way they'd come at the team after Chris Powell had been traded. Luke had learned many times over that you couldn't trust anyone whose livelihood depended on uncovering secrets.

So he'd circled up behind Holly, trying to see what she'd been typing so furiously. But she'd bobbled her phone when he'd spoken, and he hadn't managed a good look at the screen.

And then she'd turned to him, a little bit breathless, slightly flushed, and his hormones had surged like they had back in that bathroom stall. His objectivity had been effectively drowned in a tidal wave of good old-fashioned lust.

"What's up, Mags?"

Luke looked over at goaltender Jean-Claude LaCroix. Despite a long history together in the minor leagues, it wasn't until Luke had been traded to the Portland Storm after Ethan's accident that the two of them had really cultivated a friendship.

"Hey, J.C. Nothing. Just trying to get the inside scoop on what stupid interview questions we'll be enduring tomorrow. Because distraction is just what a team in play-offs needs," he added. The bitterness that laced his voice was genuine.

"Ha. Yeah, she's pretty hot, huh? If you're gonna be distracted, she's the way to do it."

Luke's head whipped toward his friend. He didn't

like the way that comment bothered him. It felt almost like…jealousy? "Do you trust her?"

J.C. seemed genuinely surprised by the question. "What's to trust, man?"

"You don't think she's up to something? As if she's putting on an act so she can snoop around?"

"Luke, be serious. Her latest question was, 'name the last show you binge watched.' I really doubt there's much to worry about here," J.C. told him. "Management hired her to be comic relief. Ask us softball questions to make us look charming and funny so we can sell more jerseys. It's not as if she's a real reporter."

"I guess. But doesn't it seem odd to you that someone with no apparent hockey knowledge would even bother to apply for this position?"

His friend chuckled. "Dude, she's a YouTube phenomenon looking to cash in on her fifteen minutes. And management is taking advantage of it. Don't overthink it."

"You're probably right." Luke frowned. "I just can't shake this feeling that she's more of a reporter than anyone gives her credit for."

"We all have enough trouble without searching for more. So keep your focus on the game and forget about this inconsequential stuff. We tanked the first game. Tonight we were out for redemption. There's a lot of series left. Keep your eye on the prize."

Luke nodded. J.C. was right. But for some reason, he couldn't get Holly out of his mind.

He *wanted* to see her again. He wasn't quite sure when it had happened, but he realized in that moment that sparring with her had become the best part of his day.

6

"Can I talk to you for a sec?"

Holly looked up from her notes about her latest piece—she was headed to the parking lot so the Storm players could answer silly questions and show off their sweet rides—to find J.C., hands shoved in his pockets, looking sheepish.

"Is this car tour optional? Because I'd rather not do it."

"Oh. You mean, ever? Or did you just want me to reschedule?"

"I mean ever. I just…there's some family stuff going on right now. I know you usually don't get through the whole roster when you're doing interviews, so I was hoping you could skip me for the car tour today. I'm happy to do the other part—the teammate question stuff."

"Okay, that's fine. I can pick someone else."

The relief on his face was almost comical, except that it was a little too extreme for someone who'd just dodged the fluffiest interview of all time.

"LaCroix! Quit flirting and go do your tour so the rest of us can get on with ours."

The rest of her interviewees were milling about the dressing room, waiting to head outside with her.

"Bite me, Kowalchuk. I'm not doing the car stuff."

"Ha! Of course you're wussing out!" Sillinger laughed. "Have you seen the piece of crap he's driving lately? Some low-end, old-man SUV. It's almost as bad as Luke's truck!"

"You got rid of the Porsche?" Luke sounded genuinely surprised to hear. Weird, considering he and J.C. seemed quite close. Holly made a mental note to add J.C.'s vehicle downgrade to his suspect file.

"Back off, guys. You do your interviews and let me do mine."

There was a bite to the usually affable goaltender's voice, and judging by the looks on his teammates' faces, Holly knew she wasn't the only one who found it odd.

Sillinger wasn't cowed. "Hey, don't take it out on us just because you're cruising around town in an old guy's ride."

"Yeah, well, sometimes you gotta make sacrifices. Dads have to think about safety, not flash."

There was a long moment of silence as the not-quite-an-announcement sank in. Luke was the first to wade into the breach.

"Tania's pregnant? Congratulations, man! That's great!" Luke and J.C. shook before Luke pulled him in for a laudatory slap on the back.

"Yeah. Not quite the plan, but what are you gonna do?"

Holly watched as the Storm gathered around their goalie, congratulating him on the big news. A new baby on the way. That was a pretty good reason to sell your sports car, she supposed. Guess she didn't need to update the suspect file after all. Maybe she could score an exclusive on potential baby names, though…

"See?" crowed the rookie. "Dad vehicle. Just like I said. Come on, Holly. I'll show you what a real man drives."

"Says the guy who rolled up to his first practice in a Ford Fiesta," J.C. shot back.

"That was my old life. Now my ride lives up to my standards. Wait until you see it," he promised, bouncing like a toddler on a sugar high. "Cherry-red Lamborghini with black leather interior. It's so sweet, you might get diabetes just looking at it."

"Jesus, rookie," Luke warned. "You remember the first three years of your contract are flat-rate, right? Pace yourself or you're going to outspend your bank account before you start raking in the big bucks."

Holly hadn't even considered that. Sillinger was only making about three hundred thousand a year. Not chump change by any means, but it made it tight to rock two-hundred-thousand-dollar cars and a place to live, on top of day-to-day expenses. And the kid was not rolling in endorsement deals. Not yet, anyway.

"Don't you worry about me. If you got the fame, there's always a way to bring in the money."

Holly tried not to react outwardly to the sentiment, but she filed it away for parsing later. Under the guise of sending a text, she typed it into the Sillinger file on her phone, but when she glanced up, it was to find Luke watching her with narrowed eyes. She shot him a bright, innocent smile and followed the rookie out to his car. .

LUKE INHALED DEEPLY and let the cool scent of arena ice soothe him. The lights were off, except for a few spotlights shining down from the press catwalk high above and all the seats in the building were bathed in shadows. No one clapped, no one jeered, there was just the rhythmic sound of the cut of his blades echoing through the empty rink as he skated a slow, easy lap. To Luke, it was heaven, a balm to his battered nerves.

There was nothing better than a moment alone on the ice. It reminded him of his early childhood, before his family had moved to Oregon when he was nine. He'd spent many a Michigan winter outside, whiling away the hours pretending he was Gretzky or Hull or Lemieux on the patch of ice his dad had made for him in the backyard.

He'd needed this, a minute to himself, so he'd bailed on Holly's car tours, suited up and come out here under the guise of breaking in his new gloves. Truth was, he wanted to clear his head. Thanks to a neatly folded piece of yellow legal pad and a certain blonde in sky-high heels, everything was too complicated right now. One of his guys was putting himself ahead of the team by playing the inside man on a point-shaving operation.

And if Holly was aware of it and just waiting until she had enough evidence to expose one of his guys, he needed to beat her to it. It was imperative that he deal with this quickly and quietly. The Storm couldn't weather another scandal.

He snagged the puck he'd brought out with him as he skated past and bounced it off the boards to himself. He'd dreamed of winning hockey's ultimate prize for as long as he could remember. But now that he was finally back in the play-offs, his play was lackluster, at best. He needed to do better, play better.

He owed that to his team, who were counting on

their captain and looking to him to set an example. He owed it to his parents, who had sacrificed so much to support him on his hockey quest. And he owed it to Ethan. His little brother had always been the better hockey player, much as Luke had hated to admit it. But it had become obvious by the time the little punk turned ten that he was destined for big things. Even through his jealousy, Luke had always been proud of Ethan, cheering him on, pushing him harder.

And since Ethan couldn't be in the play-offs himself because of the accident, it was Luke's duty to succeed on his behalf.

Yet despite the pressure, and the hoopla, and his messed-up shot, Luke was having a hard time focusing on anything but Holly.

She was ballsy. He liked that about her. Most reporter types, though dogged, kept a reverential tone when they talked to the players, as if they were trying to butter them up. Not Holly. She was a straight shooter, which he appreciated. But it was also the reason he couldn't quite buy her ditzy routine. He'd met plenty of women who couldn't care less about hockey during his lifetime, and she wasn't quite pulling it off.

He'd been unwillingly impressed that she hadn't taken the Ethan bait, though. Despite all the red flags, he *liked* her. What was that about? He hadn't been "in like" with a woman since, well, since ever. "In like" was for mooning high school students.

All his recent relationships had been about good fun, good conversation and good sex…not necessarily in that order. But when it was time for him to suit up, hockey reigned supreme. So why was she always creeping into his thoughts now?

Luke stopped at center ice and sent the puck sliding toward the net, watching until it crossed the goal line and came to a stop at the back of the net.

Maybe Sillinger was right. Maybe it was just lust and he should get it out of his system. Maybe if he spent some time with her, he could break this ridiculous and ill-timed crush on the infuriating woman who kept popping into his mind at the most inopportune of moments.

He turned to leave the ice but stopped short. As if he'd conjured her, Holly Evans was standing in the players' box, arms crossed over her chest, waiting for him. And every single reason that he should stay away from her left his brain.

"YOU CAN'T HIDE from me forever."

Luke skated over. "Who says I'm hiding?"

"You're the one out on the ice, avoiding the interview we're supposed to do. I'm the one who's here, questions at the ready, reporting for duty."

"You calling me a coward?"

"Hey, if the skate fits…"

He smiled at that, and her heart stuttered. She'd never seen him smile for real before. He'd flashed his PR smile on a couple of occasions during their on-camera stuff, but his real grin was something to behold. It was the first time he'd looked carefree. Like he didn't have the weight of the world on his shoulders. And it suited him. She had the irrational urge to make that smile come out more often.

"You think I'm gonna fall for some thinly veiled reverse psychology? I play hockey for a living. Trash talk doesn't faze me. You'll have to do better than that."

Luke stepped off the ice and over the boards like

they were nothing—God, why was that so hot?—and sat down on the bench. Holly turned her back to the ice and leaned against the boards, facing him. He set his stick against the side of the box and divested himself of his hockey gloves and his helmet. Then he ran a hand back and forth over his helmet hair. Somehow, after just a few careless swipes, his short brown coif looked photo ready. Holly lamented the hour and a half it had taken to make herself camera presentable.

"You don't like me very much, huh?" she asked.

"I don't like that you take the team's focus off the game and disrupt our routine. We need to be at our best, mentally and physically. I have to trust that every man on that ice is playing for me, and they have to believe I'm playing for them, too."

"Admirable sentiment, Captain Maguire, but there's really only one person you have complete control over. Sometimes you just have to keep it simple and play the game for you."

"I know exactly who I'm playing for," he countered. Then he went on the offensive. "So, Ms. Reporter, what kind of hard-hitting questions do you have for me tonight?" he asked, pulling his elbow pads off and setting them beside him. "What I ate for breakfast? The last song I downloaded?"

Luke pulled off his shoulder pads and jersey together and set the amorphous mound on the bench. Just like that, he was stripped down to a T-shirt—a T-shirt that was damp and clinging to his muscles. Suddenly his leg seemed very close to her bare thigh, and the fact he was wearing shin pads and hockey socks didn't deter a warm tingling from spreading through her body.

"Favorite sexual position?" he continued.

Oh geez. That warm tingling upgraded to hot throbbing in a split second.

He stood up. His skates made him incredibly tall. He loomed over her, but she didn't feel threatened. On the contrary, she felt sort of powerful—like she wanted to tame the beast. The smoldering look in his eyes said he'd let her. Somewhere, in the deep recesses of her brain, a warning light flashed.

She was here to do a job. She shouldn't get romantically involved with a story. Especially not a top suspect in a betting scandal that had the potential to rock the sports world. Her head knew walking away was the smart play right now, but her body overruled the call, especially since he'd provided the perfect opening. "So what *is* your favorite sexual position?"

His eyes darkened like a stormy sky. "Off the record?"

"Of course." Her words were a breathless rush.

"I like all of them." He reached for her, his big hands biting into her hips. She wrapped her arms around his neck as he hoisted her onto the edge of the boards and stepped between her legs. Her short skirt slid farther up her thighs, but she barely noticed the cold plastic against her skin. His mouth came down on hers, stealing her breath and wringing a moan from her.

God, she wanted him. Something about Luke Maguire called to every cell in her body.

Screw journalistic integrity, she decided. Finding out hockey players' favorite colors barely counted as journalism anyway. Then she stopped thinking altogether.

There was nothing but his lips against hers, his hands tugging her blouse from the waistband of her skirt and the sexy thrill of knowing that he was the only thing keeping her from falling onto the ice. Despite that imminent danger, she trusted he'd keep her safe.

He groaned as he slid his warm palm under her shirt and up the bare skin of her back. She returned the sound. The dichotomy of the cool, icy air and the warmth of his skin was a delicious push deeper into the sensual spell he'd cast.

She resented the T-shirt he was wearing and she tugged it up, revealing those washboard abs Paige had been so enamored with in the pages of *Sports Illustrated*. They were even better in real life, and Holly took pleasure in revealing each ridge, the definition of his pecs, his beautiful big shoulders and the flex of his muscles as he raised his arms so she could divest him of the shirt entirely. And then he was all naked torso and harsh wanting.

Holly couldn't get enough.

LUKE WAS OVERWHELMED by the desire inside him, clawing to get out. He was used to being in charge, but something about Holly unleashed the beast in him, made him want to lose control.

He let go, let himself drown in the lust, because he needed the escape. He needed her.

He wished he hadn't suited up, because there was no way he could shuck his skates, shin pads and hockey pants, but he wanted inside her too much to resist the desire. He ran his hand up under her skirt, groaning when he found her most intimate place.

He brushed his knuckles against the damp swath of her panties. She gasped and buried her face against his neck, her arms tightening around him.

Luke was certain he'd never felt more turned on in

his entire life while wearing so many clothes. There was something so amazingly sexy about the feel of her warm, smooth skin and the sounds of pleasure that escaped her throat, juxtaposed with the cool air and the familiar scent of ice and concrete that he loved so much. The heady scent of passion mixed with the comforting smell of the rink.

"Just so we're clear, this doesn't change anything," he panted. He pulled her underwear down her thighs. The first touch of his fingers on her clit made her stiffen. "I still hate that you interview my team like we're appearing in a teen magazine."

Slowly, he eased a finger inside her, and his gentle invasion was almost his undoing as he imagined himself sliding into her the same way. Her body, which had been tense, relaxed as he built her pleasure up. After a few strokes, he used two fingers to give her the friction she was craving so badly. His hips mimicked the thrust of his hand, increasing the pressure on her clit.

"Fair enough. And just so we're crystal clear," she breathed, arching toward him, unable to hold back any longer, "I'm still going to do it."

He could tell when he found her G-spot because she bit her lip and her fingernails dug into his back, pulling him closer. The sound of her breath grew choppy and it was the sexiest thing he'd ever heard. Until she moaned his name.

It short-circuited his brain and he sped the pace of his fingers, rubbing his thumb against her clit, moving his hand to the rhythm of her desire until she came apart in his arms, her cry of release echoing through the arena.

She sagged forward, her forehead resting on his

shoulder. He took a deep breath to calm his racing heart, but all he got was a lungful of her, a scent that was warm and female and sweet...like apples.

"That was amazing." Her smile was radiant, free.

He fought back a flood of testosterone that hit him so hard it was tough to think straight. He hadn't seen a smile like that maybe ever, and definitely not after sex.

The women he'd been with usually tried to act coy, or feigned modesty, or seemed embarrassed. Holly looked like a satisfied lioness who'd gotten exactly what she wanted.

"Paige was right. I definitely needed that."

He needed deep breaths and to not think about all the things they hadn't done together yet. "Who's Paige?"

"My best friend. She's been threatening to hire me a male escort because she's worried that my 'special flower' is crying out for some water. Her words, not mine."

Okay. Well, that *was as good a mood killer as any.* "She sounds like something else."

"Oh, she's something else all right."

A sudden crack followed by a loud hum echoed through the arena, and one by one, the big overhead lights fired up.

Luke swore as he, half-naked, and Holly, barely dressed, both instinctively dropped down behind the boards. It took him a moment to process what had happened.

"It's just the cleaning crew," he explained. He was about to get up, but when he looked over, instead of the panicked or angry woman he expected to find, Holly had both hands clamped over her mouth. "Holly?"

He was about to ask if she was okay when a giggle

slipped out from behind her fingers. Her shoulders were rocking and she was laughing so hard that Luke couldn't help but join her. God, she was pretty.

He leaned in conspiratorially. "Why are we still hiding?"

"Because my contract specifically states I'm not supposed to fraternize with members of the Portland Storm franchise. A clause, may I point out, that does not appear in my cameraman's contract."

Her put-out frown made him chuckle. "Well, they may not be a very enlightened bunch, but in management's defense, I've never seen Buchanan's practical white cotton panties." He grabbed said underwear from the ground beside his hip and held them out to her.

"Hey, these are really comfortable," she said, snatching them from his fingers. With a pretty blush, she glanced over at Luke's naked torso. "And touché. But I'd rather not get fired for engaging in an illicit affair with a member of the team because we were stupid enough to let the cleaning staff catch us."

"Is that what this is?" Luke asked, grabbing his T-shirt from the bench and pulling it back on. "An illicit affair?"

"This," she said, "was a mistake. A big one."

She had a point. He'd let her goad him into losing control. And boy, had he lost it. Yet he couldn't quite bring himself to regret it. Or stop himself from imagining Holly in his bed.

"I still owe you an interview. I'm going to head back to the dressing room and grab my stuff. Give me a couple minutes' head start so that no one suspects anything, and I'll meet you at the exit to the player parking lot."

"Aye, aye, captain."

She made a face at him before she hurried out of the

box and down the hallway with speed and stealth, despite her high heels.

As she disappeared around the corner, Luke leaned back against the boards, relishing the bracing sensation of cold plastic against his overheated skin. He'd never admit it aloud, but that had been the most genuine fun he'd had in a hockey arena in ages.

HOLLY WALKED THROUGH the parking lot beside the man who was responsible for her first non-self-induced orgasm in over a year. And thanks to his prowess, she found him even more attractive, something she wouldn't have thought possible before he'd unleashed a tsunami of delicious endorphins in her system. She'd forgotten how freaking fantastic sex could be. Holly vowed in that moment she'd never let herself forget again.

She couldn't help stealing glances at his handsome profile as they headed toward his black Ford F-250 pickup truck. Holly knew it was his because it was the last vehicle left in the fenced-in players' parking lot. He walked her over to her side of the vehicle and pulled the door open for her, and she crawled up into the black leather cab, waiting as he headed around to the driver's seat.

Get it together, girl. Time to focus.

"So," he said, crawling into the bucket seat beside her, "this is my truck."

He looked nervous, like he cared what she thought. She smiled and let him off the hook. "It's nice."

His answering grin was tinged with equal measures of relief, pride and embarrassment. The combination was utterly adorable.

"It's my one real indulgence. Money's been tight, so I try to keep the extravagances to a minimum."

Holly frowned. She was trying to keep it light and in standard Women's Hockey Network territory, and he just kept dumping incredible openings in her lap. Luke's latest contract was for just south of six million dollars over three years. How tight could money be? "Not a sports car kind of guy?"

Luke shrugged. "Can't haul a wheelchair in a two-seater."

Luke and Holly both froze at his slip. The blatant reference to Ethan hung there for a long moment. And after what they'd just shared, Holly felt she couldn't ignore it. "I read about what happened to your brother. I'm incredibly sorry for what your family has been through. What you've been through."

A weird pressure filled the cab. It was like she could feel Luke withdrawing into himself, but also fighting not to. She wasn't at all sure which part of him was going to win until he rolled his shoulders and tipped his head from side to side, like a boxer loosening up for a match.

After a deep breath, he finally spoke. "Yeah, it's been a tough couple of years. But Ethan's a fighter. And you don't want to hear the sob story. So how exactly does this work? You're just going to ask me some questions?"

Oh right. The interview.

"Yeah, if you can turn on your interior light, I'll just ask you about the truck, your first car, your favorite song to cruise to, that kind of stuff." She gave him the rundown while she pulled her phone out. Once she switched it to video mode, they were ready to roll. He was a good sport, and they sped through the questions.

Holly was just leaning toward him to show him the playback when the "Charge" anthem struck again.

"Sorry." Luke pulled out his phone. She couldn't quite read the expression on his face when he read the screen. "I have to take this."

She nodded, surprised to find he didn't leave the truck to answer the call. "Hey, Dad. How are you? Oh. Yeah, I heard. I was going to call and fill you in, but… uh…" He snuck a glance in her direction and flushed. "Practice ran late."

The G-rated reference to her amazing orgasm made her flush a little herself.

"Yeah, yeah. Don't worry about the money. It's covered. No problem. How's Ethan doing? Really? Well that's good, right?" He listened for a bit longer and then said his goodbyes.

He sighed and turned to her. "Sorry. That was my dad."

"Yeah, I got that." She smiled.

"Are you parked around here?" he asked, searching the near deserted parking lot.

"No, I caught a ride with Jay because my car's in the shop. It's okay, though. I'll just grab a cab."

"I'll drive you."

He looked as surprised as she was by the offer. "Oh. Well, if you're sure it's no trouble."

Holly told him her address and the big engine rumbled to life as he turned the key. She fastened her seat belt as the black behemoth rolled out of the parking stall under Luke's guidance.

"Sounds like you and your dad are close."

He shot her a look of surprise as he pulled out of the lot and onto the road. Night had fallen, and the roads around the arena had cleared.

Luke nodded. "Yeah, he's great." There was a smile in his voice that let her know he meant what he said.

The distance ticked by in ribbons of light and dark as they sped past streetlight after streetlight. There was something soothing about the calm quiet of the evening. It seemed to invite conversation, and Holly found herself saying more than she meant to, as though the residual physical intimacy they'd shared earlier was still lurking, searching for another outlet. "I'm jealous. My pop and I don't really get along that well."

"Nothing in common?" he asked.

Not for lack of trying, she thought, not proud of the bitterness that seeped in as she remembered the hours of her childhood she'd spent camped out on the couch, watching sports with her father, learning player names and stats, anything that might engage him in a more meaningful dialogue than, "What should we order for supper tonight, kids?"

"Well, he really loves his hockey."

"Is that why you took this job?" he asked, and she wondered at that.

Indirectly, she supposed, it was the reason behind every job she'd ever held. It was definitely the reason she strove to succeed in sports reporting. She craved her father's acceptance so blatantly that she was sure any psychologist worth her salt could pick her out of a lineup. Add that to her mother's long shadow, and it was pretty clear what drove Holly.

"Yes. Mostly. I stop by his place once a week to make

him dinner. I'd hoped maybe it would give us something to talk about."

It didn't work any better now than it had then, though, which was why she always timed dinner duty to coincide with a game she was covering for one of her freelance writing gigs—hockey, basketball, baseball—didn't really matter.

Keeping track of the game and taking notes for her articles always made the uncomfortable silence pass more quickly.

"I thought this job would impress him," she confessed. "But it hasn't. I'm not sure what the problem is. Maybe he hates the questions as much as you do. Before my mom died, I remember doing a lot of stuff with him. I miss that."

Holly often found herself wondering if her earliest memories were actually memories, or just dreams she made up of what a great family they'd been before cancer had stolen so much from her. "I want to ask him why we don't hang out or talk the way we used to, but I always chicken out."

Luke nodded as they took the exit that led to her neighborhood. "That's not just you. For the most part, my dad and I get along great, but family emotions can be tough to navigate. There's stuff I can't bring up with him, either." He paused. "Sometimes I worry that my parents blame me for what happened to Ethan."

Oh, God. Holly hadn't seen that coming, and it hit her like a kick to the gut. Did Luke really harbor that much guilt over an event that had been completely out of his control?

"The whistle blew. The game stopped. There was no warning when the hit came," he whispered.

He did a double take when she put a comforting hand on his arm. The startled look on his face, like she'd pulled him out of a memory, made her wonder if he'd meant to say that aloud.

He cleared his throat, motioning toward the upcoming turnoff. "This is the one?" he asked, effectively shifting the rest of their drive to a strictly navigator/navigatee dynamic.

When they rolled up to the curb in front of her house, she did her best to remove any pity from her smile, despite her breaking heart. "Thanks for the ride."

"No problem." To her surprise, he switched off the truck. "I'll walk you to the door."

They sauntered in silence up to the porch, side by side, in the chill of the night air. Their footsteps and the faint sound of distant cars were the only break in the quiet until they arrived at the front step. Her keys jangled as she pulled them from her purse and unlocked the door.

"Thanks so much for the ride, Luke. I really appreciate it."

"Not a problem. I just wanted to make sure you got home safe."

"And here I am," she said, motioning at her surroundings. "Safe."

"I guess I'll see you when we get back from Colorado then."

She nodded, and there was a weird moment where she wasn't sure if he was going for a hug or a handshake, and somehow it morphed into a bit of both, with a surprise cheek kiss thrown in for good measure.

"Good night, Holly."

"Good night."

With a smile, Holly stepped inside and pushed the door closed behind her. She dropped her purse and keys on the small table in the entranceway. Tonight had been...incredible. From the sexy encounter in the players' box, to laughing with Luke without a care in the world, to navigating some emotionally dense daddy issues while he drove her home.

Even the awkward cheek kiss had been kind of perfect. In a way, it was representative of this crazy friend-or-foe relationship they had going on. And suddenly, and with complete clarity, she knew that if she didn't do something, right then and there, to foster whatever fragile, new thing had bloomed between them tonight, then it would be lost forever.

She yanked the door back open with two hands, ready to run down the street after his truck if she had to.

Instead, she found him standing on the step, arm arrested in knocking-position.

HE'D BEEN ABOUT to rap on the door when she'd suddenly pulled it out of the way.

Luke had meant to leave, he really had, but he'd barely made it down the steps before he'd turned around. The prospect of being alone tonight was too much. Not with all that family stuff bubbling up in his brain.

He'd told her things he'd never said to anyone on the drive to her house. And the crazy part was, he was glad it'd been her.

She was addictive. A life raft in the midst of the sea of hockey that had overtaken his world. And tonight he wanted to be selfish. He wanted to do what he wanted, not what he should—consequences be damned.

"I can't stop thinking about you." He stepped toward her. And then his hand was buried in her hair, and his lips were devouring her lips, and she was pulling off his jacket as he pushed the door shut behind them. And for the first time since the Portland Storm had made the play-offs, Luke felt like he could breathe.

He was vaguely aware of the slap of his leather jacket hitting the floor, but suddenly her arms were around his neck and she was kissing him. His mind went incredibly, deliriously blank. With a growl of need, he grabbed the backs of her thighs and hoisted her into his arms, reveling in the press of their bodies as she wrapped her gorgeous legs around his hips.

"Which way's the bedroom?" he managed to ask when they finally came up for air.

"Over there," she said with a vague motioning of her head. He interpreted the gesture to mean he should turn down the hallway to their left. "Then last door on the right."

Their mouths met deeply, frantically, as he did his best to navigate without bumping into anything. He was eager to arrive at their destination but not willing to miss any part of the journey. There was something so elemental about carrying a woman to bed, kissing and touching and driving each other crazy. Luke couldn't get enough of it.

But inevitably, even through the halcyon buzz and the rushing hormones, Luke's responsible side made its presence known as they rounded the corner into her bedroom. "Please tell me you have condoms."

"Um…" She pushed her hair back from her face, brown eyes glazed with lust, lips swollen with his kisses and the rasp of his stubble.

Playing to Win

He'd never wanted anyone so badly in his life.

"I don't think so. But I'm on the pill. So if you're…"

She trailed off, and he nodded reassuringly. "I am. In my line of work, we get tested for everything—and I mean *everything*—regularly."

"I am, too," she said. "Clean, I mean."

Luke stood there, with Holly wrapped around him, and there was a breath of anticipation in the air as they enjoyed that split second of awareness that what they both so desperately wanted was about to happen.

And then that moment of restraint erupted into all-consuming flames. He crushed her mouth with his own, lowering her onto the mattress and following her down. They tugged off each others' clothes, revealing the bend of an elbow, the curve of a hip, the camber of a thigh until finally they were both naked.

She was as beautiful as he'd imagined, as he'd remembered, as he'd hoped. The kind of beauty that brought a man to his knees.

He pushed inside her, one long, deep stroke, and then, because he couldn't wait, he did it again. And again. Losing himself in the rhythm, taking everything he'd craved since they'd gotten down and dirty on the rink boards, loving that the reality of their bodies together was putting his fantasy to shame.

He braced himself on his elbows, trying to tell if she was as turned on as he was, if she liked it, if she was pissed that he'd gone straight for the main event and cheated her out of foreplay. But when he slowed the pace of his hips, she opened her eyes and whispered, "Don't stop. Just like that, Luke. Just like that."

His cock surged inside her and he increased his pace,

loving the soft, startled gasps of her pleasure and the bite of her fingernails against his back.

He buried his face in her neck and breathed, "You feel so good, baby. You make me feel so good."

HOLLY WAS BEWITCHED. Luke Maguire at peak concentration was a powerful force. It was like every cell of his body was focused on her, a visceral awareness that crackled in the air. Missionary was not usually enough to build such a powerful arousal in her, but already she could feel the telltale heat growing, throbbing. She dug her heels into the bed and met him thrust for thrust, ensuring she was taking every inch of him inside her.

She'd thought his fingers had been magical, but this, the heat of him between her thighs, the weight of him against her breasts, this was so much better.

The orgasm at the arena had been sharp, tingly and shallow, racing along her skin like flash paper. In short, nothing compared to the savage need that was building inside her with every stroke of his cock, every brush of his hands. She wanted more, and when she couldn't bear the scorching heat of it a second longer, she let go, reveling in the dark pleasure that erupted, thick and hot like lava, through her veins. All she could do was hold on, clutching Luke against her as their bodies shuddered with the aftershocks of the explosion.

7

"I THINK I HAVE a crush on my arch-nemesis," Holly confessed to Paige a few days later.

Holly did not add the fact that her arch-nemesis was a virtuoso in the sack and might be involved in illegal betting. Just because some of the Storm's games had correlated with the list didn't mean they all would. And this was not an accusation that could be made lightly.

"First of all, thank God. It's been a shockingly long time since you've had man problems." Paige popped the last bit of her cupcake in her mouth and pushed the plate to the edge of their usual table at Piece of Cake, a cute little bakery just down the street from Paige's salon. Holly had originally dragged Paige to the shop in a moment of pure fangirlism, because it was owned by none other than Eric Jacobs's grandma, but the legendary vanilla bean cupcakes kept them coming back time and time again. "And second of all, who?"

"Just this guy at work. He's trying to catch me in the charade. Thinks I know more about hockey than I'm letting on and he wants to figure out my angle. It's awful."

"Then why are you smiling?" Paige asked.

"What? I'm not smiling." But she was. Holly did her best to neutralize her expression.

Sure, Luke was gorgeous, but she shouldn't feel so infatuated. She knew it was a trick—the result of her parent issues. After she'd lost her mom, her father had never thought she was good enough, no matter how much sports trivia she memorized, no matter how insightful her comments. He'd never taken her seriously. And as for her mom…it was really hard to impress someone who wasn't even on this corporeal plane.

So to have this hockey god, a player she deeply admired and respected on the ice, with a body and a face that made her melt, to have him see through the facade that she was presenting, well…of course she was infatuated.

Still, she couldn't get too carried away. He'd been sweet the next morning, even made her breakfast. On his way out, he'd kissed her and said he'd see her after the team's away games in Colorado. But he hadn't exactly professed his undying love, or even promised to call.

Besides, she was the one who'd insisted it was a mistake. And then there was that pesky contract thing…

"Okay, now you're seriously frowning. What's up?"

"I dunno, Paige. It was just really hot."

Paige gave her a skeptical look. "What kind of hot? Taming-the-rebel hot? Corrupting-the-innocent hot? Wrestler hot?"

"What? Ew. No. What is wrestler hot? That doesn't even exist."

"Wrestler hot is when the guy is loud and confident and is kind of pulling off fringe. Besides, you know I love it when men glisten."

Holly took a sip of her macchiato. "It was black-and-white movie hot. Sexy banter, witty repartee…"

"Everyone was wearing all their clothes…" Paige joked.

Rarely had Holly hated her fair skin and propensity for blushing more than she did in that moment.

"Oh my God! Someone watered your special flower? Holly, I'm so proud of you!"

She winced. "Geez, Paige. Decorum much? Would you keep your voice down?"

"Fine, but only if you tell me *everything*."

"He's the only person who doesn't treat me like a complete idiot. He basically accused me of stepping on the Storm to get ahead and that he's sure I know more about hockey that I'm letting on."

"Ooh. I like a man who gets to the point. So what did you do?"

Holly shoved a hand through her hair with a sigh. It felt so much better when it wasn't teased and sprayed into submission. "Swore up and down that I definitely *was* an idiot and then doubled up on the act. I can't let him win! Besides, why does he care so much whether I'm asking his team some joke questions? What's he hiding?"

Besides, of course, a potential windfall of ill-gotten cash for selling out his team.

"Oh, my! Sex *and* intrigue? This is more serious than I thought! Give me every detail about the man who swept you into bed."

Holly tamped down the blush as best she could. She was not getting into the down and dirty in the middle of a crowded bakery. "He's tall, and handsome and serious, but in this appealing, cares-about-something kind of way. And he's built. Good God, the body on that man." Holly took a long, restorative gulp of caffeine.

"So what's the problem? You deserve to blow off some steam. I know this job has been a little tough on you. So if he's into it, have at him!"

"It's not that simple. We both work for the team."

Paige sighed. "Stupid ethics. They get in the way of all the best stuff. Can't you guys have a secret affair or something?"

Holly laughed at the wording, so similar to her own. "That's what I love about you, Paige. You're always full of ideas."

She smiled back. "Please. You held my hand throughout my divorce. Getting you laid is the least I can do."

"You don't think it's wildly unprofessional of me?"

Paige shook her head so hard that her ponytail swung side to side. "No way! First of all, they called you because you're a YouTube sensation and they wanted to hitch a ride on your star. They know they're beyond lucky to have you. And secondly, this is a temporary job, not your career. So if there's a hot guy who will get you back in the game, then I see nothing wrong with that."

"Back in the game?" Holly laughed as Paige took a dainty sip of espresso. "What, you're sporty now?"

"*My* inspirational speech, *my* metaphor. All the men I work with are gay. I'm living vicariously through you here."

"Excuse me?" said a voice from above them.

Holly and Paige glanced up to find a woman standing beside their table, a young girl in tow. Holly pegged the girl at around nine. She looked very nervous, the pen and napkin clutched in her fingers shaking enough to betray the tremor in her hands. "Aren't you Holly Evans?"

"Yep, that's me. Can I help you?"

The woman's smile turned radiant.

"I'm Lydia, this is my daughter, Teagan. We just love your show! Teagan was actually hoping to get your autograph." Lydia gave her daughter a little shove, and the girl held the napkin and pen out in front of her.

"Of course!" Holly made herself speak through the shock. She accepted the napkin and smiled at Teagan. "So you like sports?" she asked, scrawling a quick little message and adding her signature to the bottom. The girl just shrugged shyly and took the napkin Holly held out to her.

"Can I get a picture of you two?" Lydia asked, holding up her phone.

"Oh, sure!" She leaned in closer to Teagan, surprised when the little girl tucked right in beside her.

"Oh, that's a nice one! Thank you so much. Teagan, say goodbye to Holly."

Teagan threw her little arms around Holly's neck, and Holly was so surprised, it took her a moment to hug the girl back.

"Thank you for making my mom yell less about my daddy watching sports," she whispered. "I want to be just like you when I grow up." Then Teagan pulled away and gave Holly a timid smile before she hurried to her mom's side again.

"How adorable was that?" Paige gushed. "What did she say to you?"

"She said she wants to be like me when she grows up."

Paige placed a well-manicured hand over her heart. "I think I just died a little from cuteness!"

The shrill ring of her phone shook Holly out of the surreal moment, and she grabbed it from the back pocket of her jeans. "Jay, what's up?"

Her tablemate made a face and Holly rolled her eyes at the childish gesture. *Grow up*, she mouthed, and then said into the phone, said, "I'm just having breakfast with Paige—hey. Be nice."

Paige frowned at the unheard insult.

"What? Are you serious? When? Oh my God. Thanks for the heads-up! Yes, of course I'm going to submit my résumé right now. Yeah. I'll talk to you later. Thanks again."

"What? What's going on?"

"Jim Purcell finally retired!" The announcement came out a little high-pitched and squealy, but Holly was so stoked she didn't even care.

"Oh my God!" Paige seal clapped with glee. "Who is that and why do we care?"

Holly laughed. She and Paige might be polar opposites, but she couldn't ask for a better, more supportive friend. "Jim Purcell is the sports anchor on *Portland News Now*."

"Right! The old guy with the bad toupee."

"Exactly. And if he's retiring, that means that the one and only Corey Baniuk is most likely getting promoted to the anchor desk as we speak. And that means..."

"That they will be looking for an amazing, knowledgeable, well-spoken replacement—who is you!" Paige's seal clap was genuine this time. "We have to get you home immediately," she exclaimed, downing the rest of her espresso. "You need to email that stellar résumé of yours to them at once. At once, I say! And then later, I'll take you out for dinner and we can celebrate this big step in your quest for nightly news dominance."

Holly smiled, appreciative of Paige's enthusiasm. "A lovely offer, but I'm having dinner with my dad tonight."

"Fine. I'll eat alone. But I'm having champagne in your honor and you can't stop me."

Paige's over-the-top zeal was a nice little ego boost, but Holly couldn't afford to lose sight of the truth. There were a lot of résumés out there far more stellar than hers.

But, she rationalized, if she could be the one to break a certain hockey scandal wide open at just the right moment… that was exactly the sort of thing that could make her stand out from a crowd.

"Hey, Pop. How's it going?"

"I'm still alive."

The gruff response was a typical one, and Holly sighed as she stopped at her father's recliner and pressed a kiss to his forehead. "Well, at least you've got that going for you. Tacos okay tonight?" she asked, heading toward the kitchen.

"I could eat a taco or two."

"Perfect. Put the game on and turn it up so I can hear it from in here." Holly hefted the bag of groceries onto the counter and set about unpacking. She put the hamburger in a skillet, sliced up some toppings and dumped the cheese in a bowl, glad she'd sprung for pre-shredded.

The third game of the series had ended with an uninspired 1–0 win for Portland. She knew that because she'd ghostwritten no less than seven articles about it. Not that she was complaining. Play-offs were always a nice bump to the bank account. Tonight they were playing the second of their two-game road trip. Which meant that, except for televised interviews, she hadn't seen a certain hot captain in a few days. She missed him.

But tonight she had to focus on the game and on Pop. Judging by the announcers' lack of enthusiasm, the Storm seemed to be headed for a scoreless first period. She hoped the second period would bring more excitement, because she had another seven articles due bright and early in the morning.

What could she say? Freelancing was not the most glamorous lifestyle. You wrote what people wanted, when they wanted it. That was why she preferred op-eds. It was nice to inject a little personality and analysis into a piece every now and again. But she couldn't afford to be too choosy. It was the no-frills assignments that paid the bills.

Whenever the cooking permitted, she snuck a glance at the big TV, her father's only real indulgence. Everything else in the small bungalow was almost exactly the same as it had been when she'd grown up here. Same oatmeal-colored carpeting, same dated brass lamps, same crystal knickknacks sitting in exactly the same spots, as evidenced by the dust.

It was a house full of good memories and dismal reality. Before her mother had died, the place had been cheery and full of love. Since her passing, it had gotten stuck in time, and there was a palpable desperation to a house that seemed to just be waiting for someone who was never coming back.

With a sigh, Holly served up two plates of soft tacos

and headed into the living room to join her father. She took her usual place on the threadbare couch after she handed him his supper, which he accepted with a grunt. "Pop, you think maybe it's time to get some new furniture?" she asked, noticing that he'd finally given in and duct-taped the armrest on his recliner. "You know, spruce the place up a little?"

"It doesn't need sprucing."

"Your chair is falling apart. It's older than I am."

"I fixed it, didn't I?"

Holly sighed. There was no budging him when he was being stubborn. "Like trying to charm a pig outta mud," her mother used to say, although to Holly's recollection, Diane Evans had always managed to get her husband to come around to her way of thinking.

Holly hadn't inherited that particular gift, so instead of arguing with her father, she dug in to her taco.

As they waited for the second period to get underway, the station was showing highlights from another game being played that night. A San Jose player tipped the puck into the opposition's net, and the home crowd went wild.

"Montana's gonna blow it. Those guys can't get their defense in order." Her dad's words were muffled by a mouthful of taco.

"I don't know. Federov and Rogers are a pretty good duo when their forwards are hot."

"Your brother thinks they should trade 'em both."

Holly shook her head. "No way. If they're going to trade anyone, it should be Powell. He's not living up to his potential because they don't have anyone good enough to play with him. But he's had a decent enough season, so they'll get something in return for him. Plus, he's got a real attitude. He's not gelling with the team."

No comment. Of course. Instead of acknowledging the brilliance of her strategy, he took another giant bite of his taco.

She watched and reported on sports for a living. Her brother was an electrician. Why *wouldn't* Neil's comments hold more weight?

Holly took a sip of her beer. It wasn't unexpected, but it always stung. She couldn't figure out why she kept setting herself up for the TKO, but at some point on these visits, she always brought up sports and always got shut down.

You'd think I'd have learned by now.

For a long time, Holly had figured her father's distance had something to do with her being a girl. Maybe he couldn't relate to her without her mother there as a buffer. And that sucked. But then her niece Melissa had come along and wound her grandpa around her little finger. He went to her hockey games and cheered louder than anyone. It hurt.

As they settled into watching the second period, Holly grabbed the notebook she'd set on the small table next to her dad's chair and began taking her usual game notes. It didn't take long before she found herself nitpicking the game, though. Well, not the game so much as the players. More specifically, the players she most suspected of game tampering.

Holly started an impromptu plus/minus tally on all the potential suspects from the last game. Brett Sillinger, for a boneheaded penalty, Luke for coughing up the puck, Eric Jacobs for a heroic play that had maintained the two-goal lead. It was more in-depth stat keeping than she usually bothered with, but then again, this was about more than a couple of "last night in hockey" reports. This was about making a name for herself in the world of sports.

Each time one of them was on the ice and the Storm scored, she gave them a plus sign. If one of them was on the ice and Colorado scored, she marked a minus sign. When the final buzzer scored to herald a 3–2 win for the Storm, Eric was +1 and Luke and the rookie were both sitting at -2. Not up to the season's standards for any of them. Which wasn't to say that bad games didn't happen. Still, trends were tracked for a reason.

"I thought these guys would walk all over Colorado. None of them are playing up to snuff."

Holly nodded at her father's summation. "You're right. Even when they win, they're performing statistically worse than I'd have suspected."

Her father harrumphed. "I'm going to get another beer. You want one?"

"I'm good, thanks."

And for once, Holly actually was.

She glanced at the stats filling the left side of her notebook—the list had been right about the spread again tonight.

She might not be great at family stuff, but she was a damn good reporter. And soon, she'd have the evidence to prove it. Even if that evidence pointed at Luke.

LUKE LOOSENED HIS tie and tried to rearrange himself in a more comfortable position in the posh airplane seat. Both games had turned out just like the list in his pocket had predicted.

He glanced around the dimly-lit cabin. In fact, the

mood was pretty low-key, despite their back-to-back wins in Colorado. Probably because they'd eked out some pretty ugly victories against a team they should have crushed. He was still surprised they'd held on to a 3–2 win tonight.

J.C. was snoring beside him. Most everyone else was plugged into a movie or talking with seatmates. Except for Eric, who was sitting toward the front of the plane, all by himself, reading a book, as usual.

He liked Eric Jacobs. He was a great hockey player, and the game really mattered to him.

And he was low-key off the ice—no tabloid stories of drunken debauchery or chronic womanizing. He didn't love being on camera, but he didn't complain about the obligatory interviews, either. Still, he'd seemed particularly aloof lately.

With the weight of his *C* heavy on his chest, Luke got up and walked over to him.

"Mind if I sit down?"

Jacobs glanced up from his book. "Sure." He opened his right hand to reveal a chain looped through two expensive-looking rings. Luke watched as he placed the necklace reverently between the pages of his spy thriller like a bookmark before shoving the book in the pocket in front of him. "What's up, Mags?"

"Actually, I was going to ask you the same thing," Luke confessed, taking a seat.

"Nothing really." Eric ran a hand through his dark blond hair. "I'm fine."

"Cubs, we both know that's bullshit. How long have we been playing together?"

"Two years."

"Exactly. You think I can't tell when something's up with my linemate?"

Eric was toying with the bottom of his matte gray tie and refused to meet Luke's stare.

"Let's not make this any worse than it has to be. Just be straight with me. You know I've got your back. Are you in some kind of trouble?"

There was a long, ominous stretch of silence. The piece of yellow legal paper weighed heavy on Luke's mind.

Then Eric heaved a sigh of defeat. "It's nothing like that. It's just…family stuff."

Luke kept his gaze steady and waited.

Cubs dropped the end of his tie and turned to face him. "My grandma's in the hospital. She had a heart attack."

"Jesus. Eric, I'm really sorry to hear that." Eric's parents had died when he was really young, and his grandmother, Stella Jacobs, had raised him ever since. She'd become the unofficial grandma of the Portland Storm and when she was in the stands to cheer them, a round of cupcakes from her bakery always made their way to the dressing room to announce her presence. "Is she going to be okay?"

Eric shrugged, and the gesture had an air of helplessness about it. "The doctors won't say. She seems to be doing better. She pretty much forced me to come on this road trip." He smiled a little when he said it, and Luke had a vivid vision of tiny, white-haired Stella bossing her six-foot grandson around, even from the confines of a hospital bed.

"Why didn't you tell anyone?"

"I don't want to talk about it. And I definitely don't want reporters asking."

"I understand wanting to keep the family stuff under wraps. I won't object if you're sure you want to keep playing."

There was no hesitation in Eric's nod. "It's the play-offs. And I get that this is stupid, but I want to win for her, you know?"

Oh, Luke knew all right. It was what drove him every single day. He wanted that championship, wanted to win it so badly. Not for himself, but for the brother who'd lost his shot at the dream they'd shared their whole lives. "Yeah," he said quietly. "I get that."

And he did. Which was why he was so shocked when Holly's voice echoed in his mind. *Sometimes you just have to keep it simple and play the game for you.*

THE TEAM WAS already out on the ice for practice when she arrived at the arena the day after the Storm had knocked Colorado out of the play-offs with a 4–2 win at home. Because of the celebration and the increased media interest, the team captain had been too busy for her to snag an interview last night, but today, well, it was only a matter of time before they ran into each other, and her nerves were on edge for the reunion.

Holly was standing in the players' bench—Orgasm Central, as her dirty mind had taken to calling it. She was trying to keep her voice even, her blush under control and her eyes from wandering over to the practice happening on the ice behind her. Not because she cared about the practice but because of the overwhelming desire to check if maybe Luke was having as much trouble concentrating as she was.

It took three tries before she managed to get through the intro to the car interview montage without messing up. She could tell Jay was relieved when she finally nailed it by the speed at which he was gathering his video equipment. "Okay, I'm just going to run upstairs to get a few more angles on the practice. Give me ten minutes and we can go for lunch."

Holly nodded. "Okay. I'll text Paige and tell her we'll be at the restaurant in about half an hour."

"Aw, Paige is coming?" Jay whined.

"Suck it up, Buchanan. You know she is."

"Fine. Not sure why we have to ruin a perfectly good lunch, though. I'll meet you at the car in fifteen minutes."

She pulled her phone out of her bra, its usual storage space when she was dolled up in a skirt suit, and texted their ETA to Paige.

Her friend immediately returned the text with one that predictably read: Aw, Jay is coming?

"Holly."

She almost dropped her phone at the sound of the familiar deep voice saying her name. With a deep breath to restore her composure, she turned around. Luke, sweaty and gorgeous in his Storm practice jersey, was standing on the other side of the bench. Her stomach lurched at the sheer handsomeness of him. Clearly her body was ready to start on Orgasm Central: The Sequel.

"Hey. I didn't know we had interviews scheduled for today."

"Oh, we don't. Jay wanted to get some practice footage, and we filmed a quick intro to the car interview bit."

Luke's eyes darkened in a way that shot heat right

through her core. So apparently she wasn't the only one haunted by the sexy ghosts of lovemaking past.

He shook his head slightly, as if to clear it, and when his eyes met hers, he had the air of a man who'd come to a decision. His next words confirmed what that decision was.

"Look, I wanted to ask, do you think maybe I could buy you dinner tonight?"

Holly wouldn't have been more shocked if a hockey-stick-wielding alien had burst through the logo on his broad chest.

"As per my contract, we can't really be seen cavorting about town," she reminded him.

He nodded. "I remember. I was going to suggest takeout at my place. I'll pick you up around five thirty?"

Holly cocked an eyebrow at the time.

"Play-offs," he reminded her with a grin and a shrug. "I've got curfew, so we'll have to get an early start."

Holly couldn't help but laugh. "Didn't I go on this date in the seventh grade?"

"Yeah, well. You pick a career that twelve-year-old boys dream of, turns out that sometimes you get treated like a twelve-year-old boy."

"So there is justice in the world after all," she joked. "It's not all big paychecks, fast cars and constant adoration."

"It's definitely not all that," Luke agreed, and she caught a somber note in his deep voice. Before she had a chance to examine it, he barged through the moment. "So I'll see you tonight?"

"Sure."

His smile was endearingly self-conscious. Not the smile she'd expected from a professional athlete blessed with a big salary and the good looks to back up some swagger. "I gotta get to practice. Five thirty. Don't forget."

Holly watched him skate off to rejoin his team, her phone clutched to her heart and a single thought running through her head.

Oh, shit.

8

"He asked me out."

"Who?"

"Luke Maguire."

The answer brought two very different reactions from her lunch companions. Jay stopped in the middle of eating his nachos, his mouth agape. Paige continued the act of buttering her roll and barely glanced up as she repeated, "Who?"

Holly took a bracing chug of Heineken. "The shirtless hockey player from the *Sports Illustrated* magazine your eyes were glued to a couple of days ago."

"The superhot dreamy one with the bedroom eyes and the washboard abs?"

"He's not *that* hot," Jay countered gruffly.

"Please. That man is a god."

Jay took a huffy bite of nacho.

"Wait a minute! Is Abs Maguire your sex crush?"

Jay cringed. "Do I really need to be here for this?"

"Hush, Jay. This is important lady business. So what did you say?"

"I'm not an idiot, Paige."

"Great. So if you said yes, then I don't understand the problem."

That was the more complicated part. "The problem is that a high concentration of shame is eating through my stomach lining as we speak." Holly took the final swig of Dutch beer. "I'm contractually obligated to lie to him…about my hockey knowledge," she hedged. She hadn't told either of her best friends about her suspicions of illegal betting, and the realization that she was lying to everyone she cared about made her feel worse. "I have a guilt ulcer."

"What's to feel guilty about? You're a beautiful, single woman, and he's a rich, single man who looks like he knows how to wield his hockey stick. Let's not kid ourselves, Hol. You need to get laid. Jay and I, mortal enemies that we are, have actually discussed hiring a male escort just to put you out of your misery."

Jay winced. "No, we haven't."

Paige's raised eyebrow confirmed that they had.

"I swear, you guys. How is it even possible to be so close to your dream job and yet light-years away?"

She reached over and took an unladylike gulp of Paige's red wine, then did her best not to spew it across the table. "Oh, *gawd*! How do you drink this stuff?" she demanded, gratefully tearing the bottle of Pilsner Jay held in her direction from his hand and drowning out the obnoxious taste of merlot with luscious, cold beer.

Shrugging, Paige took a perfect, dainty sip of her wine. "Well, I'm proud of you for putting your lady bits first for once."

"Oh, man! I'm trying to eat here," Jay complained.

"And vaginas disgust you?" Paige asked. "You can't possibly ingest food around women who are discussing them, even though men talk about their penises constantly?"

"What? How did my junk get brought into this conversation? Nobody said anything about dicks."

Holly groaned. "Would you two just sleep together already and get rid of the sexual tension? It's *exhausting*."

"Ewww!" Their disgust was expressed loudly and simultaneously. "That would be like kissing my—" The words "sister" and "dog" overlapped.

Their affronted expressions were almost identical, not that Holly would offend either of them by saying so.

"Seriously, Jay? Your sister? She has a mustache."

"Kissing me is like kissing a dog?"

"Except for the fact that I could muster some enthusiasm for kissing an adorable dog, yes, I imagine so."

Jay cocked an eyebrow. "So you *have* imagined kissing me, then?"

"You. Wish." Paige held up a hand. "I'm going to pretend you're not here." To Holly, she said, "I'm still not seeing the problem."

"Paige, game analysis isn't just criticism. There are a lot of moving pieces to a game. Line matchups, hot streaks, underperforming players, team morale. And when you get millions of dollars to play a game, you have to understand that there will be some scrutiny. But I'm a professional, and that means I can't let my personal feelings interfere with my ability to do my job."

Something that she would do well to remember, Holly decided.

Paige nodded, but Holly didn't like the sly smile on her face. "Tell me more about these personal feelings you're having."

"And now *I'm* going to pretend *you're* not here."

"You'd better be thanking your lucky stars that I'm here. Otherwise you'd probably end up wearing some ripped jeans, a ratty T-shirt and a ball cap on your date tonight."

Holly looked down at her stupid skirt suit. "Well, I'm definitely not wearing this."

Paige smiled. "I'm sure we can find a happy medium. Hurry up and finish your nachos, Jay. We've got work to do."

THERE WERE BUTTERFLIES in her stomach as she crawled into Luke's truck. He'd rolled up to her curb at five thirty sharp, just as he said he would.

"Wow. You look great."

The compliment meant a lot, because it was the first time she'd hung out with Luke feeling even remotely like the real her. Paige had sanctioned Holly's pick of a pair of dark-wash skinny jeans and a white T-shirt. But in exchange, Holly had relented and worn the strappy nude heels and the jade statement necklace Paige had insisted upon.

"Thanks. It feels like I haven't worn pants in ages."

"Well, to celebrate the Portland Storm making it through the first round of play-offs and your long-awaited return to wearing pants, we can have any kind of takeout you want."

"Wow. Living the high life."

Luke nodded as he pulled away from the curb. "Tonight, the world is ours."

Two hours later, Luke, Holly, two mostly decimated pizzas and two bottles of beer were spread out across the living room floor of Luke's swanky—but not quite as swanky as she'd been expecting—apartment. They'd just finished watching a chase movie that was heavy on explosions and fast cars and light on plot. Holly was pretty sure she'd never been on a better date. Until he said—

"I have a confession to make."

Holly's stomach bottomed out and she choked on her beer.

Luke's brow creased with concern. "You okay?"

She nodded, coughing as she set her bottle back on the coffee table. "Yeah. Just went down the wrong way. Sorry. You were saying?"

The nervous look on his face made her gut twist into knots. Her palms prickled with moisture.

No. Please don't let it be Luke who's throwing games.

"I had a bit of an ulterior motive for inviting you for dinner."

The beat of silence scraped across her nerves. She hadn't realized how much she was hoping Luke was innocent of point-shaving. And now, here they were, after an amazing couple of hours together, and it was all about to fall apart.

"Tomorrow I'm heading home to Millerville for the sledge hockey finals," he said, reaching for his own beer. "These kids have worked so hard. And if they win this weekend, they're going to the state finals. I told them I might not be able to make it, but now that we've wrapped up the series and I have a week off, I asked for two days' leave," he explained.

He picked absently at the label on the bottle in his hands and took a deep breath. "And I was wondering if you'd come with me."

Holly couldn't quite process the words. There was a buzzing in her ears as she reexamined the last few minutes. "You plied me with pizza and beer because you want me to go to your hometown with you?"

Luke nodded before draining the last of his drink and leaning forward. "I was kind of hoping you'd do a little story on the team. You know, interview them, give them a taste of what it's like to deal with the media. They'd love that."

Holly couldn't hold back a smile at how animated Luke was at the mention of the kids who were part of his pet charity. She'd done a lot of research about it for her Hockey Hottie of the Month shtick.

Kids on Wheels was a top-notch organization that did an amazing job assisting kids with physical disabilities. She admired the genuine joy on Luke's face when he talked about it. It made her want to say yes, except...

"I don't have anywhere to stay. And Jay's filming a wedding this weekend."

"My parents have plenty of room. And we can just film the interviews on my phone. It doesn't have to be fancy. I just wanted to give the team some professional hockey league experience, you know?"

Holly shook her head to clear it. *Did he just say what I thought he just said?*

"You want me to stay at your parents'?"

"Yeah, well, my mother would kill me if I rented a hotel room, so consider Casa Maguire like a bed-and-breakfast, but with more parental interference."

"You had me at breakfast." The words were out of her mouth before she'd realized she said anything. Because she liked Luke. She wanted to go with him. And it scared her that, for the first time in her life, she was willing to put her job—even one as banal as asking hockey players what kind of underwear they wore—on the line for someone else.

Thankfully, Luke's dazzling smile was enough to shore up her resolve against the doubt that was trying to trickle in.

"That's great. I was really nervous about bringing this up, but the kids are going to be so excited to meet you."

"Me?"

"Yeah, they've all watched your show. They give me a hard time about my answers to your interview questions. The second your videos get posted to the Storm's site, the text messages start pouring in."

"Ah. So this isn't a nice perk, this is revenge," she joked, before downing the last sip of her own beer.

"You caught me. Gotta keep those little punks in line or they'll be out of control before you know it."

"Ooh. You're such an authority figure. That's actually kind of hot."

"What can I say? It's dangerous when things get out of control," he said, and the proof was in the way his eyes darkened.

"It can be," Holly agreed. She shivered as he moved closer. His leg came into light contact with hers. Her body flooded with warmth and sweetness, like she had syrup coursing through her veins. He increased the pressure of his knee against her thigh.

"You done with dinner?" he asked, and his voice was low and rough.

She licked her lips involuntarily. "I could be talked into starting the dessert course."

"I was hoping you'd say that."

The journey to his bedroom was a hazy, erotic blur of kissing and touching and haphazard stripping. Now he was standing shirtless beside the bed, marveling at how damn sexy Holly looked in her pale-pink lace lingerie. He watched with slack-jawed appreciation as she crawled onto the mattress, giving him a perfect view of her incredible ass.

God, he'd never seen her in anything but sensible white cotton, and the idea that she'd picked the sexy lace out just for him was blowing his mind and his restraint. And that was *before* she rose up onto her knees, her back still toward him and sent him a coy glance over her shoulder. She reached behind her back and unclasped her bra, tugging it off in the most delectable little peep show he'd ever seen.

Shucking his jeans and boxer briefs in one move, Luke joined her on the mattress, pulling her against his chest. He nuzzled at her neck, kissing the curve of her soft shoulder. She turned her head to grant him easier access, raising her arms to run her fingers through his hair. The movement made her breasts lift, and Luke couldn't resist the pretty sight. She sighed her pleasure as he ran his hands up the smooth skin of her torso and cupped her breasts.

He pressed his erection against the small of her spine and she pressed back, as if she was testing how ready to go he was. She wouldn't be disappointed.

"I want you," she said.

Luke wanted her, too. He loved her abandon, the way she went after what she wanted, be it the answer to her question, or his body.

Her breath came in soft little pants, and he reveled in how responsive she was to every brush of his fingers, every kiss of his lips. He ran his palm down the front of her stomach, his fingers flirting with the elastic of her panties. She leaned back against his chest, encouraging him to explore. He accepted her invitation, sliding his fingers down to find her wet and ready for him.

"Jesus, Holly. I want you, too. So damn bad."

Her throaty, sensual laugh made his hips jerk. "So do something about it," she challenged, reaching forward so that she was on her hands and knees in front of him. She wiggled her ass, looking back at him over her shoulder.

Luke let himself take what he wanted. With a growl, he yanked her underwear down her thighs and, anchoring his hands on her hips, plunged into her.

OH, GOD. She'd never felt anything like this.

Holly had to remind herself to breathe, the pleasure was so intense. What was it about this man that could take her so high, so fast? She'd released the beast, and there was something so empowering about making a man known for his steely control lose all sense of restraint. He was stroking her G-spot with every thrust of his hips, and the sensation that was building inside her was all-consuming.

She dropped down to her elbows, almost screaming with pleasure as the angle changed. Heat streaked through every nerve in her body, culminating in a tingling starburst of bliss that moved through her body like a wave. Luke was only a few strokes behind, and she could feel him pulsing inside her as he joined her in the most intense orgasm she'd ever experienced.

Sweaty and satisfied, she flopped onto her side. Luke lay down beside her, gathering her close so that her cheek rested against his shoulder. She reached out to trace her finger around his nipple, loving the way his pec jumped at her touch. "So much for your curfew."

"What are you talking about? I was in bed by nine."

She laughed. "You always play this fast and loose with the rules?"

"Rules were made to be broken."

She snuggled up closer to his big naked body. "After that deft display, I can't help but agree."

He ran his hand up and down her arm, and the soft, rhythmic stroking made here eyelids flutter closed.

"I'm glad you're coming with me tomorrow."

"Mmm. Me too."

"Are you falling asleep?"

She smiled as he shifted, pulling the blanket from the end of the bed up to cover them. "Maybe."

He pressed a sweet kiss to her forehead. "'Night, Holly."

She wasn't sure if she answered or not as she drifted into the best sleep she'd had in ages.

9

SINCE SHE'D STAYED the night, they'd ended up getting a much earlier start than they'd anticipated—despite the fact that their tandem shower had turned into an hour and a half of fun distraction that had necessitated another shower.

Luke grabbed the bag he'd packed, and they swung past her place so she could throw some weekend supplies into a small suitcase. One more quick stop at her brother's house—Holly needed to pick something up, and Luke was nice enough to indulge her in the last-minute errand—and they were on their way out of town.

In a scant hour and twenty minutes, they pulled up in front of a house that was small but cozy. The kind of house that any kid would be lucky to grow up in. It boasted big trees that were perfect for climbing, lots of driveway space, which, considering two hockey stars had grown up here, had probably hosted its fair share of ball hockey grudge matches and an attention to detail—potted flowers, freshly painted trim—that said the owners cared.

The idyllic scene made her a little wistful. She couldn't

remember even a handful of family memories that could match the cheerfulness of Luke's childhood. She bet he could think of hundreds without trying.

Luke slipped the keys from the ignition and unbuckled his seat belt, but he paused after that, staring at the house for such a long time that Holly didn't know what to make of it.

"Luke?"

She'd startled him, but he tried to cover it with a smile. "Sorry. Lost in thought." He scrubbed a hand across his stubbly face.

Despite the question she'd asked him the day they'd met, Holly was glad he wasn't growing a proper play-off beard. That whole "lumberjack chic" look that was sweeping the magazines didn't do much for her.

He sat there for another long moment, as if he was psyching himself up to go inside. When he finally turned to her, his smile was dimmer than she was used to and it didn't quite ring true. "Ready?"

Holly did her best to seem peppy and normal, ignoring the part of her that wanted to wrap her arms around him and soothe the pain she hadn't expected to find in his eyes. "Ready," she agreed.

She followed Luke into the small bungalow where he'd grown up. She'd never considered meeting the parents to be the big deal everyone else seemed to make it, but suddenly her stomach seemed to think it was on a roller coaster.

"Holly! It's so nice to meet you!"

She found herself caught up in a hug that blindsided her. It took her a moment to relax into the other woman's maternal embrace. She couldn't remember the last time a woman had hugged her—*really* hugged her—as opposed to the cursory, two-second greeting hugs that were all the rage these days. It was...a little unnerving, actually.

"Thank you, Mrs. Maguire. It's great to meet you, too."

The tiny dynamo of a woman flicked her fingers, shooing away the notion. She was casually dressed in jeans and a yellow T-shirt with flowers on it. Her short brown hair was streaked with gray and cut in a no-fuss style that suited her kind face.

"Please. I'm just me. You're the famous one! I watch all your shows on the internet. Luke gave me an iPad for Christmas. I even saw your interview on *Good Morning Portland*. And we don't stand on formality here. Call me Cathy. This is my husband, Ross."

Holly smiled as she shook the man's hand. He had only a hint of white at the temples of his dark hair. It made him look very distinguished. She could see Luke in him: the strong nose, the kind eyes, the rugged jaw.

Luke's smile, though—his real smile—that was all Cathy.

"Well, let's not just stand in the doorway! Luke, you take Holly's bag up to my knitting room." She turned to Holly. "It's actually a little suite over top of the garage, so you'll have lots of privacy and your very own bathroom. I already made up the bed for you."

Luke caught Holly's eye and grinned at the way Cathy had subtly stressed that the room was for her and her alone. "Sure thing, Mom." Grabbing both their bags, he leaned over and kissed Cathy's cheek, and Holly was enchanted at the joy sparkling in his mom's eyes.

As Luke headed back outside and toward the detached garage, Cathy tucked Holly's arm into hers and pulled her into the kitchen.

The highly varnished wooden table was littered with official-looking envelopes emblazoned with the logo of a prominent bank in the top left-hand corner. Some of them had ominous red stamps that said *Final Notice* on them.

"Oh my. Please excuse the mess!" Cathy rushed over to the table and began stacking the notices into a disordered pile, but not before Holly noticed that Luke's name appeared on some of them, along with his parents'. *Huh.*

"Ross and I were just paying some bills before you arrived." Cathy dumped said "bills" into the shoebox on the table and replaced the lid. Only then did her smile regain its genuine warmth of earlier.

"Now let's get some food into you. I just finished making coconut gumdrop cookies—they're Luke's favorite."

The afternoon sped by. The Maguires were warm, attentive hosts, and although Ethan did not make an appearance, Holly was drawn in by their obvious closeness. Luke seemed more relaxed here, and she liked knowing that this side of him existed—that he wasn't uptight and serious all the time.

And yet, she couldn't help but notice the blatant hockey void in the conversation. Hours of chatting had gone by with no mention of Luke's play-off run, or anything hockey related whatsoever. Considering Luke's entire world revolved around the sport right now, she found the omission very odd. She found herself growing indignant on his behalf that his parents didn't make more of a fuss about him.

"I'm going to go check on dinner," Cathy announced. "Luke, why don't you show Holly to her room, in case she wants to freshen up before we eat. I've practically held her hostage all day. I'm sure she'd appreciate a moment to herself."

Holly smiled at the false summation of their day, but the prospect of stealing a few moments alone with Luke was too great to pass up.

"Actually, Luke, I'd rather see your old room."

LUKE LED HER down the hallway to his childhood bedroom. There was still a wooden sign on the door with a hockey player and his name printed in primary colors. He'd picked it out himself in the second grade. A normal kid probably would have taken it down when he was thirteen or fourteen, but at fourteen, Luke had already been billeting with other families and playing in the minor leagues, trying to become the best.

Ethan had been coming up fast on his heels, a definite hockey superstar in the making, and it had pushed Luke to excel. He was proud of his little brother, but he was also competitive enough that he didn't want to be surpassed, either.

As always, his room was just how he'd left it. His parents had talked about turning it into a reading room, but they'd never gotten around to it. Maybe that was something he should do for them for Christmas...send his parents on a trip somewhere and get the room renovated. Just a little something to put a smile on their faces. God knew they deserved it.

"Wow, check it out. A glimpse into the life of a young Luke Maguire." She meandered around the room, staring at inscriptions on trophies and titles on book spines.

He spent the moments looking at her. He liked casual Holly, barefoot and clad in jeans and a black T-shirt, her blond ponytail swinging behind her as she snooped around his room.

He thought it'd been the short skirt and push-up bra and teased-out hair that had pulled him in, but if he was being honest with himself, he found her much prettier and more alluring today than ever before.

He was curious about the attraction they shared. It burned hot and bright and yet it wasn't all passion. They'd had a great trip down, conversing easily and laughing the entire hour and change that it had taken to get here. He enjoyed her company, both in and out of the bedroom.

"Yearbook!"

"What? No!" Luke did his best to mask the panic in his voice, knowing that would only encourage her. "You don't need to look at...too late."

She was already nose deep in the glossy pages, in search of childhood embarrassment.

"Is this you? Oh my God, you had a mullet!" She flipped the yearbook around to show him, pointing gleefully at his photo, as if he didn't remember what he'd looked like.

"I did not have a mullet."

Her pretty mouth hitched up on one side, and he was a goner. "Photographic evidence begs to differ."

"I had a flow. It's totally different. That is a well-respected and timeless hockey haircut. Jaromír Jágr had that exact hairdo."

She laughed as she shut the book and set it on the end table. "Check out this place. You ate, slept and breathed hockey, huh?" He followed her gaze around the room—

old hockey trophies and medals dominated the shelves above his desk, along with a couple of hockey biographies and an impressive collection of *Don Cherry's Rock'em Sock'em Hockey* videos.

"Wayne Gretzky, Mario Lemieux and Bobby Hull." She pointed at each of the faded, curling posters he'd tacked to the wall so very long ago. "Dreaming of the day when you'd have a poster of your own?"

"You know it." Luke tried to keep the frown out of his voice as he crossed his arms over his chest.

Wayne Gretzky, sure, his 99 was showing after all, and Mario Lemieux's name was printed on the poster. But Bobby Hull? Would someone who didn't have the first clue about hockey recognize him? He seemed a little too niche.

It was on the tip of his tongue to call her out on it, but he swallowed his retort. He wasn't going there. No, he was done being suspicious. He liked this girl. She was funny and beautiful and he enjoyed her company. He was done looking for flaws and investigating her every move.

Being home always reminded him that things could change for the worse in a split second. And it would be a disservice to forget to enjoy the things he had. Because he was all too aware that it could all disappear in an instant.

"Instead of posters, I had a signed picture of Barbara Walters on my wall," she said.

Luke smiled at the odd choice. "Really?"

Holly nodded. "It was my mom's. She was an anchor on the six o'clock news. Barbara was her hero, too. Every weeknight, my family would eat dinner in front of the TV and watch Mom tell us about the day's events. And at the end of the hour, she'd tuck her hair behind her right ear and that was our signal. Her little code that she loved us and she knew we were watching."

Her smile was sad, but beautiful, and Luke was glad she'd trusted him with it.

"When she died of breast cancer, my father let me hang the Barbara picture in my room. I'd look at it every night and promise my mom that one day I'd be a reporter on TV, just like her, and then I'd tuck my hair behind my right ear so that she knew I was thinking about her."

"And that's why you do what you do," he said, adding a few more pieces to the puzzle that was Holly.

"That's why."

"I'm sorry about your mom."

She shrugged as she sat on his childhood bed. "It was a long time ago. And it's nice to remember the good stuff."

"Kids! Dinner's ready! Wash your hands."

Luke and Holly shared a smile at his mother's summons, and he took comfort in the fact that, even in the midst of constant flux, some things never changed.

"Take a seat! Holly, you can sit beside Luke over here," his mom directed. She set a roast chicken on the table.

"Everything looks fantastic, Cathy. Thank you so much for having me."

His mother preened under Holly's praises. Luke hadn't seen his mom this animated in a long time. "Oh, it's our pleasure. It's just so nice to see Lucas happy."

Luke didn't have a chance to be embarrassed, because the hum of the back door made everyone freeze. His father walked in first, and behind him, Ethan navigated his wheelchair into the kitchen with such ease that it made Luke realize just how long he'd been using it.

Sometimes it felt like only yesterday they'd been camped out in the hospital, waiting for the swelling to go down, hoping against hope that Ethan would walk again. Other times it felt like aeons had passed since that fateful night.

"The prodigal son returns," Ethan muttered when he spotted Luke.

Luke forced a smile, trying not to be hurt by the lackluster greeting. "Hey, little brother. Looking fit." Ethan's arms bulged against the fabric of his Nike T-shirt. He must be up at least a couple of pounds of muscle since they'd seen each other last. "Katie must be putting you through your paces."

Ethan nodded at the mention of his physiotherapist. "Yeah. She's tough." He grabbed his plate and started dishing out some food.

"This is Luke's friend, Holly," his mother offered, wading into the tension.

"Hey," he said without glancing up.

"Ethan! Manners." There was a warning note in Cathy Maguire's voice that not even a sullen twenty-two-year-old could ignore. Hell, even Luke still flinched when she marched it out.

Ethan sighed and Luke watched him physically regroup. When he raised his eye, Luke recognized the battle-weary look of a man engaged in a tireless fight. "It's very nice to meet you, Holly."

Holly's smile was warm, despite the fact that the greeting had been decreed rather than given sincerely. "You, too, Ethan."

Taut silence settled over the room then, broken only

by the clank of utensils as everyone served themselves portions of chicken and stuffing and gravy and veggies.

"If you'll all excuse me, I'm going to eat in my room."

"Ethan, we have company." Ross Maguire's voice held a hint of desperation that made Luke wonder how many nights he and his mother ate at the dinner table alone.

"Oh, that's fine." If she was hurt by his brother's abruptness, Holly didn't show it. "I understand better than most what it's like to want to avoid small talk," she joked.

"Thanks." It was, by Luke's count, Ethan's most sincere moment of the night.

The world deflated when he left.

Luke could feel his mother's heart break just a fraction more, see the way his father's shoulders sagged under the weight of his youngest son's misery. He wanted to punch his brother in the face for doing this to them, and yet...

And yet, Luke's own shoulders and his own heart were just as affected at the sight of Ethan's struggle to make sense of the devastating blow he'd been dealt. His little brother was the strongest man he knew. Ethan's dedication to his recovery was beyond incredible, and even the doctors were amazed by his progress. Luke was jealous of how ripped he'd gotten and in awe that Ethan had taught himself to walk again.

But he could only stand for short periods, and his walk was a slow shuffle. Neither was good enough for his brother, who was aiming for nothing less than full recovery. But three years later, the odds of that were dwindling at an alarming rate. And his brother was angry.

Luke couldn't blame him for that, even when he wanted to.

Holly broke the ice. "I can't wait to dig into this chicken."

His mom smiled and encouraged everyone to eat. Holly was wonderful through the entire meal. She did her best to carry the dinner discussion and after the meal, helped his mom clean up the dishes so he and his father could figure out why the power opener on the back door wasn't functioning properly. Then they all sat outside on the deck with his mother's famous lemonade and talked until it was time for bed.

"Thanks," he said, as he and Holly sauntered toward the garage. The evening air was warm and damp and tinged with the scent of spring flowers.

"For what?" she asked, like she honestly didn't know.

"For handling today like a pro."

"Nothing to thank me for. Your family was incredibly kind."

He put a hand on her hip, tugged her forward a step and brushed a soft kiss to her lips. Her sigh was sweet and dreamy, and he leaned his forehead against hers. "Good night, Holly."

She smiled up at him. "Good night, Luke."

He kissed her once more before he pulled himself away, glancing behind him to watch her ascend the small staircase and disappear into the guest suite.

He waited until she'd pushed the door shut before he headed back to the house.

He had every intention of heading straight for his

own room, but instead, he found himself standing outside his brother's.

Luke rapped his knuckles against the door before he pushed it open.

Ethan didn't look up from his physio log book. "Hey."

"Hey." It was weird, seeing the wheelchair beside the bed. Unlike his own room, Ethan's reflected the passage of time. All his trophies and posters and hockey paraphernalia had been packed up and hidden away—probably in the attic, if he knew his mother. Cathy Maguire couldn't bear to throw away memories.

"I just dropped Holly off in the guest room. I'm glad Mom's still protecting our virginities," Luke joked.

A ghost of a smile played over Ethan's lips.

"Some things never change."

Luke didn't mean for his gaze to dart to the wheelchair beside the bed, but it did, and the moment of camaraderie disappeared with the blank expression that overtook his brother's face.

Luke wasn't about to let his brother shut him down that easily. Not again. "And some things change a lot."

"Yeah, well. Be thankful you're the one who got out of this mess unscathed."

Luke ran a frustrated hand over his hair. The ever-present guilt chewed at the lining of his stomach. He ignored his brother's dig and tried to take the high road. "Do you want to come to the sledge hockey game with Holly and me tomorrow? The kids would love to meet you. They keep giving me a hard time that you haven't come."

"I have physio."

"Ethan—"

"I have physio," he repeated in a tone that brooked no opposition.

"Okay, fine." Luke didn't know what to do to reach his brother anymore. Every time he came home, he felt like they grew further and further apart. "You wanna have some ice cream?" he asked. It was a last-ditch effort to connect, a ritual from back in the day. Whenever there was company staying at the house, they'd wait until midnight and sneak downstairs for makeshift ice cream sundaes, thinking they were pulling one over on their parents.

It wasn't until years later that they'd realized it couldn't be coincidence that whenever they had visitors, there was always ice cream in the freezer and an array of toppings in the cupboard. Luke didn't doubt for a second they were there now.

"I think I'm just going to go to sleep. Hit the light on your way out?"

Even though Luke had braced himself for the impact of rejection, his brother's dismissal stung more than he'd expected. "Yeah, sure. Good night, Ethan."

Luke flipped the switch and headed for his own room. He unceremoniously stripped down to his underwear and crawled into bed, but he didn't sleep. It wasn't just that he'd outgrown the bed, either. The whole house was uncomfortable. The whole family was stuck in the middle of a nightmare.

Luke was still wide-awake come midnight. He slipped out of bed and pulled the door shut behind him. Once in the kitchen, though, he decided ice cream didn't sound all that appealing.

A glance out the window showed a light burning

brightly in the suite above the garage. Suddenly, he was in the mood for a different kind of sweet.

Luke grabbed the extra key from the hook in the entryway and was careful to close the door silently behind him—a trick he'd mastered by the age of twelve. In no time, he'd crossed the small expanse of grass between the house and the garage and climbed the stairs to the door.

He knocked before he used the key. Holly looked up from her phone as he pushed the door shut behind him. She was sitting on top of the covers, her back against the headboard, feet flat on the mattress, wearing nothing but a T-shirt and another pair of those sensible white cotton panties. She was absolutely perfect.

"To what do I owe the honor?" she asked, her eyes tracking down his bare chest, boxer-briefs and thighs. If he hadn't already been up for the main event, that once-over would have done the trick.

"This is a booty call."

She licked her lips. "You don't say."

"But it's not just any booty call," he explained, crossing the carpeted floor until he stood beside the bed. "This is a booty call twelve years in the making."

She set her phone on the end table. "Oh? Sounds epic."

Luke nodded as he crawled across the bed. "Since I was fourteen years old, I've dreamed of sneaking a woman up to this bed. Tonight, the fantasy has finally presented itself. So whad'ya say, Holly Evans? Want to make a man out of me?"

"I don't know," she told him, and the uncertainty on her face made him pause. She'd seemed into it a second ago.

"I don't want to get in trouble." She cocked a wicked eyebrow. "We'll have to be really quiet."

Jesus. Lust ignited in his belly as if her words were gasoline. He understood she was just playing along, teasing him, but damn if the role play wasn't working for him in a big way.

She twirled a piece of hair around her finger. "And you have to promise not to gossip to all your friends about this at school tomorrow."

"I promise." She was so damn perfect in that instant that the words came out in a growl. He hooked his arm beneath her knees, tugging her toward him so that she was flat on her back. She let out a cute little shriek, surprised by the move, and he swooped in to kiss the giggles from her lips.

"Shhh. Wouldn't want someone to figure out that I sneaked in here."

Her eyes shone with humor as she wrapped her arms around his neck and pulled him down on top of her. "Oh right. Well, I guess I should warn you, I'm a bit of a moaner, so you'd better think up some way to keep me quiet."

Up for the challenge, Luke pressed his mouth to hers. God, he ached to be inside her. Everything around here felt so wrong, but when he was alone with her… he could turn off his brain. He could just shut it down, run on pure instinct and lose himself in her embrace. It was almost magical the way she made him forget all the pressures that dogged him when she wasn't around.

He poured everything into that kiss, his whole self, and when she pulled away from him, things were spinning so fast that it took him a moment to reorient himself.

"Luke?"

He caught his breath, braced himself on his elbows. Her smile was so pretty it made his chest ache.

"I think I'm ready to go all the way," she teased.

He grinned down at her, unable to resist dropping a kiss to the end of her nose. It was the perfect thing to say. She'd kept things light, pulling him back from the spiraling emotional abyss of moments before.

He got to his feet beside the bed and shoved his underwear down his thighs. "I'm the luckiest fake high school kid on the planet," he said, watching as she sat up and tugged her T-shirt off. He enjoyed the gentle sway of her breasts as she wiggled out of the white cotton panties. At this point, those damn panties had some kind of Pavlovian hold over his body. Just the thought of them made him hard.

"Oh, you're about to get lucky, all right."

She reached for him as he joined her on the twin bed. But he misjudged the distance, swearing when he banged his head on the headboard as he pushed her back against the pillows.

"Oh, are you okay?" she asked, giggling as she ran her hand over his hair to soothe the wound. "I'm sorry. It's not funny," she said, but she was still laughing a little, and he couldn't help but join her, even though his head stung almost as much as his pride.

"If I die, it will be from embarrassment and not head trauma," he assured her. She scooted over to the edge of the mattress so he could lie down.

"Awww. Poor thing. Don't worry. Nobody's first time goes smoothly," she reminded him, reverting to their role play. It brought a smile to his face. "Maybe you'd better let me kiss it better," she offered, leaning over and pressing her lips to his.

Her mouth tasted heavenly. She ran her tongue across his bottom lip, and he reached up to bury his hand in her hair, pulling her toward him so that he could return the kiss with more urgency. He was panting when she pulled away.

"Did that help?"

He nodded. "That definitely helped...a little."

"Only a little? Hmm. We might have to up our treatment level." She pushed herself up and straddled his hips.

He could do nothing but watch in awe as she lowered her body slowly toward his erection. He was so turned on by the time his body finally made contact with the apex of her thighs, he was crazy with wanting.

She continued moving down, trapping his cock against his stomach before rocking her hips forward and back, her wet heat sliding along his length, driving him to madness.

"How about now?" she asked. There was a breathy quality to her voice that confirmed she was just as aroused as he was.

"What head injury?" he managed to ask, his hips pumping involuntarily in an effort to maintain the sensation that had wrung a groan from deep in his chest. She was going to kill him with pleasure, Luke decided.

"Shhh. You're going to get us caught."

She pressed a finger to his lips and he sucked it into his mouth. She threw her head back at the sensation and sped up the pace of her hips. It was incredible, but he wanted more. He wanted all of her.

As if she was reading his mind, Holly reached down and placed her hand on his heart, bracing herself so she could reach between them and when she finally slipped him inside her, his world shrank to raw sensation and a string of swearwords on loop in his head, because he couldn't form anything more coherent through the bliss.

Then she started fingering herself as she rode him, and he'd never seen anything so perfect in his whole life. It was all he could do not to explode. But he needed to hold out until he was sure she was getting at least as much pleasure out of this as he was.

"Come for me, Holly."

"I'm so close…so close."

He grabbed her hips, pushing himself as high and deep as he could. He thrust once, twice, and then she fell forward, hands on either side of his head, kissing him as the contractions of her body ignited Luke's own fierce orgasm.

10

"Good morning, Holly. Did you sleep all right?"

Surely the heat prickling across her face wasn't as obvious as it felt? This was another parental milestone she'd never endured. She'd already moved out of the house by the time she'd lost her virginity.

"I did, thank you, Cathy." She accepted the mug of coffee the other woman held in her direction and took a grateful sip.

"I'm glad to hear it. Come, sit down. I'm making bacon and eggs. I hope that's okay."

"Sounds delicious."

"Oh, wonderful. There's fresh fruit on the table, please help yourself. I'll bring the rest out as soon as it's ready."

"Can I help at all?"

"Nonsense! You're our guest. Besides, that's what Luke is for, right, son?"

Holly turned to find Luke padding into the kitchen in a rumpled T-shirt, gray sweats and a seriously sexy case of bedhead and stubble. "I live to serve," he agreed.

Her pulse sped up as he stepped toward her and pressed a kiss to her cheek.

Holly ducked her head to hide her blush. Cathy's smile of approval was too much to deal with right now. She hurried into the dining room, joining Ross at the table.

"Morning, Holly. Sports section okay?"

"Perfect. Thank you." She set her coffee down and sat next to Ross, accepting the newspaper he handed to her. Combined with the incredible spread of strawberries, pineapple, kiwi and grapes piled high on the platter in the middle of the table, Holly was hard-pressed to remember a lovelier morning. It was idyllic, the kind of scene she'd imagined so many times since her mother had died.

Seemed that Luke was not the only one living out childhood fantasies this weekend. The problem was, her fantasy was a dangerous one. This family wasn't hers and never would be. Still, she couldn't help but let herself be swept up in the idle chatter and homey sounds that came with eating breakfast with people who loved each other.

"You should see that apple tree your mother and I planted beside the ramp in the backyard last year, Lucas. We'll deal with these plates and then I'll show you how much it's grown."

"No, you two go," Holly insisted. "Take Cathy with you. Spend some time with your son. I'll take care of the breakfast dishes. It's the least I can do."

"That's very sweet of you, Holly." Cathy stood, but started gathering up plates as she did. "You boys go on outside. I'm going to relish the joy of having another woman in the house. And don't you argue with me, missy," she warned, cutting Holly's protest off before she could make it. Instead, Holly stood and grabbed the rest of the plates, oddly flattered that Cathy wanted to spend this time with her.

In the kitchen, Cathy stopped at the sink. She set the dishes down before leaning forward to gaze out the window that overlooked the backyard. As Holly approached, she could see father and son, standing at the edge of the wheelchair ramp. Ross was pointing at the small, flowering tree as Luke nodded.

"I'm just so happy you're here," Cathy said, grabbing the plates from Holly's hands and adding them to the pile. Holly's eyes widened in surprise. She didn't think she'd ever received such a warm reception.

"It's such a relief to see him happy. My Lucas has always been serious. And I've been worried about him. Always takes the weight of the world on his shoulders. My little Atlas, I used to call him. Still do, just not to his face anymore," Cathy said with a wink. "I'm glad that he's smiling again." Cathy's warm fingers found Holly's and she gave her hand a quick squeeze. "And I'm glad he found you."

The warm, maternal gesture stunned Holly into immobility.

"How long have the two of you been dating?" Cathy asked.

"Oh, uh. We're not really…we're not very far into things. We only met a few weeks ago."

"Really?" Cathy looked surprised. "Well, I'm relieved Luke hasn't been hiding you from us. But you two seem so comfortable together, so in sync, that I just assumed you'd known each other for longer."

She wasn't wrong. Holly had been pleasantly surprised at just how much they had in common. The drive down had been a blast. Easy conversation, lots of laughs, they'd even established some inside jokes. If she wasn't lying outright to his face and he wasn't the prime suspect in the betting scandal she was investigating, then hey, they might actually have a future together.

The joke sobered her. Luke was a really great guy. He was completely devoted to his family, who were totally worth it, as far as she'd seen. He was confident without being cocky, serious without being stodgy and despite his intense image, he was still able to relax and make her laugh. The sex was pretty incredible, too.

He was the total package. And, she reminded herself, innocent until proven guilty, despite her suspicions. So really, *she* was the problem in this relationship. Fortnight of fun. Spring fling. Whatever you wanted to call it, she was the only verified liar in their midst.

And for what? For a job? But it was more than a job. And not just because the story she was investigating was career making. She was actually starting to come around to the Women's Hockey Network stuff. It was kind of fun.

And she'd gotten a few really nice emails forwarded to her from the Portland Storm site that said stuff like, "You saved my marriage," or, "I get why my boyfriend is into this stuff now," or just, "Your show makes us laugh." It made her feel good to know that this wasn't just three months of career limbo. She was getting exposure and she was touching people's lives.

And she was sitting on a sports scandal that would propel her into the big leagues. Especially now that Corey Baniuk's old job was up for grabs. Besides, she and Luke hadn't agreed to anything. They weren't even dating. Like the Women's Hockey Network, their time together was temporary, and it would be lunacy to put her future in the hands of a man she was having a tryst with, no matter how skilled and sexy those hands might be.

Holly glanced at him through the kitchen window.

Especially since Luke didn't trust her. And with the evidence mounting, she couldn't quite trust him, either.

The sound of rattling dishes pulled Holly back to the present, and she was surprised to find that Luke's mom had completely finished loading the dishwasher while Holly had done little more than stare starry-eyed out the window at her son.

"There, all done," Cathy said, pushing the door to the machine closed and wiping her hands on the tea towel she'd plucked off the counter. "Can I tell you again how much I love your show?"

"Aw, thank you, Cathy. That means a lot. Especially since I would imagine you know everything there is to know about hockey, whether you like it or not."

Luke's mom grinned. "I am a bit of an expert. Job hazard of being the mom of two sports-obsessed boys. I thought Luke might be the most hockey-crazed kid ever, but along came Ethan, every bit as hockey crazy. That child came out of the womb ready to outdo his older brother at anything he possibly could."

She folded the red-and-white checkered towel into perfect thirds and hung it on the oven door.

"For a while, Ross and I used to worry that it would impact their relationship. But Lucas…he's just got a special temperament, I guess. They've been thick as thieves their whole lives, until…well. We've all struggled since

Ethan's accident. But I hope one day that we'll find our way back. I catch glimpses of it sometimes, when Ethan forgets to be angry. My boy's still in there."

Holly's eyes stung, but she did her best to hold back the tears. Cathy's words were not for her—they were the words of a mother who'd come to the aching realization that her son's happiness was out of her control and it was a fact that she resented the hell out of. Holly had never missed her own mother more than she did right then, witnessing the strength and the heartache in Cathy's face, the duality of maternal love.

The Maguire men were a very lucky bunch.

Wiping her eyes, Cathy made a shooing motion with her other hand. "Oh, listen to me. We old people are always going off on tangents! I will not waste this beautiful day blathering when I could be learning all about you. I'm going to make us a pot of tea, and we're going to go enjoy some girl chat out on the deck."

LUKE FOLLOWED HIS dad around the backyard, taking in his latest updates. The old man had done a lot of work. Installed wheelchair ramps to make both the front and back doors accessible, widened all the sidewalks and his car was parked outside because he'd revamped the garage into a physio studio for Ethan. As they stopped to admire the apple tree, Luke could hear the muffled banging of weights behind the door.

Luke glanced at his dad. "How's he doing?"

Ross Maguire shook his head. "He's still so angry. But determined. He's in there every day, does his exercises religiously. Everything that made him such a great hockey player—the focus, the drive—he pours into his recovery. The physiotherapist is astounded by his progress, but Ethan has a hard time accepting praise because he's not where he wants to be. I don't know how to break it to him that he might never be."

The pain on his father's face was unbearable.

"I've never had to do that before, Luke. I've raised two extraordinary men who've accomplished everything they've put their minds to. No one's explained the protocol for when dreams don't come true."

"You're doing fine, Dad. Better than fine. Look at this place. You remortgaged the house to make every inch of it accessible. Ethan's gone to the best doctors, the best rehab clinics. His physiotherapist is practically part of the family, she's here so much. And as much as it sucks, there's nothing more we can do. The rest is up to Ethan."

Ross Maguire nodded. "I know you're right, son. But it doesn't make standing on the sidelines any easier."

Luke raked a hand through his hair. He hated himself just then, because even as he bore witness to his father's hurt, Luke had the overwhelming urge to yell, "No one's asking you to be on the sidelines of *my* life! I'm your son, too. I got named captain, my team made the play-offs and I'm struggling, playing worse than I ever have. And you haven't asked me about a single one of those things! I'm not even sure you watch my games on TV."

But he couldn't say any of those things without being a completely selfish bastard, so instead, Luke said, "I'm going to see if Ethan needs a spotter for his workout," and then he headed toward the garage.

"Got room for one more?" he asked as he entered.

Ethan barely glanced up at the intrusion. He was on the lat pull-down machine, doing heavy weights and high reps. Luke watched the sweat drip from his brother's determined brow. He was going to hurt himself if he kept up this demented pace. And yet Luke respected the hell out of him for sticking to it. For believing.

Luke stepped between the parallel bars, the spot where Ethan had willed himself to walk again. First one step, then twenty, then a few more. In that moment, Luke had wanted to believe, too, that Ethan would one day be free of the wheelchair. But after that, his brother's progress had stalled. And with each passing day it became less and less likely that he would ever fully recover. Ethan refused to accept that. But as Luke had learned as the captain of the Portland Storm, somebody had to be the voice of reason.

He understood that his parents couldn't bring themselves to dash the hopes of their little boy. And that meant that Luke would have to raise the possibility.

Stalling, he anchored a hand on each of the waist-high bars. He pushed up until his feet left the floor and his arms were straight. Then he launched into a quick round of tricep dips, pounding them out until his arms started to burn a little.

The clank of weights dropping let Luke know that he had an audience. He swung his feet back and forth a few times before dropping to the ground.

"What do you want, Luke?"

"I was hoping if my boys win this afternoon, that maybe you could attend the sledge hockey state championships with the team for me. If our series against Montana goes well, I'll be out of town."

Ethan was shaking his head before Luke had even finished speaking. "I can't. I'm training."

"You're always training, E."

"If I can't walk, I can't skate. I need to keep working. I can't afford to lose focus now."

Luke watched as Ethan pulled the pin and raised the knee pad on the lat machine. Slowly, carefully, he pushed himself into a standing position. He waited a moment, hand on the machine, to make sure he was stable. Then he backed up a step, then another, then another.

"No one's more determined than you. I know that better than anyone."

It was all Luke could do not to rush over and help him, to push the wheelchair closer, to swear at the injustice that had left this young, virile kid with the walking skills of a decrepit eighty-year-old man.

But he didn't.

Ethan made it, slowly but surely, back to his chair.

"You might be four years younger than me, Ethan, but you've always been right on my heels. Anything I ever did, you did faster and better, including hockey. And I know you miss it. But it's been three years since the accident. Three intense years, and you've been training nonstop."

Now Ethan did look up at him, and Luke could read betrayal in his brother's eyes. "You don't think I can do it? You don't believe I'll skate again?"

"I have no doubt that you will accomplish all kinds of great things in your lifetime, Ethan. You've always done anything you put your mind to. But I'm wondering at what price. As powerful as your single-minded focus is… We're just worried about you, little brother. Mom, Dad, me. You're in here for hours every day. You're only twenty-two years old. I don't want life to pass you by."

Ethan's laugh was bitter. "And what kind of life do

you think is passing me by, Luke? I spent a whole year barely able to take a piss by myself. People have to open the door for me. I can't drive. I can barely reach the damn stove. Physio is the only thing that makes me feel even halfway normal. Working out is the only thing that's helped me get better."

His voice broke. Ethan swiped at his cheek, erasing any sign of weakness. "And I fought through it. I fought through the pain and I won. I went from not being able to stand, to being able to walk five steps and then ten. It's measurable. I can see myself improving and I need that. Because that's what's going to make my life better."

Ethan shook his head. "That hit took everything from me, Luke. It took my body. It took my career. It took my dream. You can't understand what that's like because you're still playing. You're in the goddamn play-offs!"

"And I hate every minute of it! I can't concentrate, I can't score. Because I wish you were there instead of me."

"You want me to feel sorry for you? You want me to give up? Well, I won't. I'll do whatever it takes to walk again." His brother said the words like a vow.

"You're right," Luke said quietly. "This isn't about me. I want you to walk again, Ethan. I do. But I also want you to have a life. To enjoy yourself sometimes. To smile again."

"I'll smile when I can get rid of the chair and the crutches."

Luke scrubbed a hand down his face. "It's been three years."

His brother flinched like he'd punched him.

"Nobody wants to say it, but what if this is it, Ethan? What if this is as good as it gets?"

"Get out."

"C'mon, man. I just—"

"Stop treating me like I'm one of your damn charity cases, Luke. What are you even doing out here? Jesus Christ! Don't you understand? If this doesn't work out, I've got nothing!"

Luke shook his head at the injustice of that. "That's not true."

"Spare me the platitudes and get the fuck out."

With a sigh, Luke walked over to the door. He stepped outside and pulled the door closed behind him, but he hesitated to walk away.

There was a long pause, but then he heard the clank of metal that meant Ethan had resumed his workout. Luke headed back to the house.

He couldn't wait to find Holly and hit the road.

"You ready to go?"

Holly could tell something was on Luke's mind. He'd been distant since he'd come back to the house. Reading the signs, she'd packed up her suitcase and brought it down to the kitchen, anticipating his need for a speedy exit after his shower. She glanced over to where he stood, making jeans and a sledge hockey sweatshirt look good.

"Just about," she responded. "I wanted to say goodbye to Ethan before we go."

Luke tugged nervously at the brim of his black cap, and she could tell he wasn't wild about the idea. Neither were his parents, if their identical deer-in-headlights expressions were any indication. Little did they know, that was exactly the reason she was doing it.

She grabbed the bag she'd purposely left out of her luggage and headed for the back door.

With a deep breath for courage, she walked down the lovingly crafted wheelchair ramp and knocked on the garage door before stepping inside.

"Hi, Ethan. I hope I'm not intruding. My niece, Melissa, is your biggest fan and when she found out I was coming here, she asked me to see if you'd sign her jersey."

He'd looked pissed when she'd first walked in, but now there was only surprise in his eyes as she pulled the Team USA jersey from the bag, complete with "Maguire" and a big number ten on the back.

Ethan rolled his chair from the modified bicep curl machine he'd been using and approached her. He hesitated before he took the marker she held in his direction and even longer before he took the jersey itself.

"No idea why she'd want this," he muttered, scribbling his signature on the crest on the front.

"Are you kidding? You're her favorite player. Your goal in the gold medal game is what made her want to play hockey."

"That was a long time ago." Ethan clicked the lid back onto the Sharpie.

"Not so long," Holly countered. "People still remember. Just like they remember the dirty, after-the-whistle hit that took it all away."

Ethan's head snapped up at her bluntness.

"What happened to you was awful, completely unfair. But you can't let it define you. You can't spend your life focused on what you've lost."

"Did Luke put you up to this?"

Holly shook her head. "Nope. This is all me."

"You're going to walk into my house and tell me how to live my life? Like I give a fuck what my brother's new girlfriend thinks of me?"

"Oh, I'm not Luke's girlfriend. We're just sleeping together."

The expression on Ethan's face was almost comical, but Holly didn't pause to enjoy it. She had too much to say. "I'm just an outside observer, a hockey lover, someone who was sitting with Melissa when you scored that golden goal—one that will grace highlight reels for the rest of time. I saw the way you inspired my niece to try something new and the way your memory still inspires her to be the best at something that she loves."

Holly took a seat on a nearby weight bench.

"Your family loves you. They want to help you through this. And they're devastated every time you turn your back on their help."

"Leave my family out of this!"

Holly ignored him. "Luke's in the longest scoring drought of his professional career. He's playing like shit in the play-offs and beating himself up over it every single second. All because he feels like he's letting you down. But he straps on those skates every day and tries to do better, because he holds on to the hope that you might be watching.

"It kills him a little bit more with every game that you're not in the stands to cheer him on, but he'd never tell you that. Just like he'd never tell you that he's got a number ten sticker plastered to the inside of his helmet."

Holly shook her head. Her eyes prickled with unshed tears, but they were for Luke, not for Ethan, so she didn't let them fall.

"You know, I wanted to play hockey my whole life,

but I wasn't any good. I washed out. I was a horrible skater and I couldn't keep up with the other kids, so I decided to pursue hockey in a way that I *was* good at. I changed my focus to something more realistic. I took up sports journalism and broadcasting and now I get to be close to the game I love.

"There are opportunities to be part of hockey that don't involve playing. Television stations would kill to have you as a commentator or an analyst. Hell, Luke would love your help with the sledge hockey foundation. But if you're not into that, there are hundreds of sports-related charities dying for big names to bring them some much-needed press and support. There are also a ton of hockey teams out there, from the underprivileged ones all the way to the pros, who need mentors, or assistants, or coaches. And all of them would consider it an honor to have you aboard."

Holly got up and walked over to stand in front of Ethan. "So I guess what I'm trying to say is, the only one who thinks you're stuck in that chair is you." She grabbed the jersey from his slackened hands and held it up. "Thanks for the autograph, by the way. My niece is going to love it."

AFTER WARM HUGS with his parents and a promise that she'd come back to visit soon, Holly and Luke and their luggage were back in his truck and headed for the arena.

The game was amazing. Holly had never watched sledge hockey before and she was in awe. The kids were strapped into their sleds and propelled themselves around the ice with what looked like elongated miniature hockey sticks in each hand. Luke did his best to commentate for her, explaining how the butt end of the sticks had little metal teeth that gripped the ice and how a flip of the wrist was all it took to go from shooting the puck to speeding down the ice.

The logistics of the game hardly mattered as the game progressed. These kids were playing their hearts out, loving every minute of it, and by the time the Millerville Sled Dogs vanquished their opponents 3–1, Holly was cheering as loudly as anyone in the arena.

She followed Luke down to the Sled Dogs's dressing room, and they stood outside the open door waiting for the coach's cue.

"Great job today, boys! So good, in fact, that somebody special wanted to stop by and congratulate you on your big win!"

From the moment Luke stepped into the dressing room, it was obvious the kids loved him. Holly stood just outside the door, watching as he high-fived everyone. She couldn't help but be impressed. These kids weren't excited to see a premier hockey player—this wasn't a hero-worship, get-an-autograph type of joy. The bond went deeper than that. They were excited to see an old friend.

"Luke! You came!"

"Of course I did. You guys think I'm gonna miss watching you play such a big game? Not for anything. And you were fantastic! You guys just made the state finals! That's a really big deal."

"Says the man in the middle of a play-off run."

Luke brushed off the comment, and Holly really admired the way he kept the focus on the kids. "I'm proud of you guys. You've worked so hard this season, and all the practices and the focus is paying off. You have a real shot at winning the state championship, and that's why I brought an extraspecial surprise guest to get you ready for all the media and interviews you guys are going to be doing! Please welcome Holly Evans!"

She waved as she stepped into the dressing room, laughing at the excitement and all the hoots and hollers that greeted the announcement.

For the next few hours, she and Luke had a blast filming the kids, asking silly questions and watching them emulate the interview styles of their favorite hockey stars.

Holly was so caught up in talking with the kids, taking photos and answering questions, that she didn't even notice when Luke slipped out of the room. She found him sitting alone at the top of the bleachers, hands in the pockets of his hoodie, staring out at the ice as the Zamboni circled slowly, erasing the game they'd just witnessed.

"Wow. Those kids really love you."

Luke shook his head modestly, but a flush crept up his neck. His embarrassment was so endearing Holly's insides went all squishy. "I get more out of it than they do."

"Oh yeah?" she asked, taking a seat next to him. The painted wood was cold through her jeans. "How do you figure?"

"It's just awesome to see their joy. Their genuine love of the game. Lots of guys lose that by the time they go pro. The people I play with, the people I play against, there's not too many who still love it the same way they did when they were kids. Too much bullshit creeps in. Contracts, ice time, money and constant criticism from the media, armchair athletes.

"But these kids are still pure. They still play for the love of the game. And when I see them happy, it just…"

"It just what?"

Luke shook his head. "Nothing. It's stupid."

She placed a hand on his shoulder. "Luke?"

He kept his eyes firmly on the ground for so long that she was sure he wasn't going to tell her. She squeezed his shoulder to let him know that was okay, but when she pulled her hand away, he met her gaze.

"It makes me hope that maybe, someday, Ethan will find a way to be happy again, too, y'know? Some of these kids have never been able to walk, and some of them were injured, like him. But this game, this team, it makes them smile, despite all the shitty stuff they've been through. I want that for my brother. Even for a second, I want him to remember that life can be good. That we can be good. Like we used to be."

Luke pulled his hands from his pockets, tugged on the brim of his cap and continued.

"Ethan was a superstar. One of those kids that you knew was destined for greatness. Scouts were sniffing around him by the time he was twelve, keeping track, asking questions. He was just so goddamn good that you couldn't help but notice him."

Luke shook his head. "At seventeen, my little brother scored the goal that won our country a gold medal. At eighteen, he got drafted first overall to the league. People had big hopes. And even though I was jealous as hell of the kid, at how it all came so easily for him, I was proud, too.

"Anyway, as fate would have it, he and I both ended up on the Wisconsin Blades that year—his first year as a professional hockey player. Because of our age gap, we'd never officially played hockey together. Some pickup at the local rink, ball hockey in the driveway, sure, but we'd never had matching jerseys, or been on the same line. And it was awesome."

Luke laughed, and Holly realized that he'd left her. He was back in that moment, reacting to some inside joke she couldn't hear.

"Seriously, I loved every second of that season, him down the center, me on the left wing. We dominated. The Blades breezed through the regular season and right into the play-offs. We thought nothing could stop us. That championship had our name on it."

He was wringing his hands together, picking at his thumbnail, bouncing his heel on the concrete beneath his foot. Agitation that would have warned her the story was about to take a turn for the worse, had she not already known.

"And then we hit the fifth game of the second round. We were up three-one in the series, winning two-nothing in the second period. The whistle blew and I headed for the bench. Then there was this thud behind me, and it sounded like every fan in the building gasped, as if they'd all gotten punched in the stomach at the same time."

There were tears in his eyes now, and he bent over, elbows on his knees. And she knew that for him, just telling the story was a punch in the gut.

"Everyone in the Blades bench was standing up, craning to see what had happened. And when I turned, there was my little brother sprawled out on his stomach on the ice, not moving at all. Still. Deathly still. I dropped my stick and gloves and moved. I don't think I've ever skated so fast or so slowly in my life.

"It took forever to get over there, and I was screaming his name. People grabbed me, held me back. I remember them yelling, 'Don't touch him! You can't move him!' but at the time, the words meant nothing. I just wanted to get to him. I just wanted him to wake up."

The tremble in his voice stole her breath.

"Then there were team doctors, and ambulance crews and spine boards. And they took him away, and there was absolutely nothing I could do to help him. He's my little brother, Holly. I was supposed to protect him!"

Luke scrubbed his hands over his face and she could feel his struggle to pull himself together. With a sigh, he sat straight and tall on the hard wooden bench, eyes still glassy with the old pain. She doubted he knew there were tears streaming down his face.

"It was the worst fucking moment of my life. And it haunts me every single day. It's always there. And it makes me feel like an asshole. Because if that's how it feels for me, I can't even imagine how much worse it is for him."

Holly knew the chain of events, of course. She'd watched the career-ending hit. And the aftermath. But hearing Luke tell his story, to actually see his pain, still so close to the surface, it made her heart bleed.

And all she could do in that moment, high in the dimly lit bleachers of the chilly, small-town arena, was put her head on his shoulder and cry with him.

11

Holly stood at the counter of her father's kitchen, dicing onions, while Luke Maguire chopped peppers. It was like playing a surreal version of house, and Holly had to remind herself that the domesticity was just an illusion. After their trip to Millerville, they'd both wanted to continue seeing each other. But they agreed on very clear rules for their dalliance. Just sex, no commitments. Still, the lines kept getting blurred.

Like how he'd dropped her off at home at four o'clock, and by six she was on her way to his place, with only a quick stop to drop off her niece's newly signed Team USA jersey to slow her down.

Like how she'd spent the next two days at his fancy condo with him, having sex and watching movies and eating takeout.

Or how it had taken everything she had to keep her standing Tuesday night dinner date with her father and leave Luke behind. But when she told Luke why she was leaving, he'd volunteered to come with her.

Things were getting very complicated.

"Do you know what I enjoy about this?" He gestured back and forth between them with the knife.

Holly raised an eyebrow. "About the fact that I have boobs and you don't? I could take a wild guess."

Luke winced with annoyance. He was so easy to bait. "No. And keep your voice down. We're at your dad's house."

He was *adorable*, she decided. "Yeah, but he's not here," Holly reminded him, glancing at her watch. 6:20. He always ate at 6:30 on the dot. *Where on earth is he?*

"Besides," she added, "what else am I supposed to guess with you waving that blade around at chest height?"

"I was gesturing to signify us." He lowered his voice. "Our illicit affair."

"What do you like about us?" she asked, ignoring the way her heart stuttered at the topic.

"That we don't talk hockey."

She hoped her face didn't give away her disappointment at that answer. "Oh?" She turned back to the onions, dumping them into the pan on the stove. They sizzled as they hit the hot oil, releasing their fragrance almost immediately.

"Everyone in my life wants to talk about hockey. About Ethan. About the Storm. My thoughts on our last game. My thoughts on our next game. My thoughts on games I'm not even part of. Sometimes it feels like I don't talk about anything else. It's actually kind of a relief that you don't care about it."

Holly added the peppers Luke had cut to the pan, as well as the bag of stir-fry veggies she'd left in her dad's fridge last week.

She knew he meant it as a good thing. He was trying

to say he was comfortable with her, and it was a lovely sentiment. But it made her gut hurt. Because that thing that he liked about her? It wasn't her at all. She was dying to debate hockey with him. Ask him his thoughts on all those things he was tired of talking about and share hers.

She gave the veggies a halfhearted stir, forcing a smile when he stepped up behind her and kissed her neck. "I'm glad," she lied.

And it reminded her that their entire relationship was based on lie after lie. Luke might be comfortable with this woman who didn't exist, but it was Holly's real heart on the line.

There was a big commotion at the front door and while it was right on time, it was much too big to be *just* her father.

Holly groaned inwardly. Her brother and niece must've decided to come over for stir-fry. Karen was probably working a stretch of nights at the hospital, and Neil was a notoriously lazy cook when his wife wasn't around to supervise.

Holly's suspicion was confirmed a moment later when a hungry eight-year-old girl came rushing into the kitchen. "Smells good, Auntie. Dad and I were going to have McDonald's but..." Melissa trailed off, eyes round as hockey pucks as she started to hyperventilate. "You're Luke Maguire. Ohmygosh, you're Luke Maguire!" By the end of the sentence, Melissa's voice was so high-pitched only dogs could hear her.

Holly laughed. "Breathe, monkey."

"Dad, Luke Maguire is at Grandpa's house! Are you staying for dinner, Mr. Maguire?"

Luke nodded. "That's the plan."

"That is so awesome! Your brother is my favorite player of all time. No offense."

"None taken," Luke assured her.

"Aunt Holly got my Team USA jersey signed by him. How cool is that?"

"She did?" Luke's raised brow held questions she didn't want to answer.

"Luke, will you sign my hat? Aunt Holly, is there a marker around here so I can get my hat signed?"

Saved by the autograph seeker. Holly rooted through the junk drawer as Melissa flitted around like a butterfly drunk on excitement. "My team's in the play-offs, too, you know. Just like yours."

"Is that so?"

"Yep. And we're gonna win, too. Dad! Luke Maguire is in Grandpa's kitchen. He's gonna sign my hat. Dad?" Melissa disappeared back into the living room in search of Neil.

Thank you, she mouthed at Luke, tossing him the marker she'd found. He caught it easily, but he waved off her appreciation like it was no big deal. Considering he'd finished explaining to her how much he'd been enjoying his hockey reprieve, she found his kindness toward her niece even more touching.

"So that's why you went to see Ethan before we left. Why didn't you tell me?"

"Oh, you know," she said, nudging the drawer shut with her hip. "I was worried your fragile ego might not be able to handle that Melissa's heart belongs to your brother."

Luke made a halfhearted effort at a laugh, but his preoccupation was obvious. "He actually signed it, though?"

"Yeah. He signed it."

The relief on Luke's face was heartbreaking.

"I'm really sorry about all this craziness. I understand that you were trying to escape hockey. I didn't realize it was going to be a full house."

Whatever Luke was about to say was cut off as Melissa marched back into the kitchen, pulling her dad along by the wrist.

"Nice try, monkey. You expect me to believe a hockey superstar is hanging out in Grandpa's kitchen and…"

"Told you." Melissa pulled off her ball cap and handed it to the hockey superstar hanging out in the kitchen.

Holly suppressed a laugh as her brother lost all ability to speak. His complexion, every bit as fair as her own, flamed red as he recognized their guest.

"Neil, meet Luke. Luke, this is my older brother, Neil."

"Hi. Wow. Hi."

Luke grinned as he signed Melissa's hat and handed it back to her. "Nice to meet you, Neil."

"You, too. Wow. Just…wow. Why didn't you warn me, Hols?"

"Or me," added her father. "When you said you were bringing someone home for dinner, this was definitely not who I was expecting," her father said gruffly, extending a hand. "Frank Evans. It's a pleasure to have you in my home."

Luke shifted the marker to his left hand so he could return the handshake. "Thank you for having me, sir."

"Okay, dinner's almost ready. How about everyone who just got home goes and washes their hands so they can help set the table."

"The table?" her father scoffed. "The first game of

the Buffalo-Wisconsin series is on TV right now and you want us to eat at the table?"

Holly shook her head in defeat. "Why do I even bother?"

TEN MINUTES LATER, Holly was sitting on the couch, sandwiched between Luke and her brother, with Melissa on the floor at Luke's feet. Pop, as always, was comfortably ensconced in his recliner. All of them were enjoying heaping bowls of teriyaki chicken stir-fry.

The first period featured some pretty intense hockey, and her family was in fine form, heckling the refs and players alike, hypothesizing the trades they'd make if they ruled the hockey world.

"Hey, Luke?"

He grinned down at the star-struck girl at his feet, and Holly hated her traitorous heart for noticing how good he was with her.

"Hey, Melissa?"

"Um, remember the time you scored that goal against the Wyoming Stallions back on October seventeenth? You stole the puck from Alfredsson at the blue line and then you skated so fast and scored right through the five-hole? And the goalie was just lying there 'cause he couldn't even believe it?"

Luke chuckled at the description. "I have a vague memory of that, yes."

"I was at that game," Melissa told him. "It was awesome. Aunt Holly took me for my birthday."

Oh my God. As if her "I don't speak hockey" cover wasn't tenuous enough *before* the last few hours. Now a witness had placed her at the scene of the crime. Holly jumped to her feet. "Okay. I think that's enough hockey talk for today. Who wants dessert?"

The answer was a unanimous yes. When Luke tried to help her gather up the supper dishes, she shook her head firmly. "I got it," she said, hurrying into the kitchen.

Thankfully, her family was too caught up in the on-ice battle to notice Holly's odd behavior. Luke, however, followed her into the kitchen before she'd even finished unwrapping the store-bought brownies.

"You sure you're okay? You seem a little distracted tonight."

She reached into the cupboard to grab a stack of napkins. "It's fine." She tried to smile. "I just feel badly for you. You were saying earlier how nice it was not to talk hockey every moment."

"Sure, but that?" He thumbed in the direction of the living room. "That brings back memories. Yelling at the television, armchair coaching and that instant connection you can have, even with a stranger, as long as he's wearing the same jersey as you. I'd forgotten how great the game could be from this side of the boards. It's a lot different than watching game tape."

Holly was touched by his kindness. He was trying to fit in and put her family at ease.

He stepped closer to her and his hands came to rest on the small of her back. "But somehow, I don't actually believe that's the reason you're so distant tonight."

"Oh no? What, are you a mind reader now?" she joked, resting her hands on his chest.

"Maybe I am. Are you thinking of the number... four?"

She shook her head, not understanding. "Four?"

"It's numerology," he said. Holly had to forcibly remind herself to breathe during the pause that followed. "If you add up all the letters in Vancouver, you get four. Not nine, like you said. Not nine, like Jay's birthday. Four."

Uh-oh. That was not an auspicious start to the conversation. Dread seeped through her stomach lining, and the stir-fry soured in her belly. "You've known for that long?"

"I did the math that night, when I got home."

Busted. On the bright side, it was probably the nicest way she'd ever been called a liar.

"I told you the day we met that I was on to you. Hockey is not a sport for the weakhearted. You're either all in, or all out. And I had a hunch you were all in. But now... I just wanted you to know that I know. You don't have to pretend with me anymore. Okay?"

Holly nodded. "Yeah. Better than okay."

He leaned in and the kiss was sweet and filled with relief. It was nice to be assured that she didn't have to hide that part of her around him anymore. That some part of what they had was based in truth.

"Great. So let's go watch some hockey." He grabbed the plastic tray of brownies and stack of napkins she'd set on the counter.

Her phone rang, and she recognized the name of one of her freelance clients, *Sports Nation*, on the caller ID. "Right behind you. I just have to take this first."

"More brownies for me, I guess," Luke joked, heading back into the living room.

She was smiling when she answered the phone.

"Holly? It's John Marshall from *Sports Nation*."

"Hey, John." That was odd. He was the senior editor

at one of the biggest blogs she wrote for. Except for the day he'd called to offer her the freelance job, he usually stuck to email, and even then his messages tended to come through lackeys. "I'm just waiting for the final buzzer so I can finish up tonight's game wrap-up. Should have it to you within the hour."

"That's great, Holly, but it's not why I'm calling. I actually wanted to talk to you about publishing one of your op-ed pieces."

Holly's heart revved, thudding against her rib cage. "I'm sorry, what?"

"Don't play coy with me," John joked. "Every second week, you submit an article about something going on in the world of sports and beg me for a byline. I'm finally going to give you what you want."

"Oh my God! John, that's amazing. Seriously. I couldn't be happier." Holly was practically bouncing. This was a big deal. She couldn't wait to tell her dad.

"Which article finally convinced you? The one about the evolution of goaltending equipment? No, it's my analysis on the new hybrid icing rule, isn't it?"

"Actually, it's neither. Those were solid pieces, but I could publish them any time, interchangeably. There's no *oomph* to them. The one that really impressed me is not only provocative and well-argued but incredibly timely. It's the perfect storm of sports articles."

"Don't leave me in suspense! Which article are you…"

Oh no. Holly's shoulders hunched even as all her muscles braced for bad news. *He doesn't mean…*

"How Luke Maguire Is Hurting His Team."

Holly's stomach bottomed out.

"It's fantastic, Holly. Obviously, I'll have to update it a bit since you wrote it at the beginning of the play-offs—his scoreless streak has hit sixteen games now—but all in all, it's got huge potential for our site. If it does as well as I think it will, who knows? I'm always on the lookout for insightful staff writers."

The line between dream and nightmare blurred. She'd been sending in articles for two years without a word from John, and the minute she got hired by the Portland Storm, the minute she and Luke were, well, whatever they were, *this* happened? She'd written that article two months ago. Before the Women's Hockey Network had even existed.

"You can't publish it, John."

"Yes, I can, Holly. The submission guidelines clearly state that once you send it in, I own it. And I will publish this article—"

She didn't have time for legalese right now. "Fine. Publish it, but I need you to pull my name off it."

"What are you talking about? You've been begging me for a byline since the day I hired you."

"John. The article is yours, but no names, okay?"

"I guess we can go with Anonymous. Might give the article more legs if everyone is speculating about who wrote it."

Great.

"You're sure about this, Holly? *Sports Nation* is a major player. Being published with us tends to help careers."

Holly's fingers migrated subconsciously to her lips. Lips that had just kissed the mouth of a man she cared for more deeply than she'd ever expected to. There was no choice.

"I'm sure."

STANDING OUTSIDE THE Storm's dressing room with the puck set to drop in about two hours, Holly knew she'd made the right decision.

She'd been concerned about Luke, first and foremost. She hadn't even thought about this job in the moment. That meant something. Something big. Something much too complicated to dissect right now.

But as she stood with Jay and the rest of the scrum, waiting for pregame access to the dressing room, she realized she was having fun. Sometime in the last month, she'd come to really enjoy this joke network of hers. Publishing with another company would have voided this contract, and she wasn't quite ready to do that.

The doors finally opened, and she stood back, letting the rest of the reporters head in. She had a good relationship with all the players on the team now, so she never wanted for interviews. Even the big names would carve out a little time to tell her whether they preferred dogs or cats.

She was just about to head in, when Brett Sillinger pushed through everyone in his quest to leave the dressing room in a hurry. His brow was creased and his scraggly play-off beard did little to hide his frown and the determined set of his jaw. The phone in his hand was blaring the "Charge" rally.

That damn anthem had become her nemesis. Every time she heard it—which in the course of a day's worth of interviews with twenty-three players on the active roster, was a lot—her heartbeat tripled and she went on high alert. She couldn't help herself. Even though she knew it was a clue with a lot of dead ends, it remained the most concrete lead she had.

If she could just re-create that bathroom happenstance, overhear the right conversation at the right moment, she'd have her man. She'd lost her chance for a byline on that damning article she'd written because she didn't want to hurt Luke, but the silver lining was the fact that she hadn't blown her cover with the Storm. Now she was *this* close to an on-camera exposé on a betting scandal. It was the kind of hard news story her mom would have killed for. The kind of legit sports reporting that might impress her dad.

That was why, with a quick apology to Jay and directions on a few questions he should ask should the opportunity arise, Holly hurried after the rookie. His long strides had given him a pretty good head start.

When he disappeared around a corner at the end of the hallway, Holly took a quick moment to stop and take off her pumps. Television shows that portrayed their women detectives chasing down perps while wearing high-heeled boots were such a load of crap, she decided. She resumed her chase, more sure-footed and quiet with her shoes safely in hand.

The hallway came to a T intersection, and Holly stopped for a second, debating which way to go. She decided any direction was better than no direction. She arbitrarily went left. When she got to the end of that hallway, she came to a skidding halt outside the occupied room, not at all prepared for what she found.

J.C. had his hands up to protect his face, ducking and covering as his fiancée screamed and swung her fancy designer purse like a flail.

"I can't believe you did this!"

Whack.

"I can't believe you would do this to me! To the baby! How am I supposed to show my face with the other hockey wives?" *Whack*. "Why would you sell the Porsche? Who's going to take us seriously driving some low-end four-door!"

"Come on, Tania. Quit hitting me with your purse already!"

"I'm going to be a laughingstock."

Holly tore her attention from the fighting couple, backing away slowly, trying to leave unnoticed.

She almost made it, too, but Tania gave a particularly wild swing of her bag, and J.C.'s gaze caught hers. She didn't even break stride. She just spun and ran.

Cowardly? Maybe, but she was hot on the trail of a suspect, and Tania's brand of a woman scorned was more than she cared to deal with right now.

Obviously, Sillinger had gone in the opposite direction, so she hurried back to where she'd lost him and turned the other way.

She was relieved that it did not take long to locate his nasally whine.

"What the hell, man? I thought we had a deal! I told you, I just need a little more time!"

Holly stopped short at the outburst. Her scalp prickled at the realization that this might be the break she'd been searching for. She tried to recall the harsh whisper that had echoed off the tiles in the Storm's bathroom. Had it been the rookie all along?

"Dude, you can't do this to me. I'll get you your money. Just give me a week. Two, tops. My mom'll help me out. She's in Vegas on vacation or I'd have your cash right now."

Holly frowned and leaned forward to peek around the corner.

Brett shoved a hand in his dark curls, his knuckles

white, he was clutching his hair so tightly. He pressed his back against the concrete wall, then slid down until he was sitting on the rubber floor.

"You don't understand. The Lamborghini's all I've got. My teammates think I'm a joke. This is the only thing I've ever done to impress them. Just give me a couple of weeks. I'll get you your money."

There was a long moment of silence, followed by, "Yeah. I understand you've got a business to run. Whatever."

He swore, then slammed his phone on the ground before wrapping his arms around his legs and dropping his forehead to his knees. All in all, it was quite a dramatic show.

"Brett?"

He started like she'd hit him with a cattle prod. He scrambled to his feet. The pout on his face made him seem even younger than his nineteen years, despite the pitiful beard.

"How long have you been there, Holly? What did you hear?"

Holly shook her head and started toward him slowly with her hand out, like she was approaching a skittish deer. "I just wanted to make sure you're okay."

"No, Holly. Actually, I'm not okay. I just found out they're repossessing my Lamborghini, so life pretty much sucks balls right now."

She did her best not to laugh.

After such an intensely emotional weekend with Luke, his parents, Ethan…the idea that a nineteen-year-old hockey player making a salary that most people could only dream of, herself included, was pouting like a child because he couldn't make the payments on his Lamborghini seemed the height of absurdity to her. Talk about your first-world problems.

She stared at the simpering man-child before her and mentally crossed his name off the suspect list. A man raking in extra money by betting on his team wouldn't have to ask for money from his mother. Even more damning was Brett's complete inability to deal with surprises.

Point-shaving was a delicate balance, especially in a low-scoring game like hockey. The idea that the kid before her had the chops to handle and manipulate a rink full of veteran hockey players was ridiculous. Truthfully, she was a little embarrassed she'd put him on the suspect list at all.

"You're not gonna tell the team, are you? About my Lambo getting repossessed?"

"No. I'm not going to tell them about your *Lambo*," she said dully.

"Okay, great. Maybe I can make up a story about how I totaled it or something. That would make me sound cool."

Holly let Brett disappear around the corner so she wouldn't have to walk back to the dressing room with him. Then she put her high heels on again to slow her down even further.

The dressing room was packed. She sidled up to Jay as soon as she spotted him. "What'd I miss?"

He shook his head. "No idea where J.C. is. I scored some face time with Eric and Doug, asked them the stuff you wanted for the 'How Well Do You Know Your Teammate?' segment. We're up next with Luke, after Baniuk finishes with him."

Holly watched Corey and his cameraman set up the shot and launch right into the interview.

"I'm Corey Baniuk from *Portland News Now*. Here with me is the Storm's captain, Luke Maguire. Luke, *Sports Nation* has recently published an article saying that your play, in particular, might be suffering because it's your first time in the play-offs since your brother, former Wisconsin center Ethan Maguire, took a brutal hit in the post-season three years ago. What do you have to say to those allegations?"

Shit.

Holly had hoped she'd have a chance to warn Luke before the article hit the media. John must have pressed "publish" the moment he got off the phone with her.

Why hadn't she said something to Luke after dinner? On their way home? After they'd made love? Because she was a coward, that's why. And she'd wanted to enjoy what she had with him as long as possible.

The color drained from Luke's face for a split second before it returned with a vengeance. "No comment. We're done." He pushed past the camera and headed for the exit.

Holly hurried after him, but instead of the hunt she'd endured with Brett, she found Luke pacing in the hallway right outside the dressing room door.

She couldn't keep the concern from her voice. "Are you okay?"

"I just need a minute."

"I saw what just happened with Corey Baniuk, Luke. You don't have to be fine. He coldcocked you. That was way out of line."

Luke just shrugged. "Rumor has it Baniuk's about to inherit the anchor desk. I should have expected him to go for the jugular on that interview, go out in a blaze of glory."

He took a breath. "Besides, Baniuk's not the problem. He was just the first reporter to get a crack at me. The problem is the damn *Sports Nation* article." Luke shook his head. "It's going to dredge up all the Ethan questions again. That guy really hit me where I live."

He lowered his voice, leaned toward her, and Holly could only hope he couldn't smell the culpability rolling off her in waves.

Luke continued. "The article talks about how my scoring drought started on the same day the team was mathematically guaranteed a play-off spot. This guy just laid out all my neuroses. I don't even get how he could figure out half that stuff. Much as it hurts to admit it, it's a really professional and well-written article. No cheap shots, just facts.

"It's probably for the best he didn't have the balls to sign his name to the thing. I'm not sure if I should pay him for the therapy or punch him in the face."

Luke shook out his hands. He was moving around a lot.

Holly, on the other hand, was frozen to the spot under a blizzard of remorse and shame. How had she thought taking her name off the article would ease the impact? She should have fought harder to keep it from being published in the first place. Again, coward.

Luke didn't seem to notice her anxiety. "Anyway, the article doesn't matter. What matters is that I've got a game tonight and I need to calm down and get back in the zone."

He drew in a deep breath and exhaled slowly. "We really have to win tonight. Any advice?"

She couldn't make her confession now. That would only screw with his head more. As the cause of his messed-up equilibrium, the least she could do for him now was to keep quiet.

Holly tucked her hair behind her right ear as she stepped toward him. "Montana's notoriously weak on their left side, so just keep the pressure on. Forecheck hard and whenever you get a shot on Krouse, remember to shoot stick-side. His glove has been hot in the post-season."

Luke grinned at the counsel. "Man. You weren't kidding when you said you know hockey."

"Kick the Wolfpack's ass tonight and I'll show you what else I know," she teased. It was a desperate attempt to keep the guilt from winning.

It didn't work.

12

It was past midnight by the time Luke finished doing press and they'd arrived back at his place. Still, when Luke walked out of his ensuite bathroom wearing nothing but black sweatpants, Holly's weariness dissipated at the prospect of making good on her promise. Luke had kept up his end of the bargain and the Storm had come out victorious, downing Montana 5–3.

"So, what have you got in store for me tonight?" he asked, joining her on the bed. "And bear in mind that you're going to have to pull out all the stops to impress me, since I am currently a man in possession of flavored body oils and a tin of Altoids."

"Oooh! Flavored oils? Sounds fun! Where are you stashing 'em?" Holly rolled onto her stomach and reached for the bottom drawer of the nightstand closest to her.

"No! Not that one!" Luke practically vaulted over her, pulling open the small top drawer instead.

Holly shot him a frown. "What? Is that your fetish drawer, or something? You don't want me to find your ball gag?"

Oh my God, is Luke blushing? Her curiosity bubbled to new heights.

"It's nothing, okay? You wanted sexy oil, here it is." He pulled the lube out and set it on the end table. "Ooh, look! Cherry flavored."

"Nice try." She couldn't keep the grin from her face. "What's in there, Luke?"

He shrugged but it looked painful, like his skin was too small for his body. "Remember how we were going to have sex? Remember that fun plan?"

"But how am I supposed to really concentrate on doing naughty things to your body when all I'll be able to focus on is what's in that drawer?"

"You are very bad at taking no for an answer, do you realize that?"

Holly shook her head and heaved an innocent shrug. "What can I say? Our misogynistic culture has forced me to become a fighter, to believe in my dreams and power through the glass ceiling. You're part of the patriarchy, the reason I must pursue things with such single-minded determination. Face it, Mags. You're fighting a losing battle here."

With weary defeat on his face, Luke flopped back onto the bed and slung an arm across his face. "Fine. But you cannot, upon pain of death and/or laryngitis whenever there's a camera on you, tell anyone what you've seen here today."

Holly smiled graciously in victory. "What is it? What is it?" she chanted, pulling open the drawer. "What the...?" To her utter amazement, she found a pair of knitting needles attached to what she assumed was a striped scarf. But as she began to pull, the haphazardness of the striping became obvious, as did the never-ending length. "Seriously, what is it?"

Luke heaved a long-suffering sigh. "I told you. It's nothing."

Holly was still searching for the end of the navy, white and teal monstrosity. It was at least twice as long as she was tall and she still hadn't pulled it all from its resting place yet. "It's a pretty long nothing."

"It's just knitting, okay? My mom taught me."

Holly sat on the edge of the bed, yanking foot after foot of inconsistent stripes into her lap. "Okay, you have got to tell me how this came about."

Luke pulled his arm away from his face and stacked a pillow under his head. "When I was young, I used to really dwell on stuff—especially hockey games. If we lost, I'd go over it again and again, trying to figure out what I did wrong, what I could do better. If we won, I'd try to deconstruct what went right, how I could build on it. I was a pretty intense kid, especially once my little brother started climbing the hockey ranks. I'd get so deep in my head that I developed some pretty bad insomnia."

Holly ran her hand across the yarn in her lap. She could imagine a young Luke, solemn blue eyes, a determined set to his chin as he figured out how to be faster, stronger and better, all in the name of the sport he adored. He was still doing it.

"So she taught me how to knit. She said knitting would keep the chattering part of my brain occupied so I could mull over only the most important stuff and keep my thoughts really focused. She made the rule that I could only go over the game until I was done knitting five inches and then I had to put the yarn away."

He smiled. "It sounds dumb, but it worked. I would replay the game for however long it took me to knit five inches, and then I was free. I didn't have to think about it anymore. I've made one of these every hockey season since."

She held up the project in her hands. "All color-coded to your team, I hope."

Luke laughed at himself. "Yep. For my Portland Storm years, navy is a loss, white is a win and teal is a tie. Every game is five inches of knitting or purling and intense contemplation."

"So it's a good thing that this is mostly white then, huh?"

"Yeah, it was a pretty good season."

"And these thin teal lines at this end? That's the start of each play-off series?"

He nodded. "No ties in the play-offs, so that's my way of keeping track of how far we make it."

"You are a very surprising man, Luke Maguire. Just when I think I've figured you out, you change the game. Although I'm pissed at you that you told me that your secret talent was speaking French. This is way cooler."

Luke rolled his eyes.

"I'm serious," she said, with a playful punch to his arm. "I just have one more question."

"Of *course* you do."

"How do you hide it from the other guys on road trips?"

Luke grinned. "Nobody ever thinks your World Junior Championship duffel bag is full of yarn."

"Hiding in plain sight." Holly laughed. "Well done."

She set the knitted record of the Storm's current season on the end table. Every piece of himself that

Luke revealed made Holly fall in love with him just a little bit more.

How could she hurt someone she loved? And she would hurt him; that seemed inevitable. But was it better to hide the truth from him and let him have his win? Or come clean and destroy everything? There were no easy answers. She only knew that she wanted him to be happy, and tonight she could make him happy.

"I gotta say, that knitting was a much sexier find than a ball gag."

"Oh yeah?"

Holly nodded. "Yep. And now that my curiosity is sated, I find myself with plenty of naughty things percolating in my brain."

"You don't say."

"I *do* say," she countered, crawling over and straddling him. She grabbed the end of his knitting project. "So here's the plan. We're about to take your knitting to a whole new level."

LUKE LAY BACK against the pillows as she tied up one of his wrists before looping the free end of the yarn monstrosity through the slatted headboard. His body was already approving where she was going with this, even before she'd finished fashioning the woolen shackle around his other wrist.

Although his restraints could easily be slipped with a few tugs, her foray into light bondage was turning him on in a big way. He loved the satisfaction in her smile as she surveyed him, all trussed up and at her disposal.

If he'd known knitting would score him this kind of action, he would have opened the damn drawer himself.

"So now what?" he asked, unable to hide the desire that was tenting his pants.

"Now," she said with a wicked grin, "we get to the naughty stuff."

"I was hoping you'd say that."

She leaned down and kissed him with a brute force he hadn't expected. But he liked this take-charge side of her, the way her tongue plunged into his mouth, the bite of her nails on his chest.

When she pulled back, the look on her face undid him. She was this incredible mix of sweetheart and vixen, and the sugar-and-spice combo was proving to be never-ending fun.

She maintained eye contact as she stood on the mattress, stripping off her jacket, then her skirt. His breath came faster at the sight of her curves, highlighted by a purple bra and matching panties.

She dropped to her knees, then crawled forward between his legs. "Your turn."

Luke couldn't help the groan that escaped as she grabbed his pants and tugged them slowly down his legs. The torturous rasp of the elastic waistband against his hard flesh culminated in a harsh gasp when his erection was finally freed of its confines.

She tossed his pants to the floor and then stretched to grab the cherry lube. He loved her body, loved watching her move. She was a real woman, not a skeleton with boobs, and when he got free from his knitted prison, he was going to do some exploring of his own.

The lid on the oil tube opened with a soft *click*, and the intent look of concentration on Holly's face as she drizzled cool liquid on his hot flesh made his hips buck.

Dropping the recapped bottle on the mattress, she

reached for his straining cock. But then she jerked her hand back. "Wait!"

"What?" The word came out harsher than he meant it to.

"Can we jump right into this, or do you need to knit first?" she asked. The fact that she would stop to tease him just then made him want her even more.

"Only if you can't come up with a better way to get my mind off the game and tire me out."

Her smile said she had some ideas that he just might enjoy.

He was not disappointed. She wrapped her hand around his cock and pumped once, twice, three times to ensure an even distribution of the oil.

Then she put her hands on the bed beside his hips and took him in her mouth. His whole world shrank to the warm, wet pressure of her lips and her magical, magical tongue.

"Mmm."

The vibration of her sound sent another level of pleasure humming through his veins, and he flexed his hips, seeking more but unsure how things could get any better.

She lifted her head, releasing him from her mouth after a hard suck of his crown. "The cherries taste good, but next time, I'd rather just taste you," she said. Then she grasped his cock firmly in her right hand and proceeded to push him farther toward oblivion.

He was dying to bury his fingers in her soft, blond curls and set her pace, but he was also loving the torture of being restrained. The soft, suctioning sounds of her mouth were his undoing.

"Holly, I need inside you. I want to make you feel as good as I do right now."

He slipped his hands free of the yarn shackles so he could reach for her, pull her up the bed, taste her lips and move her body beneath his.

She sighed as he drove into her, slow and deliberate, but it didn't take long until he gave in to the roar of his blood and sped his pace. Holly didn't seem to mind. She drew her knees up, hooking her legs around his waist. The change in position forced him even deeper, and she started chanting his name against his lips.

He gave her everything she wanted, following her whispered orders until her breath grew choppy and her fingernails dug into his back.

Then Luke redoubled his efforts, plunging harder, faster, deeper, until he felt her body clench. And then he let her cries of ecstasy pull him over the edge right along with her.

SHE WOKE UP to find the bed empty. But the curtains blowing in the warm Portland breeze solved the mystery of Luke's whereabouts before she even had a moment to be curious. With a sleepy smile, she stretched and slid out of the bed. As she was grabbing her shirt, a familiar mix of navy, white and teal caught her eye. She padded across the hardwood floor to the chair in the corner of the room.

No way was Luke getting away with this blatant show of hubris without a goodly amount of teasing. She pulled the jersey on and headed toward the balcony.

Luke stood on the balcony wearing nothing but a pair of low-slung jeans, staring contemplatively out at the city. He looked so damn yummy that certain parts of her anatomy perked up at just the sight of him.

Down, girl.

"Seriously, Maguire. You have your own jersey in replica? That is so wrong."

He glanced over at the sound of her voice, and she could tell she'd surprised him. His jaw flexed as he took in the jersey, her thighs, calves, bare feet. His eyes tracked every inch of her and when their gazes met, there was an appealing cockiness to his expression.

"No, what's wrong is how much it's turning me on that you're wearing it. I like seeing my name on you."

"How very Neanderthal," she joked, walking over to him.

"What can I say? Me horny, you hot."

She laughed as Luke stepped behind her, placing one hand on the railing on either side of her hips. With a contented sigh, she leaned back against his chest. They stared out at the city as the sun came up over Portland.

It was romantic, standing in his arms and watching the world wake up. But after awhile, Holly couldn't silence the niggling voice in her brain, the one that said Luke was not the type of guy to indulge in blatant self-worship, and she turned in his arms to face him.

"So seriously, why do you have your own jersey? And why is the number wrong? Misprint?"

Luke shook his head. "No. It's not a misprint. It was for Ethan. I bought it for him after they gave me the *C*. I thought maybe he'd come to a game or something."

Holly's heart went a little melty. She traced a finger down his bare chest, hoping he'd say more.

Luke tightened his grip on the balcony railing. It took a moment, but he finally spoke.

"He's the reason I'm the captain now. Because I have to play for both of us. It was just my way of saying thanks. But you saw him. He's been so down, I just didn't have the heart to give it to him."

Holly suddenly realized the significance of the twenty-eight on the back of the jersey. Forget melty, her heart was liquid goo, sliding down the inside of her rib cage. "Eighteen plus ten. You added both of your jersey numbers together."

Luke shrugged, as if it wasn't the sweetest thing she'd ever heard.

"Like I said, it was dumb. It's been sitting on that chair for three months now."

"I'm sorry I put it on. I didn't realize it was so significant. I was just giving you a hard time."

"You know what? Keep it. No one else is going to wear it."

Holly had plans to the contrary, but she kept those to herself. "You're sure you don't mind?"

"Why would I mind? You look sexy as hell in it."

She smiled at that. "Well, if that's what you think about me in it," she teased, ducking under his arm and heading for the door, "then you should see me out of it." Luke followed her back to bed and she proceeded to prove her point.

AFTER ANOTHER HARD-FOUGHT win at home, they'd split away games in Montana, losing the first and winning tonight. And while Luke was glad they'd managed a win, he found he owed more of his good mood to the prospect of seeing Holly again than to the game result. Luke loosened his tie and looked out the oval window at the lights of whatever city they were currently flying over.

"Mags, you okay?"

Luke glanced over as J.C. took the aisle seat beside him.

"You're staring off into nothing. I thought you'd had a stroke or something."

"How did you know Tania was the one?"

J.C. laughed. "What?"

"I'm serious, man. You two are getting married, having a baby. How did you know she was the one you wanted to do all that with?"

Normally the stymied expression on his goaltender's face would have made him laugh, but tonight he just wanted answers.

"Where is this coming from? Wait a minute, are you dating someone?"

Luke took a deep breath. He wasn't really ready to spread the news around. He certainly didn't want to put Holly's job at risk. But he was dying to tell someone, and J.C. was his best friend. He couldn't help his smile when he said her name. "Holly."

"Holly? As in, *Holly* Holly? Of Women's Hockey Network fame? The woman you don't trust because she is undermining the sanctity of the game and threatening the team? *That* Holly?"

Luke accepted the ribbing as par for the course, but when he didn't fire back, J.C. sobered a little. "You're serious? You have feelings for this girl."

Luke shrugged, which in guy talk was as good as a yes.

"Huh. Never took you for the kind of guy who'd end up with a ditz just because she's got a nice rack."

Luke's shoulders stiffened. "That's over the line, man." His voice was all steel, and J.C. held his hands up in a gesture of surrender.

"My bad, man. Just testing the waters. I wasn't expecting to come back from the can and have you start talking about your emotions and shit. Stand down."

Luke relaxed in his chair, but not until he'd stared J.C. down, let him know he meant what he said. "And for the record, she's not a ditz. She just plays one on the internet."

"Whad'ya mean?"

"The dumb blonde routine is all an act. She's actually as smart as she is beautiful." He sent his buddy a sidelong glance. "And she knows more about hockey than you ever will."

"So then what's with all the secrecy?"

Luke shrugged. "I guess the top brass doesn't think we're good enough actors to answer the questions if we thought she was only joking."

"Ha. They believe us well enough when we line up to kiss their asses at all their hoity-toity events."

Luke smiled at the dig. Everyone was aware of how much J.C. hated putting on a tux and schmoozing with the bigwigs.

"So what's Holly's deal then?" his friend asked. "She's like, a reporter or something?"

"She wants to be."

J.C. nodded. "Cool. Good for her. And good for the two of you. I'm happy for you guys. Truth is, Mags, the fact that you're asking me how you know? That probably means you already know." J.C pushed the button that made his seat recline. "I'm gonna catch twenty minutes before we land."

"'Night." The word came out distracted, though, as Luke let the words settle in.

That probably means you already know.

13

THE GAME WAS going well until the hit. The sight of Eric Jacobs lying on the ice and clutching his knee was too much.

With a feral growl, Luke dropped his stick and his gloves and launched himself at six feet, two hundred pounds worth of smug left-winger. He grabbed a fistful of Wolfpack jersey with his left hand and landed a solid hook with his right. He only had a second to relish the roar of the crowd and the sting in his knuckles before his punching bag recovered and launched a counterattack.

But Luke wasn't about to back down. He might not have gotten the chance to punish the man who put Ethan in a wheelchair, but he wasn't going to let the one who'd just sidelined Eric Jacobs get away with it unscathed.

Despite Chris Powell's attempts to wrestle him into submission, Luke managed to land a few more good blows to the jerk's face before the two of them overbalanced and fell to the ice. Luke swore when his nose made contact with Powell's helmet, his eyes welling up at the sharp sting.

He didn't have time to worry about it, as he struggled to gain the upper hand even as someone grabbed him by the shoulders and pulled him back.

"That's enough, you two. Break it up." The ref's voice managed to penetrate the angry haze that had overtaken Luke's brain, but he was too worked up to obey.

With a final jab to Powell's left cheek, he let himself be hauled off the asshole who'd just lambasted Eric Jacobs with a dirty, knee-on-knee hit.

He watched his nemesis scramble to his feet, only to be detained by the referee.

"Nice fight, Powell," he taunted, ignoring the linesman's attempts to wrestle him over to the penalty box. "I think you might have even broken a nail trying to hug me into submission."

"You should thank me for not messin' up your face there, pretty boy. Might lose your 'hottie of the month' status and then you'd have to play hockey for a living. How many games has it been since you last scored?"

The idea that he and Powell had been linemates a mere four months ago, before the other man's giant ego and philandering ways had sent the bastard to Montana, seemed ludicrous in that moment. Obviously things changed. Loyalties faded. You couldn't trust just anybody.

"Tell your boys I said good luck in the play-offs, Maguire. It's gonna be a battle without your top scorer."

Luke followed Powell's gaze toward the net, where Cubs was being helped off the ice by the trainer. Luke didn't like the way his centerman was hunched over, his left leg bearing no weight.

The ref skated up. "Shut your mouth and get moving, Powell." Then he turned to Luke and gave him a shove. "That goes for you, too."

The other linesman skated up, handing Luke his stick and gloves. The memories that came flooding back were not happy ones, and even though Eric's injury wasn't as serious as the one that was haunting him, it was cold comfort.

With a sigh, Luke headed for the penalty box. He'd gotten two minutes for instigating and five for fighting. Powell got two minors and a game misconduct.

The Storm ended up winning the game and the series with it, but Luke barely made it through the post-game press junket. By the time he and Holly got to his place, his palms were clammy and he couldn't stop shaking.

Everything with Ethan had been so close to the surface lately. To see another talented player—another centerman, for God's sake—get taken down on Luke's shift…it made his heart feel too big for his rib cage, like it might puncture any second.

"I can't do this again."

"He's going to be okay, Luke. Here, just crawl into bed, okay?"

"But what if he's not? His grandma had a heart attack a few months ago. He needs to be able to take care of her."

"He can. He got off the ice himself. He's not as badly hurt as Ethan was. And even if he had been, there's nothing you could have done to stop it. It's not your fault." Her voice was soft. Reassuring. He liked hearing it. It made him feel better.

"I'm the captain. I'm responsible for my team."

"I know you are. But you couldn't have stopped this."

She crawled in beside him, and for the first time since the fight with Powell, he began to breathe normally.

"Maybe I could have. I should have tried. I should have done something."

"Luke. Stop. You did everything you could."

Holly wrapped her arms around him. His heart slowed to its standard pace.

"Will you stay tonight?" he asked.

"Sure, of course."

Her warm fingers stroked his hair. It wasn't too long after that, that Luke surrendered to sleep.

IT WAS SIX THIRTY in the morning when the sun streaming through Luke's window woke Holly. He was slung out on the mattress beside her, and she was glad to see him resting after his post-game panic attack. He'd been through so much lately. Too much. And there was more to come.

He shifted on the mattress, sliding his hand over her hip and tugging her closer. She turned to face him. His blue eyes blinked a few times before they opened for good. "Hi."

She smiled and ran a finger down his stubbly cheek. "Hi back."

"Sorry about last night."

"There's nothing to be sorry about."

Luke sighed. "Holly, I can recognize a panic attack when one hits. I had them really bad right after, well, right after Ethan got hurt. Last night wasn't anything compared to those ones, but I really appreciate you staying here and talking me down."

"It's not a problem, because…" she trailed off.

"Because?"

I love you. She did, but she couldn't say it yet, though, so she kissed him instead.

He kissed her back and shifted closer. Before she knew it, they were naked and entwined, his body driving into hers with such an elemental force that for the first time in their relationship, there was no need for sexy words, or woolen shackles, or flavored oils. They were beyond all that. And when her climax rolled in like soft tides instead of roaring waves, it was the most exquisite thing she'd ever experienced.

They were holding hands and trading kisses and indulging in a dreamy discussion about breakfast—he was firmly in camp bacon and eggs, while she was leaning more toward French toast—when the "Charge" anthem intruded on their blissful post-coital haze.

Luke rolled away from her so he could locate his phone, and the loss of his body heat sent a chill down her spine. It took him a few moments of searching—he'd been in such rough shape last night that most of his before-bed routines, like putting his phone on its charger, had been annexed by the panic attack.

She watched as he followed the familiar music toward the chair where she'd slung his suit jacket after she'd helped him take it off. He flipped the expensive fabric around so he could access the interior breast pocket. Finally he got hold of his ringing prey.

"H'lo? Yeah, it's me."

His whole body tensed, and Holly felt the distance he put between them even before Luke pulled on a pair of jeans. He didn't miss a beat on the phone that was expertly cradled between his ear and his shoulder.

"No way. I told you, that's not an option," he said, stalking out of the bedroom. "I don't care how you do it, just get him the money. I can't have this traced back to me."

The words stopped her heart. She jumped up with some half-formed plan to follow him, but she only made it three steps from the bed before the unthinkable caught her eye.

Dazed, she walked toward his jacket, askew on the chair back, just as he'd left it. A folded piece of yellow legal paper poked out of the inside breast pocket.

She unfolded it to find a list of letters and numbers in stark black ink.

And just like that, her perfect morning crumbled.

It can't be Luke.

The man who was so sweet and thoughtful, the man who needed hockey to breathe, surely he wouldn't do something that could earn him a lifetime ban from the game he loved?

And yet there were other things—his parents' modest dwelling and pile of bills, Ethan's intense physio regime and state-of-the-art equipment, the fact that a hockey player who should have adequate funds had said things like "money's tight" and "I can't have this traced back to me." Something wasn't quite adding up there. She'd tried her best to find a more viable suspect, but something always cleared them.

Brett Sillinger had pouted when his Lamborghini got repoed.

J.C. LaCroix had done the responsible thing and downgraded to a family car because he had a baby on the way.

And Eric Jacobs, who'd been her least likely suspect in the first place, had apparently been dealing with some intense family issues that correlated with his slightly-below-average play-off showing.

Luke, on the other hand...

Holly sat on the edge of the bed, the over/under list clenched in her fist.

He'd shown up in the bathroom moments after she'd found the betting sheet, and his ringtone matched the mystery man's.

His truck was nice, but in the grand scheme of luxury vehicles, it was pretty low on the scale for a six-year veteran who was currently earning almost two million a year.

His parents must've invested huge amounts of money into making their old house fully accessible, not to mention the cost of Ethan's physio studio and medical bills. And she'd heard several sports outlets reporting that Brad Timmons had recently filed for bankruptcy, which meant the Maguires were receiving no financial help from the man responsible for their money woes.

And she'd caught Luke twice now in the midst of suspicious-sounding phone calls, the most recent one specifically about untraceable money.

She didn't want to believe it. Luke loved the game and he was fiercely protective of his teammates. It was beyond comprehension that he would jeopardize his career or his team's integrity this way.

But even as she thought it, she knew there was one thing he loved more than hockey—his family. He would do whatever it took to take care of them. Manipulating the games a little was an easy way to help pay down his family's debts, to take care of his parents and his little brother.

And maybe that straight-arrow reputation he'd built

up—the one that made her doubt he was capable of it—was the key to getting away with the crime. He had the perfect cover.

She *had* to ask him.

She was in love with Luke and she owed him the truth about her suspicions, the right to defend himself, to give his side of the story. Before she exposed it to the world.

14

"Luke, can we talk?"

He'd barely stepped back into the bedroom after a massive fight with his brother's bank. The somber note in Holly's voice made the hair on his arms stand up. "Sure, yeah."

He took a seat on the corner of the bed opposite her. "What's going on, Holly? Is everything okay?"

"Yeah," she said, but she backtracked immediately. "No. It's not, actually." She sighed.

They made eye contact and he didn't like what he saw there.

"Luke, I'm just worried about you. I know you've had some money trouble."

"What?"

"You were obviously speaking with a bank just now. And I get it. Your family is amazing. And they needed your help, but manipulating hockey games…that's a dangerous road to start down. So if it's about money…"

His muscles tensed and his jaw hardened. This wasn't a talk. It was a cross-check after the whistle. The kind that left permanent damage.

"What are you trying to say?" His eyes dropped to the yellow paper clutched in her fingers. He shot to his feet, eyes lighting on his suit jacket, askew on the chair. "Have you been going through my things?"

"I found a list, Luke. When I was in the Storm bathroom that day that we kissed. This list. And aside from the first one, every single play-off game has ended with the same over/under as the list predicted. That's not a coincidence. Someone is manipulating the games."

"And you're accusing me?"

Her silence was all the answer he needed. Luke experienced a moment of full-body pins and needles and then…nothing. Numbness settled over him with a finality that reminded him of death. "You believe I would do that." It wasn't really a question, since she'd already said as much. More of a reckoning.

"Luke, I know how important your family is to you. You'd do anything it took to make sure they're okay."

He raked a hand through his hair. "But this? After all we've been through? I kept your secret! I introduced you to the people who mean the most to me in this world. I fell in love with you, Holly."

She looked like he'd punched her. That stricken reaction to the words he'd wanted to say for longer than he was willing to admit was the final nail in the relationship that had turned his world upside down. "And this is what you think of me."

Her brown eyes were swimming in unshed tears, and her chin trembled as she fought to hold them back. "Luke, the evidence—"

"Fuck the evidence! I would never do what you just accused me of! Not for any amount of money. I wouldn't do that to my family. I wouldn't do that to my guys.

We're a team, Holly. We trust each other. We back each other up. I can see you don't know anything about that, but that's how we operate. It's how we win games and it's how we lose games. Together."

"But the stats, and that phone call about untraceable money and Ethan's top-of-the-line rehab equipment…"

"That's your reasoning? Let me tell you something about money. Pro hockey players make around three hundred thousand dollars a year in the first three years of their contract. Unless they get paralyzed. Then they make nothing. But they still have to live, Holly. They need money to eat, to buy a wheelchair, to pay for medical bills and specialists and daily physio. Whatever it takes for the chance to walk again.

"The parents of an injured pro have to remortgage their house when they should be gearing up for retirement, because sidewalks have to be widened, ramps have to be built and garages have to be converted into rehab facilities. A paralyzed player needs a new van to accommodate a wheelchair. And when things start looking bleaker and bleaker, he has to figure out how to finance a car with hand controls so that a broken hockey player can live the fulfilling, independent life he deserves, even if he doesn't regain full use of his legs.

"So, yeah. Money's tight. My paycheck might have a few zeroes on the end of it right now, but there are millions of dollars of catching up to do. And the secrecy? The phone call you overheard? That was just for Ethan's pride. Because he's already struggling with accepting physical help, and I didn't want him to know about the financials, that the bastard who ruined his life claimed bankruptcy and that all his money is coming from me.

"He needs to focus on recovering, on himself, not

worrying about his family. And maybe I should have told him. But I'm his big brother and it's my job to protect him. I didn't do it on the ice that day, but I've damn well done whatever it takes to make up for it ever since. And that's my call. Not yours."

She was trembling now, and he hardened himself against her imploring eyes. "I'm sorry, Luke. I can see I made a mistake. I just wanted to bring my concerns to you. To be honest with you. And I realize this is hard to hear, but every prediction on the list I found has come true save one, and that is not coincidence. If it's not you, it's somebody else on the team."

His protectiveness roared up with a vengeance. "Leave my guys out of this!"

"I won't!" She came to her feet then, too, and the change in her, from meek acceptance of his lecture to formidable warrior ready for battle, was startling. "I sat here and I listened to your side. Just because you have an explanation for my evidence does not mean it was ridiculous, so don't you dare stand there and demean it. I'm an excellent reporter, Luke.

"I do my homework and I test my hypotheses. Just because my conclusion about you was proven false, doesn't let your team off the hook. This list still belongs to somebody who used the Storm bathroom that day." She held it up, and it trembled because her hand was also trembling.

"It's not mine, obviously," she said, "so by process of elimination, thanks to your ridiculous game-day superstitions, that means it's one of your teammates.

"And you want more honesty? You want to be able to trust me? You know that fair and honest article on the

Sports Nation blog? The one about how you're hurting your team? I wrote that."

Blood roared in his ears as he processed that betrayal.

"I wrote it before I ever met you and when I found out they were going to publish it against my objections, I asked them to take my name off it. Because not hurting your feelings and continuing to work for the Storm meant more to me than the byline that would have helped me reach my dream job in sports reporting.

"You think I'm out to hurt you and the team? Then why have I kept this illegal activity under the radar instead of selling the story to any number of media outlets who would pay me large sums of money and give me my pick of jobs? Your heart is not the only one that got bruised here. And while I've always admired your loyalty to your teammates, if you do not figure out who is poisoning your team right now, then you're all going to end up infected."

Luke crossed his arms, kept his voice level. "I think you've said everything there is to say. You should go."

"I agree." The tears she'd so valiantly held back spilled down her cheeks, but he refused to be moved. Holly's words were impassioned, but they didn't change anything.

All this time he'd been giving her his heart, and he meant nothing to her. Just as he'd accused her of from the start, all she'd wanted from him was a career-making story. She'd written the *Sports Nation* article. She'd been investigating them the whole time. And he'd taken her to his home. He felt sick to his stomach, like he'd just put the puck in his own net.

He'd let his heart overrule his head. Ignored the

clues—he'd caught her in her lies about not knowing hockey, listened raptly to her stories about her mother and her childhood dreams of becoming a reporter. She'd been rubbing it in his face for their entire relationship, and he was too stupid to have even noticed.

She might have kept this story secret for a couple days, but she wouldn't sit on it for long.

He should have trusted his instincts and fought harder to get her fired from the get-go. He'd had his own suspicions about the list but he'd let her distract him. And now his reputation, the reputation of his entire team, was going to be dragged through the mud in the court of public opinion. All because he couldn't keep his dick in his pants.

He was the worst kind of fool—a willing participant in his own downfall. That ended now.

"Fired?"

The word felt like ash on her tongue, chalky and bitter. The taste of lost dreams.

"I'm sorry, Ms. Evans, but it was stated very clearly in your contract that you were not to interact with players outside of your professional capacity."

"But who—?"

"I'm sorry, but we can't release that information. Suffice it to say, a reputable source came forward and we have no choice but to enforce the terms that you yourself agreed to."

Said contract sat on Hastings's formidable oak desk, mocking her. Holly raised her eyes from the blinding whiteness of the paper with binding black type marching in perfect lines that reminded her the striped prison garb in old-timey movies. She raised her eyes to the man who sat across from her.

"I don't even get to defend myself?"

"I'm afraid the informant is a rather...important member of the Storm's organization."

Hastings was one hell of a finesser, she'd give him that.

"As such, we will be terminating your contract immediately and your services will no longer be required. In return for this short notice, you will receive your full compensation, as outlined in your notice of hire. Do you agree to these terms?"

"Do I have a choice?"

"I will take that as a yes." Hastings slid another piece of paper toward her. "We do require you to sign this nondisclosure agreement, which states that you will not discuss the details of this parting of ways, or anything leading up to it, upon threat of legal action."

She grabbed the pen and with numb fingers, scrawled her signature on the designated line.

Luke had sold her out. She'd gotten too close to hurting the team and he'd turned her in.

Betrayal burned white-hot in her chest, and she had to gulp to get enough air in her lungs. The fact that he hadn't even given her a heads-up... She understood that he was angry at her, but at least *she'd* had the courtesy to bring her concerns to him first, even though it had been the last thing she'd wanted to do. She'd been honest with him. To his face. Because she loved him.

She hated herself for it, but she did. Even when she'd believed he might have been involved in illegal activity, some part of her still believed that what they'd shared was real. And now, when he'd sold her out, she was still conflicted about breaking the story.

Luke had seemed genuinely hurt by her accusation, even as he'd confirmed all the reasons that some extra money could have gone a long way. She thought of Luke's parents, of Ethan, of everything the Maguires had been through. Luke loved his family enough to do anything for them, but she hadn't considered what a betting scandal would do to them if he'd been exposed. He would never have taken that risk.

She'd interpreted the evidence, but she'd boiled it all down to numbers, to probabilities and stats. She'd been so focused on doing what it took to get the job of her dreams that she'd failed to take the man himself into account. And now she'd lost everything. Her story. Her job. And the man she loved. Unsure what to do with herself, she gathered her things and headed for her father's house. He looked up with surprise as she entered the door.

"What are you doing here in the middle of the day?" he asked.

"I got fired, Pop."

"Oh."

"Oh? That's all you have to say about this?"

All her frustration, all her anger, everything she'd kept bottled up since the night she found out her mother was never coming home again roiled up from the depths and she was powerless to hold it in.

"Everything I've ever done is to make you proud, and you just look right past me!"

"That's not true."

"It is true! I've been sitting on this couch beside you for years trying to get your attention, and all you've ever done is ignore me and watch sports! So I watched sports, too. And I learned everything there was to learn about them. Players, rules, stats, just so we could have a conversation sometime. But you wouldn't even give me that! You just act like I'm not even here!"

"Holly—"

"Don't 'Holly' me! You talked sports with Neil! Why not me? Why not me, Pop?" She was too angry to cry, too exhausted to shout anymore. She was just empty. Holly sat on the couch in her usual spot and stared at the basketball game on the television.

"When I lost Mom, I didn't think anything could ever hurt as badly as that again. But I was wrong, because Mom didn't leave me on purpose. Not like you did."

Her dad got out of his chair and joined her on the couch. In her entire life, her father had never sat on the couch. She almost jumped when he put his hand on her knee.

"You remind me of her. Especially when you're on camera. That's always been hard for me."

Holly looked at her dad, felt like she was seeing him for the first time. "What?"

"You're smart and beautiful and you're so good at everything you do. Of course I'm proud of my girl. But sometimes it hurts to look at you because I miss her so much. I didn't realize how unfair I've been to you all these years. I never meant…I never meant to push you away. I love you, Holly. I do."

The words brought tears to her eyes. She couldn't remember the last time her father had said something nice about her, or told her he loved her. Throughout the years, his sporadic comments were always externally focused: "work harder, know more, do better." And she had. She'd lived her whole life striving to be good enough for him. To actually hear that he was proud of her made her heart swell.

"They were stupid to let you go. You're an expert at that game. If they can't see that, then they don't deserve you. And you'll show them. Because when you put your mind to something, there's nothing that can stand in your way. Now don't go and cry on me. I've never been good with that."

"Well, tough beans," Holly said with a watery laugh, and she hugged him. He stiffened in her grasp, but then his arms came around her and she felt his weathered hand pat her shoulder. It was like she was six years old again. Like she had her dad back. "I miss her, too," she confessed.

"She would've been proud of you. And she would have told you to fight for what you deserve. When life knocks you down, you get up and punch it in the gut."

His arms tightened around her, and she heard an unmistakable sniff.

"You okay?"

He cleared his throat and pulled away. "S'nothin'. Just got some dirt in my eye is all. Now you gonna stop yammerin' so we can watch the game, or what?"

Holly smiled as he got up and brushed his knuckles under his eyes. "Yeah. I'll stop yammering. How about I make us some popcorn to go with that game?"

He nodded gruffly as he dropped into his beat-up old recliner. "I could go for some popcorn."

15

"PAIGE! OPEN UP! I need to talk to you."

Holly banged on the door again, this time with more force. Paige's phone had gone straight to voice mail—a regular occurrence, as her friend was notorious for forgetting to charge her phone. But Holly was desperate for counsel and she wasn't going to let a dead phone stand in her way.

"C'mon, Paige! I know you're in there. Your car's in the driveway. I really need your advice."

Finally, after what felt like a lifetime, Holly heard the snick of the lock give way. Paige's face appeared in the six-inch crack of the open door. "Holly, what are you doing here? Is everything okay?"

Holly shoved the door open all the way and barged past her friend. "*News Now* just called. They just gave me Corey Baniuk's old job. I'm the new roving sports reporter for the six and eleven o'clock news."

"Wow, Hols. That's fantastic! That's your dream job, right? Interviewing athletes on TV. That's everything you've been working toward."

Holly nodded, dropping onto Paige's couch—a sleek,

robin's-egg-blue torture device that was built for style, not comfort. "I know!" She glanced over her shoulder at her friend. "So why am I not happier about it?"

"Aw, sweetie." Paige rushed over, wrapping the lilac sheet tighter around her before she joined Holly on the couch. "What's going on?"

"I have no idea. This is everything I wanted! And since the Storm fired me, I should be doubly glad because it means I'm not unemployed, trying to scrape by on ghostwriting sports articles.

"I went for the interview this morning, and they offered me the position on the spot. But even as I was shaking hands and signing contracts, something felt… off, you know?"

Paige nodded reassuringly, readjusting her toga. All of a sudden, her new job wasn't the only thing that seemed off to Holly. "Wait a minute. Why are you wrapped in a sheet?" Holly stood. "And why did it take you so long to answer the door? Is someone here? Did I just catch you *in flagrante*?"

She walked back toward the door, cocking an eyebrow as Paige rushed after her, blocking Holly's path to the bedroom.

"Do you have a sex crush of your own? And is he, or is he not in this house right now? Do not lie to me, Paige Marie Hallett."

"What?" Paige's blush made her whole face blotchy, like she was allergic to the lie she was trying so desperately to formulate. "No, I was just… I mean I, I just…" Her eyes focused briefly on something to Holly's left before they darted back to the floor.

Holly glanced behind her. A familiar pair of worn Vans sat in the entranceway. "Those are Jay's shoes."

She whipped around to face her friend. "You're sleeping with Jay? You hate Jay! Since when are you sleeping with Jay?"

There was a long moment of silence, before a deep voice sounded from behind the door at the end of the hall. "Since she already knows, can I come out now?"

Paige sighed. "Yes. Come out."

The door to her friend's bedroom swung open, and Holly could barely process the sight of her barefooted cameraman wearing jeans and pulling his vintage Ghostbusters T-shirt over his head. His grin was sheepish as he ran a hand through his unruly brown hair. "Hey, Holly. Congrats on the new job."

The entire world had gone mad. Her dream job was making her miserable. Jay was sleeping with Paige. She was going to have to keep an eye on the sky when she left, because the odds of seeing pigs soaring over the clouds seemed pretty high right now.

"I need some water."

Holly headed into Paige's kitchen and grabbed a bottle of Evian from the fridge. She took a long swig of the cool liquid and followed it with a couple of deep breaths. "Okay, so you guys are sleeping together. I can deal with that. I'm an adult. Angry sex is a thing."

"Actually…" Jay slung an arm over Paige's shoulders. "We're kind of past the angry sex stage and on to the dating exclusively stage."

Holly knew he was telling the truth because Paige didn't slug him. Instead, her friend's bright green eyes turned imploring. "I'm sorry we kept it a secret, Hols, but we were trying to get a handle on it ourselves. I'm glad it's not a secret anymore, though, because you deserve to know. This never would have happened if not for you and the Women's Hockey Network."

"Say what now?"

Paige smiled at her. "You think the Women's Hockey Network was a joke, but the truth is you did great research and presented facts in a way that resonated with me. And with a bunch of people who aren't usually interested in sports. You gave us a foothold in a world we didn't understand. And not because we were incapable of understanding. You're not dumbing anything down. You're just coming at it from a different angle. Hockey got a whole lot more exciting for me when you snuck in a little medicine to the spoonful of sugar that is Luke Maguire's abs."

"Seriously, Paige? I'm right here," Jay lamented.

"Understanding the game made it more interesting to watch. Because of you, I suddenly understood offside, or why the whistle blew even though no one had touched the puck and why the face-off was happening somewhere other than at center ice. And that made me care more about the game."

Holly tried not to be touched, but to hear her sports-allergic best friend talking about offsides was kind of a big deal in her world. Damned if it didn't make her a bit misty-eyed.

"Basically, you made me realize what else I was missing out on. I mean, if hockey wasn't as bad as I thought, what else might be better than I gave it credit for?" Paige slipped an arm around Jay's waist. "Sometimes what you want doesn't look at all like what you thought you wanted. Nothing about Jay and I makes sense, but we just fit. And I owe it all to you because I might not have figured that out on my own."

"You think that dumb fluff is me at my most insightful? My mom is probably rolling over in her grave."

"I think she'd respect you for it as much as I do, Hols."

If she was being honest, at some point during this whole farce, the Women's Hockey Network *had* started to really matter to her. In her heart, Holly knew it was more than fluff, had known it for a long time.

It was just hard to reimagine her future, to reevaluate her priorities. She'd spent so long convinced that *real* sports reporting was her destiny. The only route to make her dad proud. The best way to honor her mother's legacy. But Paige was right, the only person who wasn't proud of her was herself.

"The thing that makes you great is that you care so much," Paige continued. "You're not supposed to be on *News Now* reading a teleprompter, you're supposed to be making real connections and improving people's lives." She remembered the little girl she'd met at the bakery. Paige was right. She *was* making a difference. Sometimes miniscule, like making people laugh, and sometimes major, like helping two people feel closer to one another. But either way, it was rewarding. It was still sports, still her passion, but it was so much more than that, too.

So she let go. All her expectations, all her goals, all her former dreams. Her chest felt light, as if her lungs were full of helium. Or freedom.

For the first time, Holly wasn't in someone else's shadow, or seeking someone else's approval. She knew exactly where her future lay and she had a phone call to make.

16

WAITING WAS A special kind of hell.

Every morning, Luke expected to wake up to an angry phone call from his agent and an even angrier headline in the paper. And every morning, there was nothing.

It was driving him crazy. He'd been sure it would have come by now. He'd worried about it through both of the Storm's out-of-town games, constantly monitoring the internet for any sign that Holly had broken her story. But she hadn't. Yet. The prospect loomed over his head like a guillotine.

And now they were back in Portland after two tough losses in Wyoming. They were hoping to even things out tonight with the home crowd behind them.

The tension in the dressing room was almost unbearable. His teammates were unusually quiet as they fidgeted in full equipment and waited for Coach Taggert to start his pregame speech. Instead, Taggert walked over to Luke, touched his shoulder pad. "Someone's here to see you."

Holly.

Her name popped unbidden into his heart. Was she here to apologize? Or to tell him she was going live with the story tonight? And why did the prospect of seeing her make his heart race with anticipation? He was mad at her. Furious, really.

"Now's not really the time, is it, Coach?"

The gruff, burly man motioned toward the door with a shake of his head. "You wanna stay a part of this team, you do what I say and trust me when I tell you, you wanna take this meeting."

Luke obeyed. But when he stepped out of the dressing room, it took a long moment before his brain could fully register the sight before him. "You came."

"Yeah, well. There's only so many places you can wear one of these jerseys, so…" Ethan shrugged.

Luke hadn't even noticed the damn jersey. The *C* on the front. The number twenty-eight visible on the sleeve. "Holly," he breathed.

His little brother nodded. "Yeah, it showed up in the mail the other day. Complete with a scathing letter that threatened me with bodily harm if I didn't get my ass out to one of your games. She's pretty incredible. Too good for you, really."

Luke couldn't even process the joke. "I'm glad you're here."

Ethan stared down at the ground. "I should have come before. It's been a really tough couple of years, Luke. Without hockey, I've got nothing. I've put everything into getting back on that ice, and every day it became clearer that wasn't going to happen, and I couldn't deal with that. But Holly helped me see that there are still opportunities to be part of hockey. Maybe not on the ice, but on the bench. Or in a studio. I can still talk about it, dissect it, coach it and watch my brother play it the way it's meant to be played." He looked up at that.

"You've always been in it for the love of the game. That's what makes you great, big brother. You do it for the right reasons. Not the fame or the fortune or the ladies. Because you genuinely love playing. You've got to stop giving a shit about my feelings, or what's going on with your teammates and just get out there and do what you do. And know that it's good enough, no matter what happens."

Growing up, he and Ethan had always been close, but the heartfelt words made Luke realize how much distance had crept between them since the accident. He'd been so busy trying to take care of things, he hadn't realized how much he'd missed his brother.

"Also, this is for you."

Ethan handed him a beat-up paper bag. Luke opened it and couldn't help but laugh. "No way!"

Ethan blushed as Luke held up a knitted replica of the Storm Jersey he wore, complete with "Maguire" and a big twenty-eight on the back and the coveted *C* on the front.

"You made this?"

"Yeah, well, I've had a lot of time to think lately. Had to break through some of that mental chatter. Figured if I was knitting, it might as well *be* something...not like your stupid thirty-foot lengths of nothing."

Luke shook his head. "You always gotta show me up, don't you, you prick?"

"It's not my fault I'm so much better than you at everything. Now got out there and win this game."

Ethan's words were still ringing in his ears as he stepped onto the ice. The game was going to be a battle. Down 2–0 in a series was not a great place to be, but for the first time since the play-offs began, Luke was in his element. He belonged there. Tonight, he was going to make sure everybody knew it.

A minute and twenty-seven seconds into the first period, Luke snapped his scoring drought with a beautiful wrist shot to the top-left corner.

IT WAS A hard-fought, physical game. Players from both teams spent their fair share of time in the penalty box, and despite the Storm's commanding first period, the Wyoming Stallions had battled back to a 3–3 draw with seven minutes left in the game.

Luke had thought they were destined for overtime, but with forty-six seconds left on the clock, the rookie redirected one of Kowalchuk's big booming slap shots, and the Storm had gone on to win it 4–3 in regular time. There was a tangible relief in the air as his weary teammates filed into the dressing room after the game. They'd held on, brought the series back to within one. Their dreams of the championship were still viable.

It took him a moment to notice that his goaltender was walking in front of him hunched over with the air of a man who'd just lost it all.

Luke grabbed his jersey, stopping him before he stepped into the dressing room with the rest of the team. "Hey man, you okay?"

J.C. barely looked at him as he shrugged. "Huh? Yeah, no. I'm fine. Good goal. You relaxed and played the game. Just like I told you to."

Luke frowned. "For a man who was just part of an epic, kick-ass win, you seem pretty down."

He shook his head. "It's nothing. Just tired. Play-offs are pretty grueling."

"Yeah, okay." Luke meant to drop it then, to give his goaltender—his friend—some space, but there was a niggling thought in his mind. A piece that wouldn't quite fit. J.C. wasn't acting like himself tonight. Hadn't been since... "You went down."

"What?"

"Third period. We were up 3–2. Johnson was coming in on his backhand and you went down. He scored top shelf. You never go down when Keith Johnson is on his backhand. You've been playing against him since we were fourteen."

"What are you talking about?"

"It's you." The realization vibrated in every cell in Luke's body. He stood facing his friend in the middle of the hallway, betrayal burning like lava in his veins. "Holly was right. You let that goal in on purpose. What the hell are you wrapped up in?"

For the first time, J.C. looked something other than listless. In fact, he looked downright panicked. He glanced around the hallway. "Would you keep your voice down?"

"What the fuck is going on?"

"Calm down. It's nothing." He put a comforting hand on Luke's shoulder.

Luke shook it off. "Are you betting on hockey? Are you betting on us?"

J.C. went from soothing to defensive in a split second. "What the hell's your problem, Mags? It's no big deal. It's over-under stuff. We've got a real chance this year. All I have to do is keep the score a little closer than it should be in a few games."

Luke's stomach churned with disgust. "I can't believe you! You could go to jail for this! You're about to get married. You've got a *baby* on the way."

J.C.'s face twisted with ire. "Why does everyone keep saying that like it's a good thing? Tania and I have been together for four years, and she wanted a ring or else. I didn't propose, I followed orders. And when the doubts took over, I was all set to tell her I wanted the damn ring back. But then she dropped the bombshell that I was going to be a dad."

J.C. ran a hand over his play-off beard and his voice turned beseeching. "A dad, Mags. Me. I'm too young to be a dad. I wanted to leave her, and now we're bonded together for the rest of time. And there's not a goddamn thing I can do about it. So I went to the track. A few times. Just to blow off some steam. And I got in a little over my head. But they offered me a way out—a way to clear up my debt. And we still win. Everybody wins. C'mon, man. We're the only ones left who know about this."

"What do you mean, the *only ones left*?" Realization dawned as soon as the words were out of Luke's mouth. "*You* got Holly fired? You son of a bitch! You used what I told you on the plane and you sold her out, you sold *me* out. I trusted you. I'm in love with this girl."

"She's a reporter, Mags."

"You're the one who insisted I was overreacting. That she was harmless."

"That was before I knew she was only pretending to be stupid! She heard Tania yelling about me getting rid of the Porsche. It was only a matter of time until she put it together. No one can find out about this. It wasn't personal, man. I was just covering my bases."

"J.C., what you're doing is illegal. You've put this whole team at risk. Jesus." Luke ran a hand through his hair. "What were you thinking?"

"I was thinking you had my back. Isn't that what you always say? Put the team first?"

Luke shook his head. He'd been so wrapped up in his guilt, so blinded by his insistence on protecting the team that he'd lost sight of what was important. "You think this is putting the team first? You crossed the line, man. You *deserted* your team, and as the captain, I can't let that stand."

"What, you're going to tell on me? Is that it, Luke? After all we've been through together, you're going to end our friendship and torpedo my career over a few goals that, in the grand scheme of things, don't even matter?"

Luke looked at his teammate, his friend, and saw a stranger staring back at him. "You're goddamn right I am."

17

"Good evening and welcome to the eleven o'clock sports wrap-up. I'm Corey Baniuk and I'd like to introduce you to the newest addition to our team, Holly Evans. Usually, she'll be on the scene, covering games as they happen," he said. "But tonight we're happy to have her joining us in studio so that you, our viewers, can meet her properly. Holly, good to have you here."

"Thanks, Corey. And congratulations on your promotion." Holly smiled big and turned to the camera. "Hi, everyone. Let's start with hockey, where earlier tonight the captain of the Portland Storm, Luke Maguire, finally broke a nineteen-game scoreless streak with this beauty less than two minutes into their game against the Wyoming Stallions…"

Holly did the entire segment and it was incredible. She nailed the scores, the camera changes, every word that came out of her mouth was crisp and precise. It was a triumphant moment, but not quite as triumphant as the moment that followed it.

"Thank you, Holly. And now—"

"Actually, Corey, I'm not quite finished."

She'd never seen the golden voice of sports at a loss for words. Apparently it wasn't good for business, because the camera operators bobbled for a quick moment before every single one of them turned to focus on her.

"When I made the Women's Hockey Network video, I was being a smart-ass. I was frustrated that people would discount opinions on sports just because they came from a woman. So I created a satirical look at how women in the sports world are perceived.

"Except when my video hit YouTube, it went viral. The Portland Storm hired me for their play-off run, and everything changed. The Women's Hockey Network grew into something unstoppable, and I was just along for the ride. For a while, I thought I was making mockery of everything I loved. Then I heard from you, the people watching, and I realized that together, we had something special.

"I want to thank everyone at this station and you, the viewers, for welcoming me with open arms. This job was a childhood dream come true and I will remember this night for the rest of my life. But my priorities have changed, which is why tonight will be my only show with *News Now*. Effective immediately, I'm tendering my resignation.

"But if you liked the Women's Hockey Network, then I invite you to join me on XT Satellite Radio, where I will be hosting *The Women's Sport Network* every weekday from one to three on Sports Talk Radio. It's going to be a show where women can congregate and talk about sports. Where we can teach what we know, or learn what we need to know."

Holly could feel her smile warming as she spoke. "It's going to be real women asking real questions. If you don't understand the rules of the game, ask me. If you don't understand why the GM of your home team isn't moving on signing that free agent who lit up the field last year, we'll discuss it. And if you want to hear what cologne your favorite player wears, I'll find out for you.

"Because there are no stupid questions. I want to help every woman, every person, find the part of the game that appeals to him or her, because when it comes right down to it, sports are about having a good time. I lost sight of that for a while, but I finally found it again. And now I want to share it with you." Holly tucked her hair behind her right ear. "I'm Holly Evans, for *Portland News Now*. Thank you and good night."

Holly strode out of the studio without a single doubt that she'd made her mother proud. It was a great feeling, one she reveled in all the way to the lobby, until she glanced over at the security station and noticed a certain hockey highlight. She beelined toward the desk.

"Can you rewind that?" she asked.

The security guard grabbed a remote off the desk and turned to the monitor.

"Thanks, just run it back to the last goal that Wisconsin scored on the Storm. Yes. There."

Her skin prickled as she watched Keith Johnson walk in and score a top-shelf backhand on J.C. LaCroix, who was sprawled across the crease.

"Son of a—"

It all made sense now. The awful goal, the lackluster baby announcement, the vehicle downgrade and the purse-wielding psycho fiancée.

It had been J.C. she'd heard in the bathroom that day. He was the mole. She had to tell Luke! And if he wouldn't listen, well, she'd make him listen.

She'd just pulled out of the parking lot, formulating a plan to get Luke to let her explain herself when the radio announcer's voice penetrated her single focus.

"And we take you now live to a surprise press conference involving key members of the Portland Storm. We've confirmed that Captain Luke Maguire, Coach Randy Taggert and GM Ron Lougheed are all present, as is League Commissioner Grant McDavid. McDavid was seen during tonight's game sitting with former Blades centerman and national hero Ethan Maguire. Needless to say, the sports community is buzzing with speculation over what the big announcement is. We now go live to the Portland Dome."

Ethan had shown up?

Her grip tightened on the steering wheel, and she changed her course from Luke's apartment to the arena. But what could they possibly be talking about at a press conference? The post-game interviews had ended hours ago.

Holly shook her head. The biggest damn story of the day was unfolding while she'd been looking pretty on TV. And instead of sending her or Corey Baniuk, *Portland News Now* had probably sent some intern to cover it. Thank the hockey gods she'd quit.

"Thank you, everyone, for coming tonight. I'm afraid we're here with bad news."

Her stomach flipped at the sound of Luke's deep voice filling the airwaves.

"As the captain of this team, I would like to begin by saying the Storm organization has always prided itself on stressing the importance of sportsmanship and integrity. However, thanks to some incredible undercover work by sports reporter Holly Evans, it has recently come to my attention that there is an individual on this team who has not been living up to the code that we, the Portland Storm, have sought to play by.

"This individual has been involved in betting, and when his debt got too big, he agreed to manipulate game results during our play-off run. As the captain of a phenomenal team, I have spoken with my teammates and we have decided, after consulting with the league, to withdraw from this year's play-off run and wish the Wyoming Stallions the best of luck as they take on the winner of the Eastern Conference."

The gasps in the auditorium were audible even through the radio, and Holly sped up as she approached the turn-off that would get her closer to the Portland Dome.

"We, as a team, in conjunction with our coach and management, feel this is the best way to keep one person's actions from tainting the entire team."

He knows. Oh God. She wondered how Luke was taking the devastating betrayal of his best friend's actions. His voice sounded even, if a little somber, but she'd need to look into his eyes to be sure.

"And with the league's support, we hope to earn our way back to next year's play-offs and claim our chance to win the championship.

"I personally would like to apologize to Holly Evans and thank her for her diligent work."

The car swerved a bit at that, as Holly tried to process the shock of Luke's very public words of praise.

"I love this game with all my heart and I could not have lived with myself if I had been part of sullying its good reputation, however unwittingly. The truth has come to light, and that's exactly how it should be. And for that reason, effective immediately, Jean-Claude LaCroix is no longer a member of the Portland Storm. Thank you. Coach Taggert will now say a few words."

Questions exploded throughout the press room, and Holly could hardly breathe as she pulled into the parking lot. She was relieved the attendant at the gate recognized her and let her through without a hassle, because she was having a hard time forming words.

Luke had done the right thing even though it had cost him his dream, and she wanted to throw up for doubting his integrity for even a split second. He'd not only taken the high road and given her credit for breaking the story, he'd even thanked her publicly. And for what? For jumping to conclusions about him? She had to get in there right away.

Holly screeched to a halt and parked in an illegal zone as close to the door as she could. She turned off the car, silencing Coach Taggert's "weathering this adversity will only make us a stronger hockey club" speech.

Then she ran—in heels—for the press room. By the time she got there, the league commissioner was handing down his ruling.

A security person stopped her. "Ma'am? I'm sorry, you can't go in there. Press only."

"I am press!"

"I'll need to see some identification."

Holly dug frantically through her purse until she came upon the lanyard she'd failed to return: her Women's Hockey Network press pass. And for the first time, her wide-eyed, helmet-haired photo wasn't an embarrassment, but a badge of honor.

The security guard let her through.

"Although there will be a further investigation by the league, the fact that the Portland Storm brought this breach of ethics to our attention immediately upon learning of it will go a long way in expediting the process. Mr. LaCroix has admitted to being the sole perpetrator and has been banned from the league indefinitely. At this time, we will be taking questions."

The room was a roar of sound as the scrum exploded with queries.

"One at a time, and please use the microphone."

As she approached the front of the room, the interrogation quieted, replaced with whispers as the gathered reporters began to recognize her.

She stopped in front of the microphone and Taggert nodded at her to proceed. "Holly Evans, from the Women's Sports Network. My question is for Luke Maguire."

The way he was looking at her broke her heart, part hopeful, part wary. It took everything she had to keep herself from running up on that stage and pulling him into her arms so she could apologize.

"Luke, I was just wondering, do you think there's any chance that you can forgive me? Because if you love me even half as much as I love you, then I think we could be a great team."

There was a long, silent moment where the world went still. Seconds ticked by to the beat of the pulse echoing in her ears.

A murmur spread through the crowd.

"Teammates, huh?" he said.

She nodded.

He leaned forward to speak into his mic. "I don't know."

Dread wound its way through her stomach and into her chest, squeezing her heart like a vise. She deserved this, she reminded herself. She'd known this was a possibility.

"You think you can handle that, Evans? Because if we do this again, I'm going to need you in it for the long haul, a hundred percent commitment. Eye on the prize."

Holly bit her lip as Luke got up from the table and pushed his way past the rest of the panel members. With every step that brought him closer, hope bubbled in her chest like a lava lamp. She was nodding before he even reached her. "I believe I can manage that, yes."

"I hope so, because I love you, too." When he pulled her into his arms, his kiss was everything—an apology, a declaration, a promise. Holly wound her arms around his neck, relief and love pounding through her veins in equal measure.

The room erupted in applause and camera flashes. But all that mattered to her was the man who held her in his arms. She was never going to let him go again.

"I thought I'd lost you," she whispered.

Luke smiled and it made her heart flutter. "Not possible."

"How do you figure?" she asked.

"You ever heard people say that love is a game?"

She nodded.

"When I play, I play to win. And just for the record, I expect my teammate to do the same."

Holly grinned and grabbed him by the tie. "Aye aye, captain," she said and sealed her promise with a kiss.

* * * * *

COMING SOON!

We really hope you enjoyed reading this book.
If you're looking for more romance
be sure to head to the shops when
new books are available on

Thursday 27th February

To see which titles are coming soon, please visit
millsandboon.co.uk/nextmonth

MILLS & BOON

FOUR BRAND NEW BOOKS FROM
MILLS & BOON MODERN

The same great stories you love, a stylish new look!

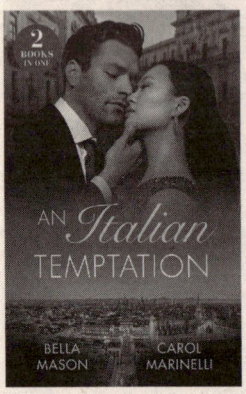

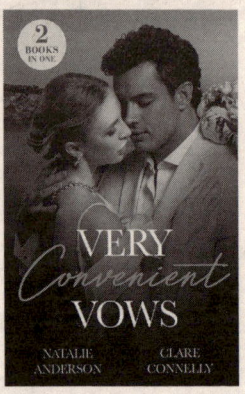

For Passion or Payback?
MAYA BLAKE — MILLIE ADAMS

Pregnant Then Wed
LYNNE GRAHAM — ANNIE WEST

An Italian Temptation
BELLA MASON — CAROL MARINELLI

Very Convenient Vows
NATALIE ANDERSON — CLARE CONNELLY

OUT NOW

Eight Modern stories published every month, find them all at:

millsandboon.co.uk

OUT NOW!

FRIENDS to LOVERS
Something More

3 BOOKS IN ONE

JC HARROWAY · LOUISA GEORGE · HELEN LACEY

Available at
millsandboon.co.uk

MILLS & BOON

LET'S TALK
Romance

For exclusive extracts, competitions and special offers, find us online:

- **f** MillsandBoon
- **X** @MillsandBoon
- **◉** @MillsandBoonUK
- **♪** @MillsandBoonUK

Get in touch on 01413 063 232

For all the latest titles coming soon, visit
millsandboon.co.uk/nextmonth

afterglow BOOKS

Afterglow Books is a trend-led, trope-filled list of books with diverse, authentic and relatable characters, a wide array of voices and representations, plus real world trials and tribulations. Featuring all the tropes you could possibly want (think small-town settings, fake relationships, grumpy vs sunshine, enemies to lovers) and all with a generous dose of spice in every story.

@millsandboonuk
@millsandboonuk
afterglowbooks.co.uk
#AfterglowBooks

For all the latest book news, exclusive content and giveaways scan the QR code below to sign up to the Afterglow newsletter:

SCAN ME

afterglow BOOKS

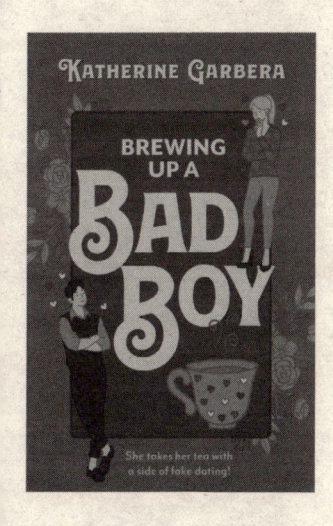

KATHERINE GARBERA
BREWING UP A BAD BOY
She takes her tea with a side of fake dating!

KARMEN LEE
BIG CITY MEETS SMALL-TOWN...AND SPARKS FLY!
The Relationship Mechanic

- Second chance
- Small-town romance
- Fake dating

- Spicy
- Small-town romance
- Forced proximity

OUT NOW

Two stories published every month. Discover more at:
Afterglowbooks.co.uk

afterglow BOOKS

Looking for more Afterglow Books?

Try the perfect subscription for spicy romance lovers and save 50% on your first parcel.

PLUS receive these additional benefits when you subscribe:

- **FREE** delivery direct to your door
- **EXCLUSIVE** offers every month
- **SAVE** up to 30% on pre-paid subscriptions

SUBSCRIBE AND SAVE

millsandboon.co.uk/Subscribe

MILLS & BOON

THE HEART OF ROMANCE

A ROMANCE FOR EVERY READER

MODERN — Prepare to be swept off your feet by sophisticated, sexy and seductive heroes, in some of the world's most glamourous and romantic locations, where power and passion collide.

HISTORICAL — Escape with historical heroes from time gone by. Whether your passion is for wicked Regency Rakes, muscled Vikings or rugged Highlanders, awaken the romance of the past.

MEDICAL — Set your pulse racing with dedicated, delectable doctors in the high-pressure world of medicine, where emotions run high and passion, comfort and love are the best medicine.

True Love — Celebrate true love with tender stories of heartfelt romance, from the rush of falling in love to the joy a new baby can bring, and a focus on the emotional heart of a relationship.

HEROES — The excitement of a gripping thriller, with intense romance at its heart. Resourceful, true-to-life women and strong, fearless men face danger and desire - a killer combination!

Afterglow BOOKS — From showing up to glowing up, these characters are on the path to leading their best lives and finding romance along the way – with plenty of sizzling spice!

To see which titles are coming soon, please visit

millsandboon.co.uk/nextmonth

MILLS & BOON
A ROMANCE FOR EVERY READER

- **FREE** delivery direct to your door
- **EXCLUSIVE** offers every month
- **SAVE** up to 30% on pre-paid subscriptions

SUBSCRIBE AND SAVE

millsandboon.co.uk/Subscribe